CLOSE ENCOUNTE

Donna scurried behind a bush, clutching her rain-coat. Her victims came into view. Looking about them, the two young men sat by the fence and waited.

'Do you think she'll come?'

'I'll make her come, all right.'

'She may not turn up, what with the rain.'

'I'm already here,' Donna said as she emerged from the bush, her long blonde hair wet. 'You may both remove my cat suit. I like to be totally naked when being pleasured by two young men.'

Moving in, they tugged on the zip running down the front of the suit. Slowly, the soft leather opened to reveal Donna's breasts, her smooth belly. Further still, and the suit was open fully. Gazing, each youth squeezed her breasts, sucked on her nipples, reached down and fondled her intimate places. Peeling the suit from her wet body, they ran their hands over the smoothness of her skin, female skin, curvaceous, sensual – naked. Learning, discovering, they gently pulled her down and lay her on the wet grass, her legs spread, her arms above her head – her body open . . .

First published in 1995 by Hodder and Stoughton
A division of Hodder Headline PLC

A New English Library paperback

10 9 8 7 6 5 4 3 2 1

British Library Cataloguing in Publication Data

Gordon, Ray
    The Uninhibited
    I. Title
    823 [F]
    ISBN 0-340-63494-4

Typeset by
Letterpart Limited, Reigate, Surrey
Printed and bound in Great Britain by
Cox & Wyman Ltd, Reading, Berks

Hodder and Stoughton
A division of Hodder Headline PLC
338 Euston Road
London NW1 3BH

The Uninhibited

Chapter One

Donna Ryan looked up from her microscope and rubbed her eyes. After another long and laborious day, she was tired. She'd worked an hour past her time, again, and couldn't wait to get home to her flat. Leaning back in her swivel chair and stretching her arms over her head, she gazed at her boss, Doctor Alan Rosenberg.

His dark hair fell over his forehead as he leaned forward and scribbled yet more illegible notes on his coffee-stained pad. A mad professor? Yawning, she wondered at the incessant compulsion driving him to work seven days a week, and often through the nights. Engrossed in his work, he had no concept of time, of the world outside the laboratory. Thirty-five years old and living alone in a squalid flat, he'd devoted ten years to research – the last three to his latest project, a new and exciting form of hormone replacement therapy.

Working closely with him for five years, Donna had developed nothing more than a brother-sister relationship with her boss. He seemed to disregard the fact that, beneath her white lab coat, she was a woman – all woman. She'd used her eyes, body language, perfumes, to encourage him to see her in a different light, but nothing had worked. Nothing, it seemed, roused his male instinct, leaving her questioning her femininity – her sexuality.

Whilst far from unattractive with her waist-length blonde hair, full, red lips and deep blue bedroom eyes, few men seemed to notice Donna, apart from David Blake, a thin, bespectacled lab assistant working in cultures across the corridor – a highly undesirable excuse for a man. Doctor Rosenberg, Donna had concluded sadly, although good-looking, masculine, well-spoken and certainly financially solvent, was asexual. She'd long since given up her futile attempts to lure him out to dinner and discover the real man – the man behind the microscope.

Living alone with her dreams of marrying, having children, a normal life outside the lab, Donna spent her evenings reading romantic novels. Now twenty-five, she wondered if she'd ever realise her dreams, experience the rich and wonderful love enjoyed by the characters in her books. Perhaps, she, too, had become obsessed with the research work? Sucked into the swirling pool of formulae, chemical analyses, endless experiments, her only escape was the well-thumbed pages of her novels.

'I'm off now, Alan,' she sighed, grabbing her bag from under the bench and running her fingers through her long blonde hair.

'Yes, yes,' he murmured without looking up. 'Until tomorrow.'

Removing her white lab coat, Donna stretched her long legs and flattened her knee-length skirt with her palms before wandering across the lab to Alan's bench. He'd been working secretly for months. Normally, they'd work as a team, but he seemed reticent to discuss the project with her now, and she'd often wondered exactly what it was that had grabbed his attention, held his fascination to the point where he rarely even spoke.

'What's that?' she asked, leaning over his shoulder. Jumping, Alan covered his note pad like a schoolboy during an exam. 'Nothing, nothing,' he grunted, staring into her big blue eyes.

'No, not your notes, that round plaster – have you cut yourself?' Following her gaze to the plaster lying by his note pad, his dark eyes widened.

'It's nothing,' he assured her unconvincingly. 'I don't know where it came from. I'll get rid of it.'

Meticulous, a perfectionist in his work, Donna thought it odd that Alan should have a plaster on his desk, and odder still that he claimed to know nothing about it. Lab conditions, as he constantly reminded her, were most important. Cleanliness, tidiness, order, were paramount to the efficient running of the lab and the success of their research experiments.

Seizing the plaster, she squashed it in her palm. 'You've spilled your coffee on it,' she remarked as a sticky substance oozed into her hand. 'I'll put it in the bin on my way out.'

Alan held out his hand, his forehead lined with anguish. 'No, no, leave it!' he barked impatiently.

Smiling impishly, she left him to his work, still clutching the plaster as she opened the door and called goodbye. He seemed agitated that she'd not followed his instruction, not returned the plaster. Quietly cursing as he stood up to give chase, he knocked his coffee cup off the bench. It smashed, loudly, on the floor.

Alan was hiding something, Donna knew. That look in his eye, the uncharacteristic secretiveness, his strange mannerisms, repeatedly glancing over his shoulder as he worked – he was up to something. She had no idea of the significance of a simple plaster, but she knew it was important to him.

Walking quickly down the brightly-lit corridor, Donna gripped the plaster triumphantly in her small hand. If it was really that important to Alan, he'd tell her in the morning. She'd discover his secret, sooner or later, but for now her only interest was her flat, her armchair and her latest book. Her little world.

She felt slightly dizzy during the short walk home. Probably hunger and the heat of the summer's day, she thought as she opened her front door and dropped her bag on the floor. Pleased to be home, she kicked off her shoes as she walked into the lounge and picked up her book, hoping to finish a chapter before cooking. Would the hero and heroine marry and live happily ever after? Flopping into her armchair with a sigh of relief, she realised that she was still holding the plaster. Peeling the sticky mess from her palm, she dropped it onto the coffee table.

The flat seemed hotter than usual, the air thick and humid, difficult to breathe. Her head spinning, she unbuttoned her blouse and fanned her breasts with the loose material, cooling herself. Slipping the garment from her shoulders, she threw it to the floor, wondering if she was becoming ill. The day had been hot, close. The pollen count would be high and the ozone layer thin.

Feeling strange, different somehow, light-headed, she pulled her bra off, freeing her full breasts from the confining red silk, allowing them to breathe. Fanning herself with her book, the cool air caused her nipples to grow slightly, harden a little. Suddenly aware of her body, her sexuality, she lightly stroked her elongated nipples with her fingertips.

Sensitive in the extreme, they responded, stiffened, lengthened. Insignificant before, nothing more than another part of her body to be washed and concealed under her clothing, her milk buds now became the centre of her pleasure. Circling her fingers round the brown buds until she began to breathe deeply with sensations she'd never known before, she pinched, pulled, twisted until the ripples of pleasure penetrated deep into her body, ran down to her pelvis to awaken her womb. Cupping her hard breast in her hand, she pushed her tongue out and tasted her nipple. The book fell to the floor as she greedily cupped both breasts and licked the hard, brown protrusions in turn, stiffening them until they ached, sucking until they grew and stood out from the dark discs of her aureolae.

Raising her hips, she slipped her skirt off and kicked it aside with a strange abandonment. Now only her panties covered her sex, hugging the contours of her swelling pussy lips, wet and stained with her juices. Quickly shedding the panties, she gazed longingly at the small triangular patch of downy hair below her smooth stomach. Wondering at her strange and sudden arousal, she ran a finger up the tightly closed groove just visible under the tangle of blonde hair. Her clitoris hardened, responded as never before, as she swung her legs over the arms of the chair, opening her swelling lips to expose the complex pinken folds of her femininity. Intrigued, fascinated by the only part of her young body she'd never before explored, she stretched her lips wide apart and examined the glistening pink flesh, the small clitoris, protruding now, hard, yearning for her attention.

Circling her fingertip around the hard nodule, she gasped as unfamiliar sensations welled up from her womb, reddening the swelling flesh between her splayed lips, dispatching tingles over her trembling, naked body. Quickening her caress, she realised that, for the first time, a real and powerful orgasm was about to break over her body, crash through her mind. Thrusting three fingers into her wetness, stretching her sheath wide, she brought her clitoris to a wondrous peak.

Enticing the pleasure from the throbbing tip with her slender fingers, tossing her head as the euphoria cast aside her chains, freed her mind of inhibitions, she revelled delightfully in her lewd act. Pulsating, throbbing, her appreciative cumbud swelled to an incredible size. Rhythmically squeezing her fingers, the silky walls of her sheath spasmed, gripped like a vice as she lifted her buttocks clear of the chair. Arching her back, projecting her hips, she laid the centre of her being open to the magical sexual power engulfing her flesh, her psyche. Abandoned, she found herself floating, flying high above the earth through swirling clouds of orgasm.

Gently stroking her clitoris as it receded, she breathed one last sigh of satisfaction and reluctantly withdrew her fingers from her sodden hole. Panting, drifting in the wake of an undreamt-of sexual high, she closed her eyes and wondered why. After futile attempts during her teens to achieve a satisfying orgasm, why was it suddenly so easy? What had changed? But more, would it be possible to attain such beautiful sexual heights again? Or would future attempts simply bring her the old familiar weak tremblings?

Whatever, nothing could have prepared her for the delights her body had yielded in return for a little attention, a gentle, loving caress. As she lay naked in her chair, almost in fear of such exquisite pleasure engulfing her again, she pushed her fingers into her satiated hole to explore the hot, creamy walls of her uncharted depths. Her soft cunt lips open, encompassing her fingers, her clitoris pulsating slightly in anticipation, she massaged her inner flesh, inducing a flow of warm juice from her womb. Trickling down her fingers, her hand, the slippery liquid glistened in the evening sunlight streaming in through the window. Withdrawing her hand, she examined the fluid, the product of orgasm, before pushing out her tongue and tentatively tasting the nectar.

Warm, creamy, lubricous, the fluid aroused her taste buds as she ran her tongue round her mouth. Sucking on her fingers, licking her hand in a sexual frenzy, she savoured the aphrodisiacal taste of her milky sex fluid. Thrusting into her body, her cunt, again and again to elicit her love-juice, she licked her slender fingers until her sheath had drained, her soft love-tube run dry.

Sprawled across the armchair, legs splayed, she thought of Alan, what he'd say, what he'd do if he saw her blatant nakedness, her supple nether lips spread, exposing her innermost secrets. Would he fall to his knees and bury his face in the wet, matted hair surrounding her open slit? Would he push his tongue between her swollen quim lips and gently sink it into the most private entrance to her body? An experience she'd never known, she quivered at the thought of her boss, a man, drinking from her inflamed cunt, licking deep inside, penetrating to the very opening of her womb.

As if waking from a dream, a strange state of intoxication, she looked down to her thighs, spread, exposing her girlish intimacy. She gazed at her swollen vaginal lips, parted, revealing the tip of her clitoris, her pleasure bud peeping out from under its protective hood as if waiting for more. 'What have I *done?*' she whispered, suddenly shocked by the sight of her shamelessly exposed womanhood. Was it the work of demons – coaxing, urging, driving, possessing?

Somehow managing to stand on her trembling legs,

she staggered to the bathroom and stepped into the shower. Eradicating the milky sex juices from her pubic hair, the sticky fluid from her thighs, was easy. But she couldn't cleanse her mind, wash away the wicked thoughts, the fantasies, the experience, the memory of the most powerful orgasm that had ever rocked her body.

In a state of near-shock, she dried herself quickly and dressed before returning to the lounge. The walls looked at her accusingly. Now her home, her lounge, had taken on a new meaning – it had become a den of sex, masturbation. In the armchair was the small white stain where the open centre of her body had spewed its fruits in response to her climax. The chair seemed to beckon her, to again sink her naked buttocks into its soft cushion. It willed her to spread-eagle her legs across its supportive arms as, once again, she massaged her magic bud and found her secret heaven.

Grabbing her book, Donna sat on the sofa, desperately trying to empty her mind of the vulgarity of her debased act of wanton self-abuse. Confused, she didn't understand what had taken control of her mind, driven her to commit such an act. Running her finger down the leather book mark, she opened the page and picked up the story where she'd left off. '. . . Emily closed her eyes as he carried her to the bridal suite and kicked the door shut.' Would the sea crash against the rocks for them, sending showers of salty spray into the air as they reached their crescendo?

The meaning had gone now. The love, the romance, tainted, stripped by the debauched and yet so beautiful experience of masturbation, of orgasm. There was nothing she could do to erase the image of her parted pussy lips, wet, swollen – her open hole, oozing, dripping with lust from her debauched caresses.

In an attempt to clear her head, she cooked herself a meal and sat in the lounge and watched television. But still she wondered fearfully at her actions. To lie in her bed on the odd occasion and induce light ripples of pleasure from her clitoris, that she could understand. But to sprawl naked across her armchair, to masturbate to such a powerful orgasm, legs spread and body crudely open, was another matter, she felt. Uncharacteristic and, though beautiful, very wrong.

Haunted by dreams of lust, masturbation, orgasm, Donna woke to the hot sun bathing her bed, her bared breasts. Tentatively touching her nipple, she felt nothing. Her fingers explored her tightly closed groove, located her sleeping clitoris, but there was no response to her gentle massage, no arousal. Sadly, she realised that her body had returned to normality – cold, barren, alien to her caress.

But she'd had a taste, at least, of the delights her body had to offer, experienced the insurmountable pleasure of her pulsating clitoris as it had reached its peak, burst into orgasm. But now, as an erotic dream, the unreal pleasure was over – but not forgotten.

Alone in her bed, she thought of the day ahead, the laboratory, Alan – and remembered the plaster. She smiled as she kicked the quilt off the bed, stretching out her shapely young body. She'd return his precious plaster in exchange for his secret, she decided, as she wandered into the bathroom and stepped into the shower.

Grabbing the sticky plaster as she left for work, Donna dropped it into her bag. The sun was hot, the air fresh, and she wondered again at her actions of the night before as she gazed at a young man jogging towards her. She'd seen him once or twice before, jogging, keeping fit. His hairy chest rippling with muscles, his shorts bulging, he smiled as he passed. Suddenly she found herself imagining him naked, his penis free, bouncing up and down as he ran. Turning, she watched as he crossed the road and disappeared into the park. Strange, uncharacteristic thoughts. Checking the time, she decided to return his smile if she saw him again – get to know him, perhaps?

'Morning, Alan,' she trilled in her summery voice as she threw her bag under her bench and walked over to him. Looking up from his work he smiled, and then frowned.

'How are you feeling?' he asked cautiously.

'Fine, couldn't be better.'

'Everything all right when you got home last night?'

It was Donna's turn to frown. What did he know of her evening of masturbation? He couldn't know. 'Why do you ask?' she queried.

'Just wondered. What did you do with the plaster?'

'It's in my bag. It's important to you, isn't it?'

Looking back to his work, he didn't answer.

'If we're to work together, Alan, I want to know everything. You've been engrossed for weeks now. What are you working on, exactly?'

'I wasn't going to tell you until I'd perfected it,' he smiled triumphantly. 'But since you are so persistent, I'll explain.' Taking a strip of plasters from his drawer, his smile turned into a grin. 'The hormone replacement therapy programme we've been working on . . . I've developed a new type of skin patch, similar to those used to aid giving up smoking.'

'That's nothing new, they've been around for years.'

'*This* one's new. I've almost perfected the idea. I won't go into the details now, it's too complex, but the patches will have a far greater effect and last longer. They're simple to use, extremely cheap to manufacture – brilliant, in fact.'

'Why didn't you tell me about it?' Donna asked, taking the strip of patches from Alan's hand.

'I was going to. Just a few more tests to do, and I was going to tell you. I asked you how you felt because you took the patch from my bench last night and squeezed the hormone into your palm. So, how did you feel?'

'Fine,' she replied, convincing herself that the patch wasn't responsible for her becoming more sexually aroused than she'd ever imagined possible – for her masturbating to a hitherto unknown climax.

'Anyway, now you know. I've got to go upstairs and have a word with Malcolm about the marketing aspects. I'll be back soon.'

Tearing a patch off the strip, Donna examined it, wondering at the implications, the money to be made from such a discovery. Unethical, against all the rules, she knew, as she stuck it to her upper arm to prove to herself that the hormone could have had nothing to do with her massive orgasm.

'You all right?' asked Alan, standing before her on his return, fifteen minutes later.

'Yes, fine.' Gazing up at him, his body, she suddenly found herself highly aroused. Her stomach somersaulted, her womb fluttered as he moved towards her and frowned.

'He wants more bloody tests,' he complained, his dark eyes anguished. 'More and more tests before we can go ahead.'

Donna wasn't listening as she glanced down at his

tight trousers, imagined his penis – thick, long, hard. She felt dizzy now, sexually alive as she'd done in her flat. Moving nearer, she kissed him, pushed her hands inside his shirt, ran her fingers over his hard body, over his chest.

'What are you doing?' he breathed as she unzipped his trousers and pushed her hand inside the warmth, against the hardness there. She smiled her reply only with her full lips, her misty blue eyes. Pulling his penis out, she fell to her knees, levelling her face with her prize. Examining the purple knob, the loose, dark skin of his shaft as he breathed deeply and held her head, she opened her lips and engulfed the hard bulb in her hot mouth.

Stunned, Alan said nothing as she sucked, licked and mouthed. He could only gasp, cling to the bench and look down in disbelief at Donna, his lab assistant. Her long blonde hair over her pretty face, her mouth full with his hardness, she moved her head back and forth, rolled her tongue, bringing him ever closer to orgasm.

Never had Donna dreamed that she would take a man's penis in her mouth, but now she wanted nothing else. Sucking hard, running her tongue round and round, she became lost in her fantasy, her dreams of his tongue deep inside her soft sheath as she writhed in ecstasy in her armchair, crushing his head between her thighs as she came and poured her juices over his face.

Suddenly Alan gasped, the thick shaft twitched and the silky head swelled against her tongue. Her reward was nearing now, she knew, as she moved her head back and forth, gripping the hard shaft in her small hand, ramming the knob against the back of her throat as he shook and groaned in his male pleasure. Her clitoris aching, her cunt spasming, she closed her eyes and drank his sperm as it spurted, wakening her taste buds, filling her cheeks, running down her chin as she discovered a new, delirious sexual euphoria.

Gasping, grunting as if in pain, he pulled away, leaning on the bench to support his trembling body as he gazed down at her.

'That was wonderful,' he whispered. 'But . . .'

'No buts,' she smiled, rising to her feet and lifting her skirt. He lowered his eyes to the tight, bulging silk of her panties, wet and stained with her creamy juices. 'Aren't you going to reciprocate?' she breathed in her words of female arousal.

On his knees now, Alan peeled her panties from her warm mound and pulled them down to her ankles. Kicking the wet material to one side, Donna leaned back against the bench, feet apart, surveying the ceiling before closing her eyes in anticipation.

Swirling in her sensual trance, she felt his warm breath against her swollen cunt lips, his mouth brushing against her pubic hair, his hands gripping her buttocks as he pressed his tongue into her groove. Now she was alone, drifting in a cloudless sky, aware only of his tongue, her cunt, as he licked, sucked at her inner lips, nibbled, buried his face in her warmth, and located her swelling clitoris. Expertly, he teased, tantalised her precious, newly discovered cumbud until she gasped, shuddering, and cried out for more. Pressing her lips up and apart with his thumbs he brought out the full, pulsating length of her clitoris as her climax erupted over the tip, the wondrous sensations ripping through her trembling body, exploding in her mind, sending her up to her blue sky and beyond, to her heaven.

Lapping at her hole, drinking her warm, sticky fluid as her orgasm subsided, he held her buttocks again, found her dark crease and buried a finger in the hotness of her bowels. She writhed, squirmed, as he penetrated her body further and began to lick at her swelling bud again. Now a thumb found its way into her hot, wet tube to massage the soft lining. Her knees weakened, her stomach swirled as he worked on her intimacy, engulfed all she had between her legs, sucked an orgasm from her body. Her hands gripped his head, forcing his face into her open slit as her clitoris exploded. As her cunt spilled its juices, she flew higher – higher this time than the cloudless sky, than heaven, even, into a land of perpetual orgasm.

Resting now as he gently withdrew his finger, his thumb, Donna sat on the stool, depleted, her life force sapped, her womb drained, milked dry, her clitoris satisfied.

'I shouldn't have done that,' Alan whispered, taking her in his arms and kissing her full mouth with his wet lips. 'It wasn't right of me to . . .'

'Yes, it was right, Alan,' she breathed, savouring the taste of her sex fluid on his lips as she returned his kiss. 'It's what I wanted. It's what all women should want.'

Pulling her panties up her long legs, Donna suddenly became aware of her recent actions. As if waking from a dream, coming to her senses, the shock of her lewd behaviour hit her. She looked around the lab. The door was closed, thank God. Turning bright red, she adjusted her skirt, wondering why she'd allowed herself to behave like a nymphomaniac with Alan – her boss! What had driven her to take his penis in her mouth, drink the sperm as it pumped from his balls? But more, she wondered why she'd opened the intimacy of her young body to his tongue. What was possessing her, driving her on? What lurked in the shadows of her mind?

'I shouldn't have taken advantage of you . . .' Alan began again. 'I took advantage of you. I'm sorry, it was all my fault.' Guilt, fear. 'It was the best . . . You must have been sent by the angels, the angels of love.' Donna frowned. Angels of lust, more like, she mused. 'I didn't realise how you felt about me, Donna. What made you . . .'

'I don't know what came over me, Alan. Something weird happened. I just lost control . . . I'm sorry, let's forget about it.'

'I can't just forget the most beautiful experience of my life.'

'You must, you have to. It won't happen again, Alan, it mustn't.'

Agonising over why she'd behaved no better than a common whore, Donna settled at her bench and tried to concentrate on her work. She couldn't believe it was simply the effect of the hormone, the patch. Were nymphos made in the lab? But all too soon she was aware of her clitoris again. What was it that was driving her, swelling her bud, causing her stomach to somer-sault?

Her libido rising as the day drifted by, she began to think about Alan's penis – hard, thick, hot in her mouth as it pumped her full of sperm. Her cunt ached for his tongue again, her clitoris engorged and tingled delight-fully as she pictured her puffy cunt lips spread wide, her hole oozing with creamy liquid as he licked, drank from her body.

If only she'd taken his penis inside her tight sheath, massaged it with her spasming muscles! If only he'd come inside her, filled her womb with his gushing sperm! Almost crazed with desire, she desperately tried to drag her thoughts away from Alan, his penis, her clitoris, and concentrate on her work.

By the time she left the lab to make her way home, her clitoris was on the verge of spontaneous orgasm. With every step she took, it swelled, pulsating deliciously between her inflamed pussy lips. Her panties filled with her slippery cream as it flowed from her body with every swing of her hips. She was alive as never before – sensually alive with sex.

Whether or not it was a weird psychological effect brought about by her arousal, she didn't know, but she had the distinct feeling that she was being followed as she walked along the street. Turning her head, she thought she saw a figure dash behind a parked car. But no – the imagination, the mind, plays tricks, she decided. She wanted to be followed, by a man. She wanted to be used, taken by a stranger.

Reaching her flat, she flopped into her armchair and thrust her hands down her panties to relieve the overwhelming desire for orgasm. Again, she felt eyes upon her, prying eyes. But only the walls watched as she rubbed her clitoris and made it swell, inducing her slippery milk to flow from her gaping sheath.

As waves of pleasure rippled over her trembling body in response to her vibrating fingertips working between her moist lips, the front doorbell rang, distracting her, sending her crashing back to earth before she'd even orbited. Her friend, Helen, stood smiling on the doorstep. 'Come in,' Donna said wearily, her hands trembling, her cunt aching to be filled with her fingers – or, better, with Alan's hard penis.

'Hi, Donna. How's it going?' the girl asked, her long, frumpy skirt billowing in the breeze like a sail, her baggy top disguising her femininity, her long dark hair tangled and knotted.

Showing her friend into the lounge, Donna wondered why Helen didn't use makeup, take more care over her appearance. She was a petite, eighteen-year-old college student – pretty, even without makeup. With a little effort, she could almost be classed as stunning.

Constantly aware of her insatiable clitoris as they chatted, Donna wondered again about the hormone. She'd masturbated and derived unbelievable pleasure from her body after squeezing a patch in her hand. She'd taken Alan, used him, almost raped him, after applying a patch to her arm. The patch *had* to play a part in her uncharacteristic arousal. The hormone had some weird and wonderful side-effect, she was now sure. Soon, she found herself speculating how Helen would respond to it.

Pulling the patch from her arm, she moved towards Helen under the pretext of admiring the ring on her right hand. 'I've not seen that before, where did you get it from?' Donna asked, settling at Helen's feet and gently pressing the patch onto her ankle.

'You have seen it,' Helen replied, 'I've had it for ages.' It was a beautiful gold ring with a big ruby stone. Images of love, marriage. Donna hated rings.

The patch securely in place, she moved back to her armchair, apprehensive, excited, aroused as never before. Helen began to fidget a little, adjusting her long skirt, her 'mainsail,' her bra, as the patch took effect, took hold of her body, her mind.

'I had a terrible panic attack yesterday,' Helen confided. 'I had to leave the shopping trolley with my mother and run out of the supermarket!'

'I thought they were getting better?'

'No. I'll never be free of them. No-one can help, it's just something I've got to live with, I suppose.'

'What does your doctor say?'

'Nothing, it's just one of those things.'

'They will probably wear off as you get older. Anyway, I'll make some coffee.' Donna moved towards the door. 'Make yourself comfortable and relax. I won't be long.'

Having filled the kettle, she crept into the hall and gazed at her friend through the crack in the door. Helen was still fidgeting, rubbing her crotch, stroking her nipples through her baggy top. Perhaps she was about to have one of her attacks and run out of the flat? The patch might have some terrible effect, send her mind off course.

Donna grinned as the girl closed her eyes and began rubbing her clitoris through her clothing. Her mouth open slightly, her breathing deep, tangibly she sank under the magical spell of the patch into a warm pool of lust.

'I'm just popping out for some milk,' Donna called as she returned to the kitchen to open the back door and bang it shut. Creeping into the hall again to spy on her friend, she had to stifle a gasp. Her skirt up over her stomach, her panties round her ankles, Helen was openly masturbating, vigorously working on her clitoris with her fingertips, moaning deeply as her orgasm approached.

Donna gazed in sheer disbelief at the girl who'd never previously shown the slightest sign of femininity, sexuality. Now wantonly masturbating, pulling her lips apart with one hand and working on her clitoris with the other, she arched her back, gasped and collapsed, quivering, breathless, satisfied. Her fingers inducing the last ripples of pleasure from her inflamed cunt, she gently drifted back into her satiated body and relaxed.

Gazing at Helen's dark bush, the swollen pink lips between her milk-white thighs, Donna's hand slid down inside her panties to appease her own swelling cumbud. A terrible realization suddenly hit her as she leaned against the door frame and massaged her clitoris – she desperately wanted Helen's body, to touch her, feel her, kiss her, sink her fingers, her tongue, into her wet hole.

Overwhelmed with lust, she wandered into the lounge and gazed at her friend's splayed thighs. Helen moved quickly, closing her legs, pulling her knickers up, her skirt down. Donna smiled as she knelt down and lifted Helen's skirt, tugged her wet knickers down again and parted her thighs. 'I was watching you,' she murmured as she pushed her face into the dark tangle of wet hair and breathed in the heady female scent.

Who was watching who? More than the walls were looking. Donna again felt prying eyes. *Whose* eyes? The effects of the patch still controlling her libido, driving her on, she became lost in her living fantasy. The walls, the eyes, faded into oblivion. Helen said nothing, responding silently by opening her thighs further and reclining in the chair to offer her open sex to another girl's mouth.

Her lips pressed against her friend's wet folds, Donna closed her eyes and lapped up the female sex fluid as it flowed in torrents from Helen's trembling body, savouring her first-ever taste of another girl's nectarous secretions. Helen writhed and moaned as her bud was sucked from its pinken cover, teased by a hot, darting tongue – a female tongue. Coming now, she panted, gasped her appreciation as her sheath cried out for attention, something to grip on during the climax, something to squeeze, rhythmically massage and bathe with its warm milk.

Groping for Donna's hand, Helen moved it to the entrance of her quivering body, desperate to push it inside. Learning quickly, the older girl thrust four fingers into the spasming chasm where they were crushed in the hot wetness, lubricated by the warm flowing juices as they thrust in and out like a hard penis.

As Helen's body poured out its orgasm, both girls began to tear at each other's clothing in a strange and uncontrollable sexual frenzy, ripping the material from their bodies to offer their nakedness to each other. Nails and teeth sinking into flesh, tongues licking, mouths sucking, fingers desperately trying to gain entrance to crevices, they writhed, then fell to the floor in a tangle of trembling limbs.

Pinning Donna down, Helen sat astride her face and lowered herself over her mouth. Rocking, gyrating her hips, running her gaping cunt over the obliging facial orifice, she shuddered as she reached another mind-blowing climax and decanted the contents of her love-tube into Donna's thirsty mouth. Slurping, drinking as the orgasm ran on and on, Donna lost herself, her mind, in a swirling mist of love, lust – lesbian sex.

Rolling over, arms, legs entwined, tangled in lust, Donna squatted over Helen's face, holding her offering inches away, lowering herself then rising again, teasing her friend until she begged to taste, to drink from the gaping chasm. Opening her vaginal lips with her fingers, Donna settled over Helen's mouth and gently slid the length of her groove back and forth, catching her clitoris on the girl's tongue now and then, pushing her hole over her mouth, filling her with her hot cream.

Reaching up, Helen pinched Donna's nipples, squeezing, pulling them until the sexual pain caused Donna to shudder, her clitoris to erupt, her womb to contract rhythmically. The relentless waves of pure sexual ecstasy rolled on and on, crashing over the girls, wet in their wetness, bathing them with warmth, unleashing their minds, their psyche, until they were both left gasping, quivering, panting for lifegiving breath.

Side by side now, they lay calm, serene. Donna frowned as she suddenly regained control, became aware of her wrongdoing. The effects of the patch were wearing off fast, making way for guilt, fear. Peeling the patch from Helen's ankle, she stood up and quickly dressed, ignoring her friend's pleas for more pleasure, dragging her gaze away from the girl's fingers which voraciously caressed her clitoris, sank into her hot body.

'I must go out,' Donna lied as she finished dressing. 'I've a lot to do and . . .'

'Don't you want me again?'

'Not now . . . I – I'm going out. Let yourself out when you've . . .'

Dashing from the flat, Donna took a deep breath. She was terrified by what she'd done with her friend, horrified by the obscenity of their debauched, lesbian union. Pleasures of the flesh, quivering, wet flesh – *female* flesh.

It was no good running away, she knew. But how could she ever face Helen again? What would her friend think when the effects of the patch had worn off? Not knowing why she'd stripped off, licked and fingered Donna's vagina, had her own vagina sucked, her clitoris brought to orgasm by Donna's tongue, she'd think the worst: Donna was a rampant lesbian – Helen was a

rampant lesbian. What would Helen do? Kill herself?
She had always been unstable, suffered terribly from
her strange panic attacks. Perhaps now she'd go over
the top and do something stupid.

Wandering down the street to the park, Donna
breathed in the warm, evening air and sat on a bench
under the sun, the birds, the white wisps of cloud. She
wanted to be a cloud, to drift away and escape from the
world. Eyes again, lurking, spying. Where?

Surely the patch couldn't be to blame? she pondered,
looking around the park. And if it was, then what other
wonderful side-effects did it have? She'd have to tell
Alan. If the patches were put on the open market,
prescribed by doctors to thousands of women, the
results could be disastrous – wondrous.

But she'd derived immense pleasure from the patch.
Could she now throw away a lifetime of unadulterated,
mind-blowing sex? Could she deny herself her newly
discovered sexuality? After twenty-five years, the
angels of lust had at last touched her and brought her
orgasm – life.

Chapter Two

Leaving Donna's flat, Helen walked home. Shocked, distressed, her body aching as the effect of the patch wore off, she crept into her house via the back door, red-faced, guilty, praying that her mother wouldn't be around.

'That you, Helen?' a voice called from the lounge.

'Yes, mum,' she replied shakily, standing before the hall mirror brushing her long, bedraggled hair and adjusting her torn skirt as best she could before facing her mother.

The woman smiled to greet her daughter, then her pretty red lips curled with anger. 'Where have you been all this time? What have you been up to?' she enquired suspiciously. Helen sat on the sofa, blushing, averting her gaze, fiddling with her fingers like a naughty school-girl. She could hide nothing from her most prim and proper mother, she knew. Her lies had always been blatantly obvious in the past and she'd long since given up trying to pull the wool over her eyes. But now she *had* to lie, to concoct a story to cover her outrageously lewd, debased, lesbian behaviour.

'I've been to see Donna,' she replied softly.

'You haven't been seeing that young Martin, have you? I've told you before to keep away from him! He's a no-good lout!'

'Of course I haven't! Phone Donna, if you like – she'll tell you.'

Her mother launched into her usual lecture. 'Donna's got a good job, she studied, worked hard. Why you mess around at college, I don't know! You should take your studies seriously. At eighteen you should be thinking of the future, not playing around with boys!'

'I've not been playing around with boys!' contradicted Helen, her guilt rising as she stormed from the room.

In the security of her bedroom, she slipped out of her skirt and wet panties. The evidence, she thought, stuffing them at the back of her drawer. Sitting on her bed, she examined her inflamed, vaginal lips, her wet and stretched hole, her tiny clitoris that seemed to smile by way of appreciation as she popped it out.

Easing a finger into her warm, creamy hole, she became confused. The sensations were wonderful, but it was wrong. Her mother had always warned her not to touch herself, never to derive pleasure from her body. But now, her precious virginity, technically, had been crudely taken, snatched from her in a wild, frantic session of wanton lust – by a woman.

Closing the bathroom door as her mother came up the stairs, she stepped into the shower. Massaging soap into her firm, perfectly formed breasts, her nipples hardened. Directing the shower nozzle between her puffy, vaginal lips, her clitoris throbbed. Her body had been awoken, at long last. Womanhood had arrived. But gazing at her violated groove, once private, sacrosanct, questions filled her mind. What had she done? Who had initiated the lesbian act? Why had she masturbated the minute Donna had left the room? She didn't want any more confrontations – her guilt was more than enough to cope with, let alone her mother's cross-examination.

Guilt? It weighed so heavily. If there were no guilt, no remorse, she reflected, she could blatantly enjoy the pleasures of her young body, her clitoris. She wanted to be an angel – free, flying naked in swirling clouds of lust. She wanted to be a woman uninhibited.

Finding Helen's bedroom door open, her mother crept into the room, her eyes scanning for evidence of the girl's obvious lies. As if led by some unnatural instinct, she opened the drawer and came across the panties, soaking wet, stained – torn. Clutching her evidence, she bounded down the stairs and rang Donna. Yes, Helen had been with her. No, nothing had happened, they'd been alone together. Yes, as far as she knew, she'd gone straight home. No, she hadn't mentioned Martin or any other boys.

Vacating the bathroom in her dressing gown, Helen blushed. Her heart sank as her mother confronted her, brandishing the wet, ripped panties – indisputable proof of her act of frenzied lust. Her mother had always been anti-sex – that's why her father had left, Helen was sure. Perhaps she was asexual? She'd often overheard the heated discussions, the complaints from her father, the distressed confessions, desperate words of frustration from her mother. 'I can't come! I've never had an orgasm in my life! It's not that I don't love you – I just can't come!'

Before her staggering awakening with Donna, Helen had never allowed her fingers to infiltrate her tight, virginal hole, never masturbated, never experienced orgasm. Until now, she'd not understood the implications of her mother's complaint, not conceived the problem. How could her mother, any woman, have sex and not come? she now wondered, meeting her mother's fiery eyes.

'Well, my girl! What have you to say about these?'
What indeed had she to say? They were wet, torn – so?
The incriminating panties swung only inches from
Helen's face. She'd have to admit to experimenting with
a boy in the park. Better to do that than to admit to
squatting over Donna's face, having her sodden hole
licked, coming in her mouth, writhing in the ecstasy of
lesbian lust.

'Donna said that you were at her flat, alone with her.
She wouldn't lie, not Donna, so how did this happen?
Why are your knickers ripped? Why are they . . .
What's this mess in them? And don't tell me that it was
an accident! You haven't been *touching* yourself, have
you?' Did angels touch themselves?

Masturbation was the answer – she'd experimented.
Her panties had been torn for some time, they were
getting old. The mother's expression softened, the
anger subsided slightly, she believed the story. 'Why did
you do it?' she asked. 'Don't you know that it's wrong?
Masturbation is . . .'

'I'm eighteen, mum! There's nothing wrong with . . .
Well, I was just experimenting, that's all. Haven't you
ever . . .?'

'Certainly not! What do you think I am?' An angel,
perhaps?

The woman's eyelids lowered, veiling the sadness
mirrored in her eyes. Her mouth fell, expressing disappointment – not in Helen, but in herself. 'It's all right,
mum,' Helen began, placing her hand on her mother's
shoulder. 'I know about your problem. I've heard you
and dad talking.'

Offering Helen the panties, her eyes tearful, the
woman turned and made her way downstairs. Grabbing
her jacket from the banister, she left the house. The

confrontation between the two women was over, but there was still the flak – each had their own private and most secret battles raging in their minds. Dressing, Helen wondered how she could ever face Donna again. Walking down the leafy avenue, her eyes tearful, her mother asked herself how she could ever again look her daughter in the eye.

Donna's heart sank at the sound of the front doorbell. It couldn't be Helen, surely? What would she say to her? Opening the door, her mouth fell open at the sight of Helen's mother. Helen hadn't said anything to her – surely? She wouldn't tell her mother what had taken place! Six years Helen's senior, Donna knew that she was responsible – she was to blame for what had happened. But there was no proof, nothing to implicate her, other than Helen's word.

'Hello, Sue, come in,' she invited, concealing her anxiety. Her heart banging hard against her chest, she opened the door wider, forcing a smile as she showed her visitor into the lounge. Watching her seat herself in the chair where her daughter had spread her legs to allow Donna to lick at her pinken folds, stiffen her clitoris, take her virginity, bring her to her maiden climax, fear mingled with Donna's guilt. Donna chose the armchair where she'd opened her own swollen lips, masturbated and come as never before.

'I'm worried about Helen,' Sue began, wringing her hands, her expression anguished. 'She's a very good friend of yours and . . . It's not easy for me to talk about this but – she's been masturbating. Will you speak to her about it, Donna? Tell her how wrong it is, that she shouldn't . . . Just have a word with her, will you?'

Relief gushing over her, as had Helen's juices, Donna's breathing became easier and she smiled,

Ray Gordon

stifling a laugh. She could still see Helen naked, writing with the sensations emanating from her clitoris. If only her mother knew! The walls knew. The poor woman had come to her for help, advice, to the very person who'd taken her daughter, sucked on her pretty little cumbud, lapped up her creamy offering – introduced her to the delights of lesbianism.

'There's nothing wrong with masturbation,' Donna asserted, wondering why Sue saw it as a problem. 'We've all done it at one time or another, it's quite normal – healthy, even.'

'I've never . . . Not everyone masturbates, Donna. And it's far from normal, healthy, as you put it. It's . . .'

'It's nothing to worry about, Sue. She's discovering herself, her body. Let her get on with it and be thankful that she's not . . .'

'Not what?'

'Not into boys and all that, yet.'

Donna wondered at Sue, an attractive woman in her late thirties, possessing such a stilted Victorian attitude. Suddenly, she remembered the patch. If any woman needed to use the patch, to experience the wonders of powerful orgasm, it was Sue, she decided. Thank God she'd not been wearing the patch herself when Sue had arrived! By now she would surely have been between the poor woman's thighs, sucking a climax from her hard, neglected clitoris, pushing her tongue deep into her frustrated hole. She imagined first bringing Helen to orgasm before moving to attend her mother's clitoris. To pleasure both women simultaneously! The very thought sent a carnal shiver up her spine.

'I'll have a word with Helen the next time I see her,' Donna promised. 'In the meantime, don't worry.'

'I'd appreciate it if you would,' Sue replied as she stood up. 'I don't want her mixed up in . . . Well, sex, I suppose. She's just not ready for it.'

'I'm sure she'll meet a nice man one day, marry and have a family and everything will be fine.' That's what she'd wanted herself, once . . . But with her new sexual awakening, the discovery of the power between her legs, everything had dramatically changed. The little, twee housewife with the proprietary husband in tow, dinner on the table at six every evening, performing her wifely duty every Saturday night, wasn't for her now. What *was* for her? She didn't know. 'Go home now, and forget all about it,' she advised her friend's mother.

Alan Rosenberg raised his eyes and smiled as Donna walked into the lab the following morning. She could feel the tension as she returned his smile and sat at her bench. Nothing would be the same again, it couldn't be. What had happened between them had changed every-thing. He was aware of this – but not of her new life outside the lab, her beautiful masturbation session, her wonderfully debauched time with Helen.

Torn, unable to decide between Alan and Helen, male and female, Donna sighed. Alan was certainly attractive, his penis, long, thick, desirable. And Helen? Naked, her legs splayed, her swollen lips parted, her body offered to Donna in lust, her inner beauty shone through the dowdy exterior. And who better to lick and suck at a woman's pinken folds, to tease a woman's clitoris and bring it to orgasm, than another woman?

'How's it going?' Donna enquired as Alan wandered towards her, his trousers somehow tighter than usual, his zip bulging invitingly. Even patchless, her mind swirled with sex. Perhaps her body, even her thinking, had been permanently changed by the hormone? She gazed longingly at his bulging manhood. Was his penis stiff? She wanted it.

'It's going very well, but I have to do a lot more work on the side-effects of the patches,' he said, dangling his long legs from the bench and abstractedly running his fingers through his dark hair. 'Now Malcolm wants to market them as soon as possible. Our grant is coming to an end, we're as good as broke. I have to know more, discover if there are any detrimental side-effects.'

She should reveal her secret, she knew. But then women would be denied the opportunity, the right, to discover orgasm, as she had, as Helen had, as Helen's mother so desperately needed to – and soon would. How many women were there out there who had never known *real* orgasm? she wondered. How many women were crying out for the aphrodisiacal effect of the patches? But was it an aphrodisiac? She knew there was no such thing. Studying for her degree in chemistry had taught her a lot, and working with Alan even more. Aphrodisiacs didn't exist. At least, no-one had yet discovered one – had they?

'What side-effects?' she asked, imagining something awful happening to her body.

'There probably aren't any. This isn't a drug, as such, it's just a simple hormone which tops up and balances the other hormones present in the female. I doubt, I very much hope, there aren't any adverse side-effects.'

Donna averted her gaze. Adverse side-effects? Destroying a woman's inhibitions, bringing out her true sexuality, enabling her to achieve wondrous orgasms, could hardly be termed side-effects – and, far from adverse, they were heavenly. The patch was an important discovery that could revolutionise women's lives the world over. She would conduct the research herself, she decided. For a start, test it on Helen again, on her mother, realise its true potential.

Alan couldn't test the patches on anyone willy-nilly: he'd be struck off if he were caught. And Malcolm's properly administered and controlled experiments would take an age. Donna couldn't wait. Highly unethical and probably illegal as it was, nonetheless in the name of science, of women's welfare the world over, her own work and clandestine research on the patches had to continue. So she justified her intended course of action to herself.

'Do you fancy a meal, or a drink this evening?' Alan asked, gazing at Donna's nipples pressing against her tight top. They were hard, sensitive – alive. At last, he'd noticed her. After all her efforts to get his attention over the years, he was actually asking her out. But, she thought sadly, it had taken her body, the intimacy between her legs, naked, open to his mouth, to lure him.

What was it with men? she wondered. Why were they so very different to women in their thinking? At the first taste of sex they were ready to wine and dine, to move mountains, in the hope of having more sex, and more sex. But then – what was it with women?

Donna imagined all women wearing patches, becoming as their male counterparts, chatting up men, enjoying sex without the need for a proper relationship, without love, just as men seemed to. Or, perhaps, having wonderful sex with each other? Were angels male or female? Who needed men when women understood each other's bodies, their minds, so much better than men? But remembering Alan's hard penis throbbing against her tongue, filling her mouth with his hot sperm, she knew that men could never become redundant. Her graphic thoughts overwhelming her with desire, she wanted to kneel before Alan and drink from the bulging head of his hard penis again. The picture stirred her clitoris, wet the warm furrow between her bloated cunt lips – to grip his shaft in her small hands, knead his balls, run her tongue around his purple, ballooning knob as he groaned with pleasure had been a beautiful experience, and one that she desperately wanted again. But no, she felt different now. Without the patch, without the strange, consuming, drug-like effect, she had some power, some control over her emotions – sadly. Later, she promised herself, she would slip a patch onto her arm and release Alan's penis from his tight trousers: in a sexual haze, engulf the beautiful head in her mouth. Her cunt, too, would receive attention – Alan's attention, his fingers, his tongue. But this time, she would also allow him to fill her tight sheath with his penis. She would lie over her bench, her legs spread wide to receive his hardness, take it deep into her body and instruct him to stretch her, fill her, come inside her – fuck her.

Despite her lustful thoughts, Donna decided to decline Alan's offer for that particular evening. Instead, she would invite Helen's mother round, borrow a strip of patches and experiment on the woman. Recalling her threesome lesbian fantasy, she toyed with the idea of inviting both Helen *and* her mother round, slipping patches on them both. But as much as the idea appealed to her, she couldn't do it, she decided. It wouldn't be fair, would it? But then, all was fair in lust and greed.

Alan hovered around Donna like a bluebottle

throughout the day, wondering why she seemed to have reverted to her old self. Why, one minute she was all over him, taking him in her mouth, drinking his sperm and giving her body, and the next, appearing indifferent, wintry cold towards him. With her racing thoughts, weird and wonderful fantasies, pictures of Helen, Sue, herself, writhing in naked ecstasy, hidden from him, he was disappointed, confused.

Observing his mood, Donna realised the full potential of her young body, the power between her legs. When she wished to be wined and dined, made love to, she now knew exactly what to do. The patches could, and would, bring her anything she desired – if only she could lay her hands on some.

All day, she'd waited for the opportunity to raid Alan's drawer until, just as she was preparing to go home, he left the lab. Grabbing her chance, she opened his drawer and seized a strip of five patches, slipping them into her handbag. As a thief in the night, she stole from the lab, walked quickly down the corridor and out into the warm, fresh air. Eyes again – piercing, gazing, watching. Whose eyes? Eyes of her imagination?

Birds singing in trees, pale faces passing, cars moving – the world going by. Overwhelmed by an incredible sense of knowledge, power, she clutched her bag tightly, like a Christmas present, grinning as she imagined the fun, the excitement that the patches would bring her – the incredible consequences. Where was the world going to in such a hurry?

She breathed a sigh of relief when Sue answered the phone. 'I need to talk to you, Sue,' she said shakily, adrenalin coursing through her veins, her legs weak.

'About Helen?'

'Yes, yes, about Helen. Can you come round?'

'Half-an-hour. Shall I bring her with me? We can all discuss it together over coffee.'

Over naked, trembling flesh, more like, thought Donna. Her stomach somersaulted, she gulped, caught her breath, almost said yes. A threesome? God, what was she thinking of? Why was she thinking like this? 'Come alone,' she forced herself to say eventually. 'I'll chat with Helen some other time. It's you I want – I mean, want to help.'

As she showered, washing her body in readiness for sex with her friend's mother, Donna wondered about the patch, how to apply it secretly. Then, fearfully, she wondered exactly what she was planning to do. To seduce an older woman, any woman, for that matter, was ridiculous, unthinkable. Drying herself, knowing that she couldn't go through with it, she quickly opened her bag and stuck a patch to her upper arm. Then, sitting in the lounge in her short skirt and tight top, she waited for the effect, for her mind to be freed of inhibitions, her thoughts to turn to sex, her clitoris to swell and demand her fingers.

She didn't have to wait long, for it came soon, the magical effect, guilt fading into an enveloping sensation of sexual arousal. The chains gone, her inhibitions cast aside, she was ready to seduce Helen's mother. Now her clitoris was the only being, nothing else mattered. Guilt, anxiety, apprehension, all had gone, blown away on the wind of lust.

The front doorbell rang. This was it. Taking another patch from her bag, Donna walked unsteadily through the hall. 'Hello, Sue,' she greeted the woman cheerily, looking down at her long skirt, imagining her tight panties flattening the soft hairs covering her puffy vaginal lips. She smiled warmly – the patch was working perfectly. Desire welled up from the deep, surfacing.

Passing Sue in the narrow hallway, Donna stopped her and lifted her long, dark hair from her shoulders. 'You've got a feather stuck in your hair,' she lied, gently pressing the patch onto her neck. 'That's got it! Let's go through to the lounge. Would you like some tea or coffee?' Declining, Sue made herself comfortable in an armchair. Donna crouched in her lair, grinning, waiting in anticipation, her stomach swirling, increasingly aware of her clitoris with every passing second.

The inevitable fidgeting started – uneasy, her hand between her legs pretending to adjust her skirt, Sue was experiencing the beautiful awakening of her body, her sexuality. To leave her alone for a while to masturbate or to move in now? Donna didn't know. She chatted, talked about the weather, her job, the flat and how she'd like to move to a bigger place. She spoke about life – what was it? Sue wasn't listening – her eyes widening, her breathing quickening, she was ready, Donna knew, as she tentatively moved across the room and sat on the floor by her victim.

'How's Helen?' she asked, pressing her body against Sue's legs, placing a hand on her knee, gazing longingly into her green eyes. The older woman didn't reply, reclining as she allowed her legs to fall open, relaxing as the patch took control, loosened the chains, released her mind. Moving her hand to Sue's calf, Donna slid it under her long skirt. Up to her knee, her inner thigh, the soft, warm mound between her legs, her hand explored, her fingers caressed. Closing her eyes, Sue drifted away. Donna knew where her mind had taken her – to that wonderful land of uninhibited sexual fantasy where warm pools of sensuality engulfed her. Where angels play.

Donna contemplated Sue, relaxed, open, calm, serene, with incredulity. How could a simple hormone, as Alan had put it, transform an asexual prude into a nymphomaniacal lesbian? It didn't matter – nothing mattered in the moment, any moment. She would discover all there was to know about the hormone later. Now, there were more important things on her mind – not least, the hidden beauty between Sue's soft thighs, her moist, swollen valley.

Her own clitoris swelling hard between her cunt lips, Donna lifted Sue's skirt over her stomach and gazed at her prize – the tight, red panties hugging the delicate contour of her mound, outlining the dividing groove where her clitoris lay, ripe, ready for her mouth, her tongue. Were the walls gazing, too? Someone was, she sensed it. A woman's intuition.

She lifted her hips clear of the chair as Donna tugged on her panties. She was aware, Donna knew. Aware that she was about to experience the ultimate sexual union, a female tongue, hot, darting between her nether lips, penetrating her body. Her panties down to her thighs, her dark bush lay before Donna's hungry eyes, the flattened, matted hair springing to life, spongy, the lips swelling, dividing, to reveal the little pleasure bud that she was sure had never known orgasm in its thirty odd years.

Further down the panties slid, over her knees, her calves, her feet. A small white stain lay in the crotch – a female stain. Free now, her thighs fell open to expose the full extent of the wet valley between her pink pussy lips. Her heart thumping, her breathing heavy with lust, Donna moved her face nearer to her goal as she peeled the soft lips apart. Glistening in the light, the soft flesh had already reddened, swollen with desire in readiness for love.

Placing a tender kiss on the warm lips surrounding Sue's vagina, Donna wondered how large her breasts were, how long were the nipples of a woman nearing her forties. Becoming aware of her own nipples hardening beneath her tight clothing, she lifted her top over her head and unclipped her bra, allowing her breasts to fall free, her nipples to grow. Cupping her breast in her hand, she rubbed her nipple up and down Sue's opening groove, lubricating the brown bud with the warm fluid oozing from the older woman's vagina. Pressing her nipple into the wet valley, Donna managed to push it into Sue's vagina where she ran it round and round, hardening the penis-like protrusion, bathing her dark aureola. If only it were longer – inches longer! Moving up the valley, she pressed her nipple against Sue's clitoris. Gently, the two hard buds rubbed against each other, caressing, massaging, bringing new and wonderful sensations to both women. Donna looked at Sue and smiled, pleased by the pleasure so obvious in her eyes – the pleasure of trembling, lesbian flesh.

Her nipple now wet, hard, aching for attention, Donna moved her breast up to Sue's mouth. Offering the milk bud to her lips, she pressed it into the hot wetness as Sue's mouth opened. The older woman suckled as a babe, licking her own juices from the elongated brown tissue, biting, mouthing, yielding Donna strange and wondrous sensations that filled her breast and coursed through her body to erupt in her clitoris. Round and round Sue's hot tongue ran, as if attempting to bring the nipple itself to orgasm. Lost in a sexual haze, Donna willed her nipple to come. But then Sue's hand was inside the girl's wet knickers, massaging the hard protrusion, matching the rhythm of her tongue against her nipple. Donna tossed back her long, blonde hair, closed her eyes and gasped as her climax welled, oscillating between her nipple and her clitoris. Terrifyingly powerful, it ripped through her young quivering body, rocking her womb, the very centre of her soul. Biting hard on the nipple, Sue caressed her own clitoris as Donna floated gently down from her heaven. She desperately needed attention – it was her turn now for love, for orgasm, Donna knew.

Sue breathed heavily, moaned her sexual moan as Donna slipped her nipple from her mouth and moved her face down between her legs to caress the soft flesh tentatively with the tip of her tongue. Older than Helen, mature, Sue's outer lips were fuller, her inner folds more wrinkled, darker, protruding. Her beautiful clitoris was longer, thicker, more accessible – a small, pink bird in a warm nest awaiting food. Pressing on the soft flesh surrounding the expectant bud, Donna eased out its full length and engulfed the protrusion. Gently sucked, it stiffened immediately, swelled even more, throbbed in response to the female tongue – the first ever tongue to explore, to excite, the sensitive, trembling flesh.

Easing her captive's legs over the arms of the chair, Donna opened the dark, dank entrance to her body, her womb. Moving down, she buried her tongue in the wet warmth, deeper and deeper until her mouth pressed hard against the surrounding flesh. The juice of love flowed in torrents from the open hole, filling her mouth with its creamy texture as she stretched the protective cushions of sex open further and licked at the small urethral opening. Sue writhed and lowered her hips to bring her clitoris to meet the girl's tongue again. She would soon come, Donna knew, as she flicked the bud with the tip of her tongue, still stretching the full lips apart, forcing her mouth against the soaked flesh, the hardness of her pubic bone.

'That's it, that's it!' Arching her back and splaying her legs wider, the triumphant cry garbled from Sue's lips – a woman lost in a sexual heaven. Grabbing Donna's head, she yanked it back and forth, grinding her body into her mouth as she shuddered and rocked with her orgasm as it rolled from her depths and exploded into a hot, female mouth. Unable to breathe, Donna tried to pull away but she was locked between Sue's twitching thighs, her face glued to her open cunt. Eyes watching the lesbian union. Eyes of her driving demon?

At last, the waves of pleasure calmed, pooled around Sue's clitoris and gently subsided, leaving her serene, satisfied beyond belief. Free now, Donna fell back and collapsed to the floor, her face wet, her mouth full of creamy fluid – hot, bitter-sweet, beautiful. Her body trembling, she'd barely caught her breath when Sue leapt from the chair and began tugging at her panties. Almost torn from her body as she raised her hips, the wet panties flew across the room as two fingers rudely thrust into her body. Three, four fingers now, massaging, stretching the soft lining of her sheath, opening her cunt to its wonderfully painful limits. Suddenly, her legs were yanked clear of the floor, her knees pushed up to her breasts, to expose the full length of her shamelessly open groove. Almost brutally, the intruding fingers penetrated to the depths of her young sex, halted only by her cervix. Full to capacity, her hole almost split open, her muscles gripped the fingers as they moved in and out like a huge penis, battering her cervix until she cried out. 'Suck my clitoris! Lick it! Make me come in your mouth!' Her hair matted, wet with perspiration, Sue flung Donna's legs apart and sank her face into her open crack, lapping up the milk fluid, teasing her bursting clitoris until the girl shuddered and let out a long, low moan of satisfaction. Her thighs splayed, her cunt decanting its hot, slippery cream, her clitoris ballooning against Sue's vibrating tongue, she convulsed, shuddering uncontrollably with every ripple of pleasure from her orgasm.

Floating gently down from her peak, Donna rolled her eyes as Sue softly circled her clitoris with her tongue to sustain the last pulses of orgasm, massaged the walls of her hot vagina, induced the last drop of milk from her love-tube.

Both drained, exhausted, they lay on the floor and gazed at each other. 'There are no words,' Sue whispered as she leaned over and kissed Donna's full mouth, saliva and sex juice mingling deliciously. 'No words to describe the pleasure, the beauty, of what I have, for the first time, experienced. It was . . . heavenly.' Where was heaven?

Donna smiled. There was no embarrassment, no regret, no explanation needed. They had both found an illicit love, a sanctified union only possible between two females. Their hands, fingers, exploring each other's wet and swollen fissures, lips, tongues pressed together, they breathed deeply, satisfied, locked in a wondrous sexual love – a female love they'd never thought possible.

'Is this what you did to my daughter?' Sue asked, nibbling at Donna's hot mouth and pushing her fingers into her wetness once more. Donna opened her eyes. What could she say?

'Yes, it is,' she breathed, biting on Sue's lips.

'Then I have you to thank for awakening Helen. If she experienced anything remotely as wonderful as I just have, then she has discovered herself, and I have you to thank for that. I've always dreaded the thought that, like me, she'd never be able to come.'

'She needs a man, not me,' Donna conceded. 'A hard, thick penis.'

'And no doubt she will find one. But hopefully, like me, she now understands her body, the pleasures it can give. Are you going to see her again?'

Donna thought for a moment. To initiate the girl into lesbian sex had certainly awoken her inner desires, but to continue to pleasure her, to love her body? She wasn't sure. Yes, she would delight in having Helen lick and mouth between her legs, drink from her love-tube again – but was it right? What *was* right, or wrong?

'I don't know,' she finally whispered. 'What do you think?'

'I'd rather you didn't,' came the soft reply. 'I'd like *us* to do this again, though.'

'We will, I promise,' Donna grinned as she stood up. 'But is this the real you? I mean, what drove you to this?'

'I don't know. I've always been so . . . It doesn't matter what brought about the change in me, I like it very much – I like *you* very much. It's strange, but I feel no guilt, no regret, only overwhelming gratification. You've brought out the woman in me, shown me love, sex, as I never thought possible.'

What was love? Sex, perhaps?

Helping Sue to her feet, Donna discreetly pulled the patch from her neck, wondering how she'd feel when the effects had worn off. Would she fly at Helen, accuse her of being a lesbian? A slut? Would she blame Donna? Whatever the result, Donna had shown her how to enjoy her body. Perhaps now she would allow her fingers to seek out her clitoris as she lay in her bed at night. Perhaps now, uninhibited, she would pleasure herself, without the need for a patch. Was not that what clitorises were for?

When Sue had gone, Donna flopped into her arm-chair and peeled the patch from her skin. Gazing at the small, round, sticky piece of thin plastic, she contemplated. What effect would *two* patches have on a woman? What would happen if a man were to use one? Would he grow breasts? Become an uncontrollable, insatiable sex-maniac, perhaps? Had Alan tried one? she wondered. Should she discreetly stick one on his arm and then open her legs to him?

Undoubtedly an incredible discovery, she wondered again at the potential, the scope. But what, exactly, did the patches, the hormone, do to the body, the brain chemistry, to drive two heterosexual women to engage in abandoned, frenzied, lesbian lust? Further investigation was needed, she knew. Again, she justified herself, her actions, to herself – in the name of science, she was researching, learning, making new and wonderful discoveries. Her campaign was to liberate women, free them from their chains, open their minds, their beautiful bodies, to the wonders of masturbation – massive orgasms. Unleash women, break down the old ideals, beliefs, and allow them to discover not only their own bodies, but each other's.

Poor Alan, this was his discovery, his baby. But she couldn't tell him, not yet. Not until her work was well under way.

Chapter Three

Lynn Bulmur sat in the café drawing hard on her cigarette. Wearing yesterday's makeup, her cropped, dark hair a mess, her nail polish chipped, Donna barely recognized her.

'Lynn? It *is* you!' she exclaimed as she neared her table.

'Ryan, isn't it? Donna Ryan?'

'Yes, how are you?'

'How do I look? No, don't answer that!'

The last person Donna had expected to run into in her lunch hour was Lynn Bulmur. She'd not seen her since the day she was thrown out of university for a variety of reasons, including holding rampant orgies in her room. The least likely candidate for a patch! Donna mused, remembering the rumours. Obviously over the eight years or so she'd gone downhill, as just about everyone on the campus had predicted. But to end up like this? Her parents were rich, well-spoken. Lynn had been the same once, but now? The Bulmurs had obviously disowned the dishevelled mess they'd once called their pretty little girl.

'So, what have you been up to?' Donna asked, eyeing her black leather miniskirt, fishnet-stockinged legs and red stilettos.

'This and that – and you? You look as if you're doing well.'

'I'm with Grunwerg Research Laboratories.'

'You got your degree, then? Live locally?'

'Thornton Road, and you?'

'Just around the corner in Park Street, next to the pub. I moved in a few weeks ago. No job yet, but who'd employ someone like me? You couldn't lend me a fiver, could you?'

Making her excuses to leave, Donna ignored Lynn's request. She was the last person she'd lend money to, and it was pretty obvious that no-one would employ someone whom she could only describe as a total failure, a down and out tart. Lynn Bulmur wasn't someone she wanted to get involved with. Several university girls had learned that lesson the hard way, ending up with criminal records instead of degrees. She was trouble, always had been, and Donna wished that she'd never set eyes on her.

'See you around sometime,' Lynn called as Donna turned to go. Donna forced a smile as she took one last look at the tramp who had tried so many times to get her into trouble, lied, cheated, made life on the campus hell for all those around her.

'Maybe. I work most of the time so . . . Anyway, bye for now.'

'Always come here in your lunch hour, do you?' Lynn pursued, blowing smoke through her thick red lips.

'No, no, never. I . . . I arranged to meet someone here. Normally I have lunch at work. I really must be going, Lynn. It's nice to see you again.'

'How about going out for a drink tonight?'

'I can't, I'm afraid. I take a lot of work home with me. I have to go now, I'll be late. Bye.'

Escaping into the street, Donna breathed a sigh of relief. Lynn Bulmur, of all people! she thought. Here in my town, living around the corner from the lab, from home! She shouldn't have told her where she worked, where she lived. Lynn was the sort to ruin people's lives without flinching an eyelid, if it suited her. In the hot midday sun the feeling of being followed, watched, suddenly returned, haunting.

'Hi, Donna.' The soft female voice took her by surprise as she turned to see Helen smiling, her young face glowing with life. Had she been following her? Someone had.

'Oh, Helen! How are you? You look great!' she added hesitantly.

'I feel great – how are you?'

'I'm fine, thanks. I'm just off back to work.'

After Lynn Bulmur, all she needed was to bump into Helen! The tension was just as she would have expected it to be. Guilt, confusion – what could she say? What had her mother said to the girl? But more to the point, what did Helen think of her rude sexual awakening? A precocious awakening, premature – a bud forced to flower beneath ultra-violet light. A clitoris forced to explode under a caressing, female tongue.

'You in this evening?' Helen asked, much to Donna's surprise. Surely, she didn't want sex? But after her fantastic orgasm, their wonderful time together, why not?

'Yes. Come round for a coffee,' Donna replied nonchalantly, her thoughts a technicolour feast of eroticism.

'Okay, I'll see you later, then. By the way, I've bought some new clothes. I'll wear them tonight, I hope you'll like my new image.'

'I'm sure I will. See you later.'

Watching Helen walk down the street, Donna smiled. New clothes? New image? She was fast becoming a woman, discovering herself, her body. She knew it was wrong to use the girl, to use a patch on her and take her in the name of lesbian lust. But there again, they'd been friends for a long time, this was only a natural extension of their friendship. To give each other comfort, companionship, sex was part of their new-found relationship, Donna tried to convince herself, unsuccessfully.

Walking back to the lab, she wondered about her future, the patches, where it would all lead, what would happen between her and Helen. And there was Sue, who seemed to think that she'd found a lasting relationship with her. Where would *that* take her? To many glorious sexual highs, she hoped. But she had to be careful. Too many relationships on the go and . . . Well, she thought, it makes a change to be part of the action instead of reading between the lines of a book.

Breaking her reverie, she looked behind her. Who was that, that figure peeping from behind a tree across the road? Imagination running wild again, no doubt – or Lynn Bulmur's evil thoughts lurking, haunting, manifesting.

Alan had spent the morning upstairs with Malcolm discussing the project, leaving Donna alone to contemplate. Now he was waiting in the lab for her, a big grin across his face, his arm outstretched, a large bouquet of flowers in his hand. Helping her off with her jacket, he smiled.

'I want to talk to you, Donna,' he began as he hung her jacket up and passed her the flowers. She knew the conversation was inevitable. Wishing she'd never seduced him, spoilt everything, she wondered why he'd said nothing earlier, not confronted her about her uncharacteristic, nymphomaniacal behaviour.

'For me?' she asked, smiling her summery smile. 'What have I done to deserve these?'

'I was hoping that we could go out for that meal this evening,' he said softly, obviously not used to talking to women.

'I can't, Alan, not tonight,' she replied regretfully.

'Oh, right. Is there someone else?'

'No, no, of course not,' she laughed, wondering why she'd said of course not.

Why shouldn't she have someone else, a boyfriend, a girlfriend, even? What was this? 'Someone else,' meaning besides him, as if he were her man, had some claim to her. Flowers, a meal, helping with her jacket – no, she decided. Although Alan was attractive, sexually desirable, solvent, her debased actions in the lab had changed the perspective. He only wanted her for sex, she was sure. She'd made the mistake of giving him her body, taking him in her mouth, and now that's what he was coming back for – sex. He must think her nothing more than a tart, the way she'd acted. Perhaps she was? After the episodes with Helen and her mother, she could hardly call herself an angel. No doubt he'd even chase after the likes of Lynn Bulmur if she'd behaved the way Donna had, which no doubt she would, with or without a patch.

It was ironic, Donna reflected. The very man she'd wanted to get to know over the years was virtually begging her to go out with him, and she had to say no. Why did it have to be like this? Why did anything have to be the way it was? What had brought about the change in him? It was obvious, she reflected. His hard penis throbbing, coming in her mouth, his tongue between her swollen cunt lips, licking, sucking at her clitoris, bringing her to orgasm – what man in his right

mind wouldn't come back for more? What normal man
– or woman?

'I'd like to see you outside the lab for a change,' he
persisted. 'We've worked together all this time and not
once have we had a drink together, let alone . . .'

'Not for want of trying on my part,' she blurted out.

'What do you mean?'

'Come on, Alan. You've never paid the slightest
attention to me, other than in connection with work,
and now you're all over me. Why? One wonders.'

'I just thought . . . I don't know, I'm not very good at
this sort of thing. I suppose working all the time,
engrossed in the project, I'd never thought about anything else, about you as a woman – and a damned
attractive woman, too.'

She was weakening, but she was determined to stand
her ground, for a while, at least. Sitting at her bench she
watched him move about the lab, pretending to busy
himself, trying to conceal his obvious disappointment.
She surveyed the flowers by her microscope – chrysan-
themums, hardly romantic. He'd never married, probably never had a girlfriend, even. Living alone, working
all hours, his life was ridiculously sheltered. As far as
she knew, he didn't even have any friends, let alone a
social life. Conjuring visions of their incredibly erotic
encounter, she grinned – he must have had *some*
experience with women. Perhaps he'd read books,
masturbated over dirty magazines? A meal would be
nice, and perhaps coffee afterwards at his place? And
then maybe . . . One day, she promised herself – one
day.

The afternoon wore on, dragged on. Donna herself
wore on, wondering why she was there, at the lab, what
she was doing with her life. The sun was hot, the grass

green, the sky blue – why spend all day indoors? Money, she supposed – the root of all evil.

Five o'clock arrived. What was time? Some intangible thing that dragged by in the company of boredom, but with happiness, flew faster than the birds. Leaving the lab, and Alan, she warmed her body under the sun as she made her way home, clutching her flowers – her tainted symbol of love.

Donna waited in her lair for Helen to arrive. The scene was set – the flat tidy, soft music playing, her own patch intact and another at the ready. Her clitoris stirring expectantly, her stomach somersaulting, she paced the lounge floor wondering about Helen's new image, her new clothes. Short skirt, perhaps? That would be nice. Her long slender legs should be on display, not shrouded by that awful granny skirt. And her shoes – had she discarded those terrible clogs for something more feminine? Eight-inch red stilettos, perhaps? She hoped so.

Seven o'clock. Where *was* Helen? Perhaps she'd told her mother where she was going and had been grounded. Lifting the phone to ring Sue, Donna remembered being grounded herself. Confined to the house for a week for failing her Grade V piano exam. She hadn't kept up her five-finger exercises – not the exercises her mother had in mind, anyway.

Helen was out with a friend, a girlfriend from college, Sue enlightened her. God! Jealousy! Of course Helen had friends of her own. Sue rambled on – could *she* come round? She needed to talk. God, no! Tomorrow, maybe, but not tonight. It was Helen's turn to come. It was only fair to take it in turns. Perhaps Helen would turn up with her friend? That would be interesting. Three girls together could never be a crowd.

The doorbell eventually rang. Her heart thumping, her head spinning, Donna raced from the lounge, 'Hi!' she drawled, flinging the door open. Leaning against the wall, chewing gum, smirking, Lynn Bulmur raised her eyebrows.

'Hi, Donna. I've found you, at last! Can I come in?' she asked, pushing her way inside.

'No, no! How the hell did you get my address? I'm expecting someone, you can't . . .'

'I've only come round for a coffee, what's the problem? Anyway, who are you expecting, anyone I know from the uni?'

Throwing herself onto the sofa, Lynn made herself comfortable. Her red microskirt rode up her thighs, revealing her stocking tops, the tight, triangular patch of white material covering her mound. Obviously not wearing a bra, her long nipples pressed invitingly through her tight T-shirt. A whore if ever there was one, Donna reflected, her clitoris stirring delightfully in anticipation. A new victim?

She cursed herself, the patch. Becoming involved with Lynn Bulmur would lead to trouble, she knew. But she couldn't resist the temptation to seduce her, to strip her naked and bring her to an orgasm of such magnitude that she'd probably pass out. Perhaps it was an unconscious desire for revenge? To take Lynn, use her body with a vengeance, have her begging for more, pleading for her clitoris to be licked and sucked, would bring about a certain gratification.

Vengeance, not justice, Donna told herself. A potent cocktail of hatred and lust had her in its grips now. Lynn Bulmur, the bitch of bitches, was about to be brought to her knees – literally. Donna smiled as she discreetly took the patch in her hand and moved towards her victim, ready for the kill. All thoughts of Helen faded as she moved in to admire her earrings, all six of them. Inspecting, enquiring where she'd had her ears pierced, she pressed the patch onto her neck and sat back triumphantly.

'Where's the coffee, then?' Lynn asked churlishly. Donna said nothing as she left the room, concealing a wicked grin. 'Any chance of that fiver you said you'd lend me?' Lynn called as Donna filled the kettle. 'Money's a bit tight at the moment, I'll pay you back when I get my giro next week.' She still owed her ten pounds from eight years ago, Donna remembered. The cheeky bitch could do with a good . . . 'Hey, I've just had a thought, you haven't got a spare room, have you? I could move in with you. It would be like old times.' It would be hell. Where was hell?

Returning with two cups of coffee, Donna placed them on the table and contemplated Lynn. Old times? I'll give you old times! she thought. I'll give you something you won't forget for the rest of your miserable days!

Lynn's hand was hovering ominously between her thighs, stroking, touching, creeping ever nearer to her mound. Was she wet between her lips yet? Had her clitoris woken, hardened? Was she ready to be crudely taken, used by another woman? Her body alive with lust now, Donna was more than ready.

'Do you have a boyfriend, anyone special?' Donna asked, watching Lynn's hand, her fingers, pulling at the tight material of her panties, excavating their way between her leg and the elastic – seeking out the hidden treasures within the dark cave.

'No, no-one. Men aren't worth bothering with if you ask me.'

'A girlfriend, then?'

'Girlfriend? What, a lezzy friend? Of course not! Mind you, there was that Carla Jenkins at the uni – the big blonde, remember?'

'How can I ever forget? She was thrown out when you . . .'

'It was a laugh. We were playing around in bed together when old Nightingale caught us. God, you should have seen her face when she discovered Carla under the sheets between my legs! Anyway, how about you? Anyone special?'

'No, not really.'

The dirty little bitch hadn't changed – did they ever? Seemingly oblivious to her friend, Lynn breathed deeply as her fingers found their way inside her knickers, between her lips, and located her clitoris. To Donna's delight, her legs parted a little as she began her caress, affording a better view of her bulging panties. Her eyes rolling now, she was almost there, ready for the taking – for orgasm.

Moving in, Donna sat on the floor at her feet. Practised in the art of female seduction now, she knew exactly what to do, and when. 'Now, my girl, you are under my power, my spell,' she whispered as she moved her hand to Lynn's inner thigh, her fingernails stroking the smooth surface of her black stocking as the tart closed her eyes and relaxed. Talking dirty, she pushed her finger beneath the tight material of the girl's panties and into the moist warmth beneath her lips. 'Remember Carla Jenkins between your thighs? Playing with you, was she? Pushing her fingers into your little cunt hole and making you come, was she? You liked that, didn't you?'

Lynn said nothing as Donna tried to gain entry to her

body, to slip her fingers into her vagina, but the restricting material allowed her to go no further. The girl's suspender belt secured her panties like a chastity belt, a portcullis, defending, barring entry to the inner sanctum. There was only one thing for it.

'Get up and lift your skirt!' Urgent, in a sexual frenzy now, Donna helped her victim comply as Lynn staggered to her feet, her eyes still closed, to display her red suspender belt. Unclipping the belt, Donna rolled her stockings down over her slim thighs, over her knees to her ankles. Now her panties, already wet with her girlish cream, were wrenched to her ankles, unveiling the full beauty of her thick bush. Standing with her feet apart as Donna pressed her face between her thighs, Lynn sighed and pulled her pussy lips up and open in readiness for her aggressor's hot tongue.

A rare and beautiful sight, a young woman standing with her skirt pulled over her stomach, her slender fingers stretching her vaginal lips apart to expose the moist femininity within! The pink flesh spread appetisingly before her, Donna pushed her tongue out and licked hard. 'God! You're good at this!' Lynn breathed as she stretched her lips open wider to expose as much of the sensitive flesh as possible.

'I didn't know that you were a real lesbian,' Donna said impishly. 'I thought that time with Carla Jenkins was just fun.' 'I'm not . . . I'm not,' came the confused reply as Donna located Lynn's clitoris and sucked, discovered her hole and pushed three fingers deep inside.

'You are a lesbian, you must be if you like a woman's tongue licking you like this, a woman's fingers inside your girlie hole.'

'I'm . . . No, no! Ah yes! That's it! Lick me just

there . . . Oh, that's nice, don't stop!'

Her legs giving way as her climax approached, Lynn gasped and grabbed Donna's head, forcing her mouth into her cunt as she writhed and screamed her appreciation. Her juices pouring, running down her thighs over Donna's hand, she crumpled, shuddering, convulsing as she hit the floor. Donna fell with her, her mouth still locked onto her sex as Lynn brought her knees up to her chest and rolled over to escape the beautiful sexual torture. Wiping her mouth on the back of her hand, Donna grinned wickedly at Lynn Bulmur, quivering, weak, brought to the ground, vulnerable, defenceless – broken.

Slipping her skirt and panties off, Donna stood over her prize, her feet either side of her head, her open valley looming above her face. Lynn opened her eyes and looked up at the creamy slit, gasping as she reached up and parted the soft lips with her thumbs, opening the hole to gaze into the darkness – the cave of untold pleasures. Bending her knees, lowering her body, squatting, Donna's cunt lips splayed as they neared the waiting mouth, ready to impart their creamy offering. Ever nearer came the awesome crack to Lynn's mouth until, settling over her lips, the warm fluid oozed, the hot, pink flesh covered her face. Instinctively, the recipient's tongue pushed its way inside the gaping hole to explore the hot, velvety darkness – the cavern of lust.

'Now lick me!' Donna gasped as she pressed herself down harder. 'Suck my cunt! Make me come in your mouth!' Rocking to and fro, she rubbed her slippery flesh over Lynn's face, soaking her with her juices, engulfing her mouth with her swollen vaginal lips. 'Push your tongue further inside, suck out my juices!'

Lynn gasped, choked, as Donna's climax approached

and her sheath decanted more sticky fluid. Barely able to breathe now, she spluttered, trying desperately to push the ravenous cunt away. Riding her face, Donna shuddered, crying out in sexual euphoria as her clitoris exploded, sent a tidal wave of pleasure crashing over her consumed body, and tore at the very fibres of her mind. Where was the mind?

Moving aside, Donna collapsed to the floor, gasping, panting for breath as Lynn staggered to her feet and fell onto the sofa. 'God, what have you done to me?' she asked as she reclined on the sofa, her cunt open, dripping, her face wet with Donna's sex fluid. 'I don't know what happened. I'm not . . . I'm not a bloody lesbian!'

'Then what are you?' Donna asked, eyeing the girl's soft inner thighs, her dark triangular bush, wet, glistening in the light.

'I . . . I don't know.'

Grabbing her panties, her stockings, Lynn tottered from the room. Satisfied in every sense of the word, Donna lay still, breathing deeply, fingering her hot hole, appeasing her clitoris, planning her next move as she waited for her victim to return. She'd take her again, she decided, finger her, bring her to her knees with her tongue, her new-found power – deliver Lynn Bulmur the ultimate humiliation.

Her clitoris nearing another beautiful peak, Donna began to wonder what was taking Lynn so long. She didn't want to bring out her orgasm, not yet – she wanted to save it for Lynn, for her mouth. Desperate now, she needed to lick and drink from Lynn's body again, to have her lick and mouth at her pussy, for them to lick and drink, together.

But the fantasy would have to wait. Searching the

bathroom, bedroom, kitchen, her clitoris screaming for attention, Donna sighed despondently – the bitch had escaped. But she'd return, she knew. Come back for more, lured by memories of licking between another girl's legs, attaining massive orgasms with another girl's tongue deep between her swollen lips. For sure, the lurking demon would drag her back to the lair.

Smiling at the prospect, Donna suddenly gasped. 'The patch! Shit, she's still wearing the patch!' How long the effect would last, she had no idea. What Lynn would get up to under the influence of the hormone, she couldn't even hazard a guess. Grab a man from the street and rape him? God forbid! But there was nothing she could do, it was too late. All she could do was hope, pray, that Lynn would go home and masturbate – masturbate until the hormone faded, releasing her from its incredible, beautiful, drug-like spell.

Peeling her own patch from her arm, she carefully placed it on the mantelpiece and began to wonder about Helen. What was she up to? Having sex with her mother? The situation had become serious. What had been a game was fast becoming a problem. And the consequences? Dire, no doubt. Her thoughts returning to Lynn, she knew she'd have to discover the effect of wearing a patch over a long period of time – and there was only one way to find out. 'Suck it and see,' she whispered, retrieving the patch from the mantelpiece and pressing it to her smooth skin.

Engulfed by sexual frustration and an overwhelming sense of boredom, Donna wandered around the flat aimlessly. Soon she became desperate for company – for someone to talk to, be with, kill the loneliness with – and for orgasm.

Alan took some time to answer his phone. Working,

Donna surmised, tapping the receiver impatiently. 'Hi, Alan, it's Donna,' she offered to his abrupt "yes?".

'Donna, what can I do for you?'

'I haven't disturbed you, have I?'

'No, I'm just working – as usual.'

'I thought I'd come round and see you. My previous engagement's off, so . . . But if you're busy . . .'

'Well . . . The flat is a bit of a mess right now.'

'Isn't it always? Sorry, I shouldn't have said that.'

'No, no, you're right, I'm afraid. I need a good woman, you see,' he laughed. 'Don't know any, do you?'

Good in the kitchen? In bed? A bad woman was better than a good one, she reflected.

'Come round here for coffee, if you want to,' she invited.

'Sounds good to me. Give me fifteen minutes.'

Donna paced the floor wondering where he'd got to, where Helen had got to, what Lynn was up to. It was an hour since she'd called Alan. Her clitoris swelling, her juices soaking her knickers and streaming down her legs, she needed to relieve the swelling between her wet cunt lips. Alan, Helen, Sue, anyone's tongue would do. Male or female, a tongue was a tongue.

Finally giving up all hope of company, she settled in her armchair and pulled her knickers down. Swollen beyond belief, her outer vaginal lips were open, exposing her wet, inner labia, red and inflamed. Her clitoris, sensitive as never before and almost bursting, hardened like a rock as she lightly brushed its tip.

Gently massaging her pinken folds, she began to breathe deeply and relax as the now familiar sensations emanated from between her thighs to engulf her entire body, her mind. Almost oblivious now, she heard the doorbell, far off like a train whistling somewhere in the hazy distance – someone banging on the letter box, calling her name, invading her privacy. Opening her eyes before reaching her peak, she leapt from her chair, her soft love-tube oozing with milky fluid, and pulled her knickers up. Trembling, flushed, gasping, she opened the door to Alan.

'Sorry I've been so long,' he apologised. 'Problems, I'm afraid.'

'Problems?' she repeated, leading him into the lounge, her breathing easing a little.

'I've been talking to an old colleague on the phone for half an hour, Professor Winmann. He's at the Gardener University. He's been working on hormone replacement therapy, as we have. But instead of patches, he's been looking into administering the hormone in tablet form. There are some strange side-effects, it seems.'

Now in dire need of sexual relief, Donna took her seat opposite Alan and crossed her legs, squeezing her pussy lips together in an effort to squash her clitoris, to calm her pulsating bud. Gazing at him, she tentatively asked about the side-effects.

'He didn't say,' Alan began, eyeing her short skirt riding up her thighs as she wiggled her hips and squirmed in the chair. 'All he said was that it affects the libido. God knows how. Anyway, I'm hoping to meet him soon to discuss it.'

'Has he discovered any other effects?'

'Yes, but again, he wouldn't say too much over the phone.'

'How does he know, anyway? Has he tested the patches, I mean tablets, on anyone?'

'All he said was, make sure the hormone remains safely under lock and key until we speak and investigate further. You all right? You look as if you need the loo or something.'

'I'm fine, just feeling rather passionate, I suppose. Living alone, I . . . Well . . .'

'You get lonely, is that it? Need some company, a little physical contact now and then? I know I do.'

Desperate to come, to quell her dangerously rising sexual tension, Donna uncrossed her legs and aligned her wet, bulging panties with Alan's staring eyes. He had to respond, make a move. She couldn't allow herself to seduce him, rape him, not again. Her thighs opening further, his eyes became transfixed on the soft mound of her panties. Come *on* then, she thought impatiently, pushing her hips forward to display the full triangle of damp material closely hugging the swell of her nether lips. Almost delirious with sex now she closed her eyes, praying for his fingers, his tongue, his penis.

The soft brush of his face against her inner thigh caused her to catch her breath – she hadn't heard him shift across the room. Kissing, nibbling the warm flesh, he moved nearer to the centre of her trembling body until licking, tasting her smooth skin, he finally reached his goal – her goal – and pressed his mouth to her panties.

She couldn't wait while he teased and tantalised. Sopping with her female wetness, she needed him *now*. Tugging her panties down her legs, she lay back, swung her legs over the arms of the chair and peeled her lips apart. No teasing, no torturing, Alan dived for her clitoris and began to lick vigorously. Crying out, pleading, begging to come, she tossed her head back and squeezed her eyes shut as her cumbud swelled and burst in his mouth, sending shock waves of agonising pleasure through her body, tingling every nerve ending, tightening every muscle. On and on ran the relentless waves until she thought she would die from the overwhelming pleasure emanating from her aching clitoris. Gripping his head, she tried to push him away, free her bud from his circling tongue until her eyes rolled and she collapsed, semi-conscious, a heap of trembling limbs in her chair.

Barely recovered, she suddenly felt something fill her hot sheath, press into the depths of her pelvis to rest gently against her cervix. Opening her eyes, she gazed through her long, blonde hair to see her bloated cunt lips encircling the base of Alan's thick penis, rolled neatly around the hard shaft.

Kneeling between her legs, his rod impaling her completely, he smiled as he began his fucking motions. Back and forth his shaft slid, wet with her come, hard with his desire. Meeting his thrusts she gripped the chair, her body taking every delectable inch of his hardness until, again, she cried out in orgasm. Shuddering, gasping as the sensations rose to an incredible peak, her cunt suddenly swelled, filling with Alan's sperm as he groaned and mercilessly rammed her womb. 'Enough!' she cried as her milk mixed with his sperm and spewed from her hole, ran down the massive, glistening penis, trickled over his balls, her buttocks, to pool in the chair.

Gently withdrawing his fleshy weapon, allowing her sheath to shrink, her pinken petals to fold and close to retain his sperm, he sat on the floor, gasping, murmuring his appreciation for her beautiful body. She opened her eyes and smiled, her sexual appetite quelled, for a while, at least.

'That was wonderful, Alan,' she whispered. 'God, it

was wonderful! Much better than . . .'

'Than what?' he asked, frowning now, his forehead lined, staring deep into her eyes. 'There's no-one else, is there, Donna?'

Why did he have to spoil everything? Couldn't he just enjoy her, her body? Better than Lynn, she had been about to say – much better than Lynn, Helen, Sue. Perhaps she should tell him? Tell him how she'd squatted over Lynn's face that very evening, filling her mouth with her hot come. But no – what would be the point of upsetting him? He was her boss, after all, and she had him to thank for the patches.

Where to now? she wondered as he zipped up his trousers, concealing his magnificent thick penis. Was that it? Beautiful as it had been, was she to receive no more pleasure? She lay still, her body open, her dripping hole exposed. Alan gazed at her intimacy and moved nearer as she peeled her lips back, inviting his tongue to drink the fruits of their union from her hot depths.

Expertly, he licked the full length of her gaping valley until she was dry. Moving down, he sucked at the entrance to her love-tube and drank the wondrous cocktail of milk and sperm until he'd drained her. Her clitoris approaching another climax, she pulled his head up her valley and manoeuvered his open mouth over the hard epicentre of her pleasure. The tip of his tongue flicking the sensitive tip of her cumbud, she suddenly gasped as her womb quivered and her orgasm rose from her pelvis and exploded into his mouth once again. Riding the wave of pleasure, she gripped his head between her thighs until she could take no more and was forced to release her clitoris from her torturer.

'No more, please no more!' she gasped as he tried to

resume his mouthing. 'I can't take any more, please!'

'I think you've had enough for now,' he whispered, stroking the smooth plateau of her stomach, kissing her inner thighs. 'Tomorrow, I'll come round again tomorrow – then you can have more,' he promised. 'Every night, we'll make love, Donna. I want you, I need you, you're all mine – I love you.'

Opening her eyes, Donna surveyed the man proclaiming his love for her. All mine – a possession? Covering her inflamed pussy with her moist panties, she stood up and walked to the kitchen.

'Coffee?' she called.

'Please,' came his voice from behind as he wrapped his arms around her waist and pressed himself against her back. Feeling her stomach, her hips, pulling her closer, he kissed her neck, breathed in the scent of her hair, nibbled her ear.

'I can't make coffee unless you let me go,' she complained, pulling away.

'I'll let you go for five minutes,' he whispered in her ear. 'And then I'll hold you again. Forever, I'll hold you – love you.'

What was love? Just a few days ago Donna would have dearly loved to hear those words, be with Alan, build a permanent relationship with him, live together, even marry him. But now, after all that had happened so quickly – sex, devoid of love, cold, hard, pulsating pleasure without emotion – it was too late. Joining her on the sofa with his coffee he began his banter again, unknowingly building her defences against him – brick walls.

'This weekend, we could go out into the country, a picnic, perhaps?' he suggested enthusiastically, trying to hold her hand. A picnic in the woods? Donna liked the woods, the trees. Sex beneath the trees had always been a suppressed fantasy – but only a fantasy.

'I can't, Alan. I've a lot to do,' she replied, thinking of Helen, wondering where she was, if she'd enjoy sex under the trees.

'The weekend after, then?'

'We'll see. You have to realise that I can't just drop everything, disrupt my life overnight, and begin a relationship with you.'

'But I thought . . . After . . . I'm not asking you to disrupt your life. All I suggested was a picnic.'

'A picnic, a drink, a meal, flowers . . . It's all too much too soon, Alan. I'm not free to simply . . .'

'There is someone else, then?'

'Only a girlfriend. We're very close, do everything together.'

'How close? Not too close, I hope,' he laughed. A girl, it seemed, was not a threat to his manhood, his ego. Why not?

Glancing at the clock as the phone rang, Donna wondered if it was Helen, calling to apologise. Eleven-thirty, time had gone so quickly. Helen wouldn't be round now, she thought sadly, picking up the receiver under Alan's scrutinising gaze.

'Donna, it's Sue. Is Helen with you?'

'No. She was supposed to be coming over for . . . for a chat this evening but she didn't turn up.'

'Oh God, I wonder where she's got to? Oh, hang on, she's coming in now, thanks Donna, I'll . . . I'll see you . . . Are you doing anything tomorrow night?'

'Nothing planned, why?'

'Just thought I'd pop round, if that's all right with you?'

'Er . . . Yes, yes, okay. See you tomorrow. Bye.'

What had Helen been up to? she wondered. Maybe she'd found someone else? God, that was Alan's line. Perhaps Sue was lying as a ploy – a reason to phone and make an appointment for lesbian lust?

'Time to go, Alan. It's been nice, thanks,' Donna smiled. 'More than nice,' he elaborated as he rose to his feet and held her in his arms. 'It was wonderful.'

Wonderful it was, indeed, as it had been with the three women. God, how many more were in line for the patch? Anyway, why count? It was all research work, after all. She was a scientist – and wasn't the art of lesbian love also a science? Closing the front door, she breathed a sigh of relief before turning her thoughts again to Helen. Should she phone her, ask her where she'd been? Why she hadn't come round for . . . No, it was late: time for bed, time for loneliness.

She'd not really wanted a ground floor flat, she reflected as she climbed under her quilt. Was there someone outside in the night, peeping, spying on her? Imagination again, maybe, she didn't know, for soon dreams came, engulfing her, taking her from her body and lifting her to another world. Dreams come true, when dreamed.

Chapter Four

The weekend had arrived, at long last. Waking at nine to a hot Saturday morning, Donna lay in bed planning her day. She'd be free of Alan's persistent words of love for two days, at least. But what to do? How to spend the weekend?

Reaching under the bedclothes for her clitoris, she touched its hardness and realised that the patch was still in place. 'I can't masturbate, I can't come again!' she whispered as she ran her fingers along her warm groove and located the wetness of her entrance. Pushing a finger inside, she closed her eyes as she gently massaged the hot flesh, losing herself in the dark corridors of her mind where fantasies drift, waiting to be realized. Sliding up her damp furrow, lubricating the sensitive skin, she arrived at her clitoris and gasped as she encircled its base. The little bud swelled under her caressing fingertips as she quickened her movements, pinched her nipple with her free hand and allowed herself to sink into the warmth of her bed, her femininity.

Thoughts of Lynn suddenly filled her mind. Was she in her bed, masturbating, caressing herself as she was – coming for the umpteenth time? How many women were masturbating at any one time?

Her clitoris beginning to tingle and throb, Donna

decided she would enjoy a weekend of wanton lust. 'I want a damn good fuck,' she gasped aloud as her womb contracted, extruding her orgasm to the root of her clitoris where it quickly rose and burst over the hard tip. 'Ah, my cunt – I love you! Ah! ah! I've come! I've come!'

Relaxing, her fingers gently caressing her receding clitoris in appreciation, she breathed easily, trying to decide on her next victim. The effects of the patch had worked throughout the night – she'd dreamt of two men taking her naked body, both attending her, pleasuring her, her mouth filling with sperm from the bulbous head of a hard penis as her sheath squeezed the fruits from another throbbing shaft.

Two men, two women, who cares? she thought, leaping from her bed and standing before the mirror. 'I want two slaves to pleasure me this weekend,' she decided aloud. Admiring her slim, curvaceous body, she smiled. 'No knickers today,' she promised herself. 'And who needs a bra?'

Sexually alive, aware as never before, she tugged at her pubic hairs and decided to trim them, to unveil the dividing groove between her swollen vaginal lips in readiness for two days of wonderful sex. Her life centred around her body now. Her world was her cunt, her clitoris. The mere thought of shaving brought her new and exciting sensations, stiffened her tiny pleasure bud, caused her juices to flow.

Stepping into the shower, she began to cut away her curls with a pair of scissors. As the hair fell around her feet, the fullness, the sheer beauty of her pussy lips became visible. Shaving either side of her valley, she left only a small patch of down below her smooth stomach – a heart-shaped, tiny beard of youth. In her new enlightenment, she was young again – a teenager in the bloom of sexual discovery. Pubescent, changing, evolving.

Now, her pussy lips lay naked, bared, ready for love. Soaping her breasts, her hardening nipples, her smooth mound, massaging the lather into her folds with her fingertips, exciting her clitoris, she began to quiver uncontrollably. Directing the shower nozzle between her splayed nether lips, she leaned back against the wall and closed her eyes. The sensations welled up from the depths of her pelvis, exciting every inch of her wet, naked body as she imagined two women kneeling before her, attending her, pleasuring her with their fingers, their tongues. Like a thousand tiny fingers caressing, playing on her sensitive skin, the hot water brought her to a shuddering climax. Sliding down the wall, she sat crying and trembling with the immense pleasure, satisfaction, wondering which two women she would take and use as her sex slaves. She would shower them, have them shower her. She would have them wash her body with their tongues, lick clean every inch of her glowing skin.

Drying herself before her bedroom mirror, she smiled as she gazed lovingly at her shaven cunt lips, smooth, soft, swollen. Again, she imagined two female tongues licking and sucking each lip, four hands running up her thighs, countless fingers seeking out her crevices, pressing into the velvety warmth of her lovemouth as she writhed in ecstasy. But who? she wondered as she pulled her miniskirt up over her naked pussy and slipped her T-shirt over her bare breasts, her elongated, aching nipples. Who would she conscript as her lesbian sex slaves?

Pouring her coffee, Donna caught the tail end of the

news on the local radio station. '. . . blatantly soliciting outside the Dog and Duck public house in Park Street and was arrested last night on charges of prostitution.' Her eyes widened in horror: instant cognition. 'Lynn Bulmur!' she breathed. 'God, the bloody patch!'

Grabbing her summer jacket, Donna left her flat and made her way the short distance to Park Street, praying that Lynn was at home and not in a police cell. The patch wasn't amenable to solitary confinement! Cool air wafted up her skirt, refreshed and dried her wet, naked labia as she walked. Next to the pub, she remembered Lynn saying, as she turned the corner and crossed the road.

Passing a group of men who were staring at her slender legs, her nipples pressing through her T-shirt, she smiled. Ultimately, women ruled, held the power. They were unaware of her nakedness beneath her skirt, her shaven vaginal lips swelling in the cool air. She thought of lifting her skirt, showing off her fresh young pussy to their hungry eyes. But no – as much as the idea appealed to her, stiffened her clitoris, she had more important things to do right now.

Leaning back against the front gate, Lynn was standing with her legs apart and her short skirt pulled up, barely covering her knickerless pussy. 'What the hell are you doing?' Donna asked, running up to her.

'Earning some money,' she snapped, eyeing up a young man as he passed by with his dog.

Cars sped by, the rat-race. Where were they all going? And why?

'It's prostitution! I heard the news on the radio, you can't *do* this, Lynn! Let's go inside, for God's sake!'

The small flat was untidy, with nothing in the way of furniture, other than the bare essentials. Lynn was an untidy person – Donna liked organization. Sitting on the sofa, she looked at Lynn and shook her head. 'You fool! What the hell do you think you're playing at?' Her anger was directed more at herself than at Lynn – she should have ensured she retrieved the patch.

'I'm broke, so what's wrong with earning some tax-free cash?'

'Have you ever done this before?'

'No, no. It's unlike me, despite what you may think. But since I was at your place last night, I . . . Well, you know what happened between us. The thing with Carla Jenkins was only fun, but with you, God! I've had sex on my mind all bloody night! I honestly don't know what's happened to me. The things we did were incredible! What with that *and* being arrested for prostitution. What the hell's going on?'

Reclining on the sofa, Donna wondered how she could pull the patch from Lynn's neck. The hormone had obviously affected her far more than it had herself. But why? Perhaps it was because Lynn was naturally a randy little bitch and the patch had heightened her already excessive libido. Rather ironic, though, she thought. Here was Lynn Bulmur having her comeuppance after all these years. But then, the tables always turned, didn't they?

'I want you again,' Lynn whispered softly, eyeing Donna's naked slit as she inadvertently allowed her legs to fall apart. 'Then take me,' Donna replied, her stomach swirling, her clitoris tingling delightfully as she lay back and opened her legs wide to display her shaven lips – her girlishness.

'God, you look beautiful!' Lynn gasped, falling to her knees to examine the naked feast spread so invitingly before her. Gently kissing, nibbling the warm cushions of flesh, she began to lick each lip in turn, swelling them even more, causing them to part, to unfold ready for penetration. Drenched, hot, Donna's cunt desperately needed stretching, opening, filling to capacity. She needed a penis.

'Put something in me and fuck me hard until I come!' she ordered as Lynn continued her torturous licking. Four fingers obligingly found their way between the reddening folds and into the slippery hole. 'Something bigger!' Donna begged, her muscles gripping, rhythmically massaging Lynn's fingers as they thrust in and out. Had she thrust them into her own hole? Perhaps, when she was young and tight and the summers long and carefree? Didn't all young girls have their secrets – dark, hot, velvety secrets?

Returning from the kitchen, Lynn grinned as she knelt between Donna's legs again and introduced a huge cucumber to her gaping hole. Her cunt lips yielded, opened, encompassed the massive shaft as it gently sank into her body. Donna's eyes closed, she could only guess what was stretching her, penetrating every inch of her throbbing sheath, pressing gently against her cervix. 'This was for my lunch salad,' Lynn whispered, thrusting the cucumber in and out like a huge penis. Cool, thick, solid, the impressive phallus sent wondrous tremors through her womb as she raised her hips, opened her legs wider and sucked in the solid member.

'Lie on the floor!' Lynn commanded, pulling the glistening weapon from the other girl's shaking body. Prostrate on the carpet, Donna opened her legs to their extremity, a ballerina practising her box-splits, to display her gaping groove, her wet hole, open, waiting for the phallus to fill her, take her to her peak. Slowly, she felt her body opening, the taut walls of her sheath straining to contain the massive intruder as it filled her beyond belief, beyond capacity. As Lynn attempted to push the monster further into her quivering body, Donna grabbed her hand and gasped. 'No more! No more! Just fuck me with it!'

Aware of Lynn manoeuvring herself, placing her legs over hers, Donna lifted her head to see Lynn pushing the other end of the cucumber between her own pussy lips, easing it into her hole. Their hips pressed together, their bodies joined by the phallus, they lifted their buttocks and began to move back and forth. The cucumber gently fucking them, filling them, ramming their cervixes, they slammed their groins together in a frenzy of lust, abandoned in their abandonment. Flowing, their juices mingled, trickled between their buttocks to pool on the carpet, a slippery pool of orgasm.

Their timing perfect, their crotches meeting, slapping at each thrust of their hips on the half cucumber, they cried out their pleasure. Fucking, coming together, their hot, slippery juices lubricating the hard, green shaft, they shuddered and reached their orgasms in unison. Their cunts almost torn open, their lips stretched and inflamed, their wombs decanting milky fluid, they fell back onto the carpet. Their bodies still bound, joined in lust by the double-ended phallus, they lay panting, satisfied.

As they gently gyrated their hips, pressed their mounds together, the cucumber massaged their soft tubes, relaxing their muscles, allowing their orgasms to subside slowly. Gently moving apart, they staggered to their feet together as the wet, glistening phallus fell to the floor, lifeless. 'That was fantastic!' Donna breathed as she sat on the sofa, her hole gaping, oozing with milk.

'Better than that, it was bloody brilliant!' Lynn

laughed, pulling her short skirt down to conceal her wet, matted hair, her bulbous, pink pussy lips. If they could speak, what words would fall from the soft lovemouths between women's thighs?

Basking in her sexual afterglow, Donna began to fantasise about having two women, two sex slaves at her feet. Bent on the notion, she decided that it would have to be Helen and her mother. Right or wrong, it didn't matter, she didn't care – she desperately needed two women cowering as her slaves between her legs as she gave her instructions. Perhaps Lynn would like to meet Helen?

'I must be going,' she said, finding her wobbly legs and placing her arm on Lynn's shoulder to discreetly try and retrieve the patch. Lynn backed away and crossed the room.

'You'll have to let yourself out,' she called, diving for the bathroom. 'I need the loo.'

'I'll wait for you,' Donna answered, desperate for the patch, her heart pounding.

'Don't bother, I'll be some time, I'm going to have a shower. See yourself out and I'll ring you later.'

Picking up the wet cucumber, Donna slipped it into her bag and left the flat, praying that the wretched plaster would come off as Lynn washed.

Her body still aching from the sheer size of the wonderful phallus, she wandered home, dreading to think what Lynn would get up to next if the patch remained on her neck. Time will tell, she thought, removing her own patch as she walked, desperately needing a rest from her insatiable clitoris – for a while, at least. How many orgasms could a woman have in one day?

She was surprised to find Helen waiting on her doorstep.

'There was a man hanging around your flat when I arrived ten minutes ago,' the girl volunteered.

'A man? What did he look like?'

'Thirties, darkish, I don't know. He seemed to be watching the flat. He kept walking by and watching.'

'Strange. Oh well, there are some strange people about, I suppose. So where were you last night?'

'I went to the park,' Helen began, blushing, averting her eyes. 'I was going to come round but . . . I don't know, I just couldn't bring myself to . . .'

'Your mother rang me. She was worried about you.'

'I know. I was only sitting in the park, thinking. Can't I do anything without her asking questions?'

Admiring Helen's new short skirt, Donna led her into the kitchen and filled the kettle. 'So you were sitting in the park all alone, were you?' she asked, dumping the sticky cucumber on the table.

'I'd take that back, if I were you, it looks as if it's gone off!' Come off, more likely, Donna reflected as Helen picked up the cucumber and examined its slippery surface. Perhaps she'd like it inside her?

'You were alone in the park, were you?' Donna repeated, taking the cucumber and placing it in the fridge to cool it, preserve its hardness.

'I was with Sophie, a friend. We always confide in each other, share our secrets.'

'You didn't tell her about us, did you?'

'No, no. We were just talking about sex and I mentioned lesbians. She's done it with another girl.'

'And did you do it with her in the park?'

'No, I didn't. I told her about you, how it helps me to talk to you.'

Donna poured the coffee, speculating on her chances of talking Helen into bringing her friend round to meet her. My young sex slaves, she thought wickedly, leading the way into the lounge.

'So it helps you to talk to me, does it?'

'Yes. I've grown very fond of you, Donna. I don't know why, but when I was with you the other night I felt different, really attracted to you. I was looking forward to seeing you again . . . Well, it's strange, but it sort of wore off.'

'And how do you feel now?'

'I'm not sure. I mean, I really like you a lot, but I can't understand why I did what I did with you, if that makes sense?'

'Oh, yes, it makes sense all right,' Donna smiled, still aware of the magical effects of the patch and debating whether or not to slip one on Helen.

Deciding as they sat down together on the sofa, Donna reached for her bag. Helen deserved a little more love and affection – just once more. Employing her old trick to apply the plaster to Helen's neck, she lifted her hair, pretending to remove a piece of cotton. Discreetly, she stuck a patch to her own upper arm before settling back.

'Give your friend, Sophie, a ring. Tell her to come round here and meet me, if you want to,' she suggested.

'Okay, she only lives five minutes away. I'd love you to meet her, she's great.'

Donna grinned as Helen lifted the phone. Her dream was about to come true, her sex slaves soon to be instructed in the art of pleasuring her as she stood over them as their mistress. She wondered what the girl looked like – blonde? Pretty? Fat? Thin? Blonde and very slim, she hoped. But she daren't ask Helen about her, take too much interest.

Helen smiled sweetly, unconsciously rubbing her

hand between her legs as she replaced the receiver. 'She's on her way,' she informed Donna, much to her delight.

'How old is she?' Donna couldn't resist asking.

'Same as me, eighteen.'

'Oh, good. Is she . . . It doesn't matter. So, she's done it, as you put it, with another girl, has she?'

'Yes. She used to stay with a friend at her parents' house. They shared the same bed and . . . Well, they did it, I suppose.'

'Have *you* ever done it with another girl?'

'Only you. There was a girl at school who . . . We touched each other. Nothing much, just compared each other's . . .'

'Did you masturbate when you were younger?'

'No, I've never done that. Last night I did, though.'

'Did you come?'

'Yes, twice. But I still don't understand what's happened to me, why I've changed so quickly – overnight.'

Strange things happen in the dark of the night – in the dark of strange nights.

'You're growing up, becoming a woman,' Donna reassured her.

She was pleased that Helen had masturbated, brought her clitoris to orgasm. All the riper to eat you with, she found herself thinking. The doorbell rang, just as Helen began to squirm and fidget a little, rub between her legs, her vaginal lips. 'That'll be her,' she said, going to answer the door. Donna grinned as she waited in anticipation for her second sex slave to show herself.

'This is Sophie,' Helen announced as she showed a pretty little blonde girl into the room. An involuntary gasp of appreciation escaped Donna's lips as she cast her eyes over the girl's body. Big blue eyes, a slim, curvaceous frame hugged by a tight, short, red dress displaying the slenderest of legs – she was perfect in every way. Perfect for loving – intimate, female loving.

'Hi! Like some coffee?' Donna asked nonchalantly as the girl sat down.

'Thanks. It's a nice flat, have you been here long?'

'A few years. Oh, here, let me just move that cushion for you.'

Sticking the patch on the target was a fumbled process, but it worked, and Donna left her slaves alone to talk while the hormone took effect.

Returning to the lounge with the coffee, she smiled and chatted cheerfully as she sat in her armchair, her clitoris demanding attention more than ever before. How to instigate sex with a stranger? she wondered, eyeing Sophie's young legs, her pretty face, her small, firm breasts. She'd be tight, wet, hot, youthful down there, between the softness of her thighs. But how to initiate the lesbian proceedings?

Helen answered Donna's question for her. Her hand on Sophie's knee, she smiled and asked about her nights in her friend's bed. 'We were pretty young,' Sophie began, holding Helen's hand. 'All we did was play with each other, really.'

'How, exactly?' Donna asked, her womb contracting delectably at the thought.

'Rubbed each other, I suppose.'

'Were you both completely naked?'

'Oh, yes.'

'Did you both come?' Helen asked.

'Many, many times. It was wonderful.'

'Did you both rub each other together or take it in

turns?' Donna enquired, her heart beating faster, her misty blue eyes widening.

'Took it in turns. We timed it to make it fair. I'd slip under the bedclothes and play with her cunette for fifteen minutes, and then she'd . . .'

'Cunette? What a wonderful word,' Donna remarked as Sophie settled back on the sofa and parted her legs slightly in response to Helen's fingers encircling her knee.

Sophie closed her eyes as Helen's hand ran up her leg and found its way under her dress. She was trying to get a finger under the girl's knickers, into her young pussy, Donna surmised as she watched the wondrous spectacle. They were both ready for love, to be instructed, she concluded as she stood in the centre of the room, the word 'cunette' floating in her mind as a leaf upon a river.

'Both come here,' she ordered softly, sexily. Looking up to her, they climbed obediently to their feet. Standing before them, she told them to remove each other's clothes. Skirts, dresses, tops, tights, girls' clothes. Their hands all over each other's bodies, Donna watched as Sophie's dress was lifted over her head, Helen's top unbuttoned and discarded, her skirt unzipped and kicked aside.

Standing only in their bras and panties now, Donna nodded her head for them to continue. Her heart thumped in her chest as she waited to see Sophie's young breasts, the soft down below her stomach, the hungering in her womb. Turning, they unclipped each other's bras, freeing their firm, rounded breasts, exposing the growing milk buds to Donna's appreciative gaze. Tweeking all four nipples in turn, she cupped the young spheres as if weighing them, adjudicating them.

Kneeling, Sophie tugged on Helen's knickers, pulling them down to her ankles. Now, at last, Helen fell to her knees before Sophie and slipped her fingers between the tight elastic and her shapely hips. Donna knelt, too, gazing at the bulge between Sophie's legs – the bulge of her girlish sex. Slowly, the red silk panties fell, peeled from the swelling to expose her soft hair, and then, the most exquisite, fresh, young groove imaginable. Like freshly mown summer grass, sweet, scented, callow, the wonder imbued Donna's senses.

Standing up, she instructed her pretty young sex slaves to remove her clothes. As Helen lifted her top off, Sophie pulled her skirt down, unveiling her breasts, her naked mound, her feminine beauty. All three naked now, Donna smiled and told the girls to cup her breasts, suck her nipples. Following her orders, they each took a breast and kissed and mouthed at her nipples. Her hard buds responded delightfully, transmitting ripples of pleasure deep into her body, her womb. Her head swimming, her breathing unsteady, she instructed them to kneel before their mistress. This was it – two pretty young girls grovelling at her feet, her dream about to come true!

'Kiss and lick my inner thighs!' she commanded, standing with her feet wide apart. Two warm mouths pressing against her thighs, gently kissing. Two hot tongues licking, bathing the smooth skin with their saliva. The mistress rolled her eyes, trembling, inhaling, then, in an outrush of breath, ordered the girls to move up her thighs, slowly. Licking, kissing, they complied with their teasing caresses sending quivers up her spine, tingles through her now solid clitoris as they neared her swollen pussy lips. 'Now lick the creases between my legs and my lips!' she ordered explicitly, gazing down at

the two naked bodies working solely to pleasure her –
their mistress of lust. Twisting and pinching her nipples
she felt the urgency in her womb, the desperate need to
come, to outpour her juices from her sheath and drench
the girls as a reward for their tender love. 'Let your
hands run all over me! My legs, my bottom, my stomach
– touch me all over with your fingers!' she panted.
Silently, the girls fondled her buttocks, gently caressed
the baby-soft skin between the tops of her thighs, ran
their fingers lightly over her smooth stomach as they
continued their licking, mouthing, nibbling, sucking.

'Now my cunt lips, each suck a lip, hard! Pull them
open with your mouths!' The pleading words of desperation bubbled from her pretty mouth. Biting, nibbling the soft swell of her lips, the girls moaned deeply,
purred their purrs as they clung to their mistress's
thighs. Pulling the vaginal lips apart with their teeth,
their faces became wet with the milky fluid now trickling
from the open hole. Donna moaned deeply as she
gasped her next instruction. 'I want your tongues
between my pussy lips now! Lick my cunette!'

A pair of tongues lapped at the luxuriant flesh, both
urgently seeking entry to the source of the flow of
slippery juice. Sucking, drinking the fluid as it decanted,
the girls began to massage each other's clitorises, finger
each other's crevices, stroke each other's spheres.
'Don't touch each other!' Donna scolded. 'Pleasure *me*,
not yourselves! Now I want as many fingers inside me as
possible!'

Two, three, four fingers pushed their way deep into
Donna's writhing body, exploring, massaging the wet,
inner walls of her tube, inducing her cream to flow in
torrents. 'Move behind me, Helen,' she whispered as
she felt the birth of her orgasm deep within her

contracting womb. Sophie licking at her clitoris, fingering her hot hole, and Helen licking the dark crease between her firm buttocks, she shuddered and cried out. Tongues licking, fingers teasing, caressing her trembling body, she collapsed into a crumpled heap on the floor. Squirming, she could do nothing to fight off her young slaves as they locked their mouths between her legs, sucking out the last ripples of her climax, drinking from her spent body. 'Enough!' she cried as a finger rudely penetrated her smaller hole, wiggling and twisting as it explored her hot bowels.

Donna lay still as Helen and Sophie moved away from her consumed body and turned their attention to each other. Licking at each other's sticky slits, exploring, burrowing deep into the hot wetness within, they began their purring again. Their soft moans filled the air as they writhed, locked themselves in lesbian ecstasy, brought their clitorises to shuddering climaxes, drank the hot milk from their bloated holes.

Moving to the sofa, Donna watched the girls, wondering at her desire to have slaves – female sex slaves. She'd been bossy at school, a natural leader, always in charge of the games they'd played. Perhaps that was why? But they'd never played games such as these.

'Stop!' she ordered sharply in the realisation that her slaves were pleasuring each other without her permission. 'Sophie, roll over onto your stomach! Helen, thrash her for her impertinence!' What impertinence? – no matter. They gazed at her, their wet mouths open in disbelief. 'Do as you're told!' she shouted. Obediently, Sophie lay on her stomach, trembling, awaiting her fate.

Helen smiled at Donna as she began to stroke and knead the slave-girl's firm young buttocks. Slapping each buttock in turn, she looked to Donna again with a fire in her eyes – a fire of passion, lust. 'Harder!' Donna ordered. 'A proper thrashing!' Following her instructions, Helen slapped harder, reddening the pale crescents as Sophie whimpered. 'Harder!' Donna repeated. In full swing now, Helen beat the girl's buttocks with all her might, Sophie crying out and squirming exquisitely with each stinging blow. Wary of a possible escape attempt, Donna leaped to the floor and sat on the girl's back, pinning her down as Helen continued the thrashing.

At last, Donna ordered the beating to stop and Helen fell to the floor, her perspiring body exhausted. 'Want your revenge?' Donna asked, rolling Sophie onto her back. The girl's tearful eyes widened, her lips turning into a slight smile as she surveyed Helen's naked, heaving body.

'Yes,' she whispered, moving towards Helen, her eyes glowing with desire.

'On your front, Helen!' Donna ordered. 'You must be punished for punishing Sophie!'

Doing her mistress's bidding, Helen lay on her stomach waiting for her beautiful punishment to commence. They were loving it, Donna knew, as she watched Sophie raise her hand over her friend's taut buttocks to bring it down with a sharp slap. Much to her delight Helen jumped and groaned with each blow until she cried out that she was coming. Thrusting her hand between Helen's legs, Donna located her wet groove and massaged her hard clitoris as Sophie continued the thrashing.

'I'm coming, don't stop!' cried Helen as she was flown high up to her heaven. Would she discover the angels of lust there? They didn't stop – on and on Sophie slapped her buttocks, Donna rubbing for all she was worth between her bloated cunt lips until, crying out her pleasure, crawling across the floor, Helen escaped and rested her used, sated body.

'That was beautiful!' she gasped, gingerly rubbing her inflamed buttocks.

'Did you enjoy it, Sophie?' Donna asked, gazing at the girl's hard young nipples.

'It hurt, but yes, I loved it.'

'Good, now you may both thrash me – one to each buttock,' she instructed, taking her position on the floor and stretching out her naked body.

Settling either side of Donna's naked, outstretched body, the girls raised their hands and began their thrashing, their beautiful spanking. Donna's stomach swirled and her clitoris hardened as she winced and gasped with each hard slap. 'One of you make me come!' she breathed, raising her hips to allow a hand to slip between her thighs and locate her desperate bud. Who the caressing fingers belonged to, she didn't know or care. Pinching, massaging, they stiffened her cumbud until she thoughts it would burst with ecstasy. Her buttocks burning, stinging, she gasped as several fingers rudely thrust into the open centre of her sex. As if shocked into action, her clitoris speedily gathered momentum and soared to its peak, her hot come spattering onto the carpet.

Desperately she tried to stop the girls, to put an end to the painful pleasure but, as she had done with them, one of them sat on her back. The hot pussy lips rubbing up and down her spine, she could feel the warm juices decanting, trickling over her back, heightening her pleasure as the punishment continued. Begging for her freedom now, she tried to wriggle free but could do nothing to save herself from another orgasm. Rocking her body, tearing at her mind, her shuddering climax almost rendered her unconscious.

Finally, the girls collapsed, exhausted, wet with the perspiration of sex. Free at last, Donna rolled onto her back and covered her face with her hands. 'You're good,' she gasped. 'Both very good. I'm pleased with you. But there's one more thing before we dress. Sophie, come here and kneel astride me, my face. I want you to come in my mouth – bubble your cream into my mouth.'

Sophie moved over Donna's face, her soft, wet vaginal lips hovering above the older girl's mouth, her pink, inner petals unfolding in readiness for her tongue. Lowering the open centre of her young body, Sophie settled her lips over Donna's hot mouth, gasping as her tongue pushed its way into her wetness. Helen moved between Donna's legs and began to pleasure her there, licking, sucking on her clitoris. Donna's body burned with desire. Grabbing Sophie's hips, she moved her back and forth, rubbing the length of her groove over her mouth, eating her slippery flesh, drinking her warm milk.

Floating on a sea of lesbian lust, Donna sucked hard on Sophie's clitoris as the girl's body shuddered and her open cunt poured out its juices, swelled with orgasm. Her own love bud exploded in sympathy with Sophie's, pulsating, sending ripples of pleasure through her body to mingle with the pleasure pouring into her mouth – pleasure sustaining pleasure.

After their writhing, their perspiring, the girls relaxed their spent bodies as their climaxes subsided, leaving them wet, panting with satisfaction. Sophie climbed from Donna's mouth, her gaping slit oozing with the cream of orgasm, and fell to the floor. Marvelling at the wondrous display of complex folds of wet flesh, Donna remembered the cucumber. What better way to end a session of limitless lust than to take the girls simultaneously with a thick, cool cucumber? One at each end, each end in one. But no, they'd had enough, she decided, rising to her feet.

'That was very nice,' she praised, slipping her skirt and top over her moist body. 'We'll do this again, tomorrow.'

'I'd like that,' Sophie smiled as she dressed.

'And you, Helen?' Donna asked. 'Will you be joining us tomorrow?'

'Try and keep me away,' she giggled. 'I'll be here every day, if you want me to, that is.'

'I want you both to be my sex slaves and attend my body whenever I ask you to,' Donna declared, kissing each girl in turn, placing her arms around them to discreetly remove the patches. 'I have a little surprise in store for you both. Well, quite a big surprise, actually. But you'll have to wait until tomorrow.'

'What is it?' Sophie asked excitedly.

'Wait and see,' Donna teased, picturing the cucumber connecting the girl's naked bodies, fucking them as they lay on the floor with their wet buttocks caressing.

Alone in the flat, Donna peeled the patch from her arm and wandered into the kitchen. Salad for lunch, she thought, taking the sticky cucumber from the fridge. Preparing the food, she wondered what to do with her sex slaves the following day. Something really exciting. Tie them down, perhaps? Have them eat the cucumber from her pussy? The thought sent daggers through her sore clitoris as she placed the cucumber back in the fridge to keep it cool and hard.

Taking her salad into the lounge, she settled in her

armchair, picked up her book and opened it at the leather marker. She smiled as she read the familiar words. '. . . her arm round his neck, she closed her eyes as he carried her to the bridal suite and kicked the door shut'. Closing the book, in her mind's eye she wrote the scene in the bridal suite. 'And then he slipped her wet panties off and fucked her as she'd never been fucked before until she screamed, lost in her orgasm.' That was the way to do it, she thought, as she began her salad. Wish I had another cucumber. Anyway, who was the man Helen had mentioned, watching her flat, lurking?

Chapter Five

Donna was delighted when Lynn rang and invited her round for the evening. She increasingly resented her own company. 'Bring a bottle of wine,' Lynn drawled. 'We'll have some sexy fun tonight.'

Perhaps Lynn wasn't so bad after all, Donna reflected as she reapplied the patch to her arm and left her flat. People changed, especially after so many years, didn't they? And besides, Lynn had a beautiful body that shouldn't go to waste. Sexy fun? Obviously her patch hadn't come off in the shower. What had she been up to? Masturbating, probably. Secretly masturbating, as women do – as women deny.

Greeting Donna with a huge grin, a scantily clad Lynn invited her in and immediately began to undress her. 'I thought we'd spend the evening together, naked,' she purred, slipping her visitor's top off.

'Sounds good to me.' And feels good, too, Donna thought as Lynn unclipped her bra, freed her breasts and took a nipple in her mouth. A shiver ran up her spine as she surveyed the action objectively – a girl, rampant with desire, cupping her breast, engulfing her aureola with her pretty mouth, sucking hard on her sensitive nipple! Now kneeling, sensuously easing down her skirt and panties, burying her face between her soft vaginal lips, kissing them . . .

'You taste nice,' Lynn murmured, licking at the moist valley as Donna sank into a subjective, sexual oblivion. 'I want you.'

Taking her hand and leading her to the sofa, Lynn sat her down and spread her legs. 'What are you *doing?*' Donna panted, anxious in her arousal, as Lynn pulled her legs even wider apart and secured her ankles to the feet of the sofa with a length of rope.

'Having some sexy fun,' Lynn whispered mischievously, pulling two ropes over the arms of the sofa and tying them to her friend's wrists.

Naked, her arms outstretched, her legs spread wide, her body open, vulnerable, Donna pushed her hips forward as Lynn stuffed several cushions behind her back. Her naked, gaping valley over the edge of the sofa, she closed her eyes as Lynn positioned herself between her splayed thighs and stroked her swollen pussy lips. Nibbling the soft cushions of flesh, Lynn pushed two fingers into her hot hole and kneaded the silky walls of her vagina.

'That's nice,' Donna breathed as the sensations welled up from her womb. 'Make me come with your tongue!'

Without warning, Lynn withdrew her fingers from the dank cavern and stood up. A cucumber, Donna thought dreamily as her friend left the room. Returning fully clothed, Lynn grinned wickedly as she fixed her stare between Donna's legs.

'Comfortable?' she asked, sitting in the armchair opposite.

'Very,' Donna replied, somewhat mystified. 'But why have you got dressed? Aren't you going to make me come?'

'Later. I want to talk to you first.'

'What about?'

'This,' she said, holding up a patch. 'Stuck to my neck, it was. It came off when I was in the shower. Strange, that, don't you agree?'

Donna laughed nervously as she tugged on the ropes. Lynn couldn't possibly know what it was. There was no way she'd have been able to discover the truth.

'I know it was you because I felt something when you stuck it on my neck. I didn't give it much thought at the time, thinking that you'd caught me with your nail. But after my shower, I sat down and thought about everything that has happened recently. Our little sex sessions, being arrested for prostitution, having sex on my mind all night long, having to masturbate every hour or so to calm myself . . . It's all got something to do with this little plaster, hasn't it?'

'That's ridiculous!' Donna laughed, uneasily, wriggling and pulling harder on the ropes. 'A plaster? Why on earth would I want to stick a plaster on your neck?'

'Let's prove this once and for all, shall we? You seem to be a horny little bitch which, from what I remember, isn't you at all. I wonder why you've changed so much? I wonder what's changed you – a plaster like this, perhaps?'

Moving towards Donna, Lynn knelt and lifted her hair. Examining her neck, she moved down to her shoulders. 'Where is it?' she demanded, running her fingers over the firm young breasts. Progressing to Donna's arms, Lynn smiled triumphantly. 'Ah, here it is! So, what's this all about?'

'I cut myself.'

Lynn pulled the patch off. 'So, where's the cut? This makes you randy, doesn't it? I don't know how or why, but it turns you on! I'll just stick it back for you.'

Reapplying the plaster to Donna's arm, she had a sudden inspiration. 'And you can have this one on your other arm! There, now you'll be a real bitch on heat!'

The second patch took effect almost immediately, causing Donna's clitoris to swell, her juices to flow. Still she insisted that she knew nothing of the plasters. 'How can an ordinary plaster turn anyone on?' she asked as Lynn rummaged through her handbag.

'Ah, more plasters!' Lynn cried triumphantly. 'Let's see how randy you become with four – stuck to your legs, I think,' she said, pressing the patches onto Donna's calves.

'No, no! Take them off!'

'Why? You said that they're only ordinary plasters.'

'No, they . . . Look, let me go, let's forget all about this. I should never have come here.'

'But you *are* here, as my prisoner. Now, listen to me: I want more of these, lots more! I could earn myself a fortune, and have some bloody good fun in the process.'

'There are no more.'

'I hope there are, for your sake. Oh, and I want the formula, too. Not that I would understand it, of course, but someone would probably pay me well for it. At least I know what you do in that research lab now – make aphrodisiac plasters.'

'No. There are no more, they're just ordinary plasters.'

Leaving the room to answer the front door, Lynn told Donna that she'd planned a little surprise for her. She liked surprises – sometimes.

'Don't bring anyone in here!' Donna pleaded. 'For God's sake, Lynn! What the hell are you doing?'

'Getting my own back, and earning some money in the process.'

'You've set me up, you bitch!'

'Yes, I have – and extremely well, too,' Lynn called back over her shoulder as she opened the front door.

Muffled whispers came from the hall as Donna struggled to break free, to cover her crudely exposed femininity. The voices growing louder, she became terrified as she realised that Lynn was talking to a man. Yanking hard on the ropes, she knew she'd never escape from Lynn Bulmur – and whatever it was that she had planned for her. She was aware, too, that she didn't *want* to escape now. The sexual force rising at an alarming rate, she desperately needed orgasm – a man.

'Donna, meet Steve, a photographer friend of mine,' Lynn grinned, showing a young man into the room. Tall, dark, good looking, he stood and gazed in awe at Donna's open body. Brushing back his thick black hair, he smiled.

'She's absolutely beautiful! We'll earn more than a few bob from the photographs,' he said, setting up a tripod in the centre of the room. 'You're a real stunner, aren't you? And what a wonderful pose! I congratulate you both.'

'Thanks. But Donna doesn't need congratulating – she's not exactly willing, you see,' Lynn volunteered, pulling a blonde wig over her cropped hair.

'Bloody hell! You've tied her up against her will?'

'Sort of.'

'Won't there be trouble?'

'You're bloody right there'll be trouble!' Donna spat.

'No, no, there won't. I've got something on her, you see. And I'll have even more on her when you've finished taking the photographs.'

'I hope you know what you're doing, Lynn,' Steve said fearfully.

'I know, all right. In fact, I'm so confident that you can give her a good fucking afterwards. She'll be more than grateful, she'll even beg you for it. Do you want to?'

'Want to? I'd love to! I'll just go and get the rest of my stuff from the van.'

Humiliated, degraded, and yet incredibly aroused, Donna stared hard at Lynn. She hadn't changed at all: she was still the little bitch she used to be – worse, even. Donna cursed herself for using the patch, for seducing her, for meeting her again. Lynn flashed her captive a salacious grin as she settled in the armchair and gazed between her splayed legs. 'There's a good market for photos of this kind,' she bragged. 'And an even better one for the type of pictures Steve will be taking later.'

'I'll get you for this, Bulmur!' Donna threatened.

'How? The photographs will be published in certain seedy magazines for all to see. There'll be no mistaking you, your identity, I assure you. How can anyone possibly connect me with your dirty little side-line? Anyway, Steve's great at poster-size blow-ups. I think I'll send one to that research lab where you work. They can stick it on the wall and all have a good laugh. You were saying that you are going to get me. How, exactly?'

Donna said nothing as Steve lugged his equipment in and began to set it up. Her embarrassment rising, she squeezed her eyes shut as Lynn settled between her legs and stroked her clitoris. 'I think I'll make you come,' she said, caressing the swollen bud. 'When you're nice and wet and panting with delight, we'll start taking the pictures.'

Despite her desperate attempts to fight her over-whelming desire for orgasm, Donna could do nothing to halt the wondrous sensations emanating from her clitoris as Lynn mouthed and sucked. The soft hair from the blonde wig lightly tickled her stomach as the tart licked between the wet folds of her pussy and stiffened the hard protrusion. Ramming four fingers into the hotness of her open hole, Lynn fingered and sucked the beginnings of a powerful climax from Donna's trembling body just as Steve started to take the first few photographs.

'Keep her going!' he ordered, adjusting the lighting. 'Make sure you get her face in every shot!' Lynn spluttered, surfacing for air. 'And be sure not to get mine!' On and on ran the banter, the caressing, the tonguing, the fingering. Her entire body quivering uncontrollably, Donna was oblivious to Steve, the lights and the camera as it clicked and whirred. Moving her head aside, Lynn thrust her fingers in and out of Donna's body, massaging her clitoris faster and harder as her climax erupted.

'Ah, my cunt! My beautiful cunette is coming!' Donna heard herself cry as she swirled in the warmth of her orgasm.

Her body absorbing the hormone from the four patches, she begged to come again as soon as her climax had waned sufficiently for her to gasp her plea. 'Do you want your beautiful cunette, as you call it, filled with this?' Lynn asked, wielding a huge candle in the girl's face.

'God, yes! And quickly – I need to come again!'

Gently easing the candle into Donna's open hole, Lynn twisted and pushed until it could penetrate her body no further. Moving the camera in, Steve clicked away at Donna's thick wet cunt lips, stretched and swollen, encircling the solid wax phallus. Careful to keep out of shot, Lynn reached out to thrust the candle in and out, to bring Donna ever nearer to her sensual heaven as the camera recorded every spasm, every grimace. Her milky fluid oozing from her bloated hole, bathing the candle, running down the dark crease between her buttocks, at last she shuddered and cried out her gratification. There was no thinking, no thoughts. In a swirling river of sex, her mind departed her body to swim in dangerous, churning currents. Her clitoris throbbing incessantly, massaged by its pinken hood as the candle stretched and pulled on her labia, deeper and deeper she sank into the dark warmth, the engulfing sexual euphoria of orgasm.

Yet still, mysteriously, she wanted more. 'Fuck me!' she cried with her last strength as Lynn pulled the candle from her trembling body, leaving her hole gaping, outpouring its creamy fluid. 'Tell him to fuck me!'

Steve needed no further invitation. Slipping his jeans down, he knelt between her thighs and pushed his hard penis home, forcing its entire length into her hot, wet body, devouring her very soul as he began to thrust in and out as a man possessed. Positioning herself by his side, Lynn stretched open Donna's inflamed lips and massaged her clitoris, quickly bringing her to another climax as Steve mercilessly rammed her cervix.

Tossing her head, gasping, crying out for more, Donna thought she'd die as Lynn bit hard on her nipple and Steve filled her with his sperm – hot, gushing, spewing from the bulbous head of his throbbing penis. Her sheath filled with his hot, bubbling seed until it overflowed, spilling the slippery product of orgasm over her lips where it trickled down between her buttocks and pooled on the sofa.

Withdrawing his shrinking penis, Steve gulped and

fell to the carpet, apologising for coming so soon. 'I couldn't stop it, I was so worked up, I just couldn't . . .'

'You did very well,' Lynn consoled him. 'Now get back to the camera and let's get this over with!'

Donna opened her eyes as she slowly recovered and gazed at her captor. 'What are you going to do?' she asked fearfully.

'Take some really good pictures now!' grinned Lynn, leaving the room. Returning with a box, she knelt between Donna's thighs and clipped two clothes pegs to her sore nipples. 'They'll love these shots at your lab,' she laughed, pulling a thick carrot from the box and pushing it between Donna's gaping vaginal lips. Taking another carrot, she pushed it in alongside the first. 'And now two more,' she giggled.

'No, no! Not four, you'll never get them in!'

'I will, you'll see,' Lynn assured Donna confidently, twisting and turning the thick shafts until the girl's muscles yielded. 'There, I told you I'd get them all in! Now, just one last thing, and we're ready.' Taking Donna's lipstick from her bag, she drew an arrow on her stomach pointing down to the carrots and wrote her phone number above it. 'What a sight! Your telephone will be ringing non-stop before long. I don't know what your work colleagues will have to say about you!'

Behind the camera again, Steve focussed on the four carrot heads protruding from Donna's body, stretching her lips open as never before. On his third roll of film now, he clicked the shutter, adjusted the lighting, changed lenses every so often, ensuring that he had every delectable inch of her abused body in frame.

'Right,' he finally said. 'I'm packing up now. I'll do the developing when I get home and let you have the prints tomorrow.'

'Thanks, Steve, it's been fun. I'll see that you're paid well. You've done a brilliant job – hasn't he, Donna?'

'I need to come again! Take these bloody patches off, for God's sake!' Donna cried as her insatiable clitoris swelled and pulsated again, her wet sheath gripping the carrots rhythmically.

Peeling the patches from Donna's perspiring skin, Lynn placed them on the table and withdrew the carrots from her victim's sore vagina. Still trembling, in dire need of orgasm, Donna pleaded for her freedom, promising some patches in return for the photographs – promising anything.

'No, the photos are going to earn me a lot of money. You'll give me as many patches as you can get your hands on, and the formula, in exchange for your freedom.'

'I'll give you nothing unless I have all the pictures, and the negatives. This is blackmail, you bitch!'

'No can do, I'm afraid,' Steve interrupted as he dismantled the lighting equipment. 'I need the money too, you see.'

'Then no patches!' Donna yelled.

'What are these patches, anyway?' Steve asked.

'Nothing,' Lynn replied, brusquely, helping him to carry out his equipment.

Returning to the room, Lynn closed the door and walked over to Donna, smiling. 'He's gone,' she said, kneeling between her prisoner's thighs and stroking her wet valley. 'I want the patches, Donna. I mean it, I must have them.'

'You'll get nothing from me!'

'Then I'll keep you here indefinitely.'

'Don't be stupid, people will come looking for me.'

'Maybe, but I plan to move as soon as I get some

cash. The people who own this place are abroad so perhaps I'll move out and leave you here alone – tied up.'

'Don't talk rubbish.'

'The flat's self-contained with its own front door. No-one will be able to get in, no-one will know you're here, bound and gagged. The owners won't be back – not for a few months, anyway.'

'I'm not listening.'

'Look, I'm desperate for money, I owe hundreds, and the patches can bring me money, more than enough . . .'

'How?'

'I know people in London who will make good use of them.'

'I'll bet you do! Filthy perverts who will . . .'

'The photographs will be sold the minute I get hold of them, so you'd better agree to come up with the goods. I wasn't really going to send one to your lab, by the way.'

'How can I get you the patches if I'm tied up?'

'When you agree, I'll free you. Oh, and no funny business. You'll have to come up with the goods because I'll have the pictures, won't I? Anyway, I'm off out for the evening. If you've any money in your handbag, that is.'

'You're a thief, a whore, a bitch!'

'Oh look, fifty pounds – that'll do nicely. Thanks, Donna, see you later – I'm off to a club to enjoy your cash. I'll turn the T.V. on so you won't get too bored. You do look a sight with your pretty little cunette hanging open like that and your phone number scrawled across your belly! That's a thought, I might bring someone back with me, several people, perhaps? You never know, this might be your lucky night! Do you feel

Ray Gordon

like having a man or a woman playing with you later? Or, should I say, men or women? No comment? Oh well, it'll be a nice surprise, something to look forward to – 'bye.'

With the effect of the patches wearing off, Donna began to realise the severity of her predicament. She remembered a pretty young girl at the university who'd got herself mixed up with Lynn and ended up being sexually used by her disciples. Lynn Bulmur, she reflected fearfully, was renowned as the devil's daughter – Lucifer's daughter. Was the demon that had possessed her Lucifer? Was *he* the driving, sexual force?

Tugging on the ropes again, Donna tried desperately to free herself. It was more than likely that Lynn *would* round up a bunch of punters and charge them for taking her body. And with the patches in place, she couldn't help but enjoy it. As she writhed in orgasm, cried out for more as they took it in turns to use her, no-one would realise that she was a prisoner – taken against her will.

To her delight, she managed to slip the rope over her slender wrist. Quickly, she freed herself and dressed. But before leaving the flat she searched through the wardrobe, dressing-table and cupboards. She didn't know what for until she found it – an address book. Slipping it into her bag along with the patches, she ran from the flat into the street and breathed in the refreshing evening air.

People were gathered outside the pub enjoying the warm summer evening, unaware of what had been going on so close to them. Donna stopped and watched as they sipped their drinks under the moon. The men laughed and joked, the women sat and talked. Talked about what? Sex? Orgasm? Their husbands, each other's husbands? Who was screwing whom? They all seemed happy, so did it really matter?

She rang Alan the minute she arrived home. She had to tell him the truth, ask his advice – it was her only hope. No reply. 'Damn it!' she cursed, banging the phone down and rummaging through her bag for Lynn's address book. The photographer wasn't listed, but there were several phone numbers at the back of the book with initials alongside. She tried S.J. – no reply. S.H. was answered by a woman. 'Is Steve there, please?' Donna asked.

'You must have the wrong number,' the woman said, before hanging up. Third time lucky – she dialled S.W.

'Speaking,' a male voice replied in answer to her question.

'Steve, it's Lynn,' she said, muffling her voice as best she could.

'Hi, what can I do for you?'

'The photographs, can I come and pick them up tomorrow morning?'

'It's a terrible line, I can hardly hear you. Look, I'll bring them round to your place. You don't want to come all the way out here, do you?'

'I don't mind, it's not that far.'

'Not far? It's a good ten miles, isn't it?'

Donna bit her lip. She daren't ask for his address.

'That girl, Donna, is she still with you?' he asked.

'No, she's gone. She's not very happy, but who cares?'

'Look, this is all getting out of hand. You told me that you had a model willing to do the session, not an unwilling naked girl tied to your sofa. Anyway, I'll drop the pictures round tomorrow and that'll be the end of it as far as I'm concerned.'

'And the negatives?'

'No way, they're mine. I need something to use in case she . . . I really must go, the wife's just come in. See you tomorrow.'

She had to act quickly, she knew. Steve and Lynn would soon discover that she'd phoned and they'd . . . God knew what they'd do to her. She waited a few minutes and rang the number again, praying that his wife would answer.

'Hello,' a soft female voice said.

'Hello. I don't know if this is the right number, only I'm after a photographer, Steve someone, Steve . . .'

'Wilkins. Yes, hold on, I'll get him for you.'

Hanging up, she breathed a sigh of relief. 'Got you, you bastard,' she murmured as she flicked through the phone book. 'Wilkins S. Photographer. 21 Forsythe Avenue, Ringwood. That's about ten miles. So, Wilkins S., I think I'll pay you a visit!'

Taking a quick shower, Donna lathered her stomach, removing the greasy lipstick scrawled across her smooth skin. Bulmur was right, she knew, the phone wouldn't stop ringing if the pictures got out. Imagining under-cover police arriving at her flat, or worse still, tabloid newspapers reporters, she sighed. Quickly drying her-self, she prepared herself mentally for the confrontation with Mr and Mrs Wilkins.

Driving away from her flat, she passed Lynn walking towards it. What had happened to the night clubbing? she wondered. And what would Lynn do when she got no reply? Break in? 'This is bloody ridiculous!' Donna cursed, banging the steering wheel. 'All this bloody trouble because of that bloody Lynn Bulmur!'

Pulling up outside the photographer's house, she sat in her car contemplating her next move. Should she knock on the door? Confront him? Tell his wife? As she was about to climb out of her car, the front door opened and Steve walked to his car parked in the drive. Keeping her head low as he backed out and drove past her, she glanced at her watch. Ten o'clock. Where was he off to? How long would he be? Where did young men go at night?

Uncertain of what she was going to say, she walked up the drive and rang the bell. An extremely attractive woman in her early thirties opened the door and smiled sweetly.

'Is Steve in?' Donna asked.

'You've just missed him. Can I help?'

'Oh, no. I've got a roll of film for him, will he be long?'

'Knowing Steve, he'll be hours. He's gone to deliver some photographs, but he's bound to stop off for a drink on his way back. I'll give him the film.'

'I must give it to him personally. My name's Donna, by the way. May I come in? It's very important.'

'Er . . . Yes, I suppose so. I'm Debbie.'

Sitting in the expensively furnished lounge, Donna remembered that Steve had said he needed money. Observing Debbie, well dressed, obviously well educated, and not short of a penny, she became confused. 'Steve is your husband, isn't he?'

'Yes, he is. How long have you know him? Are you a client?'

'Yes, a client. I must speak with him about a job he did earlier this evening.'

'He's not worked today, he never works at weekends. You must be mistaken.'

A secret life, Donna mused. A man of secrets. How would his wife react to a patch? What would he say if he were to come home to find her tied to the sofa? Would he take photographs? Sweet revenge – the idea was good, she decided. But to execute it?

Holding her head, her eyes closed, feigning faintness, she asked Debbie for a glass of water. Slipping a patch from her bag as the woman left the room, she grinned. She was becoming quite adept at treachery and deception. But wasn't it all in the name of women's rights – orgasms? Holding Debbie's arm to steady herself, Donna pressed the patch to her skin as she took the glass of water. The dirty deed was done – almost.

'Thank you,' Donna said, handing the empty glass back and secreting a second patch onto the woman's arm. 'Sorry, but I must sit down for a minute, I don't know what came over me.'

'If you give me the film, I'll see that Steve gets it,' Debbie promised, sitting down beside her.

'Oh, I seem to have left it in the car,' Donna replied, wondering how to stall for time.

Smiling, she watched as Debbie began to adjust her short skirt and fiddle with her bra – the tell-tale signs of female arousal. Knowing the effects of the patch only too well, that Debbie was more than ready to be stripped and pleasured, Donna sat on the floor between her legs and lifted the other woman's skirt without saying a word. Reclining, her eyes closed, Debbie breathed deeply and opened her legs – a prisoner of her own subconscious desires.

Again, Donna wondered at the power of the patches, the hormone. After just minutes, a woman, any woman it seemed, was putty in her hands, opening her legs, begging to be licked, sucked – pleading to come. How long would the hormone last? The patches had been used several times now and, judging by the chosen few's sexual appetites, there were no signs that they were on the wane.

Gazing at the triangular patch of tight pink material between Debbie's thighs, Donna realised that she hadn't equipped herself with a plaster. Maybe she didn't need one, she reflected as she tugged at the silk panties and pulled them down the slender legs to expose her goal. Having awoken her basic instincts, perhaps she no longer needed the hormone.

Blonde, trimmed, Debbie's sparse pubic hairs barely covered her ample pussy lips. Parting the fleshy folds, Donna examined the pink, glistening pads forming the moist valley. Leaning forward, she began to lick the length of the fissure causing Debbie to push her hips forward, open her legs wider and gasp.

'Like it?' Donna asked.

'Oh, yes, yes. I've never . . .'

'Never been licked by another woman?'

'No. God, yes! Keep going, keep licking!'

'Shall I tie you down and really make you come?'

'No, just keep licking! What's happened to me? I don't even know you and yet . . . Ah, that's good!'

'I'll only make you come if I can tie you down.'

'Anything, but be quick, I desperately need to come!'

Searching the house for something to tie her victim with, Donna opened a door and found herself in the garage. Soft moans emanated from the lounge as she returned with a length of rope. Holding her cunt lips wide open, masturbating her hard clitoris as if there were no tomorrow, Debbie was already nearing her climax. There was no time to lose. Working quickly, Donna tied Debbie's feet to the sofa legs, as Lynn had done with hers. Oblivious to the world, Debbie continued to masturbate as Donna ran the rope under the length of the sofa, bringing the ends over the arms in readiness to secure her victim's wrists.

Coming, her fingertips frantically vibrating her clitoris, gasping for breath, Debbie shuddered and cried out before falling limp as a rag doll as her climax faded. Seizing her chance, Donna fastened her wrists, completing her job of bondage. Her arms outstretched, legs wrenched asunder, Debbie opened her eyes and stared wide-eyed at her bonds.

'Let me go! I want to make you come!' she pleaded, pulling on the ropes, desperate to appease her aching bud again, to pleasure Donna, to lick between her legs.

'I can't let you go,' Donna said dolefully, peeling the patches from Debbie's arm. 'Sorry, but I have to leave you like this, I'm afraid. Steve will understand when he discovers you later. Just tell him Donna sends her love.'

'No! You can't leave me like this! Please, please!'

Discovering Steve's darkroom, Donna grabbed a Polaroid camera and returned to the lounge. She didn't know how to use the camera, but that didn't matter. As long as Debbie and Steve thought that she had taken pictures, she would be safe.

'What the hell are you doing?' Debbie cried as Donna opened her blouse and pulled her bra up, allowing her ample breasts to hang free, ready for the photographs. Her nipples were long, hard, wonderful and Donna couldn't resist taking one into her mouth and sucking, bringing out the full length of the brown protrusion. Debbie sighed and closed her eyes. But time was of the essence, Donna knew.

Standing back, she took several shots. 'What's going on? Who put you up to this?' Debbie asked shakily. Donna said nothing, but couldn't conceal a huge grin as the camera whirred and the pictures rolled out. 'Look, if it's money you want . . .'

'No. Look, I'm sorry. None of this was your doing. You shouldn't be involved but . . . Blame that bastard of a husband of yours!'

'Steve? What's he done? I don't even understand what *I've* done. What's happened to me?'

Closing the lounge door, Donna was about to make her escape when the sound of a car pulling into the drive halted her in her tracks. Trying to listen above Debbie's cries for help, she dived into the dark of the understairs cupboard just as the front door opened.

'What is it?' Steve called as he dashed through the hall. 'Who the hell did this to you?' she heard him ask. Couldn't he guess? Hadn't he come across the same scenario that very evening? Hadn't he fucked a woman tied to a sofa, just as his innocent wife was tied now?

'Someone called Donna – she raped me! Untie me, quickly! She took photographs of me like this. We must call the police!' Debbie sobbed.

Donna listened with amusement as Steve did his best to calm his wife as he untied her. 'We don't need the police,' he said shakily. 'I know who the girl is. Leave it to me and I'll deal with her.'

'Who is she, then? What's she to you? You'd better explain what you're into or I'll call the police right now! And I'll tell you something else – we're finished!'

'What were you doing with your knickers down and your tits hanging out, anyway? Surely, you played some part in this?' he asked accusingly.

'I . . . She forced me. I had no power to resist her.'

'No power? This rope is from the garage. What were you doing while she went to get it, waiting for her, knowing full well what she was up to? Or did you get it yourself so that she could tie you up and . . . You disgust me!'

'You've disgusted me for years! You and your bloody silly photographs! Where the hell do you get to most evenings, anyway?'

'Bloody working, unlike some people!'

Leaving the unhappy couple to their problems, Donna crept through the front door clutching the camera and pictures and made her escape. Steve hadn't had a great deal of time to develop the photographs, but she was sure that they were the ones his wife said he was delivering. But now she was armed, too, ready to retaliate – to blackmail Debbie, at least.

Driving home, she thought about Debbie, what she'd done to her, what Steve would do. She knew it was a mistake, a stupid mistake, to do that to the poor, blameless woman. She should never have been dragged into the mess, it had nothing to do with her – she was just an innocent victim of the patches.

Lynn wasn't waiting on the doorstep as she had thought she would be but the phone started ringing as she let herself in. Dashing into the lounge, she grabbed the receiver. 'Donna, it's me, Steve.'

'Ah, Steve. The pictures of your wife came out very well.'

'Look, what is all this? My wife will go to the police, you do realize that, don't you?'

'Then you'd better stop her. It's all down to you. Get the photographs back from Lynn, give me the negatives, and I'll return the ones of your wife.'

'This is crazy. Why on earth did you drag my wife into this? Anyway, how the hell am I supposed to get the pics from Lynn?'

'That's your problem. You're the cause of all this, not me.'

'It was Lynn, she said that she had a girl willing to pose for me. Had I known the truth . . .'

'You did know the truth, she told you that I was unwilling and you still went ahead, didn't you?'

'Look, we must talk about this. God, my marriage, everything . . .'

'Marriage? Huh! You were quite happy to screw me behind your wife's back so don't give me any crap about your marriage! Just sort it out!'

No sooner had she banged the phone down than it rang again. Before she'd pressed the receiver to her ear, she could hear Lynn yelling at her.

'I've nothing to say to you, Bulmur!' Donna blasted back.

'You'll get me some patches or these pictures will all be published, and copies sent to your lab!'

'Ring Steve, your precious photographer friend. I think he's got something to tell you about Debbie, his poor wife.'

'I don't give a toss about him, or his bloody wife, stupid, naive bitch that she is! I've got the pictures, Ryan! So you'd better come up with the patches – and some cash.'

Donna sighed as the line went dead. She was in a bad position, she knew. Her only chance was Steve – her job, her friends, her life depended on him. Why had she been cursed with Bulmur again? After all the years that had passed, why run into the devil's daughter? Did Lucifer rule her destiny?

Preparing for bed, she wondered about Alan. Should she tell him? No, she was in far too deep to involve him. If the pictures were published, could she sue? No chance. Who'd believe her story? She couldn't tell anyone about the patches, not without incriminating Alan – and the entire research laboratory.

As sleep engulfed her, she thought of running away. She could grab what little cash she had in the bank and disappear. Praying that the answer would come to her that night, she drifted away into a land where young female slaves cowered at her feet, begging to pleasure her with their fingers, their tongues. She dreamed her dreams, her fantasies – and the wet patch on the sheet between her legs grew bigger as the night grew darker.

Chapter Six

Sunday morning came all too quickly. The moment Donna opened her eyes, the serene gentleness of sleep turned to fear as the whole sordid affair filled her mind. Leaping from her bed, she glanced at the clock. Eight-thirty.

Unable to eat breakfast, she paced the lounge carpet, wondering what on earth she could do to put things right, to sort out the horrendous mess. In a matter of days, her world had been turned upside down, torn apart. Her job at risk, she found herself thinking of running again, but where to? Her parents lived eighty-odd miles away, and besides, they'd ask awkward questions. Thinking of Sue, Helen and Sophie, she began to realise exactly what the patches had done to her life. Things would never be the same, she thought, with a mixture of sorrow and happiness. With or without Lynn Bulmur, they would never be the same again.

The phone rang at ten. She hesitated – best to know the news, even if it was bad, she decided. Her head heavy with worry, she eventually lifted the receiver.

'It's Steve,' a deep voice whispered.

'So?'

'Look, I've spoken to Lynn and . . . Well, short of beating it out of her, she won't tell me where the pics are. Hidden in a safe place, that's all she'd say. Obviously she's not stupid enough to have them hidden in her flat. Anyway, there's no way she'll give them back to me – no way.'

'So, what do you propose to do?'

'Debbie . . . She's the one with all the money. I get what she calls an allowance. All I've got is my photographic work. If I lose her, I can't survive.'

'And if I lose my job, I'm finished, too. Look, this is your doing, your problem and . . .'

'No, no, it's not. Lynn told me about the patches. Come on, think about it, be honest and admit to the fact that you started this bloody mess.'

He was right, she knew only too well.

'But what do we do? My fault, your fault, Lynn's fault, what's the difference?'

'I wish I'd never met her.'

'Shit! That goes for me, too! Where *did* you meet her, anyway?'

'In a bar. We got talking and . . . Well, that was three months ago. I thought we'd get something going between us but she wasn't interested.'

'Serve you right for trying to commit adultery.'

'I've had an idea. Give her some dummy patches. That'll keep her quiet.'

'No, no, it won't. You said yourself that she's not stupid. Anyway, who's to say she won't hang on to some pictures? Even if I supply her with the patches, I can't be sure . . .'

'Let's meet. I can't talk with Debbie roaming around the house. Things are really bad between us now, thanks to you. Sorry, I shouldn't have said that. What do you say? We're in this together, like it or not. Let's meet for lunch at that place by the river.'

'The Bowlers?'
'That's the one. Meet you there at twelve, okay?'
'Okay.'

To tell Alan? Ask his advice? The more Donna thought about it, the more confused she became. At least Lynn Bulmur wasn't in possession of any patches, that was one thing to be thankful for. Suddenly remembering that Lynn had skinned her of her last money, she decided to call on Alan on her way to meet Steve. He'd lend her fifty pounds until she could get to the bank.

Knickerless and braless, dressed in a red miniskirt, dark stockings and a white lace blouse, Donna rang on Alan's bell, praying that he was at home and not at the lab, as usual. To her great relief he opened the door, shocked to find her there, looking stunning, seductive, smiling at him – all woman.

'Come in, come in,' he said enthusiastically, unable to stop grinning as he looked her up and down several times.

'A favour, Alan,' she began as he led her into the kitchen and filled the kettle.

'Anything, anything,' he smiled, thinking it was his lucky day.

'I need to borrow some cash, just until tomorrow.'

Disappointment in his eyes. 'Oh, right. Yes, of course, how much? Ten? Twenty?'

'Fifty, if . . .'

'Fifty, no problem. You, er, off out somewhere?'

'Lunch.'

'Alone? Only, I'm free so we could . . .'

'A friend, actually. But we'll have that meal sometime, I promise you. Tomorrow night, perhaps?'

'Yes, that'll be nice. There's so much we have to talk about.'

'Is there? Oh, yes, right. Anyway, I really must dash.'

'I'll get the money. You've not got time for coffee, then?'

'No, I really must be going, I'm already late.'

'Your close girlfriend, is it?'

'Who?'

'Your lunch date, the close girlfriend you mentioned, is it her?'

'Girlfriend? Oh, yes, yes. We, er, often have Sunday lunch together.'

'That's nice. I don't bother with Sunday lunch, cooking and all that. Anyway, I'll get the money for you.'

Donna surveyed the kitchen. 'He certainly does need a good woman,' she sighed, eyeing a week's worth of washing up and a pile of dirty clothes heaped against the washing machine. A good woman – not her, though, not any more, not now she was mixed up with . . .

'Fifty,' Alan said, bounding into the kitchen. 'Are you all right? Only, you seem worried. There's nothing wrong, is there?'

'No, nothing I can't handle, anyway.'

'You can always come to me if you have a problem, you know that, don't you? I'll always be here to . . .'

'Yes, thanks, Alan. I'll remember that. Look, thanks for the money. I must dash. I'll see you at the lab tomorrow, I hope.'

'Hope?'

'I mean . . . I'll see you tomorrow, Alan. Thanks again for the money.'

Close to tears, Donna walked out into the street, wishing she'd gone out with Alan instead of seeing

Bulmur the night before. He'd have wined and dined her, cared for her, made passionate love to her – not resorted to blackmail. 'Blackmail!' she breathed as she climbed into her car. 'Worse than blackmail, Bulmur's selling the pictures anyway. Patches or no patches, she's going to sell the bloody pictures!'

Pulling into the restaurant car park, she thought about Alan. Was he only after sex? No, she decided. He was different. He'd be there to pick her up when she fell. To make her laugh when she was down. To wipe the tears from her eyes when she cried. He was a humanist, she remembered him once saying – whatever that meant. 'A workaholic, if you ask me,' she sighed as she locked the car door and walked towards the restaurant. 'Shit! It's all gone so wrong!'

Dressed in tight blue jeans and an open-neck shirt, Steve was leaning on the bar, chatting up the barmaid and swilling down lager from a pint glass – not Donna's idea of a husband. Especially as he screwed young naked women behind his wife's back. But didn't they all? She pictured the sordid scene, saw herself naked, tied to the sofa, licked by Lynn, savaged by Steve – abused. God, bondage! Whatever next? Whatever better?

'Hi,' he greeted her, finishing his pint before asking her what she wanted to drink.

'Hi,' she returned coldly, wondering what the hell she was doing having Sunday lunch with the man who had as good as raped her the evening before. 'I don't want to be here with you,' she said honestly. 'But we seem to have a problem and . . . I've no choice, I suppose. Gin and tonic, please. You say your wife has money – how much?'

'That's our business.'

'And mine. If we're to deal with Bulmur, we have to look at all the possibilities. She's broke. She'll have her price.'

'Doesn't everyone have their price?'

'Yes, exactly – everyone, even your wife. How much is she worth?'

'Quite a lot. Her mother left her . . .'

'I'm not interested in her mother. Can you get your hands on her money? Or are you so pathetic that she makes sure that your allowance only covers the cost of your rolls of film?'

'There's no need to turn sarcastic on me.'

'No, you're right. I'm sorry. It's just that all this has pissed me off. God, why did I have to bump into Lynn bloody Bulmur?'

'Let's go through and order, shall we? I haven't eaten since yesterday lunch time.'

'Neither have I.'

Roast beef, carrots, parsnip, cauliflower, cabbage, roast potatoes – Donna contemplated the food piled high on her plate and turned her head. 'I'd rather have a cigarette,' she sighed despondently.

'Sorry, I didn't know that you smoked.'

'I don't. I gave it up three years ago, but now . . .'

'Have one, it'll calm you down.'

'It'll give me bloody lung cancer,' she complained, taking a cigarette and placing it firmly between her lips. 'But that's no worse than this mess, is it?'

'No, I suppose not. Although they do say that there's always someone worse off than you,' he ruminated, lighting her cigarette.

'Do they? I'd like to know who.'

'Me, for a start. I stand to lose a bloody good way of life, and a lovely house. You hold the key to my problem – you've got the pictures of Debbie.'

'With all due respect,' Donna whispered as the waiter approached with the wine. 'Fuck you – and your bloody problem.'

Stubbing the cigarette out, she picked at her food and sipped her wine. Steve gulped his food down as if he hadn't eaten for a week. How could he eat at a time like this? she wondered. Uncaring, no conscience, no guilt. His only concern seemed to be for himself, his way of life, his wife's money. She thought of Alan again. Why did he keep coming back to haunt her? What was it about him that constantly dragged her thoughts to him?

On the third glass of wine, Steve suddenly bombarded Donna with a battery of questions.

'Did my wife struggle when you tied her down?'

'No, of course not.'

'Only she says that you raped her.'

'Rubbish, she was only too willing.'

'So all that crap that Lynn came out with about the patches is true, then?'

'Depends what she told you.'

'About the aphrodisiacal effect they have on people. Listen, if this is true, do you realise the potential?'

'Oh, yes, of course I do – and so does Bulmur!'

'My wife has always been – how shall I put it? – a prude, kind of non-sexual, if you know what I mean. She's never even tried oral sex, she won't consider anything other than the missionary position. These patches changed her, didn't they? Think of all the marriages there must be like mine where the old man has to find it elsewhere because the wife's frigid, inorgasmic or whatever it's called.'

Sipping her wine, Donna reflected on the numerous magazine articles she'd read about sex. Female

Orgasm – What Is It? Is Orgasm Really Necessary?
How To Achieve Orgasm. Facts About Female Masturbation And Orgasm. Multiple Orgasm – Fact or
Fantasy? Orgasm During Sex – How To Fake It. The
articles were endless, but with a common theme – the
problem of achieving orgasm. Men didn't give women
orgasms – women had them. Gifts from the angels,
maybe?

Steve had a point, she conceded. After the way Sue
had reacted to the patch, transformed from a prude to a
rampant nympho, marriages all over the world could be
saved – or ruined. But Lynn Bulmur was standing in the
way of everything, blocking any progress that might be
possible – any money that might be there, for the
taking.

'You've got something on me, well, indirectly, as it's
my wife who's at risk of being exposed,' Steve whispered thoughtfully. 'And Lynn has something on you.
The answer is simple – get rid of Lynn Bulmur.'

'What, kill her?'

'I don't know. Imprison her until all this is sorted out?
Kill her, like you said? Perhaps she could have a fatal
accident, why not? The world wouldn't miss her. Anyway, it would certainly solve the problems, yours and
mine.'

'This is real life, Steve, not a bloody movie.'

'Yes, and in this so-called real life, we are both in the
real shit.'

Shocked by Steve's idea, Donna began to wonder
how far he was prepared to go to save his pathetic
marriage, a useless liaison based on money – Debbie's
money. What was the point of getting married if you
were going to play the field? she reflected. But then,
didn't contemporary marriage open up the field – signal

for play to commence? Sadly, happily, she didn't have that problem.

'Let's go to Bulmur's flat now,' she suggested, desperate to deal with the problem once and for all. 'You go in, stick a patch on her, and when it's taken effect I'll turn up and we'll tie her to the sofa and really give her what for.'

'What's the point?'

'To take pictures of her. Tie her down, clothes pegs, carrots and all, and take photographs. Blackmail *her*.'

'And what would the threat be?'

'Exactly the same as she's doing to me – threaten to let the world know what she gets up to.'

'The world doesn't give a toss about her. She's out of work, got no real friends, her family have disowned her so they wouldn't care what she gets up to. It's no good, is it?'

'Yes, it is. There *are* people who care what she does or doesn't do. Come on, let's get round there now.'

'Okay, anything's worth trying, I suppose. I just hope you know what you're doing.'

Lynn Bulmur stood back and admired the pictures of Donna propped up on the table. 'Bitch!' she spat. 'Turn me into a bloody lesbian, would you? See me arrested for prostitution! I'll show you!' Addressing an envelope to the Head of Grunwerg Research Laboratories, she slipped a picture of Donna inside. Clothes pegs on her nipples, thighs splayed to accommodate four carrots protruding between her bloated, shaven cunt lips, her phone number clearly displayed across her stomach, she would not only lose her job but probably find herself in court, Lynn guessed. One last chance to deliver the goods, she decided, dialling Donna's number.

'Hi, this is Donna Ryan. I'm not available to take your call just now. But if you leave your name and number after the tone, I'll get back to you as soon as I can.'

Like hell you will! thought Lynn, before leaving her message. 'You can get the patches to me, Ryan! I've just put a photograph of you in an envelope. It's going to your lab first thing on Tuesday morning. I want the patches, the formula, and five hundred pounds delivered to me at my flat by Monday night, or else!'

Armed with two patches, Steve rang Lynn's doorbell.

'If you've come for the pictures, forget it! I've told you, there's nothing doing!' she stormed as she opened the door.

'Of course I haven't. I've come to the conclusion that this little game of ours could earn us both a fair amount of money. Let me in and I'll tell you my plan.'

Walking into the lounge, Lynn threw herself on the sofa and waited for Steve to join her. She was dressed in a purple suede miniskirt and matching waistcoat, and Steve thought her unusually attractive as he stood in the doorway, his penis coming to life as he pictured her young body – tethered, naked. Her hair was styled, for a change, her makeup recently applied and her nails freshly painted – she'd made an effort, but why? Casting his eyes appreciatively up her slim legs, he noticed the small patch of her panties just visible between her smooth thighs. Imagining what delights her panties were concealing, the warm, wet delights between her pussy lips, his penis twitched in anticipation.

'You look nice,' he remarked. 'Going out somewhere?'

'Yes, later. I'm meeting someone about the pictures.

I've been busy today, I've done quite well.'

'It's Sunday. No one's around on a Sunday.'

'The people I know are always around, midday, midnight, Monday, Sunday. Anyway, what's this plan of yours?'

'A business proposition. I've got contacts, as you have. How about taking pictures of girls, videos even, and making a fortune? With those patches you told me about, we could . . . Well, the sky's the limit. I know a photographer who's into . . .'

'Why do you need me?'

'Because you'll have the patches and you've got a flat. I could hardly run a business like that from home, could I? Debbie would throw me out. She probably will, anyway.'

'Don't tell me – your wife doesn't understand you. Pathetic.'

'Okay, if you're not interested . . .'

'I didn't say that. I'll tell you what we'll do. Just to prove that you're not bluffing, trying to trick me into something – set up your gear and lure that Donna Ryan here. I want some better shots of her anyway, so . . .'

'You're on. I'll set up and then ring her. Get the rope ready for the best porno pics session ever!'

Setting up his equipment, Steve grabbed the opportunity to slip a patch onto Lynn's arm as she helped with the lighting. Within minutes, her blatant sexual awareness was apparent as she gazed longingly at Steve's tight jeans, pressing her body against his as they worked. Soon, she was rubbing her fingers between her legs, kneading the soft swell of her panties, breathing heavily as her clitoris responded. The spell was cast.

Inexperienced as he was with the patches, Steve could only pray that she was ready as he pushed his hand up her short skirt and cupped her warm mound in his palm. 'Shall we move to the sofa?' he asked, thinking it odd as he guided her across the room that she'd not suspected the presence of the patch. Surely, he thought, she'd wonder at her sudden arousal? But seemingly not.

Slipping her panties down, she spread herself over the sofa and closed her eyes as Steve settled between her legs. 'Take your top off,' he whispered as he brushed his face against the soft, girl-scented hair between her thighs and pressed the second patch onto her leg. Her ample breasts free, her dark brown nipples grew and hardened as she threw her waistcoat and T-shirt to the floor. Raising her eyes to the ceiling and spreading her limbs, she listened to Steve's hypnotic murmurs as he licked at her opening groove.

'I'm going to make you come. I'm going to lick your cunt, your clitoris and then I'll screw you as you've never been screwed before. And then I'll lick you again, suck your clitoris until it's stiff, hard and throbbing with pleasure, until you come and come and come.'

Tying her hands and feet as he worked on her naked body was far easier than he'd imagined. Without a word of protest, she allowed her body to be taken prisoner, her mind to be totally engulfed in her wanton lust. Squirming, she opened her legs wider, pushed her hips forward, begging to be licked, fingered, opened – fucked.

'Shall I take some pictures of you?' he asked as he pushed his fingers deep into her wet body. She replied with only a gasp as he forced her open wider and began to massage the entrance to her womb. 'Do you realise that you're tied to the sofa?' he whispered. She said nothing as he leaned forward and took a nipple in his mouth. 'You're my prisoner, I can do anything with your naked body – anything,' he breathed, sucking hard on the elongated milk bud until she opened her mouth to bubble words of sex.

'Yes, do anything you want to me, but make me come! Open my cunt and fuck me! I desperately need to come!'

Aware that Donna was waiting outside in her car, Steve still couldn't resist the temptation to take Lynn, screw her tethered body until she screamed in orgasm as he filled her with his sperm. Slipping his jeans down, he moved the bulging head of his penis towards her and stabbed at her wet, pinken folds. Smoothly, silkily, the head slipped into the welcoming warmth, and then, inch by inch sank into her wetness, until she was completely impaled on his solid rod.

Stretching her swollen nether lips open with his fingers, he moved slowly back and forth, filling her vaginal sheath to capacity and then withdrawing, allowing her soft love-tube to close between thrusts. Hardening her exposed clitoris, bringing her ever nearer to her compulsory orgasm, he looked down at the stretched pink flesh, so tightly encompassing his hard shaft. Her stomach rose and fell with each thrust, her womb rhythmically contracted, sending ripples of sex through her body as she gasped, tossed her head and begged for more.

Wondering what was taking Steve so long, Donna edged her way up to the front door. Finding it ajar, she crept in and walked through the hall to the lounge. Spying through the crack in the door, her eyes took in the lewd spectacle – gasping, her naked body roped across the sofa, Lynn Bulmur, the bitch of bitches, Lucifer's daughter, was about to receive her just reward.

Stealing into the room, Donna sat in the armchair,

unnoticed. Eyeing Lynn's handbag on the floor, she opened it and quietly lifted out her purse. Thirty pounds, that'll do nicely, she thought as Lynn cried out, her body erupting with the most powerful orgasm she'd ever experienced. His rock-hard shaft ramming the gaping centre of her trembling body, Steve grunted and gripped her hips, pulling her closer, penetrating deeper into her sex. His face contorted, he shuddered, lost himself in her cunt as his sperm gushed, filled her swollen sheath, lubricated their debased union. The last thrust done, he convulsed and collapsed over her smooth stomach, biting hard on her nipple. The copulators lay spent, heaving, panting, perspiring, as Donna watched and waited in the wings, her own clitoris aching.

'How long have you been there?' Steve asked guiltily, turning his head as he slipped his penis from Lynn's dank cavern.

'Long enough to watch you use that whore's body. How does it feel to be tied up, Bulmur? Have you got any carrots in your kitchen?'

'Come and play with me,' Lynn spluttered, a woman drowning in lust. 'Get a cucumber and play with me – make me come!'

Stunned at Lynn's lack of concern for her situation, Donna perceived a new aspect of the patches. Lynn was their prisoner, but she didn't seem bothered. She was about to have lewd photographs taken of her naked tethered body, yet she showed no sign of anxiety. Her only thought seemed to be for her clitoris, her desperate need for orgasm. She must be aware of what's happening, Donna reasoned. Obviously the overwhelming desire for orgasm suppressed her fear, her anxiety.

'Are you ready, Steve?' Donna asked as she left the room. 'When you are,' he replied, making some final adjustments, praying that Donna knew what she was doing. Focussing on Lynn's swollen and very wet cunt lips, he thought of his wife – tied to the sofa, her legs splayed, her precious femininity betrayed. 'Couldn't spare any patches, could you?' he called to his accomplice.

Returning from the kitchen wielding a wine bottle, a length of string and two clothes pegs, Donna grinned as she settled between Lynn's thighs. 'What do you need patches for?' she enquired, presenting the neck of the bottle to Lynn's gaping hole.

'Debbie, my wife. Our sex life needs a boost, to say the least.'

'I'll see what I can do.'

Pressing the bottle into Lynn's quivering body, Donna pulled her thick pussy lips apart and arranged them neatly around the glass phallus. Lynn gasped with the pleasure running through her womb as Donna caressed her clitoris and clipped the pegs onto her hard nipples in readiness for the first shot.

'Just one thing, and we're ready,' Donna grinned wickedly, taking the length of string and tying it to the pegs. Shortening the string, she pulled the stinging nipples together, stretching the aching flesh until the two hard protrusions almost touched each other.

'That hurts! Ah! What are you . . . Ah, take it off!' Lynn complained.

'It's *supposed* to hurt. Anyway, you look good like that, just right for the camera.'

Standing to one side, Donna watched the lewd display as Steve clicked the shutter, mumbling about the cost of film and his lack of cash. 'If our little business venture works, we'll be rolling in it,' he observed as he moved the camera in for some close-ups. Her muscles spasming and ejecting the wet bottle from her sheath, Lynn writhed and pleaded for more.

'What business venture?' Donna asked as she pressed the bottle home again and stroked Lynn's clitoris to appease the hard bud.

'Don't stop, make me come!' Lynn cried, her body shuddering uncontrollably.

'I was telling Lynn that we could lure girls here and use the patches for porno photo sessions – a nice little earner, don't you agree?'

'Oh, so you're in league with her now, are you?'

'No, no. I thought that perhaps *we* could get together. You have your own place, don't you?'

'Fuck me with the bottle!' Lynn ranted as her orgasm threatened to erupt. Thrusting the bottle in and out, Donna enquired if she was enjoying herself.

'I can't feel it, it's too thin!' she panted desperately.

'How's this, then?'

Slipping the bottle out, she turned it round and began to press the thick end against the sodden folds of flesh. 'God, no!' Lynn cried as her muscles suddenly yielded and the bottle slipped in an inch or so. Twisting, gently applying pressure, Donna slid the monster deeper into the stretched cavern until she'd buried it a good five inches. Her face contorting with the wondrous sexual pain, Lynn begged to be fucked by the huge phallus. Steve stared in amazement as the bottle moved gently in and out, forcing her pink lips open, exposing her hard, protruding clitoris as the hood receded, until he thought she would split open. 'That's it, harder, faster!' she cried as the birth of her precious climax stirred deep within her contracting womb.

Keeping her face out of camera shot, Donna thrust the wet bottle deeper into Lynn's consumed cavern as

Steve's camera clicked and whirred. 'More – harder!'
she cried, oblivious to the camera as her orgasm spilled
from her cunt, sending ripples of debased pleasure over
her tingling body. Arching her back, she opened her
mouth and threw her head back, gasping her pleasure as
her spasming cunt threatened to crack the phallus.

'Move!' Steve yelled. 'I want a full shot of her
writhing like that.'

Donna crawled across the carpet leaving Lynn tossing
her head, begging for more as her cunt squeezed so
tightly that the bottle shot from her body like a bullet.
Her hole lay open, exposing the little pink stalactites
dripping with the creamy product of her orgasm, inviting Donna to drink the milky fluid as it flowed. Moving
in, Donna stretched open the glistening folds of female
sex, licking and sucking the nectarous offering, elevat-
ing the tethered girl to another euphoric, sexual high.
Opening her legs to capacity and thrusting forward her
hips, Lynn presented the full, open length of her
swollen crack to Donna's hungry tongue, crying out as
her clitoris flowered yet again to send shock waves of
agonising pleasure through her exhausted body.

Allowing her prisoner some quarter at last, Donna
moved away. Wiping her mouth on the back of her
hand, she wondered why she'd not needed a patch
herself to lick and suck between another woman's legs,
why her lesbian craving, so powerful under the influence of the hormone, was still riding high, unaided. Had
the patch had a permanent effect, disabling her natural
heterosexual instinct for good? More research was
necessary, she knew. And Alan should be told of the
momentous side-effects of his miraculous creation.

'So, who are we going to threaten to send the pics to?'

Steve asked as he packed up his equipment.

'The DSS for a start. She's on the dole and they won't take kindly to her offering her body in return for money, will they?'

Lynn opened her eyes as Donna peeled the patches from her perspiring skin, seemingly unaware of her impending doom – the dark cloud of blackmail that was about to descend upon her.

'Who else?' Steve pursued.

'I thought we'd place a few small pictures in telephone boxes, you know, as the prossies do. The police will soon be onto her and, as she's already been pulled in for prostitution, they'll bang her up, as they say.'

'Now who thinks this is a movie? You've been watching too much television!'

'I never watch television, I read books – or I used to. Anyway, can you print her phone number on each photograph?'

'No problem. I'll have them ready in the morning.'

'I want the patches!' Lynn murmured, reason beginning to loom again from the mist of lust. 'Get me the patches tomorrow!'

The morning, Donna thought with a sudden rush of anxiety. The lab, Alan – how could she concentrate on her work after a weekend like this? A weekend of sadism, lesbian lust, blackmail. She gazed at Lynn, her body tied, her legs open, displaying the centre of her girlish sex for all to see – uninhibited in her abandon. The hormone was already wearing off. What next? Would she come to the flat and wreak havoc? With the devil's daughter, anything was possible.

'The patches, Ryan, get them!' The mist fading fast, Lynn's reason was returning rapidly.

Untying the ropes as Steve loaded the van, Donna

was aware of her own clitoris calling. Reaching out, Lynn pushed her hand up her skirt, gently rubbing her swelling panties, easing a finger between her hot flesh and the tight material. Donna breathed a sigh of pleasure, pulling away. Was Bulmur up to her old tricks – or still under the influence of the hormone? She stared hard at Donna, her eyes wide and fiery with the beginnings of rage rather than desire, Donna fancied. Lynn was returning to her normal self – a cold, hard bitch who would stop at nothing for money. Leaving the flat, Donna handed Steve two patches and smiled. 'These will sort your wife out.'

'Great, thanks, Donna. I'll be in touch.'

'I hope so. Enjoy your marriage,' she called, climbing into her car.

The afternoon had gone quickly and the weekend was drawing to a close, bringing Monday morning even nearer. She'd give Lynn a few patches, she decided as she drove away. If she could take them from Alan's drawer without his knowing, that was. Lynn had to be appeased, somehow. Besides, what could she do with only a handful of patches? A hell of a lot of damage, no doubt.

Wandering into the lounge, she switched the answerphone to 'play.' 'Hi, Donna, it's me, Helen. I was wondering if Sophie and I could come round this evening – it's Sunday afternoon, three o'clock, now. I've tried to contact you several times over the weekend. Anyway, ring me if it's okay. Bye.'

'Hello, Donna, Sue here. I haven't heard from you and . . . Well, I was looking forward to seeing you over the weekend. I'll call round and see you later. Bye for now. And, well . . . I miss you. Bye.'

'You can get the patches to me, Ryan! I've just put a photograph of you in an envelope. It's going to your lab first thing on Tuesday morning. I want the patches, the formula, and five hundred pounds delivered to me at my flat by Monday night, or else!'

'Hello. You've got a sexy voice. Are your knickers wet, or aren't you wearing any? Can I lick your cunt and make you come?'

Donna didn't recognize the soft male voice. Her heart thumping, her hands trembling, she sat down. Who the hell was that? The watcher, the follower? What did he want? No, no-one had been watching, following, she was sure. She sighed, tried to reason, find some logic. Whoever the man was, there was nothing she could do. He was just a dirty old man who enjoyed making dirty phone calls – he didn't know her, he couldn't. Perhaps he'll go away, she thought. No, he won't, they never do. The stench of evil clings.

Her thoughts returned to Lynn Bulmur. Would the fact that she now had pornographic pictures of her really change anything? Probably not, she thought fearfully. The DSS, the police, nothing would stop Bulmur. Even from a prison cell she'd radiate her malice, send out her evil – trouble. Shit, the photograph! She imagined Malcolm, the head of the lab, opening the envelope to find Grunwerg's up-and-coming research assistant sprawled naked over a sofa, clothes pegs adorning her nipples, carrots peering out from her bloated hole – and her phone number scrawled over her stomach. Shit! Intercept the postman? Undoubtedly Bulmur would deliver it by hand on Tuesday morning. She'd have to, if she was waiting for delivery of the patches to her flat on Monday evening. Leaving the lab at five, Donna would not be at Lynn Bulmur's flat until five-thirty at the earliest – too late for Lynn to catch the post.

Five o'clock. With Sue coming round, and Helen and Sophie awaiting her call, she didn't know what to do. The prospect of Sue's company sent a quiver through her body – the thought of her two young sex slaves between her thighs, a hot tingle through her clitoris. Remembering the cucumber, she grinned. Her obedient slaves would be delighted to have their bodies yoked by the thick, green phallus. But what to do about Sue? Ring her, put her off? Invite her to join the orgy?

No good worrying – might as well have my slaves here to attend me, Donna decided, lifting the receiver and dialling. Pressing a patch onto her arm, she replaced the receiver. Helen must be in the park with Sophie, she speculated. And Sue will be on her way round here.

Still with no reply as the evening wore on, she decided to go to bed to appease her aching clitoris. Just my luck, she thought as she climbed under her quilt, naked, imagining a hot tongue darting between her thighs. No slaves, and Sue didn't bother to turn up. Bulmur should have been whipped, beaten with a cane for her sins. Donna herself wanted to be caned, tied over her bed and whipped like a naughty schoolgirl until her clitoris erupted in orgasm.

Gently massaging the wet folds of flesh between her legs, imagining her buttocks splayed, thrashed with a thin bamboo cane, she brought her hard clitoris to an excruciating climax. Her fingers moving up and down her naked groove, she teased the last ripples of lust from her bud, wondering about the angels. Would they protect her from the likes of Bulmur? Probably not.

Her body calming now, she closed her eyes and drifted into a land of erotic dreams – dreams so real that her juices flowed and her clitoris pulsated as she tossed and turned in her sleep. Who was lurking in the shadows – watching? Do women have wet dreams? Do they wet the sheets during the night? When uninhibited – yes.

Chapter Seven

Dreamily pulling the quilt over her shoulders as she woke to Monday morning, Donna realised that her bed was wet. Half opening her eyes, she lifted the quilt and gazed at a large sodden patch on the sheet – a pond of love. Her thighs were sticky, her swollen pussy lips hot, encrusted with white, starchy cream. 'The patch,' she breathed, realizing that she'd been wearing it all night. Instinctively, her fingers found their way between her lips and began to explore the wet flesh. 'God, I can't go to the lab feeling like this!'

There was no time for masturbation, for pleasure – Monday mornings weren't for pleasure. Her mind swirling between her aching clitoris and the lab, she tore the patch from her arm and leaped out of bed. Stepping into the shower, the warm water coaxed her from her sleepy state and she remembered Lynn Bulmur, the photographs. Steve. Steal some patches, first priority, she decided. Get to work before Alan, that was the answer.

Emerging from her flat, she stepped out into the world – another hot day. The sun beat down onto the pavement, shimmering, the heat reflecting, beaming up her skirt, warming the soft nakedness between her legs. The park looked tempting, the grass, the sun – to lie naked and bathe in the enveloping warmth, to masturbate under the trees. But work, the lab, blotched the horizon.

Alan was already working as Donna breezed into the lab.

'Don't you ever have any time away from this place?' she snapped.

'Wrong side of the bed?' he asked, raising his eyebrows at her unconfined breasts, her nipples pressing through her tight red top. She felt a power in his noticing, his arousal. No bra, no knickers. That was a part of her enlightenment, her freedom – her potential as a woman. She smiled, revelling in her seductiveness, her femininity.

'No, no. I'm just a bit fed up, that's all,' she replied.

'What time this evening? I'll pick you up about eight, is that okay with you?'

She frowned.

'The meal, tonight, remember?'

Memories – Helen, Sue, the weekend. Lynn Bulmur.

'Oh, yes, about eight, I suppose.'

'You don't seem very keen.'

'I'm tired, that's all.'

'Had a good weekend?'

'Different, I suppose, but I wouldn't call it good.'

'I've got to spend the morning upstairs, a meeting, so I'll leave you to it. By the way, there's a new girl starting today. Look after her, will you?'

'New girl? Why didn't you say anything earlier?'

'I've only just found out myself, you know what Malcolm's like.'

'What's she supposed to do?'

'She's a neurologist. Malcolm's borrowed her from Gardener University. He wants the effect of the hormone studied further. She's done a lot of research on the chemistry of the brain. Show her the ropes, will you? I must go, see you later.'

A new girl, dammit. Donna didn't want a new girl hanging around, trying to make conversation, asking about this and that. Opening Alan's drawer she took out several strips of patches and slipped them into her handbag. She knew only too well what would happen if she were caught, but she had no choice. Praying that Alan hadn't a record of how many patches he'd manufactured, she settled at her bench and tried to turn her thoughts to her work.

The new girl was in her early forties, wearing her dark hair in a bun, no makeup, and with a stern, expressionless face. Sporting a long tweed skirt and a blouse buttoned up to her neck, she reminded Donna of her English teacher – a strict, strait-laced, Victorian governess type. She wore knickers, Donna surmised – heavy, thick, full knickers to conceal her pussy, to deny her femininity. A woman inhibited.

Introducing herself as Elizabeth, she frowned at Donna as she entered the lab and enquired why her lab coat wasn't buttoned. Dismissively, Donna offered her a cup of coffee, wondering what secret desires Miss Prim was suppressing, what unconscious fetishes were lurking, waiting to surface, to be freed. Clad in leather, wielding a whip, she'd make an ideal mistress, Donna reflected. A correction mistress for the disciplining of young girls – didn't all young girls need correcting and disciplining? She was tempted to serve Miss Prim up a patch with her coffee then and there, but no – there was a time and place.

'What, exactly, are you going to do?' she asked, trying to be friendly.

'The female brain secretes a chemical which controls

the libido, acts as an inhibitor, stops women from becoming oversexed,' she began authoritatively. Donna didn't want to know. She wanted to be in the park, under the sun, beneath the trees, naked, masturbating. 'When dealing with hormones, we must be sure that the chemical inhibitor remains unaffected or . . . Well, from the research I've done so far with Professor Winmann, there is some indication that the natural hormones in the body sometimes tend to counteract the chemical inhibitor, giving some clue as to why one female may have nymphomaniacal tendencies, whereas another may be almost asexual.'

That was it, Donna knew. The hormone in the patches obviously eradicated the chemical, allowing the woman's libido to rise unchecked to astronomical heights. 'What about the male? Is there a chemical that controls the libido in the male brain?' she asked, forgetting about the park, the summer sun.

'No. Well, there's only a minute trace of the chemical, an insignificant amount.'

'So what would happen if the chemical inhibitor in the female was eradicated completely?' she pursued anxiously.

'All hell would be let loose! Can you imagine women acting like their male counterparts? Or worse, possibly?'

Donna could do more than imagine.

'Surely, this could help thousands of women who suffer from frigidity, or other sexually related problems?'

'On the contrary, I am looking into the possibilities of *increasing* the chemical inhibitor in the female brain, and introducing it into the male's. Society today is suffering terribly from oversexed men, and many oversexed women too, I'm afraid. I intend to balance the libido between male and female, to rid the world of prostitution and pornography.'

A world full of Miss Prim-and-Propers? Wimpish men? The thought was terrifying. Did Elizabeth possess a cunt? Did she know what it was for? Probably not, Donna decided, resolving to do her own research work, to exploit the incredible findings to the full, so that woman could *enjoy* their bodies, their sexuality. Elizabeth knew only half the story, she mused. She had no idea that the patch retracted women's natural heterosexual instinct, allowing them to enjoy each other's bodies. But she might well soon find that out at first hand!

'Are you married?' Donna asked tentatively.

'No, no need for marriage. My career comes before anything else.'

That figured. She couldn't imagine Elizabeth allowing a man to make love to her, settle between her thighs, lick between her cunt lips and make her come. Again, she thought about sticking a patch on the woman – luring her to her flat and giving her the incredible experience of female-induced orgasm.

'Do you live locally?' Donna enquired.

'No, I live near the university. I'm hoping to find a boarding house this afternoon. I'll only be here for a few days, but it's too far to travel from home every day.'

'I've got a spare room,' Donna offered, imagining Elizabeth dressed in leather, wielding a whip.

'That's nice of you. I'd pay you, of course.'

'That's all right. It will be nice to have some company, for a change.'

Donna was jubilant. Not only would she now have the chance to learn more about the hormone and its effects but she would also have the benefit of a prime guinea pig living under her roof. She could live out her fantasy

– dress Miss Prim in rubber, in leather, discover her repressed sexuality, strip her of her inhibitions, release her from her chains.

Throughout the day, she fantasized about Elizabeth – and worried about Lynn Bulmur. Thankfully, Alan had remained upstairs in the meeting. She didn't want to have dinner with him that evening. With a new victim moving into her flat, her lair, she had better things to do than listen to Alan's words of love, words of spending lives together. Mundane now, after the change, the experience of the hormone-orgasm.

Five o'clock, at last. Armed with the patches, Donna walked to her flat with Elizabeth in tow, the older woman chatting about the research work and her idea of neutralising the libido. She would soon think differently, Donna reflected. Once she was under the influence of the hormone, she'd become her ally and help liberate women the world over.

Donna still sensed that she was being followed. She turned her head several times, but there was no-one there. Her heart beat faster as she remembered the phone call. Who was it? A pervert, she decided. Should she lure him to the flat? Bring him out from his hide, his dirty little room where he sat by the telephone making his dirty little calls, dribbling over dirty magazines, masturbating?

Installing her victim in the spare room, she explained that she had to pop out for ten minutes. 'I'll make us something to eat when I get back,' she promised.

'I'll have a shower while you're out, if that's all right?'

Donna found it difficult imagining Elizabeth in the shower, her long hair loose, her body naked.

'That's fine,' she called, closing the front door, wishing she could spy on her as she washed her mounds, her crevices – the pink, wrinkled butterfly wings between her vaginal lips.

Lynn Bulmur was out. Praying that they'd be enough to appease her, for a while, at least, Donna pushed two strips of patches through her letterbox. Perhaps she was delivering the envelope? She'd surely not do that until the morning. Besides, she might not make a move now, not until she knew the destiny of her own incriminating pictures.

Returning to her flat, she planned Elizabeth's seduction. To cane or be caned? To lick or be licked? Had she masturbated in the shower? Directed the jet of water between her nether lips at her clitoris and writhed as her juices flowed and her bud flowered? She thought not. Asexual, inhibited women didn't masturbate, didn't allow their fingers to caress between their pussy lips and induce orgasms from their hard clitorises.

'May I call you Liz?' Donna asked, finding her in the lounge going through some lab notes.

'I prefer Elizabeth, if you don't mind,' she replied stuffily.

'Elizabeth it is, then.'

Just as Donna was wondering how to plant a patch, the opportunity materialised like a gift from heaven.

'Ooh! My hair's caught up in my zipper again! Would you be so kind as to untangle it?' Elizabeth asked.

'Your hair looks lovely down,' Donna remarked, pressing a patch onto Elizabeth's neck as she freed the flowing tresses. 'You should wear it like this all the time.'

'I can't, not at the lab, it would get in the way. One has to be practical, Donna. I really must have it cut off, it's far too long.'

'That would be a shame,' Donna smiled, impatient

for the hormone to release the woman and allow her secret desires to surface from the murky well of her subconscious.

Leaving Elizabeth to her lab notes, Donna applied a patch to her upper arm and began to prepare a salad. What to do once the patch was working? she wondered. What to do once the victim was in its grip – and hers? And what if Elizabeth suspected that she'd been subjected to the hormone? Donna decided that she would suggest that Elizabeth had inadvertently absorbed some of the hormone whilst working in the lab. The idea wasn't brilliant, but it would suffice.

'It's hot in here,' Donna remarked, noticing Elizabeth's flushed face as she returned to the lounge. 'Why don't you take your dress off? You'll feel much cooler.'

'I think I will,' she replied. 'I do feel rather strange, it must be the heat.'

'Allow me,' Donna smiled, unzipping Elizabeth's dress and tugging it down her body to her ankles. Faced with a heavy basque covering her curvaceous frame, Donna frowned. 'I'm not surprised that you're hot with all these clothes on. Let's take that off, too.'

Peeling the thick garment from Elizabeth's body, Donna was amazed to encounter a pair of heavy breasts adorned with large, dark aureolae, topped with huge, elongated nipples. Unfamiliar, mature fruit – full, rounded, but firm in their ripeness. She felt the stirrings of an appetite for something untried.

But still the epitome of the woman's womanhood, her sex, was covered, concealed by a substantial pair of woollen knickers which rose to her navel. Donna dropped to her knees and tugged on the material as Elizabeth began to breathe heavily.

'I don't know what's come over me,' she complained.

'What are you doing? What am *I* doing? I don't understand! Why are you undressing me? Good God, I'm virtually naked!'

Slipping another patch from her bag, Donna quickly pressed it onto Elizabeth's back before attempting to remove her knickers. Normally one patch sufficed, she reflected – obviously the level of the woman's chemical inhibitor was way above average. Almost immediately Elizabeth relaxed, closing her eyes as she fondled her breasts, squeezed her nipples, revelling in sensations she'd never known existed. Donna dropped to her knees and tugged at Elizabeth's knickers again, the older woman now only too willing to participate in unveiling her virgin pussy. Her thick, black, tangled bush had obviously never been trimmed and Donna's first thought was to shave away the hair to expose the lips that had probably never been parted by Elizabeth herself, still less by a man – let alone by another woman.

Leaving her victim to explore her uncharted body, Donna went to the bathroom to prepare the necessary equipment, wondering what Elizabeth was thinking, what strange, oppressed emotions and desires were surfacing. Returning to the lounge, she placed a towel over the sofa and told Elizabeth to sit down with her legs open wide. The walls were watching, listening. Someone lurked in the shadows, pried – someone, somewhere.

As Donna lathered the foam into the thick hair, Elizabeth stroked her nipples, hardening the brown buds until they stood to attention, aching to be sucked into a hot mouth. Dragging the safety razor down her stomach and over her full cunt lips, Donna smiled as the curls fell away, revealing smooth, unblemished skin. Again and again, she dragged the razor over Elizabeth's outer lips until their full beauty was exposed, naked youth returned to the mature virgin groove. Finishing off between her thighs, Donna pulled the skin taut and removed the last vestiges of hair before washing the foam away with a hot flannel.

'Now your cunt is unveiled, my beauty,' she whispered as she nibbled on the thick, inner lips protruding from the deep, moist valley. 'Have you ever been fucked by a man's hard penis?'

'No, never,' breathed Elizabeth. 'I don't understand what I'm feeling.'

'You're feeling my mouth between your legs, sucking your pink lips, bringing life to your body. There's no need to understand, just enjoy the sensations. Have you ever masturbated, rubbed your hard clitoris with your fingers and made yourself come?'

'Never, never. It's not right to . . . Ah, that's nice! God, what are you doing to me? I . . . I've never . . .'

'Have you not wondered what your clitoris is for?'

'No, it's not right . . .'

'Its sole purpose is to bring you pleasure, it has no other function. I'll suck it into my mouth now: tell me if you like it, tell me what it feels like.'

'It feels like heaven!'

Pinching the fleshy lips between her fingers and thumbs, Donna pulled them up and apart, exposing the virginal folds, popping out the neglected clitoris that had never pulsated with orgasm. Engulfing the stiff bud in her mouth, she sucked hard and flicked the tip of her tongue over its sensitive tip.

Immediately, Elizabeth arched her back and cried out as if in pain. Relentlessly, Donna continued her sexual torture, bringing the stiffening nodule closer and closer to fruition. Pressing her fingers into the indentations at the tops of her thighs, Elizabeth pulled on the flesh, stretching and opening her valley, her sexual centre, to Donna's hot mouth until suddenly, the solid protrusion throbbed against the girl's tongue and the beginnings of Elizabeth's maiden climax took its grip on her trembling body. Thrashing her limbs as the sensations welled, she screamed as her juices poured in torrents from her vaginal hole, running down Donna's chin, her neck.

Gently licking her shrinking clitoris, Donna induced the last few ripples of pleasure from its throbbing tip, bringing her ever-willing pupil slowly down from her first trip to heaven. Her body crudely splayed, her valley yawning, Elizabeth gave one last shudder before relaxing completely.

'And now for your virginity,' Donna whispered. 'You don't want to be a virgin, do you? You want your cunt free of the veil that protects her – open to receive the pleasure of sex.'

'Yes, yes. Do it to me again! I've never known such . . . Just do it to me again – please!'

'Repeat after me,' Donna said impishly. 'I want my cunt fucked.'

'Yes, yes, I want my cunt fucked.'

'I want you to fuck my cunt.'

'Yes, please fuck my cunt.'

Lesbian mumblings, beginnings.

Fetching the cucumber from the fridge, Donna was surprised to find it still fresh, still hard – succulent. 'I'll be gentle with you, as they say,' she whispered, presenting the thick end to Elizabeth's swollen groove. Gently pressing the phallus between her bloated pussy lips, she grinned. 'This is what it's like to have a man's stiff penis entering you, penetrating your vagina, only this is much bigger – and better.'

Elizabeth breathed heavily and dug her fingernails into the sofa as the phallus pressed further into her body, opening, for the first time, the protective curtain of youth. Deeper and deeper into the hot depths Donna pushed the cucumber until Elizabeth reached out and halted the intruder. Pausing, Donna stroked the woman's clitoris, taking her attention, allowing her to become accustomed to the filling sensation of the phallus.

'A little more, now,' Elizabeth breathed as she removed her hand and opened her legs wider. As Donna filled the last two inches of the swelling cavern, the telephone rang.

'Just rest for a while,' she said softly. 'Just allow the sensations to penetrate your body, your mind, and I'll be with you in a minute.'

'Where's the money, Ryan?' Lynn's voice screamed down the wire.

'I have no money. You've got what you wanted, so what's your problem?'

'I need money.'

'Don't we all? Look, I've got photographs of you now, so this blackmail thing works both ways.'

'You don't frighten me.'

'And you don't frighten me. Anyway, we're not trying to frighten each other, are we? We're not bloody kids.' Gazing at Elizabeth tentatively moving the phallus in and out of her body, discovering, learning, she turned away and lowered her voice to a whisper. 'Just be happy that you have a few patches, will you? You're bloody lucky that I was able to get those.'

'I'll send the photograph to . . .'

'Yes, yes – and I'll send the ones of you to the DSS with a note saying that you charge fifty pounds a time.

How does that sound to you? And I'm sure the Inland Revenue would be more than interested in talking to you about your undeclared income.'

Donna smiled as the phone went dead. Round one to me, she thought, moving back to her victim who was doing very well with the phallus. 'Now I think you're ready to be properly fucked,' she declared wickedly, grasping the cucumber. Ramming the solid shaft in and out of the hot, wet hole, she grinned impishly at the beautiful sight of the fleshy inner lips clinging to the green shaft as it withdrew, only to be sucked deep inside as it thrust home again. She marvelled at creation – the mysterious, perfectly accommodating vagina, the natural, fitting shape of the phallus, Mother Nature's gift to women.

'I think it's happening to me again!' Elizabeth cried as Donna caressed her clitoris with her free hand. 'Yes, yes! It's happening again! Oh, oh, yes! Ah, more, harder, deeper! Ah, ah!'

Placing her hands either side of her trembling body, she pushed down, lifting her buttocks clear of the sofa, bringing her hips forward to meet the thrusting phallus as she reached her second climax and smothered the green shaft with her hot come. Donna's arm aching, she managed to sustain the thrusting until Elizabeth collapsed in a trembling heap, clutching the cucumber as a child clutches a toy, gasping her satisfaction.

Lying there, her virginity gone, taken in the name of lesbian lust, her trembling hands pulled the phallus from her consumed hole and dropped it to the floor. Donna gazed at Miss Prim and smiled. Serene, her eyes closed, her nipples thick, long and hard, her cunette sagging open, dripping with the juices of orgasm, she had found true satisfaction. Brushed by the magical touch of the angels, she'd been given her sexuality – her womanhood.

'Come here,' Elizabeth breathed, opening her eyes and beckoning Donna with her finger. 'You've been naughty, taking advantage of me like that. I'm going to have to give you a good spanking, my girl!'

Donna's clitoris stirred as she positioned herself over Elizabeth's lap and allowed her to pull her short skirt up to her hips. Leaning forward, Elizabeth kissed her taut buttocks before lightly tapping each one in turn with the palm of her hand. Donna felt her juices flowing as her buttocks were slapped progressively harder, and she imagined Elizabeth as a dominating mistress dressed in a tight leather cat-suit with cut-outs for her long nipples and an open crotch. As the first hard slap hit home, she pictured the stringent mistress disciplining her, punishing her for her sins with a long, thin, stinging cane.

'You're a naughty little girl!' Elizabeth scorned as she mercilessly thrashed Donna's buttocks until they burned crimson, glowed with girlish desire. The pain and pleasure mingled to produce a strange new feeling of abandonment. There was no love, no bond – only two females lost in a sexual ecstasy, a dream-like world of unsurpassable sexual pleasure. How could she find love with Alan now – with any man, or woman? What was love? Complete and utter giving of the naked flesh to another, in the name of love – or lust?

Donna's buttocks were rudely parted and now a finger toyed with the tiny entrance to her most private being. Gasping with delight, she waited in anticipation for the exploration of her bowels to commence, as she knew it would. The circlet of brown, sensitive skin between her splayed buttocks spontaneously tightened in preparation to defend as the finger twisted and pressed. Harder now, in desperation, the finger pushed past the muscles and buried itself deep in her hotness, causing the girl to flinch and squirm. Deeper and deeper the probe penetrated, stretching the tissue, invading the privacy. Now a second finger stabbed, attempted to find its way in alongside the first to open the portal even more and massage the hot, velveteen walls within. Donna squeezed her eyes shut as the intruder slipped in, filling her with delight. But her clitoris demanded Elizabeth's attention now. Swelling, throbbing, the tiny cumbud stiffened and protruded, searching for fulfilment.

'Make me come, now!' Donna panted. 'Please make me come!' Elizabeth smiled at her pupil, her bared buttocks, her open body.

'Don't tell me what to do! I'll say when you can come!' she barked as she opened Donna's wet lips with her free hand and thrust three fingers inside. Cruelly neglected, her clitoris begged for release, swelling to an incredible size with its desperate need for a climax. Her body full now, Donna whimpered her pleas for orgasm, only to be rebuked by her cruel mistress. 'I'll thrash you again if you don't behave yourself, you naughty little girl!' Suddenly ripping her fingers from the small, tight hole, she spanked the bare buttocks again. Still thrusting her fingers in and out of Donna's hot pussyhole, Elizabeth granted no concession to her desperate need for climax as her bud yearned to explode, without so much as a caress to relieve the sexual agony bursting within the hard nodule.

Her mind saturated with lust, Donna climbed from Elizabeth's lap and manoeuvred her body into a position to give all she had between her thighs. Her knees either side of the older woman's head, her legs over the back of the sofa, her buttocks against Elizabeth's breasts, her back between her legs, her head to the floor, the open centre of her body lay inches from Elizabeth's mouth.

'You're very clever,' Elizabeth remarked as she nibbled on the wet flesh. 'I suppose you want your clitoris sucked now?'

'Yes, yes – open me with your fingers and suck a climax from me!'

'You have a wonderful cunt, my lovely. I'll drink from you before I attend your little spot. Drink your girlie juices.'

'No, just make me come, please!'

'When I'm ready, I will allow you your orgasm. Now be quiet and relax like a good girl – or you'll have nothing!'

Each long lick of Elizabeth's tongue sent waves of desire rippling through Donna's contorted body. Lapping up the creamy offering, spreading the bloated nether lips wide, Elizabeth explored the silky sheath with her tongue before moving up the bared groove to the summit. Pressing on the pinken hood, she popped out the little protrusion and vibrated her tongue over the swollen tip. The work of a virgin? Animal instinct? Or an innate, lesbian proclivity that all women harboured – and suppressed?

Sucking now, engulfing the cumbud in her hot mouth, she quickly elicited the girl's orgasm, releasing her from the omnipotent sexual force, draining the tension, quelling the painful desire until Donna fell limp with gratification, words of sexual appreciation bubbling from her gasping mouth.

'Tell me, do you have other women? Do you open your body like this to other women?' Elizabeth asked as

Donna slid to the floor and brought her knees up to her chest.

'Yes, yes.'

'And are they as good as me, or better?'

'They are my sex slaves – they do as I say.'

'And I do as I wish. Do you have men, too?'

'Yes, men too.'

'I've not had a man – I'd like to.'

The sexual haze clearing, Donna thought of Alan. Would he enjoy the neurologist's naked body? Would he delight in having two women pleasuring him? Or perhaps Elizabeth would appreciate two young female sex slaves at her beck and call? As the sexual force rose and her clitoris stirred once again, she became desperate with desire, burned with a passion for a man's hard penis in her mouth, withdrawing just before orgasm then thrusting into her quim and filling her trembling cunt with sperm.

'I'll get you a man,' she told Elizabeth, climbing to her feet.

'What man?' Elizabeth asked, her eyes widening at the prospect of losing her virginity properly.

'If he's got a big, hard penis, does it matter?'

'No, I suppose not.'

Did anything matter when a big, hard penis was buried within the hot depths of a woman's love sheath?

Being careful not to mention his name, Donna rang Alan and invited him round for the evening. Delighted, he accepted the offer, promising to bring over a bottle of wine. 'I've got to pop out for a while so if I'm not here when you arrive, Elizabeth will let you in,' Donna said.

'Oh, she's there, is she? Well, in that case . . .'

'Don't worry, she won't be staying, she's going out,' she lied.

'Oh, all right, I'll see you soon.'

The trap baited, Donna grinned as she replaced the receiver. Step into my parlour, said the whore to the man. Slip into my hotness, mouthed the vaginal lips to the throbbing penis.

Elizabeth frowned, looking at Donna. 'Where are you going?' she asked, patting the sofa for her to join her.

'Nowhere. This particular man wouldn't come round if he thought there were two of us here, so I had to lie. Anyway, slip your skirt and top on and, when he gets here, let him in.'

'And then what?'

'I'll be in the other room while you seduce him.'

'Seduce him? How?'

'Go with your instinct, the flow. Believe me, the way you're feeling now, you won't have to ask what to do. If he's a normal man, and I believe he is, he'll respond, don't you worry.'

Wearing only her short skirt and top, Donna shot into the kitchen when the doorbell rang. Elizabeth gasped as she found herself facing Alan, but with the hormone stripping her of her inhibitions, she would play the part of the seductress only too well, Donna knew. Peering through the crack in the door, she watched them settle on the sofa and listened as they chatted about work. Pulling her skirt up to her thighs, Elizabeth reclined on the sofa, completely relaxed. Not particularly subtle, Donna reflected as she pulled her skirt even higher, but under the magical influence of the hormone, subtlety didn't exist. Could there possibly be room for subtlety in the urgent, swirling mist of female lust?

Alan gawped in amazement as Elizabeth parted her legs and lifted her skirt up over her stomach to reveal

The Uninhibited

her shaven lips – smiling, wet and inviting. What was he thinking? Donna wondered. Would he reach out and touch? Was his penis stiffening in anticipation? Were his thoughts male thoughts? Thoughts of sex?

'You may touch me,' Elizabeth proffered, pushing her hips forward and opening her thighs further. There were no words as the man slipped off the sofa and fell to his knees to observe the smooth, naked cushions of flesh – swelling, opening, soliciting him. Parting her soft lips, he pushed his tongue between the silky folds and licked. Elizabeth threw her head back and lost herself in her ecstasy as he encircled her clitoris, bringing out its pleasure. 'Do it to me!' she begged as he engulfed her little cumbud. 'Put it in and do it! Fuck me!'

His trousers down now, his long, thick penis stood proud, ready to take her virginity, to fill her barren cunt with his hot seed and bring life there. As he pulled the loose skin back to expose the hard, purple knob, Donna felt a pang of jealousy. Remembering her own body impaled on his throbbing shaft, she became conscious that she didn't want to share him with another woman. Was it love? she wondered as his bulging knobhead slipped neatly between the pinken petals of Elizabeth's opening.

Suddenly, Elizabeth let out a long, low moan of pleasure. Alan's shaft was driving further into the hot darkness, filling her, stretching her sheath. Donna could do nothing to stop him now. She hated him – loved him. Deeper he entered the virginal tube, opening Elizabeth's flesh, opening her mind with his hardness.

Slipping into the room, Donna knelt by Alan's side and kissed his cheek. Flushed with guilt, he frowned as she pressed a finger against his lips and smiled. 'It's all right,' she whispered as she kissed his mouth. 'You

149

may fuck her.' His penis buried in another woman's body, she had no option but to join in. Gently, she parted Elizabeth's swollen labia with her fingers to expose the root of Alan's shaft – thick, glistening with the juices of another woman's pussy. Moving back and forth, he began to breathe heavily, moan his pleasure as Elizabeth's muscles gripped the first-ever penis to invade her dark cavern.

'It's beautiful,' Elizabeth sighed as he began to thrust harder and deeper into her body. 'Do it harder!'

'You like it, then?' Donna asked, massaging her clitoris.

'Yes, yes! Rub me there, that's it, rub me there! Ah, ah, yes!'

Leaning forward, Donna kissed Elizabeth's smooth stomach, licked around her navel and pushed her tongue into the little opening. Moving her mouth down to the wet, yawning valley as Alan continued to ram his knob against her cervix, she stretched the reddening flesh to expose Elizabeth's clitoris, licking and sucking until the cumbud swelled and burst in unison with Alan's bulbous knob. Their climaxes mingling, sperm gushing around the entrance of her barren womb, her sex-fluid lubricating the taut skin of his shaft, they pressed their genitals together, locked in lust. On and on flowed the magic of their orgasms, filling their bodies with unbridled pleasure as they shuddered with the last few thrusts of lust and collapsed, heaving, panting, satisfied.

As Alan slipped his glistening penis from Elizabeth's invaded cavern, Donna lowered her head and took it in her hand before sucking it into her hot mouth, stiffening the shaft, swelling the head with her rolling tongue to entice another fountain of sperm. Sucking hard,

kneading his heavy balls, she moved her head back
and forth, using her mouth as she would her vagina
until, grunting, he came and his second offering of
sperm erupted to fill her cheeks. Hot, salty, pumping,
the glutinous mass bathed her tongue, aroused her
taste buds – blurred her mind.

Watching the spectacle whilst massaging her clitoris,
Elizabeth moved to the floor and pushed Donna aside.
'*I* want to try that,' she said like a spoiled child, taking
the flaccid penis in her hand.

'It's too soon,' Alan pleaded, but she wasn't listening
as she lowered her head and pushed out her tongue to
lick up a globule of sperm before taking the head of his
prick inside her mouth. Her eyes rolling, she moaned as
she sucked, willing the shaft to expand, to swell in her
mouth, to balloon and explode with gushing sperm.

'You'll have to wait,' Donna said placatingly, placing
her hand on Elizabeth's buttocks and slowly running her
fingers down the dark crease. On all fours, still sucking
her prize, Elizabeth pushed out her buttocks, exposing
the bloated lips of her vagina, hanging appetisingly
below the small, dark entrance to her bowels. Parting
the soft cushions of flesh, Donna eased four fingers into
the warmth. Massaging the soft walls of Elizabeth's
love-tube, she suddenly remembered the cucumber.
Relinquishing her fingers, she rushed to the kitchen,
grinning wickedly, and returned with the hard, cold
phallus. Still sucking in vain on Alan's spent penis,
Elizabeth moaned as Donna presented the cucumber to
her wet hole and rudely rammed it deep inside. Full to
capacity, her cunt gripped the invading shaft, lubricated
the green surface with juices of lust as Donna thrust it in
and out like a woman possessed.

Watching the blatant blue act, Alan soon felt his penis

swell in Elizabeth's hot mouth. 'Now you'll have what you want!' he panted. 'Now I'll come in your mouth!' Imitating Donna, Elizabeth swung her head to and fro until Alan gripped it and started thrusting, ramming the back of her throat with his hard knob. Quivering uncontrollably, Elizabeth rocked her hips, meeting the thrusts of the cucumber as Alan let out a cry and shuddered. Yet again his hot sperm gushed, pumping into her mouth, filling her to the brim as her orgasm swelled and burst between her legs, her puffy cunt lips. Rolling her tongue round and round the swollen plum, swallowing hard, she drank the bitter-sweet offering until Alan, too, was totally drained.

Writhing in the wake of her beautiful climax, Elizabeth reached behind her back to halt Donna's hand. Her ravaged sheath burning, her pussy lips pouting, dripping with her copious come as the mighty phallus slid out, she collapsed to the floor, still clutching Alan's shrinking penis.

'That was incredible,' he breathed, pulling away from Elizabeth and zipping up his trousers. 'What's happened, Donna? I mean, first you, and now Elizabeth – are you both on an aphrodisiac of some kind?'

Donna laughed as she helped Elizabeth to the sofa.

'There's no such thing, you should know that. I suppose it's the time of year – summer, the heat, and all that.'

'More like the mating season, if you ask me.'

'More like the effect of the hormone on the female inhibiting chemical, if you ask me,' Elizabeth interrupted, pulling her dress down.

Donna cringed. She had to retrieve the patches from Elizabeth before she discovered them – but how? Sitting by her side, she slipped her arm over the back of the sofa and straightened Elizabeth's dishevelled hair, artfully removing the patch from her neck. Recovering in an armchair, Alan asked when they'd all meet and do it again. 'Tomorrow, perhaps,' Donna volunteered, wondering how to remove the remaining patch from Elizabeth's back.

'I must be going,' Alan sighed, glancing at his watch. 'It's been . . . Well, I'm not sure what it's been.'

He looked puzzled. Donna knew that he suspected something. He must do, she thought. Women didn't act as they had – especially women like Elizabeth! And what would Elizabeth think when she was free of the patch, when her reasoning returned? But, there again, why free her?

Following Alan to the front door, Donna said her goodbyes and kissed his lips. Pulling him close to her, she buried her tongue in his mouth and ran her hand up his inner thigh. 'Until tomorrow,' she whispered.

Something was happening to her. Love, perhaps? She hoped not. Love brought jealousy, lies, and eventually deceit and infidelity. Infidelity? But was not love – bodily love – to be shared? Should it not be shared with many, rather than just one?

The night was late, the moon keeping watch over the park – over the lovers. Who was lurking under the moon, watching, peeping? Someone was out there, Donna was sure as she closed and locked the front door.

'Bed time,' she announced as she returned to the lounge.

'Together?' Elizabeth enquired expectantly.

'Together.'

Chapter Eight

Donna had removed her patch before going to bed. But in the night the quilt had tented, hands had moved, fingers had caressed. She had been sleeping, or so she had pretended, as Elizabeth licked between her pussy lips, drank from her soft tube, sucked on her clitoris, invaded her vagina with her fingers to massage the creamy walls and induce even more cream. But now morning had come and the telephone was ringing.

'Hello,' Donna whispered sleepily.

'It's me,' Lynn said.

'And?'

'About those pictures you have of me . . .'

'What about them?'

'You're not going to send them to anyone, are you?'

'I don't know yet. I haven't decided what to do with them. What do you want? I've only just woken up!'

'I'm not sending one to your lab. I thought I'd just let you know. Steve's threatened me with . . . Shall we swap?'

'Good for him. All right, we'll swap, but I want all of them.'

'Yes, of course. I'll come round tonight, shall I?'

'Yes, bring them here tonight – and no funny business.'

Elizabeth stepped into the shower as Donna made the

bed. Would the patch come off? she wondered, covering the wet sheet with the quilt. How long would the
hormone last? Days, weeks, months? Noticing that the
patch on her back was still intact, she smiled as Elizabeth
walked back into the bedroom. The sun streamed in
through the window, shining on the two women's naked
bodies, highlighting their curves, their furrows.

'I prefer being shaved,' Elizabeth confessed, admiring
her smooth, pouting quim lips in the mirror.

'You look nice like that,' Donna agreed.

'You can kiss me there, if you want to. Lick me, make
me come.'

'No, we're already late for work. Later, perhaps.'

Patchless, Donna didn't want to kiss and lick
Elizabeth there, or anywhere else, for that matter. If
she could, she would have liked to kiss her own vaginal
lips – kiss, lick and suck her own clitoris. A major design
flaw in the human species, she concluded.

'Do you have something a little more summery?'
Elizabeth asked, holding her heavy tweed skirt to her
hips. Donna gauged her measurements, compared
waists.

'Yes, only my skirts are all rather too short for . . .'
No, they weren't too short for Elizabeth – not the new
Elizabeth. She rummaged through her wardrobe and
came up with a red miniskirt.

'Oh yes!' Elizabeth enthused, grabbing the skirt and
pulling it up over her hips. 'No knickers today,' she
announced with a glint in her eye.

'No knickers,' Donna echoed.

Walking to the lab against a strong wind, Donna
noticed Elizabeth gazing at the young passers-by – male
and female. What were her thoughts? Sex? Her knickerless pussy? Was she wet? Oozing? Perhaps she'd like to

receive Steve, take his hardness between her thighs, between her swollen pussy lips and deep into her fleshy cavern? Must give him a ring, invite him round.

She looked up to the sky, to heaven. A puffy white cloud drifted aimlessly overhead. Was there a face there in the cotton wool, a face watching? Another cloud sailed past, blown on the wind. Ships that pass in the night. Elizabeth was a passing ship – she would return to her home town soon, to her loneliness. But Helen and Sophie would remain – and Sue. Where was Sue?

Alan smiled sheepishly as the women entered the lab. Tension, anxiety – guilt. Where was his love now? Donna wondered. After the events of last night, where was his love? Only his lust shone in his dark eyes, mirroring his inner thoughts – his male desires.

The day would be long, she knew. Lab work, research, experiments – long and boring. Funny how when one door opens, another closes. The door to her body had opened, the door to the lab had closed. She had no interest now, no enjoyment, no job satisfaction. The lab had been her world, but now she was orbiting another world, a new and exciting world of uninhibited sexual freedom.

How would Elizabeth manage to work under the influence of the patch? she wondered. With difficulty, no doubt. But that was her problem. Donna wanted the day off: she had to get away from the lab, from Alan, Elizabeth – everyone and everything. Fake an illness? No, she'd not taken a day off sick in five years and it would not be good to raise suspicion.

'Professor Winmann is coming to see me today,' Alan announced. 'Hopefully, we'll discover something about the hormone's side-effects.'

'I haven't had a chance to tell you about the libido and

the female chemical inhibitor yet, have I?' Elizabeth said.

Donna winced. Change the subject – but how? Alan would put two and two together and realise that she had stolen some patches – and used them on Elizabeth. Talk about the shit hitting the fan! The phone rang as Elizabeth launched into her explanation of the chemical inhibitor. Saved by the bell, Donna mused.

Alan picked up the receiver. 'Okay, I'll be up in a minute, Malcolm.' Replacing the phone, he motioned that he was going upstairs. Donna breathed easily again, her stomach settled. The time would come when she'd be exposed, she knew. As soon as Professor Winmann arrived and opened his mouth, the game would be up – she'd be caught with her knickers down. But, for now, she wasn't wearing any.

Sitting at her bench, trying to concentrate, she decided to leave the lab, go home. The wind howled outside – she hated the wind, it blew her thoughts away. Besides, she had too much on her mind to think, to work, to wait for Professor Winmann, and the inevitable.

'I don't feel well,' she told Elizabeth. 'I'm going home. Tell Alan, will you?'

'I must say that I feel a little bit strange myself. But where there's work . . .' Left alone, would she seduce Alan? Donna wondered. Would she slip her hand up her short skirt and masturbate?

Walking down the corridor, a short, grey-haired man carrying a briefcase stopped her. 'I'm looking for Doctor Rosenberg,' he said. Professor Winmann, she guessed.

'He's, er, not around just now. But if you'll come with me, I'll show you where you can wait,' she replied hesitantly. Shit, why now?

Much to her relief, the small canteen was deserted. Showing the professor to a window seat, she asked if he'd like coffee.

'Only if it's decaffeinated,' he replied with a smile.

'It's not, I'm afraid. I'm Donna Ryan, by the way. I work with Alan . . . Doctor Rosenberg.'

'Yes, he's told me a lot about you. He thinks very highly of you. So you know all about the hormone, do you?'

'Yes, I do. But not a great deal about the side-effects.'

'That's why I'm here, as you probably know. There are several side-effects, I'm afraid.'

'Afraid?'

'Yes, the side-effects, well, one in particular, are rather alarming. The female brain secretes a chemical . . .'

Donna gazed at his lined forehead, his bow-tie, as he rambled on. A typical professor, she reflected. Lectures, boring lectures from boring mouths. She knew about the female chemical inhibitor. He was becoming unbearable, as, no doubt, most professors do. Automatically nodding her head to show her interest, she sat up and listened intently as he began talking about the natural heterosexual inclination of the female.

'Male and female are attracted – why? Because there are hormones at work in the body, secretions in the brain. Hormones are fascinating. They weren't discovered until early this century and over fifty have been identified so far. New ones are being discovered all the time. Made up of chemicals which react with cells and organs, hormones control us more than we control them.'

For a moment, she thought that she was back at the university, slumped over her desk, taking notes. 'They affect nearly everything we think, say and do. Particularly in the case of the female, as the oestrogen and progesterone levels fluctuate wildly during the monthly cycle. This new hormone, as I have said, cancels out the chemical inhibitor, leaving the female's libido to run wild. But more, it *enhances* the libido, increases the sex drive beyond measure.'

'Testosterone,' Donna thought aloud.

'No, not testosterone. That would explain things very nicely, of course, the heightened sex drive etcetera. But that is not the answer. I have discovered another effect – a surprising, almost frightening effect. The hormone disrupts the natural attraction the female has for the male. She still feels that attraction towards the male, but also towards other females. To put it bluntly, she becomes bisexual.'

'How do you know? I mean, surely you haven't tested the hormone on a woman, have you?' He shuffled, shifted in his chair, guiltily. He was a professor – surely he hadn't experimented on a human being? 'Have you?' Donna repeated.

'Yes,' he replied, gazing into her big blue eyes as if asking for forgiveness.

Her heart fluttered, thoughts swirling in her mind like leaves in a windy courtyard. Who had he tested the hormone on? Had she consented? Why was he telling her? To unburden his unbearable guilt?

'Who?' she asked.

'I can't tell you, I'm afraid.'

'Did she realise what you were doing? What she was doing?'

'She did agree, yes. Actually, it was me who agreed. She suggested the idea. It was quite safe. After all, it's only a hormone.'

'Is it?'

'Yes. Anyway, we carried out the experiment over a period of weeks and . . . It's rather worrying. She decided to take matters into her own hands, ignoring the carefully administered doses I'd calculated. Taking more and more, increasing the dosage over the weeks, she discovered that something terrible was happening to her body.'

Horrendous images filled her mind – swirling images of monsters, vile creatures roaming the earth, once known as women.

'What was happening to her body?' she asked fearfully.

'Her clitoris grew.'

Donna placed her hand over her mouth to stifle a giggle.

'How long?' she asked, rather too excitedly.

'Normally, only the tip of the clitoris is exposed as, er . . . as you know. The shaft or body of the clitoris is actually three to four inches in length. But, in answer to your question, incredibly, within a few days of taking the hormone, her clitoris protruded a good half-inch. As the weeks passed, it grew over an inch.'

She had to meet the woman, look at her clitoris, ask her questions. How strong were her orgasms? 'I don't believe you,' she said.

'It's true, it grew . . .'

'No, I don't believe that you tested the hormone on a woman. A man of your standing, your position, you wouldn't do that.'

The professor lowered his eyes and sighed.

'How old is this woman?' she enquired.

'About the same age as you, I believe, twenty, twenty-one,' he smiled, gazing at her short skirt.

'You flatter me,' Donna said, wondering if the

professor had seen the girl's clitoris – sucked it. Although sixtyish, he was still a man, with male thoughts. Dangerous thoughts.

'Don't tell Alan,' she blurted out.

'But that's why I'm here. I have to tell . . .' He broke off suddenly, frowned, looking into her eyes. 'You haven't . . . Have you?'

'I won't use such words as unethical,' she began. 'But if you are telling me the truth, you do realise that what you have done is . . .'

'Yes, yes. I realize only too well. Look, I'll be honest with you. The young lady in question took the hormone without my knowing. It was only when her clitoris grew that she came to me and confessed. You're right, I would never have administered an untried, untested hormone to a human being. But you haven't answered my question.'

Too many questions, searching questions. She daren't tell him the truth. 'I've tried it myself,' she babbled involuntarily. 'Just once, I tried it. It will help women, you know. Inorgasmic women – it will help them to . . .'

'What happened when you tried it?'

'I . . . It affected me. I masturbated.'

'Do you normally?'

Was he enjoying this? In his maleness, was he enjoying it?

'No, never. Don't tell Alan – I'll lose my job.'

She wondered whether she wanted the job anymore. She didn't know what she wanted. Did anyone, really? She wanted to be in the park.

'The girl I mentioned, she left the university, went abroad somewhere. I'm about to retire. I have to tell Alan everything: there is no-one else working in this field, only Alan.'

'Elizabeth?'

'She wants to increase the chemical inhibitor in the female brain. She's a prude, old-fashioned. I can't think why she . . .'

'She's changed. I think you'll find that her ideas are very different now.'

'Not her, she'll never change. Not unless . . . She hasn't taken the hormone, surely?'

'John, good to see you,' Alan beamed, holding his hand out as he crossed the room. 'What are you doing in here?'

'Waiting for you and chatting with this delightful young lady. How are you?'

Slipping from the room, Donna returned to the lab, knowing that her days, her minutes, were numbered. Elizabeth wasn't around. Probably in the loo, masturbating, she guessed. Grabbing several strips of patches from Alan's drawer Donna left the building, wondering if she'd ever return.

The wind had dropped, allowing her thoughts to settle as she walked towards the park, swinging her handbag, enjoying her freedom. What were they discussing, Alan and the professor? Donna? Elizabeth? Did it matter when the sun was shining in a clear sky and the birds were singing?

Sitting on a bench near a clump of trees she relaxed, thought of her future, examined the patches. How many had Alan manufactured? Why so many? Surely, he'd realized that some were missing? A train trundled through the cutting behind the trees, bringing her back from her thoughts. The park was a thinking place, somewhere people came to think – a place for thoughts. Helen had thought there, in the park, and her friend Sophie. What else had they done? Parks were for young courting couples, too. For sex.

'All alone?' a soft, female voice asked. Donna turned.

'Sue, how are you? What are you doing here?'

'Looking for Helen. You haven't seen her, have you?'

'No, I haven't. Sit down, tell me what you've been up to. You didn't come round on Sunday evening. I thought . . .'

'No, sorry. I had a problem with Helen. Young girls, you know the sort of thing. It's all right now, all sorted out, thank goodness. I'm looking for her because . . . Never mind.'

Parks were for young courting couples, Donna found herself thinking again, taking in Sue's see-through summer dress. And for not-so-young women wearing patches. 'There's a bee in your hair, don't move,' she exclaimed, slipping a patch onto Sue's neck. Simplicity itself. Too simple?

Manoeuvring a patch onto her own arm, she waited for Sue to make the first move. How delightful to lie naked on the soft grass under the trees – legs spread, tongues licking, fingers delving, cream flowing. Another train trundled through the cutting, the valley, like a huge, steel piston, and entered the tunnel – dark, dank, musky.

Standing, Sue wandered towards the trees, the sun shining through her thin dress, outlining her slender legs, the small bulge of her sex between her thighs as her bottom wiggled. Donna let out a rush of breath as her clitoris suddenly stirred and awoke with a throb. Following Sue into the wooded area, into the privacy afforded by the trees, the canopy of foliage, she smiled. Time for love, for sex.

At the edge of the railway cutting, they stopped and

The Uninhibited

gazed at each other. No words were spoken as hands moved swiftly, silently, their clothes falling away like autumn leaves in the wind, baring their slender bodies, their curves and clefts – their nakedness.

The grass was warm, soft against Donna's back as she lay down and spread her body, freed her mind. Her eyes closed, she gripped tufts of grass in her hands as Sue moved between her legs and kissed the smooth skin of her calves. Licking, tasting, devouring the firmness of her flesh as she moved higher to Donna's knees, Sue ran her fingers up the younger girl's legs, to the creases between her vaginal lips and her thighs and stroked her there. Wider now, Donna opened her legs. Higher now, Sue kissed, nibbled, licked. Another train glided through the cutting towards the dark opening of the tunnel as Sue's tongue glided between Donna's warm thighs towards her open valley, the wet entrance to her pleasure.

Running her fingers over her trembling body, Donna pinched her nipples, squeezed the pleasure from them as Sue's tongue neared her quim lips – wet, glistening, pouting lips of hot flesh. Her body swam with sensations, floated under the warm sun as the woman's tongue reached her valley and licked the moist warmth there. A quivering filled her love-tube as the hot tongue penetrated, pushed aside the pink curtains and entered the wetness within the cave. Donna raised her hips, forcing her lovemouth into Sue's face as her clitoris swelled with a powerful desire to erupt into orgasm.

Moving her naked body round, Sue settled her wetness over Donna's face. Her cunt lips pressing against Donna's mouth, Sue leaned forward and buried her own mouth between Donna's nether lips. Both licking, sucking, drinking the fluids of lust from the other's body, they writhed in harmony, unaware of the figure lurking in the bushes – watching, peeping.

Crouching behind his camouflage of green leaves, the young man gazed open-mouthed at the wondrous spectacle. Wandering through the park, he'd strayed into the wooded area, thinking, pondering on his girlfriend's infidelity. Listening to the gasping, watching the licking, he breathed silently as his penis hardened within the tightness of his jeans. In the naivety of his eighteen years, he'd believed such a scenario existed only in fantasy. Yet here he was, witnessing wanton lesbianism under the summer sky – rapidly recovering from his sadness.

Donna caught a fleeting glimpse of him as Sue briefly raised her bloated pussy lips from her face. Excitement coursed its way through Donna's veins, thrilling her as never before, as she opened her legs wider for his eyes. She wouldn't tell Sue about the voyeur, she decided, her open valley pressing more urgently against the other woman's mouth. But she would emphasise the sounds of orgasm when it came – shout words of lust. Men, peeping Toms, liked that. Was he the man Helen had seen outside her flat? she wondered.

Her cumbud about to burst, Sue rocked her hips, sliding the slippery flesh of her open vagina over Donna's mouth as her milky fluid poured out. Trembling, rigid in the grip of her climax, she bit on Donna's clitoris as her own blossomed, exploded, sending electrifying shock waves through her consumed body. Erupting in synchronisation, Donna babbled words of appreciation through the creamy folds of flesh engulfing her open mouth. 'Fuck me with your tongue!' she cried. 'Open my cunt and lick my cream!' The voyeur would appreciate the dirty words of lesbians in orgasm.

Gripping his rock-hard penis in his hand, the young man began his wanking motions, rousing his sperm pump, waking his balls as he watched the women licking each other clean, sucking the remnants of orgasm from their nodules of pleasure. Looking to the bushes, Donna beckoned him. Stunned, he zipped up his jeans and, emerging from the foliage, walked towards her. Frowning, hesitating, he couldn't believe what was happening – or what was about to happen.

Relaxing in her afterglow, Sue lay with her eyes closed, unaware of his presence – male presence. Opening her eyes to see him standing over her naked body, she gasped, covering her breasts with her hands. Tall, tanned, rugged, he gazed down at the naked women, their curves, their clefts, beautiful as young wood nymphs.

'I think it's time we had a man,' Donna whispered in her husky voice. 'What's your name?' Smiling slightly, he looked around him as if checking that the coast was clear. Returning his wide eyes to Donna, his smile broadened.

'Barry,' he replied as Sue uncovered her breasts and encircled her hard milk buds with her fingertips.

'Well, Barry, why don't you take your clothes off and join us? I'm Donna and this is Sue, by the way.'

Silently unbuttoning his shirt as Donna unzipped his jeans, he glanced around him again as if half expecting someone. Donna lowered his boxer shorts and gazed at his massive penis as it catapulted to attention only inches from her face. Silently, she parted her red lips and, pulling the loose skin back as far as she could, she took the plum into her hot mouth.

Gasping, he looked up to the canopy of green leaves, broken here and there by patches of blue sky. Shafts of sunlight played on Donna's golden hair as she moved her head back and forth, sucking, mouthing, licking his hardness. He looked down to her nakedness, her open mouth engulfing his penis, shining like a golden angel of lust – a dream, dreamed by men, come true.

Kneeling by Donna's side, Sue gently kissed his stomach, bit on the base of his shaft, breathed in the male aroma from his thick, black bush. Unselfish, Donna offered her the purple knob – wet, glistening, bulging with lust. Sucking it between her wet lips, Sue rolled her tongue around the knob, gently sank her teeth into the hardness of the warm flesh as Donna moved behind Barry and kissed his firm buttocks. Opening the dark crease, she pressed her finger into the tight hole, bit on the roundness of his buttocks, causing him to gasp with delight. Closing his eyes, he breathed deeply, let out a low moan and gripped Sue's head. Near to his orgasm now, his rigid body trembled with pleasures only possible from the intimate attention of two women – pleasures attained only when sandwiched between two lesbians in lust.

'Barry!' A distant, female voice drifted through the hazy air, lost among the trees like a leaf floating on the ocean. He opened his eyes and looked around him. But the pleasure between his legs outweighed his concern. Swelling now, twitching, his penis exploded in Sue's mouth, douching her tongue, filling her cheeks with hot, gushing sperm as Donna employed her miniature phallus, her finger, to explore the hotness of his bowels. Groaning as if in agony, he threw back his head as his pump pulsated and his balls drained. Gripping Sue's head harder in his passion, he moved his hips back to escape the tormenting mouth – but he was trapped between his lesbian captors.

'Christ!' the girl shrieked as she stumbled upon the threesome. 'What the hell are you doing?' He looked at her, expressionless, as Sue sucked the last drop of sperm from his rod, withdrawing it from her mouth. Donna relinquishing her finger, all three gazed up at the young girl.

'What does it look like?' he returned sarcastically.

'But I thought we . . .'

'Well, you thought wrong, didn't you? You put it around, screwed that bloke, so what's wrong with me having a little pleasure? Besides, these two know how to treat a man – unlike you.'

'Why don't you join us?' Donna invited. Her pretty face flushed with disgust, the girl turned and fled with tears in her eyes. Suddenly filled with remorse, Barry grabbed his shirt and gave chase with his jeans around his knees.

'Talk about ships in the night,' Donna laughed. 'We hadn't even the time to let him sail in us.'

'Who is he?' Sue asked.

'I don't know.'

'But I thought that you knew him?'

'What made you think that?'

'I thought you'd arranged to meet him here or something.'

'I wouldn't have asked his name if I had, would I?'

'Weren't you having me on, playing around? Shit! What must he have thought?'

'That it was his lucky day, I suppose.'

Their bodies wet with lust, they relaxed on the soft grass, whispering their plans to meet every day and make love in the park, under the trees, to suck the pleasure from each other's bodies. They hoped to meet the young male stranger again, to take him in their vaginas, their mouths – to drain him of his sperm. Touching, fondling, they closed their eyes and half dozed, drifting in the strange mist that lies between reality and fantasy until approaching voices roused them.

Dressing hurriedly, they left the woodland and walked out into the hot sunshine where people were walking dogs, pushing prams – people unaware of the echoes of passion still reverberating under the trees.

'See you tomorrow,' Sue smiled as they parted company at the park gates. Yes, Donna thought – and Helen, and Sophie, and Elizabeth. All five would writhe in lesbian lust, reach wondrous sexual heights together – as one. Sue was still wearing her patch. But now, thoughts of Alan returned – and the professor. All had been revealed, she was sure. Her time at the lab had come to an end. All things came to an end – good or bad.

Remembering her sex-slaves between her legs, licking at her open groove, fingering her hot cavern, Donna decided to buy some rope, a leather strap, handcuffs, a thin bamboo cane – the tools of bondage. She was sure the man in the shop knew why she wanted four pairs of toy handcuffs. He only had plastic – not very strong, but they would do. To the ironmongers now. Rope? Yes, thick, strong, long. And a cane – only one? Only one – thin, stinging, wincing. Leather straps? There was a strange look in the man's eye, a male look of sex – he knew. No leather straps – sorry. A candle, two candles – thick, long. No, she daren't ask him.

Elizabeth didn't appear at Donna's flat that evening. Probably still discussing the patches, and her future, she speculated. Lynn Bulmur arrived at eight, chewing her gum, grinning in her triumph. Donna opened the front door to find her leaning against the wall clutching a large brown envelope.

'You'd better come in,' she said coldly. 'I don't want you to stay. We'll swap the photographs and you can go back to whichever hole it is you've just crawled out of.'

'Actually, the hole I've just crawled out of is called Grunwerg Research Laboratories.'

'Don't talk crap.'

'Your boss, Alan Rosenberg – he was quite shocked when I showed him the picture of you this afternoon. "Christ!" he said. "I didn't realise that she's a whore!" I told him that you've been earning on the side ever since you were at university. And that you'd got your degree by sleeping with the lecturers.'

She'd done it, Donna knew. But the lab was history now, a chapter finished, closed, so what did it matter? She smiled as she closed the door and showed the devil's daughter into the lounge. 'Well, all I can say is that I feel less guilty now,' she smiled as she sat in her armchair.

'What do you mean, less guilty?'

'The DSS, I sent them a picture of you.'

Lynn looked into Donna's eyes, searching for the truth. Pools of misty blue light, her big eyes mirrored only her inner desires.

'Why did you do it?' Lynn asked.

'Why did you? Good fun, this blackmail business, isn't it?'

'I don't believe you, and frankly, I don't care.'

'Then why are you here?'

'I need more patches, lots more.'

'How can I get them if I don't work at the lab? And I'm sure I won't be working there any more, not now that you've pulled that bloody stupid stroke. You've gone and shot yourself in the foot, Bulmur – pathetic little bitch that you are.'

Relief washed over Donna as Lynn stormed from the flat. No more threats, no more blackmail, now that her job had gone. Would Alan remain a friend? A lover? What would Elizabeth say when she returned, if she returned? She should have been home by now.

Still wearing her patch, she wandered into the kitchen and filled the kettle. What to do with her empty days? Masturbate? Lie in bed all day, every day, enticing wondrous orgasms from her insatiable clitoris? Money reared its ugly head. Another job, perhaps? Or set up alone manufacturing patches – a consultant helping inorgasmic women such as Sue, maybe? Such as Sue *used* to be, she corrected herself. Again, the magazine articles came to mind and she pictured hundreds of women queuing to see her, to pay her for her services.

The idea gripping her more firmly with each passing minute, she returned to the lounge with her coffee and sat down. The walls gazed at her as her head whirled with thoughts of money, success. Excitement churned her stomach as she thought of the spare room becoming her mini-laboratory. But she needed money, lots of money, to set it up.

Answering the door to Alan, she felt a rush of adrenalin course through her veins and her face redden. He was smiling, at least. But what did he want? To give her her notice? To ask questions about the photograph? To pull her knickers down and spank her for her naughtiness? She hoped so. Standing speechless for several seconds, she could only stare at her boss.

'Come in,' she eventually invited. Returning her smile, he walked into the lounge as she closed the front door. 'Where's Elizabeth?' she asked, following him in.

'Where were you? That's what I want to know,' he returned, seating himself on the sofa.

'I felt ill. Didn't Elizabeth tell you?'

'No, she didn't. Anyway, are you better now? You look all right.'

'Yes, I'm better now. Something I ate, I expect.'

His dark eyes scanned her body, her breasts, her nipples, her thighs. Was *he* the perverted telephone caller? What did he want? What did *she* want? The zip of his trousers had folded as he'd sat down, giving the impression of an eight-inch erection. Perhaps it *was* an erection? Decisions. Should she open his trousers and suck the sperm from the silky, purple knob of his rock-hard penis? Keep her job by keeping him happy?

'Elizabeth left the lab at five. Hasn't she been here?' he asked, his eyes transfixed between her parted thighs.

'No. I hope she's all right,' she frowned, remembering the patch.

'She'll be okay. It was you I was worried about. I rang earlier but there was no reply.'

'I went to see my doctor. What did Professor Winmann have to say? Anything interesting?'

'Oh, we talked, swapped notes. He told me a little about the libido and the hormone's effect on the female chemical inhibitor, but he has no conclusive results. I had a visitor, by the way.'

Lynn bloody Bulmur, Donna thought fearfully, her stomach churning. Why was Alan so cool, calm? Was he trying to prolong her agony? Perhaps he was a sadist, enjoying her pain – waiting for her to ask who his visitor was. Guilt hurt – she might as well play his game.

'Who?' she asked softly, dreading, knowing the answer.

'Lynn Bulmur. She knows you, or so she said. She wanted to see Malcolm, but he was out. She left an envelope for him.'

Her heart pounded, hands trembled.

'What was in it?'

'I don't know. I didn't open it. I left it on his desk. Who is she, do you know her?'

'Someone I was at university with. She's . . . She's not a friend, just someone I know.'

The bitch hadn't shown Alan the picture. But what was she doing poking around the lab? Why not drop it through the letter box, or post it? Trying to steal some patches, no doubt. And what of the professor? Surely he hadn't kept her terrible secret from Alan?

Her clitoris ached with desire. Recovered by now from her wondrous session with Sue and the stranger in the park, she wanted more sex. Did Alan want sex? she wondered. Didn't all men, all the time?

'So, everything's all right, then?' she asked hesitantly.

'Fine. I only came to see you as you mysteriously disappeared from the lab. By the way, Elizabeth has been acting strangely, have you noticed?'

'I wouldn't know. I mean, she's only just arrived so how would I know what she's like normally?'

'She's changed overnight. When she first arrived she was sort of frumpish, old-fashioned, and the next day, well . . .'

'Mood swings. Women and their hormones and all that, I expect. You should know about hormones.'

'Do you love me?'

Caught off guard, she didn't know the answer. What was the difference between love and sex? Between loving a man or a woman? She loved Sue. Sue loved her. What was love? Alan seemed to love her, but he'd

174

stretched open Elizabeth's vagina with his stiff penis, filled her with his sperm. Perhaps he loved Elizabeth, too – loved all women?

'What a funny question,' she laughed, acutely aware of her stupid reply. Why shouldn't he ask if she loved him?

'Why?'

Was that really an erection? Or just a fold in his trousers? There was only one way to find out.

'I like you very much,' she smiled. 'But love? I don't know if I've ever been in love.'

'I hadn't,' he said sullenly.

'Oh. Are you now?'

'Yes, I think so.'

On the verge of asking who with, she thought better of it as she heard the front door open. Shit, Elizabeth! What the hell did she want to turn up for, just as she was about to open Alan's trousers and suck him into her hot, hungry mouth?

'You're late,' she remarked as Elizabeth staggered into the room, her hair over her face, her clothes dishevelled.

'I've been out . . . I had a few drinks in a bar and . . .'

'You're drunk!' Donna shrieked as Elizabeth fell over the arm of the sofa and landed in Alan's lap.

'Only a little bit. I met two men and we . . .' Giggling uncontrollably, she couldn't finish her sentence, much to Donna's relief.

'I'd better be going,' said Alan, pushing Elizabeth from his lap as he stood up. 'Now do you agree that she's changed? Just look at her! Anyway, I was hoping to have a serious talk with you about us but . . . Another time, maybe.'

'Yes, another time,' Donna echoed as she saw him

out. She didn't like serious talks – who did?

Returning to the lounge, she gazed at Elizabeth lying on her stomach over the sofa, her short skirt hiked up over her buttocks, her shaved, knickerless pussy lips bulging invitingly between her open legs. 'My God, she's been fucked!' Donna breathed, eyeing the sperm oozing between Elizabeth's sagging inner quim lips. 'You randy little whore, you've been screwed!'

Leaving Elizabeth to sleep off her drunken state, Donna grabbed her jacket and left the flat. The keys to the lab in her hand, she walked down the street wondering what she'd say to the security guard when he asked her what she was doing there at ten o'clock at night.

The moon was shining in the darkness, lighting Donna's way, bathing her body in its silvery glow, for all to see. Who was watching? Who the hell was spying on her? Someone, somewhere, was watching, she was sure.

Chapter Nine

Unseen things move in the night. Thieves steal, cats roam, people lurk in shop doorways – Peeping Toms peep. Donna moved down the street, silently, stealthily, rehearsing her lines. 'I forgot my handbag – no. I forgot to post an important letter – no.' Was someone following her?

The security guard wasn't in his office. Slipping across the foyer and up the stairs, she breathed a sigh of relief on finding Malcolm's office unlocked. In the dim light from the corridor, she could just make out the brown envelope, large, plain, ominous, lying on his desk, waiting to reveal its sordid contents. Somewhere – on the ground floor, she surmised – a window smashed loudly, crashing, tinkling in the night. Her heart nearly stopped as she grabbed the envelope and rolled it up. Where was the guard? Guarding?

Palms wet, hands trembling, knees weak, heart racing, she ran down the stairs. Voices echoed in the night, male and female, emanating from the far end of the corridor. She slipped into the lab – familiarity, safety. What was going on? Grabbing a couple of test tubes containing the hormone, she stuffed them into her bag and crept back into the corridor. Voices coming from the security guard's office now. The back way, she thought, through the fire exit and out into the car park, out into the night.

Two police cars sped past her as she walked unsteadily down the street, the envelope in her hand and enough of the hormone in her bag to produce thousands of patches. Blue flashing lights swirled around the buildings, lighting the night sky. A break-in. Someone after money, or drugs, she reflected as she ran the short distance to her flat, turning to look into the shadows now and then – shadows that followed her. Closing her front door behind her, she leaned against the wall and slid to the floor, her breathing unsteady, her stomach seething.

Elizabeth was still slumped over the sofa as Donna walked into the lounge. Her skirt still up over her buttocks, her drenched quim lips still oozing with sperm, Donna imagined taking a photograph of her, just for fun – just in case. Her snoring was punctuated by mumblings of sex, hard penises, thrusting, sperm spurting, filling her fleshy cavern. Surely she'd not been taken by two men? But then, why not? One man, two men, or women, why not?

She had just made some coffee and was about to wake Elizabeth when the phone rang.

'There's been a break-in at the lab!' Alan announced excitedly before she could say hello.

'When?' she asked coolly.

'Tonight. Malcolm has just phoned me, he's at the lab now.'

'Have they caught him?'

'Not him, her. I just thought I'd let you know that they've arrested that friend of yours – Lynn Bulmur.'

'Lynn Bulmur? She's not a friend!'

'Whatever – she's been arrested. The security man caught her. She'd broken a window and climbed in.'

'Why?'

'To get into the building, I suppose.'

'No, I mean, why break in? What did she want?'

'I don't know, do I? I thought perhaps you'd be able to throw some light on it.'

'Why me? I don't know anything about it.'

'Well, I'll see you tomorrow, anyway. We'll find out more then, I suppose. 'Night.'

Donna felt as if she was being sucked into the mire, digging her fingernails into the slimy walls of a deep well of trouble as she slid further down towards the black water. She contemplated her position, planned her alibi. The police would question her, her connection with Bulmur. She'd been at home all night, with Alan and Elizabeth. Alan had seen Elizabeth come in and flop onto the sofa. She couldn't leave her in her drunken state. Not one hundred per cent, but a good enough alibi.

Her mind reeling, Donna tried to reason, to pull herself together. 'They won't question me about the break-in, for Christ's sake!' Suddenly she remembered the patches, Bulmur's patches, hidden somewhere in the bloody girl's flat. 'Shit!' Glancing at the clock, she left the flat. Midnight, the witching hour. Bulmur was a witch. Break into her flat and remove patches, photographs, anything relevant, anything that connected Donna with the devil's daughter.

The night was dark. There was no moon now, only clouds of swirling blackness overhead as she walked to Bulmur's flat. Would Lucifer be there? The police? Or would they arrive to catch Donna red-handed? How to break in? She had no idea. Tears welled in her eyes as she thought about the patches. They were supposed to bring fun, excitement, money – not a living hell. The blackness seemed to close in – was it the devil?

'This isn't the movies,' Donna whispered to herself, discovering that Bulmur's place wasn't surrounded by rifle-wielding cops yelling through loud-hailers. Perhaps Steve had been right. Should they have killed her? 'This is bad enough without murder,' she murmured, creeping around the back of the flat.

The kitchen window was closed. She tapped the glass – it sounded thin. Thin enough to break quietly, she prayed as she groped around the garden and picked up a large stone. Tap, tap – nothing. Harder this time. Shattering, the glass tinkled to the ground in pieces only to break again, noisily. Cats fighting in a nearby garden sent a shudder up her spine. A light came on in an adjoining house. 'Get out of it!' a man shouted. Something crashed through the bushes. 'Bloody cats!' Cooking fat, Donna thought, remembering a film she'd seen, but not which one.

A dog's bark echoed somewhere in the night as she managed to lift the sash and climb inside. A police dog, she suspected as she felt her way through the kitchen to the doorway, where she found the light switch. The fluorescent tube flashed several times, illuminating the room like lightning streaking across the sky, before buzzing softly. The shadows disappearing, her eyes met with a mass of filthy dishes and mouldy, half-eaten food. Dirty cow.

Rummaging, pulling open drawers, cupboards, tins, she eventually moved her attention to the lounge to continue her search. Slinging the cushions from the sofa, she heaved a sigh of relief – the patches! But the photographs, where the hell were they? She vaguely remembered Steve's words about Lynn not being stupid enough to leave them in her flat. So where? Pulling out CDs, tapes and records from a cabinet, she flung them across the floor. The photographs would be there, somewhere – Bulmur *was* stupid.

About to give up after wrecking the place, she lifted a corner of Lynn's bedroom carpet. There it was – a large, brown envelope containing not only the photographs but two hundred pounds in cash. Dashing to the back door with her spoils, she heard a key turn in the front-door lock.

Making her way through gardens, bushes, over walls, upturning dustbins in her panic, she didn't stop until she was out in the street, well away from the scene of the crime. Bulmur? No – it would have been the police searching her flat, she was sure. Someone was following her, she could feel them, their prying eyes. Who? Through alleyways, edging along paths, dashing into driveways at the sound of passing cars, she finally reached her flat and quickly let herself in.

Guilt, fear, sheer terror. Was this the bottom of the well? she wondered. The black water? You had to hit the bottom before going up. But it seemed some wells were deeper than deep – bottomless.

Elizabeth lay snoring, unaware of the events of the night, as Donna climbed the stairs clutching her spoils. What if the police arrived? she thought fearfully. Burn the pictures? No, they wouldn't come, not in the dead of night. If only Bulmur was dead! But no – she had nothing on her, not now. She knew of her, yes, but that was all. They'd met in the café, chatted about old times, had a coffee together at her flat, no more. Innocent – until proved guilty.

Tossing, turning, sleep didn't come easily. Her mind surging this way and that, lurching from one terrible thought to another, she lay in her bed until the sun appeared low on the horizon, bringing another day.

Roused by soft moans drifting up the stairs, she dragged her naked body from the warmth of her bed and stood before the mirror. Cupping her breasts, she smiled, happy with their fullness, their roundness. Pulling at her nipples, she wondered if they'd grown. Imagination, perhaps? Remembering the professor's words, she parted her soft lips and pressed out her clitoris. Was it bigger? She thought so – hoped so. Yes, it was bigger.

More moans emanated from the lounge, louder, desperate now. Creeping down the stairs, Donna pushed all thoughts of the previous night from her mind. Spying at Elizabeth through the crack in the door, she opened her blue eyes wide and wondered at the spectacle – at the patches, the hormone and its incredible capacity.

'Come inside me, in my cunt, in my mouth! I want you both to come in me!' Openly masturbating, lying naked on the sofa, Elizabeth breathed her dirty words of sex. Her mind brimming with sexual fantasy, gasping as she stretched her lips open wider, massaged her swelling clitoris harder, her lovelips overflowed with the creamy nectar of sex. Donna pictured her session with the two men and her thoughts turned to disgust. Jealousy? She wanted Elizabeth, wanted to lick her, to suck her. But suddenly, she wanted to punish her. For all that had happened, for masturbating, for everything, she wanted her to pay.

Fetching the bag containing her tools of bondage, Donna returned to the lounge with an uncharacteristic glint in her eye – a glint of evil. Lucifer was near, she knew – and the angels had fled. Fear, sex, revenge, love, lust, hatred – all were interwoven in her mind to create a consuming desire to punish. And there was

Elizabeth, naked, wet with sex. Staring at her used body, trembling, vulnerable, lying on the floor now, she issued her instruction. 'Stand up!' Without a word, the woman climbed to her feet and stood naked before her mistress – her tormentor.

Dragging the sofa to the centre of the room, Donna ordered her victim to stand behind it and lean over the back. Like a puppet on a string she complied, exposing her firm buttocks as she bent over and rested her head on a cushion. The walls watched Donna tie a length of rope to Elizabeth's foot and secure it to a leg of the sofa. Had the angels of lust returned? Were they watching? Taking another length, she secured her free foot to the other leg. Her feet wide apart, her lips swelled beneath her buttocks, glistening with milky fluid, inviting Donna's tongue. But no – pulling a pair of handcuffs from the bag, she secured Elizabeth's wrists and stood back to admire her handiwork.

There were no soft beginnings to the caning, no light strokes to gently tempt and excite. Instead, Donna swished the cane through the air and landed the first wincing blow across the taut buttocks with a vengeance. To her surprise, Elizabeth yelped and cried out for more as the thrashing continued, reddening the pale flesh, causing her buttocks to twitch delightfully. Begging her tormentor to spank her harder, make her come with the cane, she shook and writhed in a strange, painful ecstasy. Would she come? Would the caning bring her to orgasm? Or would Lucifer enter her from behind, fill her with his erect horn of evil to suck her soul from her very womb?

Harder and harder Donna thrashed her victim, burning her buttocks with each gruelling swipe of the thin bamboo, causing her to cry out in her orgasm as it rose and shook her tethered body. Her juices spewing from her gaping hole, trickling down her thighs, at last she begged Donna to stop the torturing bliss.

'No, you need more!' she asserted, thrashing even harder.

'No more, please. I can't take . . .'

'You'll have to!' Donna cried gleefully, landing the hardest blow yet.

Her arm aching, she finally discarded the cane and knelt behind Elizabeth, gazing at the result of her work. Kissing the weals, stroking the crimson flesh, she pushed her thumb into the small hole and massaged the velveteen tube, causing Elizabeth to shudder slightly. Locating the other, larger entrance to her body, Donna's fingers pressed into the hotness where they, too, massaged the wet silky walls. Heaving now, begging to come again, Elizabeth breathed heavily, writhing and wriggling to the gentle, inner caresses.

Withdrawing her fingers and thumb, Donna lifted Elizabeth's buttocks up and apart to expose the small fusion of pinken skin where inner lips meet to conceal Mother Nature's girlish secret. Moving her hands down, she dug her fingernails into the warm spheres and stretched them open again, this time exposing the wet, milky entrance to Elizabeth's vagina. Pressing her face into the warmth, Donna pushed her tongue out and licked the delicate pink cushions before pressing her tongue inside the dank cavern to taste the musk there. Hot, wet, creamy, she drank the fruits from the hole of love as they flowed and trickled down her chin. 'My clitoris!' Elizabeth gasped in an outrush of breath. 'Lick my clitoris now!'

Releasing her victim, Donna turned her around and lay her over the back of the sofa with her open quim lips appetisingly spread. Her body upside down, her hands still cuffed, she looked up at Donna and smiled. Returning her smile, Donna bent forward and licked the wet slit from end to end, lapping up the slippery fluid, stiffening her prisoner's clitoris. Her stomach rising and falling rapidly with her increasing excitement, Elizabeth watched Donna's tongue licking, exploring between the bloated lips of her vagina. The wondrous sight heightening her arousal spectacularly, she opened her legs further to expose her femininity in its entirety.

Pressing her thumbs into the swollen cushions, Donna opened the crease and ground her mouth hard into the pink flesh, engulfing Elizabeth's stiff, throbbing clitoris, sucking out her orgasm. The blood rushing to her head, Elizabeth's face reddened and contorted, her breathing heavy, deep with the pleasure between her legs as Donna continued to mouth and suck her flowering cumbud. Spilling into Donna's mouth, her orgasm coursed its way through her body to stir her own clitoris. Donna's turn would come, soon. Shudders, trembles, soft moans emanated from Elizabeth's gasping mouth as her climax subsided, giving way to serene satisfaction.

'That was wonderful,' she whimpered. 'Let me go now and I'll do the same to you.'

Donna said nothing as she went to the kitchen and returned with the cucumber. 'No, not that!' Elizabeth pleaded as Donna gently pushed half its length deep into her splayed body. Protruding, encircled by Elizabeth's swollen lips, the vegetable stood proud between her legs like a hard penis. Standing on her toes between Elizabeth's legs, Donna opened her nether lips and lowered her body onto the phallus, sinking it deep inside her tightening cunette. Grabbing the three exposed inches of green shaft, she thrust it up and down, filling each hot hole in turn. Clinging to the back of the sofa, she gyrated her hips as her climax neared, moving the phallus in circles, stretching the wet flesh of their trembling holes until in unison, they shuddered and reached their goals as one.

Shaking, panting, they writhed, sustaining the pleasure between their thighs, their stretched lips, until Donna pulled away and lay over the sofa, wet, exhausted, satisfied as never before – adrift on a sea of sex. Squeezing her muscles to eject the hot, wet phallus from her inflamed hole, Elizabeth rolled to one side and staggered to her feet. 'Take these off now,' she said, offering her cuffed hands to Donna. 'We must get ready for work.'

'I think not. I haven't finished with you yet.'

'There's no time,' Elizabeth objected as Donna knelt on the floor and began licking her wet valley. 'There's no time for . . . Ah, that's nice! Yes, yes! Make me come again!'

As Elizabeth neared her climax, Donna moved away and stood up. 'You're right,' she said. 'Time to go to work.'

'No, you can't leave me like this, I'm nearly coming! Please, lick me, I'm almost there! Please lick my cunt!'

Falling to her knees again, Donna peeled Elizabeth's quim lips open and sucked hard on her throbbing bud until it erupted in her mouth and expelled its orgasm, releasing the sexual tension, bringing a serene satisfaction where there had been pulsating desire. Falling to the floor, Elizabeth murmured her appreciation, trembling as the pond of love settled and stilled.

'What happened last night?' Donna asked as they washed each other in the shower.

'Two men, I met them in a bar and we . . . Well, we

went to the park and we drank wine and made love. I really don't know what's come over me lately.'

'Two men came over you, by the sound of it.'

'No, I mean I've changed. I used to be . . .'

'I know what you used to be.'

'It's as if I've taken the hormone,' Elizabeth reflected, stepping out of the shower, deep in thought.

Donna followed her to the bedroom and watched her closely as she dressed. Elizabeth was beginning to understand now, to perceive. 'Perhaps you've been affected by the hormone,' she suggested tentatively. 'Maybe handling the patches, coming into contact with them has affected you.'

'I'm always careful to wear rubber gloves, it can't be that.'

'Perhaps a patch got stuck to your arm or something?'

'Perhaps, but if that was the case, where is it now? And why do I feel like this now if the patch has fallen off?'

Donna shrugged her shoulders and finished dressing. There was little more to say, and besides, to take too much interest, to discuss it further, would arouse suspicion. Let sleeping dogs lie, she thought, before changing the subject.

'I'm going home tomorrow,' Elizabeth revealed as they left the flat and walked out into the hot sunshine.

'So soon?' Donna felt relieved. If she could just get through the day avoiding further discussion about the patches she'd be free of one problem, at least.

'Yes, it's a shame. I've really enjoyed myself. Staying with you has been fun – enlightening. We'll keep in touch, shall we?'

'Shit!' The early morning jogger running towards them, shorts bulging, hard, tanned chest rippling with muscles, looked all too familiar. As he passed, he caught Donna's eye and stopped and turned. Grabbing Elizabeth's hand, she walked quickly on, chatting about the weather, her summer holiday. Glancing over her shoulder, she watched the young man cross the road and run into the park. Had he recognised her as one of the angels of sex who'd pleasured him so delightfully in the park? She smiled. She'd take up early morning jogging, she decided. And early morning loving.

'And who are you?' Entering the lab, she was confronted by a police officer. She turned to see another officer talking to Alan.

'Ryan – Donna Ryan,' she answered tonelessly. 'And this is Elizabeth . . .'

'Wellings,' Elizabeth said. 'What's happened?'

'A break-in, miss. We're just about finished here. Nothing's missing, according to Doctor Rosenberg. Would you both have a look round, just to make sure?'

Obviously no-one had mentioned the envelope, the test tubes containing the hormone, the missing patches. Should the theft come to light, Donna thought, then they would look to Bulmur. 'Nothing's missing as far as I can see,' she said, examining her bench.

'And I wouldn't know,' Elizabeth rejoined. 'I've only been here for a few days.'

The police gone, Alan turned to Donna. He looked tired, agitated – annoyed, probably, at the disruption of his precious laboratory. 'Apparently, the girl's flat has been turned over,' he told her.

'Girl?' Donna enquired nonchalantly.

'That Bulmur girl, her flat's been ransacked.'

'Oh, has it? Well, there's poetic justice for you. What else did the police say?'

'Nothing much. They've got her at the station and will be charging her with breaking and entering, but as there's nothing missing they can't do her for robbery. I wonder what she was after? Apart from the envelope.'

'Envelope?'

'The one she brought here yesterday. I left it on Malcolm's desk, but now it's gone.'

'There's the robbery, then. Bang her up behind bars for life.'

'No, she didn't have it when the security guard caught her so there's no saying that she took it. Anyway, why deliver it if she's only going to come back and steal it?'

The day wore on slowly, with little conversation. Elizabeth fiddled with herself continuously beneath her bench, massaging her clitoris, rubbing her sore buttocks. Alan muttered the odd word as he came and went from the lab while Donna spent her time thinking about Lynn Bulmur, the park and the sexy jogger. Had his girlfriend forgiven him? Probably not. She'd take up jogging in the morning, meet him in the park and pull his shorts down, she decided – really give his girlfriend something to complain about. How sweet to have her naked under the trees and lick between her young, wet lips as her boyfriend watched! One day, maybe – one day.

Skipping lunch, Donna called into the local newspaper office to place her advertisement – *Counselling and genuine help for women suffering problems of a sexual nature. Ring Donna – 839754.*

She was in time for that week's paper, the girl behind the desk said, adding that she wouldn't mind seeing her about her problem, if that was all right. All right? It was more than all right. She was young, attractive, and Donna didn't mind at all. She longed to ask what her problem was, but that wouldn't be professional. Perhaps she had discovered her latent lesbian tendencies, and considered it a problem? Maybe she masturbated three times daily while imagining another girl licking her and thought that to be abnormal, excessive? Everything in moderation – except for masturbation, lesbian fantasy and orgasm.

'Call round and see me at eight this evening,' Donna invited, silently adding, 'And I'll show you what your beautiful body can bring you – and me.'

'If I don't turn up, well . . . It's not easy . . .'

'Just be there at eight and you'll be pleased you came, I promise you. If you don't, you'll be letting yourself down, not me.'

Walking back to the lab, Donna couldn't believe her luck. To stumble across such a young and vulnerable victim was no coincidence – more a gift from the angels of lust. *The first of many young girls to be honoured by my sensual touch,* she speculated, wondering about the girl's body, how she'd administer the patch, get Elizabeth out of the way. Ideas, plans, came swirling out of the mist of her mind as she wandered along the street, full of life – sex.

Elizabeth said her goodbyes to Alan before leaving the lab at five o'clock. Why she hadn't discussed the patches with him, Donna had no idea. In all the excitement, the sexy fun, she'd done little in the way of research to help him in his quest for the truth about the hormone. But that was just as well, she concluded. The less said, the better. It was almost as if they both knew about her, the patches, her debauched world.

Donna liked the evenings, the sun-hazed, warm evenings. Walking home with Elizabeth, she listened to her plans to get out and about more, to meet people once she was back in her home town. The patch would wear off to leave her cold and frigid as before, Donna thought sadly – as brown and barren as the fields in the grips of winter. Winter – by the fire, on the hearth rug, naked, writhing in the heat as the cold scratched at the window. She didn't have a hearth rug, or an open fire – sadly.

By seven-thirty, Elizabeth had taken herself out – to a seedy bar, no doubt. Alone in the flat, Donna wondered whether the girl from the newspaper office would turn up or not. Pushing the sofa back against the wall, clearing away the ropes and handcuffs, she decided on the professional approach. No messing about, Ryan, she thought as she pressed a patch onto her arm. Dress properly, with knickers, and listen intently to her problem – even if your only interest is in what's up her skirt.

The doorbell rang at eight on the dot. Losing no time, Donna pressed a patch onto the girl's arm as she greeted her. Introducing herself as Charmaine, she said that everyone called her Charlie – pretty, feminine in its masculinity, Donna thought, looking into her deep, dark eyes. Eighteen years old? Certainly no more. Her short black hair framing her sweet baby-doll face, she seemed unreal somehow, a fairytale picture.

Stage one complete, Donna showed her into the lounge, admiring her little red summer dress which hugged her body and flared out below her hips like a pelmet – concealing her panties. Cotton? Silk? Red? White? Wet, sticky with the juice of love? Had she allowed her slender fingers to roam down the front and settle in the groove of her sex? Donna quivered at the thought. Did she masturbate? She hoped so.

'So, what's the problem?' Donna asked, gazing at her pretty little face. Sitting on the sofa facing her, Charlie smiled nervously. She needed encouragement, Donna surmised. 'Take your time. I see all sorts of people with all sorts of problems. There's nothing to worry about. Just relax and make yourself comfortable. When you feel ready, just start chatting – it's easier than you think.'

Fidgeting and fiddling with her dress, her hand pressed between her legs, Charlie looked to Donna and opened her mouth as if to speak. But no words came. What did she want to say? That she loves hiding in the bathroom and masturbating there, that she uses the electric toothbrush to vibrate her clitoris to orgasm? Perhaps her mother had caught her with her knickers down? Donna smiled and waited for the inevitable, anxious to discover her problem.

'It all started when I met Tony,' Charlie began at last. 'We'd been seeing each other for a few weeks and we began to indulge in petting – nothing much, just fiddling around, I suppose. Anyway, as time went by, we got more and more into sex and ended up doing it. He was my first so I didn't know what to expect. It was nice, pleasant, and I enjoyed it – but nothing ever happened to me. My problem is . . . I can't come.'

'Have you tried masturbating?' Donna asked, her clitoris swelling at the thought of the girl lying in her bed at night, her hand between her thighs, rubbing her clitoris, massaging her tight little hole and writhing in her orgasm.

'I've tried, yes, but nothing happens. For hours on end I've . . . Absolutely nothing happens.'

Donna moved to the sofa and sat beside her client. Placing her hand on Charlie's knee, she told her that she had a special form of therapy that would allow her to enjoy sex, not only with her boyfriend, but alone in her bed at night with her fingers. Running her hand up her inner thigh, she smiled as Charlie opened her full lips and breathed deeply, responding to the intimate touch of another woman's fingers as they neared the epicentre of her femininity.

Leaning towards her, Donna kissed her full lips, praying that she'd given the hormone enough time to work. Instinctively, Charlie pushed her tongue into Donna's hot mouth and breathed heavily through her nose, closing her eyes as she melted into her ecstasy. Inhibitions falling away, dropping like autumn leaves, their tongues caressed, touched, as they felt and explored the intimate contours of each other's bodies. 'Take your clothes off,' Donna breathed as she nibbled Charlie's red lips. 'Stand up and take them off for me.'

Obediently, Charlie rose to face her mistress. Reaching her hands up behind her back she unzipped her dress, the top falling from her suntanned body to reveal her brief, red bra. Donna gazed at the silky material, tempted to reach out and lift it clear of her breasts, but no. Wiggling her hips, Charlie eased the tight dress down to her thighs. Now, her matching red panties were in full view – petite, alluring in their female beauty. Bulging with her tightly closed pussy lips, they contained Donna's hot, wet prize, her one and only goal. The dress down to her ankles, Charlie kicked it aside with an abandonment that sent a tingle through Donna's clitoris. The walls watched the seduction – would they remember? Would they tell?

Her hands behind her back again, her breasts pushed forward, she unclipped her bra. Firm, small, well-formed, her breasts were tipped with two little milk buds nestling in the dark discs of her aureolae – eminently suckable. Again, Donna was tempted, but managed to restrain her urge, her wanton desire.

And now for her panties, she thought, her stomach swirling in anticipation. Moving forward, she watched closely as Charlie placed her thumbs between the elastic and her shapely hips and slowly pushed her arms down. Springing to life, free of the confining panties, the sparse, black bush came into view at last. Groomed to perfection, the short hairs did nothing to conceal her full lovelips, Donna observed – never had she seen such wondrous, thick, girl-pouting nether lips. As the girl lifted her knee to slip her panties over her foot they became even fuller, parting slightly – smiling longingly at Donna, she was sure.

'So, you want to come, experience orgasm, do you?' Donna asked as she reached out and stroked the dark hair between Charlie's thighs and ran a finger up her closed groove.

'Yes, I want to come,' she breathed, her hands wandering all over her body as if she'd only just discovered the beauty there.

'Then lie on the floor and show me how you masturbate when you're alone in your bed at night.'

Were the walls still watching as the young girl lay down and spread her legs, reached down for her young, inexperienced clitoris? Were they listening? Why hadn't the phone pest rung again? Donna half hoped he would so she could tell him what was going on in her flat, how she was watching a young, naked girl masturbating on the floor. Would he listen to the noises of female orgasm emanating from the receiver as he, too, masturbated and spilled his sperm on the carpet? 'Now masturbate,' she said softly as Charlie opened her lips wide and settled her fingertips on her protruding bud. Totally uninhibited, she began her caressing, breathing a small sigh as Donna moved in between her legs. 'Is it hard, your little cumbud? Is it stiff?' she asked.

'Yes, yes. It's really hard, nice, silky . . . Ah, ah.'

'Come on, make her come, massage her tip and bring out her pleasure.'

'I will. Bring out her pleasure, that's nice – hard, nice.'

Peeling open the girl's cunt lips, Donna eased a finger into Charlie's tight vaginal tube and felt the hot wetness there, deep within. Charlie opened her pretty little mouth, licked her red lips and moaned her first deep moan of pleasure as her fingers vibrated over her clitoris and Donna thrust between her folds, pounding her cervix. 'You're coming now,' Donna said, as if instructing her to come, ramming her fingers harder into the spasming sheath. 'For the first time in your life, you're going to come.'

Opening her slender legs further, breathing desperately, Charlie parted her swelling quim lips, stretching her young, pink folds as she brought her cumbud to fruition. 'It's coming!' she gasped as her womb contracted. 'It's coming in my cunt!'

Slipping another finger into the tightening sheath, Donna thrust and twisted against the gripping muscles as Charlie lifted her hips off the floor, shuddering and emitting a final cry of unrestrained sexual pleasure. Her eyes rolling, her fingers between her wet, crimson pussy lips, she finally relaxed in the wake of her first-ever orgasm.

'That was wonderful,' she sobbed. 'Absolutely wonderful.'

'I know it was, and there's more to come, my angel,' Donna whispered, stroking the girl's smooth, flat belly. Leaning forward, circling Charlie's navel with her tongue, Donna licked the soft, warm skin of

Ray Gordon

her stomach, moving ever nearer to her young, inflamed groove – her open sex. Charlie shuddered and spread her legs as Donna reached the top of her fleshy furrow and teased the sensitive nerve endings there. Licking, nibbling at the girl's engorged lovelips, she could restrain herself no longer and pushed her tongue into the hot, creamy hole. The juices of youth flowed from her womb as Donna explored the velveteen walls of her tunnel of lust with her tongue.

'My spot!' Charlie gasped. 'Do it to my spot!'

Engulfing the pink protrusion in her hot mouth, Donna sucked, licked and mouthed until a second orgasm grew in the girl's womb. 'I'm coming!' The words bubbled from Charlie's sweet lips as she squeezed her eyes shut and tensed her body in readiness for the exquisite eruptions of lust. Exploding now, her cumbud ballooned and pulsated against Donna's tongue, her vaginal lips swelling, her milky fluid decanting as, again, she flew to her heaven.

Donna gazed longingly at Charlie's young body as she lay trembling uncontrollably in the wash of her climax, her pert mouth open – ready now for Donna's body. Slipping her skirt and panties off, she crawled towards Charlie and knelt astride her head. 'Now *you* will pleasure *me*,' she whispered huskily, gazing down to the girl's hard niplettes. 'Now you will taste the juices of love, drink from my cunette and make *me* come in your pretty little mouth.'

Lowering the epitome of her femininity over the young girl's face, Donna peeled her cunt lips open and settled her wet, pinken curtains of flesh around Charlie's mouth. Immediately, Charlie poked her tongue out and savoured her first-ever taste of female sex fluid as it trickled from the older girl's pulsating sheath. Rocking her hips, Donna looked up to the ceiling as if calling on the goddess of lesbians to carry her away. Gasping, her eyes rolling, she rose quickly to her sexual heaven where she floated upon her orgasm, swirled in the sensual mists of Venus. Unselfish in her giving, Charlie revelled in her mouthing and sucking, experiencing the delight of another woman's clitoris against her tongue, pulsing its pleasure, quelling the tension within her pelvis, her womb.

Gently floating down, breathing her gasps of gratification, Donna shuddered her last shudder and rolled from Charlie's wet face. Kissing her red lips now, pressing her tongue into her mouth, she tweaked Charlie's nipples, ran her hand between her legs to fondle her wetness.

'Did you like that?' she asked.

'Yes, very much,' Charlie whispered faintly as her clitoris responded delightfully to Donna's caress. 'Make me come again, please.'

Rubbing the pinken hood gently over her hard nodule, Donna quickly brought out the girl's third orgasm. Her heart pounding, her stomach rising and falling, her breasts heaving, she tossed her head from side to side before letting out a cry of submission. 'Enough!' she sobbed as her entire body slowly submerged into a velvety pool of orgasm. 'No more – I can't take any more!'

'Then you shall rest, my sweet,' Donna whispered as she kissed each hard niplette in turn and rose to her feet.

When Charlie had recovered, Donna helped her dress. Slipping her red panties up over the younger girl's wet cunette, she invited her round the following evening. 'I'd love to come again,' Charlie smiled.

'But I'm supposed to be seeing my boyfriend, Mark.'

'Bring him with you, if you have to,' Donna said coolly, cupping Charlie's breasts in her hands as she fastened her bra. 'But you'll have to watch him pleasure me – make love to me.'

Charlie said nothing as she pulled her dress on. What were her thoughts? Did she own Mark? Was he a possession to be possessed? Did he possess *her?* Donna would free the girl of her teenage thoughts and liberate her – bring out the lesbian in her. Slipping the patch from her neck as she zipped up her dress, Donna asked Charlie if she'd ever sucked her boyfriend's penis. 'No, I haven't,' the girl replied solemnly. Donna guessed that he'd asked her to take him in her mouth, to suck the sperm from the swollen head of his manhood, and she had declined.

'Then you will suck him tomorrow evening,' she announced.

'But . . . I don't . . .'

'Tomorrow evening you will learn of new things, Charlie. Go now. Go home and pleasure yourself in your bed and think of me, my body as you come. I have given you your body – use it.'

Alone in her flat, Donna looked to the walls and wondered. If only they could speak, they would tell stories of sex and lust, whisper the murmurings of the lesbians they had shrouded from the world. But secrets remain secrets when only the walls know.

The phone rang as she settled on the sofa and closed her eyes, contemplating her new life, her body, and all the delights the future held. Sleepy now, she let it ring. Whoever it was, whatever they wanted, she, lost in her dreams, didn't want to know.

Chapter Ten

Donna woke to another day, a day of sun, warmth – sex. Elizabeth had risen early and left her with the dawn, leaving only a dent in her pillow in memory of her presence – a happy, sad day. Stirring, stretching her legs under her billowing quilt, Donna opened her eyes a little wider and sighed.

Her thoughts wandered as her fingers of love wandered, roamed around her body seeking out the crevices, the contours, the curves as her warm, silky-smooth skin tingled with life beneath her fingertips. Rough, stubbly hair was returning to cover the naked girlishness of her mound. Why? she wondered. Mother Nature's blunder – ugly, tangled hair concealing the beauty of the female form. Everything had a reason for being, a reason for everything being. Did angels have pubic hair – genitals?

Dreamily wandering into the bathroom, she returned to her bed clutching a tube of depilating cream and a damp flannel. Her groove opened, demanding attention as she sat in the middle of the bed examining her body, vibrant with lust. Massaging the cool cream into her mound, her swelling lovelips, she lay back on her pillow and kicked the quilt to the floor. The sun bathed her, warmed her nakedness as the cream dissolved her camouflage, the heart-shaped symbol of youth growing just above her little slit. Her clitoris swelled as if in appreciation of its freedom from the veil of hair. Eyes peered, she was sure.

In her sleepy haze, she wiped away the cream and brushed her fingertips over the smoothness of her mound, her puffy quim lips. Looking down between her breasts, over the creamy plateau of her stomach, she smiled at her 'front bottom,' as her mother had called it. Reminiscence of adolescence – a return to the eve of womanhood. Blossoming years – the ripening of breast buds, the swelling vaginal lips of young girls, the awakening of cumbuds beneath inquisitive little fingers.

Where were Helen and Sophie? she wondered. Why hadn't they been in touch? Slaves on the loose weren't slaves – they needed to be handcuffed, chained, used. They should be naked, wet, prepared always to follow instructions – to love and pleasure their mistress. Regularly punished, they wouldn't disappear. Cane them daily – tie them over the back of the sofa and spank their pretty bottoms for their disobedience. Side by side, their young buttocks would glow crimson, burn with desire under the cane. Correction was the only way to control naughty slaves.

Picking up the bedside phone, Donna called Sue. Helen answered. 'Do you know,' she began immediately. 'I haven't had one panic attack since . . . since that first time with you. Strange, that, isn't it?'

'Very,' Donna replied coldly. 'Where the hell have you been? What have you been up to?'

'Around and about with Sophie. We do everything together now.'

'Everything?'

'Yes, everything. I have a great deal to thank you for, Donna.'

'Indeed you have, so why don't you both come round and thank me?'

Hesitation – didn't Helen want her body anymore? The attraction of a younger girl, a tighter, unblemished young girl such as Sophie was understandable, but not acceptable. Jealous, Donna's heart sank as she imagined the girls enjoying each other's bodies, without her. Kissing, writhing naked as they licked between each other's thighs, lapped up the cream from their hot, swollen slits. Girls would be girls – but would be punished for being *naughty* girls, she decided.

'Are you working today?' Helen asked.

'Yes, I am. Why?'

'Sophie and I have nothing to do, we could have come round.'

'I can't really take the day off, things have been happening at the lab – I must go in.'

'This evening, then?'

'Yes, about seven.'

'Okay, I'll tell Sophie. See you later.'

Charlie? Poor Charlie, she'd have to be initiated as a slave somewhat sooner than Donna would have liked. Thrown in at the deep end – was she ready? With a patch or two, she'd be ready for anything, Donna decided. What would her boyfriend do? Confronted by one, two, four naked girls, what would he do? How hard would his penis become with four tongues licking? Donna quivered lasciviously at the thought. But first there was the day to get through, she realised, glancing at the clock. Five past eight. Was Lynn Bulmur enjoying her breakfast? In her police cell, probably not.

After a quick shower, she was ready for her workout in the park. Rummaging through her wardrobe, she pulled out her pink trainers, shorts and T-shirt. He'd better be there, she thought as she dressed and pressed a patch onto her arm. Did she need the hormone to enjoy her body? Now that she'd become sexually aware beyond belief, discovered her clitoris, did she need the patch? Twenty past eight. 'He'd better be there. I'm not going to be late for work for nothing,' she thought aloud as her clitoris stirred expectantly between her wet, puffy lips.

As she opened the front door, the phone rang.

'Donna, it's Steve,' a male voice whispered.

'Steve, how's your marriage?'

'Don't ask. Listen, did you hear about Lynn's flat?'

'I did, and the break-in at the lab – what's she trying to do?'

'Get herself into a lot of trouble, if you ask me. I was just wondering if . . . Well, the photographs she has of you, do you know where they are?'

'Why should I know?'

'It's crazy, I know, but it occurred to me that it might have been you who did her place.'

'Put it this way, I didn't *do* her place, as you put it, but I do have the photographs in my possession.'

'Great, I knew it was you the minute I heard the news. Any chance of returning the ones of Debbie?'

'There might be.'

'Might?'

'We'll see. I rather like having things on people, having people over a barrel, it gives me a sense of power.'

'Oh, great! Look, the wife's lurking so I can't talk for long. If it's power you want, then why not do something with the patches? Debbie's become a nymphomaniac since you gave me a couple.'

'I thought you said not to ask about your marriage?'

'Yes, I did. It's not good. Debbie's become a nympho-maniac all right, but not only with me. She'll have absolutely anyone, whether in skirt or trousers, she doesn't care.'

'So? Why not join in? It'll brighten up your sex life.'

'No, I don't want to share her.'

'Right, so you screw around and she can't, is that it? One rule for men and another for women?'

'Something like that – it's tradition, isn't it?'

'Tradition, my fanny! Anyway, things are going to change. Women are about to become powerful. Look, I'll call you sometime, I've got to go out now.'

'Women need men, they always will. Anyway, think about the pics, won't you? I need them. See you.'

Rather than jog, Donna walked to the park to conserve her energy. Women need men. The words echoed in her mind. No, they didn't – women needed each other. Why had Elizabeth left so early? She could have said good-bye, kissed goodbye, loved goodbye. Perhaps she was with Alan, loving him, sucking him? Donna hoped not, prayed not. But Alan was not a possession, he didn't belong to her, did he? Apprehension fluttered in her stomach. Would she meet Barry the jogger, pull his shorts down and eat him for breakfast? Would he eat her? She had to admit, she needed a man – Barry.

The park was deserted, but Donna felt eyes upon her, burning her skin as they stared. Breathing in the fresh air she relaxed, emptied her mind as she wandered across the freshly mown grass and sat on the bench by the trees. What is this life? she mused, thoughts of Alan filtering into her void. Jealousy again – he had taken Elizabeth, screwed her without feeling or emotion. So had she, but that was somehow different. Love? They sing about it, write about it, make films about it, search for it – kill for it. So what was it? That sinking, fluttering feeling in the pit of your stomach when you think of having sex with one special person, she thought – that was love. The stirring in the womb when a special tongue licks, probes between swollen, pinken folds. Shit! Why now? Why the dawning now, when she'd just discovered her body, her cunt, other women's bodies – orgasm? Donna supposed that she'd always loved Alan, fallen in love with him the day she'd met him. So what had changed? A wild need to suppress the emotion, the feeling, push it away and taste life – sexual freedom – she supposed.

The jogger coming into view, Alan disappeared from Donna's thoughts. Moving towards her across the grass as if expecting her, he quickened his pace and waved. Was his penis stiffening as it bounced under his silky shorts? Nearer now, she could see his hard, tanned chest, his muscly legs. Nearer still, she could see his shorts, full, bulging with her prize.

'Anyone would think you were expecting me to be here,' Donna smiled as he collapsed on the seat beside her.

'Perhaps I was,' he panted. 'Been waiting long?'

'About ten minutes. I'm often early when I meet my boyfriend.'

'Boyfriend? But I thought you were a . . .'

'Lesbian? I can be, when I want to be. What are you?'

'A man, a normal man.'

Normal? Follow the masses and you're normal – were sheep normal? she wondered.

There were things people did and things they didn't do in relationships, she decided. Being in love with Alan – and Helen and Sophie and Sue . . . It was sometimes necessary to look outside a relationship for things – those certain things that certain people couldn't or wouldn't do. Barry, she knew, with his hard, rugged body, his ample penis, his dark, deep-set eyes, wouldn't hesitate to do those certain things. He was totally irresistible – to a woman wearing a patch, anyway.

Wandering into the trees, she waited for him to follow. Who was in control, really? Who called the shots? She wanted him as much as he wanted her – but was she in charge? The all-powerful patch brought power – control.

'How's your girlfriend?' she asked as he joined her, leaning on the fence at the edge of the railway cutting.

'She's still my girlfriend, if that's what you mean. How's yours?'

'Which one?'

'How many are there?'

Her hand by her side, she reached out and felt the hardness within his shorts. 'Enough,' she answered, wondering when he'd last screwed his girlfriend, whether his bulging shaft was still wet with her come juice. 'Is she good in bed?'

'Good enough, I suppose.'

'Had she really screwed someone else?'

'I think so. She denied it, of course, but I think so.'

One rule for us and another for them, she reflected. When a man lays a woman, he's a hero – turn it around and she's a whore. Why? But the tables always turned. The patches would see to that – turn women into people with minds of their own. One day, one fine day, women would rule.

His penis grew harder and he breathed heavily as she manipulated the bulbous knob through his silky shorts. To leave him like that would be fun, she thought. Bring him close to orgasm, suck him until he begged to come and then leave him stiff and panting. Perhaps he'd masturbate in the bushes when she'd gone? Or go home to screw his possession, his girlfriend, fill her with his hot sperm whether she wanted him or not? Lie back and think of England – not anymore. Women would be on top, realising their wants, their needs.

'Why waste time?' Donna breathed as she fell to her knees and pulled his shorts down to his ankles. Free now, bathed in the hot sun, his penis wavered, swung from side to side, like a tree in the wind. Long, thick, hard, Donna examined the shaft, admired the loose skin, pulled it back to reveal the silky-smooth head.

'My sentiments entirely,' he replied, clinging to the fence as she pulled back his foreskin as far as she could to engulf his purple bulb in her hot, wet mouth. Birds singing in the trees above, a dog barking somewhere in the distance – all became lost as Donna sucked, licked, rolled her tongue round and round and drifted into a sexual haze.

A diesel engine rumbled through the cutting, pulling trucks of road stone, heavy rocks. His balls were heavy in her hand, heavy rocks of desire. She kneaded them, cupped and weighed them, took one in her mouth to explore the wrinkled skin with her tongue. Back to his shaft now, she gently bit the hardness, teasing her way up to his silky knob, her tongue darting and licking all the time. His shaft twitched as she licked around the rim of the head before taking it in her mouth again and suckling like a babe at the breast.

'Does she do this to you?' Donna asked, pulling away.

'No, she won't,' he gasped as she again engulfed him.

'And does she do this?' she enquired, standing up and

pulling her shorts off. Barry gaped as she turned her back to him, straddled her feet and touched her toes. Wide-eyed, disbelieving, he gazed in wonder at the spread buttocks, opened delightfully, the bloated quim lips, smooth, naked, wet and swelling beneath the dark crease, revealing the centre of her girlishness.

'She won't do that, either,' he murmured as he pushed the head of his penis between Donna's pink cushions and drove it deep into her hot, trembling body.

'Then what does she do?'

'Missionary – ah, that's good! Mission . . . Ah, God! You're hot, tight, wet!'

Penetrating deeper than she would have believed possible, he rammed his rod home time and again, filling and stretching the delicate lining of her love sheath until she thought she'd split open. Her hand between her thighs now, she located her clitoris and massaged the hardness, bringing it out from its hood, swelling it to capacity. Was it larger, longer now? Or was it her imagination? Remembering Professor Winmann's words, Donna hoped that her clitoris was growing. Her orgasms were getting better, stronger, more sustaining, all the time. How would they be in a few weeks' time?

Suddenly Barry grabbed her hips and groaned as his ballooning knob exploded deep within her fleshy cavern, gushing its sperm, throbbing, filling her. Donna vibrated her fingers faster over her clitoris, bringing it to fruition in time with Barry's climax. 'Ah, yes! Fuck my cunt! Fuck me!'

As her lustful cries echoed through the wood, disturbing the summery hazy air, the birds, the trees, the spasming tube of her cunette crushed his shaft as she reached her peak and poured out the slippery fruits of her orgasm, bathing, lubricating the piston within her cylinder. She trembled, her legs weak as he finished his thrusting, spurting his last spurt. Done now, he withdrew and fell to the soft grass where he lay moaning in his ecstasy, gazing at the creamy offering between Donna's gaping cunt lips.

'Lick me now!' she gasped, reaching behind her buttocks and opening her wet hole to his wide eyes. Moving forward, he knelt behind her rudely exposed body and pressed his tongue into the dark hotness, licking, slurping as he drank his sperm from her intimacy. Pushing his thumb into her smaller hole he stirred new life within her bowels, woke the nerves there to bring her overwhelming sensations of lust. Gently massaging her solid cumbud with his fingertips, he continued his mouthing and sucking and thumbing until shuddering, she decanted her cream into his thirsty mouth.

Trembling as her young body locked in the grips of a multiple orgasm that seemed to go on and on, Donna eventually collapsed to the ground, her face buried in the soft grass, breathing in the smell of summer – savouring the sweet sensations of orgasm as they drifted from her body, leaving her calm, serene.

Wiping his mouth on the back of his hand, Barry pulled up his shorts and crept through the trees and out into the park, leaving her with only the grass and the sound of trundling trains. Writhing, panting, milky fluid oozing from her inflamed tunnel entrance, Donna breathed deeply, her heart slowing – Eve abandoned on the soft grass in her garden of love after Adam had done with her.

Lucidity fell from the morning sky like hail, stinging her into waking from her dream-like world. Why had

Barry left without a word? Sneaked off through the trees to disappear like a sly fox? Guilt, perhaps? Was he jogging back to his girlfriend, rehearsing his lies, his words of unshakable loyalty – words of love?

Picking herself up, she pulled her shorts over her swollen, naked cleft and staggered through the trees into the park, her sheath oozing, dripping its satisfaction. People moved about the paths, the grass, some wandering aimlessly, some with an urgent direction. What was the hurry? Work, reality, money – nine-fifteen.

Trotting now, warm fluid trickling down her inner thighs, there was an increasing urgency in her step. The police, Lynn Bulmur, the lab – Alan. Thoughts blew in circles, whipped up in eddy currents of hope, fear, danger, excitement. Opening her front door, she slipped inside and went into the kitchen to find a note from Elizabeth. Panting from her exertion, she read aloud: 'Thanks for everything, it was fun – beautiful. Ring me sometime – 436782. All the best – Liz.'

Liz? What had happened to Elizabeth? Miss Prim and Proper, straitlaced Elizabeth! Dashing upstairs, she threw a skirt and top on and rushed from the flat. Excuses, lies. What to tell Alan? Concoct some fantastic story? Yes, he'd believe anything, she was sure. Blinded by love, he'd believe anything. Poor, trusting Alan. Had he masturbated alone in his bed, thought of her squatting over his face, sucking sperm from his penis as he licked at her cunette? Poor, used Alan.

'Sorry I'm late,' she gasped, flying into the lab. 'I was caught up in . . .'

'Miss Donna Ryan?' A policeman walked towards her from the corner of the lab where he'd been waiting, lurking. She flashed a questioning look at

Alan. Shrugging, he half smiled, raising his eyebrows.

'Yes, that's me,' she replied, placing her bag on the bench.

'I'd like to ask you a few questions concerning Lynn Bulmur. I believe you know her?'

'I know *of* her.'

'She tells us that you're blackmailing her.'

'What? Blackmailing her! How?'

'She also claims that you broke into her flat on the evening of the twenty-second.'

'I was at home all the evening. Elizabeth, she was staying with me for a few days. She came in drunk – I couldn't leave her alone.'

'And I was at Miss Ryan's flat, too,' Alan interrupted.

'How long did you stay there, sir?'

'Until the early hours. We were . . . We were discussing our research work.'

'So you didn't leave your home at all that night, Miss Ryan?'

'No, not at all.'

'Well, everything seems to be in order. Thank you for your time.'

Alone, Donna looked to Alan and asked why he'd lied. 'I don't know,' he replied. 'I suppose I didn't want to see you get into trouble.'

'Trouble? So you think that I broke into her flat?'

'I don't think anything. I don't want to know anything. Let's leave it at that, shall we?'

He was hurt, upset about something, she knew. But why? What had she done to him? What did he know? He couldn't know anything, could he? The episodes in the park were a well-kept secret, and besides, he didn't know Sue or Barry. He couldn't know about Steve the photographer, or Elizabeth. Well, he knew her intimately, but that wasn't a problem. Anyway, Elizabeth had gone, flown on the wind – the wind of lust.

'Is anything wrong?' Donna asked.

'No. Should there be?' Alan replied indifferently.

'You tell me. You seem different today. Have I done something to upset you?'

He looked down, to hide the truth mirrored in his eyes, she surmised. Was her red miniskirt too short? Too long? Her nipples too blatant without a bra? She looked down to the floor. No sperm dripping from her knickerless pussy, no tell-tale signs that she had just been fucked in the park, had a hard penis ram her cervix, fill her cunt with orgasm. God, he didn't know about the patches, the missing hormone, surely? What was his problem?

'I'm leaving the lab,' Donna blurted out, unsure why. To shock, perhaps?

'For good?' Uncaring words – why?

'Yes, I suppose so. I've been here too long. There are things I want to do, important things. Important to me, anyway.'

'Things?'

'All sorts of things. I want to become someone, do something with my life. Stuck here all day every day . . . I need more time.'

'What will you do for money?'

What indeed? Sell patches? Charge women for consultations? Fifty pounds an hour – reasonable for the gift of orgasm, the best orgasms they'd experienced in their lives, if indeed they'd had any at all before. The newspaper ad would be out tomorrow, she remembered. She'd have to be at home to take the calls from the hordes of desperate women.

Still wearing her patch, she was only too well aware of

the need between her legs as she looked at Alan. Fulfil
desires – his, hers. Why not? she thought ravenously,
moving towards him, tugging her skirt up a little higher.
Sitting on the corner of his bench, her shapely thighs
parted enough to display her smooth, puffy quim lips,
she smiled sweetly, childlike.

'I'm very fond of you, Alan,' she whispered.

He looked up to her eyes before lowering his gaze to
the sweet, creamy temptation between her legs.

'And I'm fond of you, Donna,' he replied coolly. 'I
must get on, I've a lot to do today, if you don't mind.'

Slipping off the bench, she picked up her bag and
flounced from the lab. Fair enough, she thought, have
it your own way – don't have it at all. Were the
all-powerful patches losing their touch? Anger rising
now, she decided never to return to the lab, to change
her life, to do something exciting – naughty.

The summery breeze drifted up her short skirt, cooling her wet pussy lips as she walked down the street.
Power, she ruminated. Power between my legs, to do
anything, have anything – except Alan. Walking up the
steps to the railway station, she smiled. That was it.
Another brazen decision – a decision that would change
everything, permanently.

'Return to Brackly Heath, please,' she said to the
pale-faced young man behind the glass. Was he
married? Did he masturbate in his ticket office when
there were no people around? Yes, she thought. He'd
watch the people coming and going from the station –
women, young girls in short skirts, and then, when all
was quiet, he'd pull out his stiff penis and masturbate
while fantasising about the female passengers.

'Due in two minutes,' he replied mechanically. 'One
pound fifty, please.'

Wandering onto the platform, Donna gazed at the dozen or so people milling around. A man with an umbrella and a briefcase. A woman trying unsuccessfully to control her two children. A vicar. A couple of college students, laughing, joking, pretending to try and push each other onto the railway line. She moved towards the students as the train pulled in – towards her prey. One opened the door for her, admiring her legs as she stepped into the train. Chivalry? Or sexual expectation?

Making her way to the rear of the train, Donna was aware that the young men were following her, probably hoping to sit opposite her and catch the odd glimpse of her knickers. Chivalry deserved reward, she decided as she sat in the deserted carriage and parted her legs slightly. Assuming an angelic look, she gazed out of the window as the train lurched and pulled out of the station. She liked trains – rocking, vibrating, stimulating. Excitement welled in her womb as the young men sat opposite her, gazing wide-eyed at her shaven nether lips. What were they thinking? Had they ever seen swollen, shaven pussy lips before? Had they ever seen a pussy?

Were they virgins? Donna wondered, imagining, at eighteen or so, their nice growth of black hair, fresh, unblemished shafts, well formed, hard knobs. What to do? The fifteen-minute journey left little time for playing around, teasing, tantalising. Opening her legs as wide as she could, she grinned provocatively at her young prey. 'You may touch,' she proffered seductively, parting her wet cunt lips with her slender fingers to expose her hard clitoris, her wet hole, to their disbelieving eyes.

Donna's juices flowed in torrents, her clitoris making

urgent calls as they watched, nudged each other, whispered. One fell to his knees and roughly stroked the wet, pinken flesh. Obviously inexperienced, he attempted to push a finger into the hot hole, but failed to locate her entrance. Taking his hand, she closed her eyes as she gently guided him into her sheath. Exploring, feeling, groping around in the wet warmth, he lowered his head to examine her intimate, complex folds. His first time, she reflected, as he pushed another finger into her quivering cunt and began thrusting with a frenzied urgency. 'Gently, slowly,' she breathed. 'Take your time, finger me, caress me.'

Moving aside, he chivalrously allowed his friend to discover the delights of a young woman's body. Now they both silently fingered, toyed, stroked as the train lurched again and gathered speed to enter the cutting – Donna's cutting. Looking up, she noticed the fence by the trees and smiled. Secrets lurked there, high above. Only the trees and the soft grass knew of her sexy secrets.

'Your turn, boys,' Donna said huskily, scanning their expectant faces. 'Both stand up and lower your trousers.' Power. Hesitantly, they stood and fiddled with their belts as she waited, her patience wearing thin, her frustration rising, her mouth hungry. Helping them now, she tugged on their trousers and pulled them down to their knees to expose their youth in its youthful stiffness. Gazing longingly at her prizes, she reached out and grabbed the hard penises in her hands. Rigid, young, fresh, virginal, they twitched delightfully as she pulled the foreskins back and exposed their hard, purple knobs. Had their hands played there, toyed with their foreskins, masturbated? Yes, daily, nightly.

Pulling on their rods, Donna moved them nearer and opened her mouth. Sucking hard on one, she heard a delighted gasp – a gasp of young male pleasure. Now the other – another gasp. Sucking, licking, mouthing both in turn, she elicited their full stiffness – her young, male slaves. Her mouth wide, her mind afire with lust, she took both heads together and sucked them into her hot mouth where she savoured the taste of their sex. Side by side they twitched, throbbed as she moved the skin of their shafts back and forth with her hands, tickled their balls with her fingernails, enticed their sperm to pump and fill her. Gasping, the boys gazed down at their penises, at her lips, stretched, her mouth full, her cheeks ballooning.

To Donna's delight, they came together, spurting their fresh sperm into her mouth, filling her to the brim as she gulped and swallowed and ran her tongue round and round the young knobs. Her eyes rolled, her clitoris pulsed as she drank from her young slaves. What would they tell their friends? Whatever they boasted, they'd not be believed – not in a million years. Milking the solid shafts between her fingers and thumbs, she grinned, allowing them their freedom only when they were completely drained. If only she could give them a memento, something to prove to their friends that they'd been sucked off by a woman on the train, had come in her mouth together.

Allowing them to lift her top off, examine her breasts and each suck a nipple, Donna waited until their stiffness returned, until their young shafts had recovered from their milking, before making her next move – before giving them the ultimate delight a woman's body has to offer. Sliding down in her seat, she beckoned one to kneel between her legs. Grabbing his hardness, she guided him into her body, instructing him to move his hips back and forth and give her his virginity. Gazing at his shaft, sinking, disappearing into her cunt to reappear again, wet and glistening with her juices, he groaned and shuddered and all too quickly filled her with his second coming. Rubbing her clitoris, she, too, reached her climax, crushing the young penis within her hot hole until he collapsed over her belly – a man.

As soon as he withdrew, Donna beckoned her second fledgling. Kneeling on the floor he grinned sheepishly, his penis standing to attention, awaiting its first-ever taste of a woman's vagina. Quickly, he thrust it in and began his fucking motions, looking to his friend for confirmation that he was actually doing it to a woman, and not dreaming. Lasting longer than his friend, he rammed Donna's cervix until she shuddered and arched her back, emitting her wail of orgasm. On and on the waves of sexual euphoria rolled, sustained by the rocking and swaying of the train. Crushing him, lubricating him with her juices of lust, she thrust her hips to meet his grinding as he spurted deep within her love sheath, mingling his sperm with his friend's until he fell to the floor, his virginity gone forever.

Tugging their trousers up as the train pulled into the station, they smiled at her but said nothing. The class was over, the lesson of love learned.

'Do you live near the park? Greenford Park?' Donna asked as they opened the door.

'Not far,' one replied.

'I might see you both there once in a while.'

'Our train gets in at four from college. We usually cut

through the park on our way home, around quarter past four.'

'I'll remember that. I often walk through the trees by the railway cutting. I may well see you both.'

Running along the platform, they'd disappeared by the time Donna had adjusted her clothes and climbed from the train. She'd be there in the park, she knew, as she stood and watched the train move off. Milky fluid dripped from her open hole onto the sunbaked platform as she watched the train grow smaller, until it was just a shimmering speck in the hot distance. Parks in the summer were for loving, fucking. Probably every afternoon, she'd be there.

But now, Donna had other things on her mind. Quickly, she left the station and walked into the town. The man in the shop grinned as she entered and closed the door. 'What can I do for you?' he asked, eyeing her short red skirt. Nothing, she thought, sickened by the sight of his fat belly hanging over his trousers. Filthy old man – did he masturbate? Definitely. Didn't all men – and women?

'I'm just looking,' Donna replied, gazing at the leather catsuits, vibrators, whips, creams, gels and a host of other equipment designed to bring untold pleasure to the flesh. She'd read about the shop in the local paper, about a group of women protesting with banners, but she never thought she'd be standing there, selecting a vibrator and inspecting leather bondage gear. They had to be women who didn't like sex, she mused. Or women who didn't want others to have orgasms and enjoy their bodies just because they couldn't. Selfish, narrow minds, unhappy in love – unknowing in lust.

'Don't you have better quality vibrators than these?'

Donna asked, holding up a pink, plastic phallus. He pointed to the rear of the shop.

'Over there. A bit costly, but you get what you pay for, love.'

'This one will do me,' she said, taking a huge, chromium-plated vibrator from the shelf. 'And these,' she added, dumping a leather catsuit, a whip, chains, and a leather collar on the counter.

'Looks as if you're in for a good time,' he quipped as he rang up the till. 'A party, is it?'

'No, not a party. These are for my young female slaves,' Donna said impishly. 'They need correcting, punishing when they don't pleasure me properly – you know what young girls are like.'

She could almost feel the arousal in his expression, in his trousers, as he stuffed the items into a bag. Power. 'Can you put some batteries into the vibrator for me, please? I'll be needing it on the train,' she explained, grinning at the disbelief in his eyes. 'The hot weather makes me very wet and sticky, and as you'll know, that means I need to come.'

Roaming around the shop while she waited, Donna picked up a length of wood with metal rings at either end. 'What's this for?' she asked, determined to shock him. 'What do you do with it?

'It goes between the feet, or hands, to keep the limbs apart,' he enlightened her as the vibrator burst into life. 'You fix handcuffs or whatever to the rings and ankles or wrists.'

'Interesting. I'll take it. And these?' she enquired, holding up a pair of metal clamps.

'Nipple clamps – they're for . . .'

'I know what they're for, thank you. I'll take three pairs.'

'Three?'

'Six nipples – three pairs, right? Or can't you add up? What have you got in the way of clamps or whatever for men?'

'Men?'

'Penises – clamps, restraints, I don't know.'

'Oh, right. I've got these rings for clamping . . . Well, self-explanatory, really.'

'I'll take two, please.'

'Two?'

'Two penises, two rings, yes?'

Stifling a laugh, Donna paid for her bondage equipment and left the shop, hoisting her skirt up as she closed the door to give him a good view of her firm buttocks by way of thanks for his help. If only he knew her young cunette had just been filled with sperm by two young strangers, she thought. He'd probably join the ticket man and spurt his sperm all over the floor, or use a blow-up doll to relieve himself.

On the train home, Donna found an empty carriage and pulled the vibrator from the bag. Opening her legs, she switched the phallus on and slipped it under her skirt. Pushing it between her wet lips, gently resting the cool metal tip against her expectant clitoris, she lay back and closed her eyes as the sensations swirled in her clitoris, wet her soft sheath and stiffened her cumbud, quickly taking her to the trembling verge of orgasm. The vibrations were powerful, delightful, transmitting their music of lust down through her clitoris and into her womb, where they stirred new sensations – female sensations of erotic pleasure. Swelling, pulsating, her bud suddenly burst, sending rapturous waves of ecstasy over her shuddering body as the train swayed and lurched.

Her climax subsiding, Donna's bud suddenly burst again, the pleasure from the vibrator reverberating through her love tube and deep into her pelvis as she cried out in her wondrous moment of euphoria. The sensations tore through her body before declining, letting her down from her ecstasy, only to take her up again to another mind-blowing peak. Her body, her mind, was torn, ripped apart, opened by the painful pleasure between her ballooning pussy lips, her rock-hard clitoris, her rhythmically tightening cunt. Coasting along a valley of wanton sex, she finally came to a halt, panting, perspiring after her first real multiple orgasm. Who needs men now? she pondered, slipping the sticky vibrator into her bag. Who needs anyone?

Looking down between her legs as the train pulled into the station, she gazed in awe at her inflamed lips, drenched with the liquid of sex, swelled by the wondrous tingling of the vibrator. How would Sophie and Helen respond to her new toy? she wondered as she staggered from the train into the hot sun. Charlie would writhe in ecstasy on the sofa as the vibrations rocked her young body. She'd come and come again, producing torrents of milky fluid for her consumption. Handcuffed, dressed in the leather suit with her nipples pushed through the cut-outs, her quim lips swelling through the open crotch, she'd cry out her pleasure as her body trembled with the most powerful multiple orgasm imaginable. Lucky Charlie.

The ticket man smiled as she passed with her bag containing her new and exciting future. What was his future? Selling tickets for the rest of his life? Bounding down the station steps she held her bag, the ticket to her destiny, tightly under her arm as she planned her evening of seduction.

The strange feeling of being watched, followed, roused her from her reverie. She turned her head, but saw-no one. Perhaps it was Lucifer, lurking invisible somewhere – goading, coaxing. What did he want? Her body, her soul – or both?

Chapter Eleven

Thunder rumbled somewhere in the distance – hot, summery thunder. Donna looked up to see a huge, dark cloud drifting across the sky – ominous, heavy, evil in its blackness. Perhaps it was a symbol, an omen, warning of what was to come, what was in store for her? As she turned into her street, the cloud burst as if acknowledging her presence, releasing its cooling rain to freshen the hazy air and cleanse the hot, dusty pavements. Cleanse her. She liked the rain and hoped that it would be falling from the sky in the morning. How exquisite to make love with Barry naked on the wet grass, bathed, stroked by the sensual fingers of the falling rain.

Lynn Bulmur was sitting on the doorstep chewing gum when she arrived at her flat. Her hair wet and matted, her nipples pressing against her wet T-shirt, she looked forlorn, dejected, an unwanted child – a washed-out tart. Looking up, she half smiled. A truce? Or was the devil's daughter planning something? What was she hiding up her sleeve? Or up her skirt? Lightning shot across the sky, thunder crashed, echoing between the buildings.

'Can I come in?' Lynn asked as Donna opened the front door.

'What for? To blackmail me?'

'I want to talk to you.'

'Then talk out here. You're not coming into my home, not after all the trouble you've caused me!'

'You're in more trouble, you'll be pleased to hear,' Lynn began with a strange glint in her eye. 'I've been chatting to Debbie, Steve's wife. We got together and decided that you need sorting out, dealing with once and for all.'

'Really? And how do you intend to sort me out – deal with me?'

'You've got fire insurance, haven't you? I hope so for your sake, because fires start so easily. When you're out at work, the place could go up without warning and you'd suddenly become homeless. My flat was wrecked the other night, by the way. A thief, a burglar, a bastard – or a bitch. Of course, you'd know nothing about that, would you? But there's a good example of how break-ins happen when you're out. Anything can – and probably will – happen when you're out.'

'Idle threats don't bother me, Bulmur. I've got the photographs of you, and Debbie – and you've got nothing on me, absolutely nothing.'

'True, but until we get the photographs back, there's no saying what might happen to your precious little flat. Anyway, I thought you'd sent a picture of me to the DSS?'

'No, I didn't bother – but it's still an option I'm considering. And unless you stop pestering me and get out of my life for good, I will send them one – and the Revenue. They'll assess you, of course. How much could a tart like you earn in a week, I wonder? No, you'd be safe enough with the taxman. A fiver a week is well under taxable income – and with a body like yours, you'd be lucky to earn that from half-a-dozen men.'

Watching Lynn strut down the street, Donna bit her

lip. The devil's daughter *would* set fire to the place, there was no doubt about that. She'd stop at nothing to get her hands on the photographs. But what to do? Return the pictures and have no ammunition? With the advert coming out in the paper the next day, she didn't want the likes of Bulmur hanging around. Suddenly, Donna panicked.

'Lynn!' she called. 'Come back and we'll talk.'

Lynn turned and headed back, grinning triumphantly.

'I thought you'd see sense,' she sneered as she followed Donna into the hall and shut the door. 'No patches, though. You won't get at me like that.'

'I'm wearing one now, why not talk and have some fun at the same time?'

Donna knew Lynn was tempted as she pulled a patch from her bag and held it out. Tie her up, chain her and thrash her with the whip – keep her imprisoned, forever. 'Come on, just because we have our differences, it doesn't mean to say that we can't have some fun. And I didn't mean what I said about your body.'

'No. I know your sort of fun. You'd probably tie me up and . . .'

'Please yourself. I'm going to get changed out of these wet clothes. I'll be back in a minute.'

Lynn seemed overly worried, Donna thought. Why come round to the flat with threats of setting fire to the place? Surely, she wasn't that bothered about the DSS or the Inland Revenue? Unless there was something else on her mind. What or who was she frightened of? What with being pulled for prostitution, and then the break-in at the lab, things weren't looking good for her. But she sensed there was more. With the sort of people Lynn professed to know, she could well be in serious trouble. What was she hiding?

Dressed in her leather catsuit, her nipples protruding beautifully through the neat holes in the soft cups supporting her hard breasts, her pouting cunt lips bulging from the triangular cut-out between her legs, Donna wandered into the lounge and grinned at Lynn. Was she lubricating? Would Lynn stand before her and suck on her nipples? Pull on the metal ring beneath her neck and unzip the suit?

Donna decided to call Lynn's bluff, to make out that she knew more than she did. Hopefully, Lynn would fall into the trap and spill the beans – then lick the soft flesh so appetisingly presented between her slim thighs. Why didn't she want to wear a patch, to experience the intoxicating heights of lust possible only between two girls? Donna wanted to – desperately.

'I know that you're not bothered about the DSS or the Inland Revenue,' she began as Lynn lowered her gaze to Donna's swelling pussy lips, to the smaller, pink folds protruding like young birds from the nest, awaiting food. 'I know what, or should I say, *who* it is that you're afraid of.'

'You haven't had a call, have you? Has someone been round to see you?' Lynn asked, her eyes bulging with fear.

'I'm not saying anything other than I know a damn sight more than you realise. I've spoken to Steve and . . .'

'Steve doesn't know the half of it.'

'Doesn't he? He knows more than you think.'

'Look, the photographs, I must have them back or . . .'

'Or what? Will you mysteriously disappear one night without a trace? Perhaps you'll be found in the river? Unless you fill me in on the details, I won't help you.'

Lynn stood up and walked to the window. Moving the net curtain aside, she looked up and down the street with terror in her eyes. 'I told someone about you,' she began hesitantly. 'I mentioned the patches, that you'd taken photographs of me. I told them everything.'

'Who?'

'A man. I met him at university, years ago when I was . . . I thought he was a friend. Anyway, he wants the patches. He said that unless I give them to him, he'll . . . He knows that you've got the pictures of me and he's determined to get hold of them so he can blackmail me.'

'Does he know where I live?'

'Yes. He wants the pictures, Donna – and he'll do anything to get them.'

Bulmur would be trouble, she'd known it from the outset – but not this sort of trouble. 'If I give you the pictures, he'll still come here looking for them. He'll come here and . . . God knows what you're going to do, what I'm going to do!' Donna exclaimed, looking out of the window, wondering what she was looking for. 'What's happening with the police, anyway?'

'I'm in court next week.'

'It's a bloody mess, isn't it? What have you done with the patches I gave to you?'

'Sold them to some girls I know. I broke into your lab to get some more. I had no choice. Can you get me some? I have to keep this man happy or . . .'

'I've left the lab for good. The best you can hope for is that the judge throws you in prison for a while. At least you'd be safe there.'

'No, it doesn't work like that, believe me! I've been in prison before and I'll be there again for the break-in, I

227

know. I'm not safe anywhere. You don't know this man
– or his friends.'

'No, but he knows me, thanks to you! What the
bloody hell am I going to do?'

Donna was in danger. The realisation suddenly hit
her, churning her being as she imagined a gangster
turning up at her flat wielding a gun. And it wasn't the
movies, but for real. 'The best thing I can do is give him
the pictures when he turns up,' she said, tossing her long
blonde hair over her shoulder.

'Oh, thanks a lot! That'll really help me, won't it?'

'I'm not trying to help you! It's me I'm worried about.
You got me into this mess, you silly cow. And now I've
got to get myself out of it!'

'He only wants the pictures so that he can blackmail
me into giving him some patches. No pictures, no
blackmail, so he'll come to you for the patches.'

'I'll just explain that I've left the lab and that I haven't
got any patches. He'll believe me – he'll have to.'

'I wouldn't bank on it.'

'When do you think he'll be here? I mean, when did
you give him my address?'

'This morning, he came to see me this morning. I'm
surprised he's not here now. Are the pictures here?
Perhaps he's already been and taken them?'

'No, they're not here,' she lied. 'But I've got some
patches. I'll check the bedroom and make sure they're
still there.'

The photographs were still under the bed with the test
tubes as she had left them. She'd have to hand them
over, there was no other way. Bulmur would just have
to sort her problems out for herself, deal with her own
life – or death. Perhaps she *will* end up in the river,
Donna speculated.

Lynn had gone when she returned to the lounge, run off somewhere in the pouring rain. Perhaps she'll throw herself down the railway cutting, Donna thought fearfully. She looked at the walls. 'This whole thing is a bloody mess!'

Remembering that Charlie, Helen and Sophie were coming round that evening she spread the pictures of Lynn on her bed and placed the test tubes in her handbag, praying that the mysterious man would discover them while she was out rather than that she would have to confront him. Three-fifteen. Charlie would arrive around seven – nearly four hours.

Slipping her raincoat over her leather catsuit, Donna left her bedroom window wide open and the key in the front-door lock and walked to the park. He'd get in and find the pictures, and that would solve that problem – for a while, at least. Perhaps he'd believe Lynn when she told him that Donna had left the lab, that there were no more patches. If he didn't, he might well come to her, but she'd cross that bridge when she came to it.

The rain had eased off into a fine drizzle, leaving the air clean and fresh – summery fresh. Walking across the park, Donna suddenly remembered her young male fledglings and glanced at her watch. About a quarter past four, she vaguely recalled them saying. Better give them a treat on their way home for tea. May as well christen the catsuit before the arrival of her young female slaves. Only half-an-hour to wait.

Leaning on the fence at the edge of the railway cutting Donna watched the trains go by, some creeping along the deep valley like caterpillars, others speeding like bullets. Where were all the people going to? she wondered. To the sex shop? Home to their husbands and wives? Away to see their lovers, their mistresses?

Slipping her raincoat off, she hung it over the fence and allowed the drizzle to dampen her arms, her legs. Her skin tingled delightfully, glowing in response to the cooling water as she lay down on the wet, velvety grass and teased her clitoris in preparation for the fledglings. How to have them pleasure her? Mount her from behind? Take one in her mouth and the other in her love sheath? Her clitoris quivered at the thought. Perhaps take them both between her legs? Is it possible? she asked herself. Two hard, ripe penises throbbing side by side in her wet tightness – coming, pumping her to the brim with their creamy offerings? Anything was possible, she concluded, if you wanted it enough.

Voices echoing through the trees, twigs snapping underfoot sent Donna scurrying behind a bush, clutching her raincoat. She would wait, watch, listen to the excited banter of her victims as they awaited their mistress. First one and then the other came into view, carrying their bags, drinking fizzy orange from cans. Looking about them, they sat by the fence – her fence – and waited.

'She's a tart,' one said.

'I know that, stupid.'

'Just as well, I suppose. Do you think she'll come?'

'I'll make her come, all right.'

'I wonder where she lives? Perhaps she runs a brothel? Yeah, a brothel with dozens of birds, all naked and dying for it.'

'Course she doesn't. She's just a sex-starved tart who can't get enough of it. Who's going first?'

'It's up to her, I suppose. Anyway, she may not turn up, what with the rain.'

'I'm already here,' Donna said as she emerged from the bush, her long blonde hair wet, matted, her nipples long and hard, her slit oily with slippery sex juice. 'You may both remove my catsuit. I like to be totally naked when being pleasured by two young men.'

Moving in, they tugged on the zip running down the front of the suit. Slowly, the soft leather opened to reveal Donna's breasts, her smooth belly. Further still, and the suit was open fully. Gazing, each youth squeezed her breasts, sucked on her nipples, reached down and fondled the hot swelling of her moist quim lips. Peeling the suit from her wet body, they ran their hands over the smoothness of her skin, female skin, curvaceous, sensual – naked. Exploring, examining, they felt the delicacy of her crevices, the symmetry of her firm buttocks, the girlishness between her thighs. Learning, discovering, they gently pulled her down and lay her on the wet grass, her legs spread, her arms above her head – her body open.

The rain falling harder now, stinging her body with its pinpoints of lust, Donna closed her eyes, floated in the wetness. Tongues now, mouths, teeth – biting, tasting, licking her breasts, hardening her nipples. 'Take your clothes off,' she murmured as a tongue found its way into her navel. 'I want you both naked.'

Quickly, they undressed, flinging their clothes around them in a wild abandonment, exposing their erections – wavering, upright, ready to penetrate. 'Lie down!' Donna ordered one. Obedient, he lay on the wet grass, his penis pointing skyward, a symbol of his manhood. Straddling the shaft to face his feet, Donna gently lowered the centre of her body, impaling herself completely upon its hardness. Lying back over his chest, she looked up and beckoned her other slave to kneel between her legs, their legs. 'Put it inside me,' she breathed as he gazed at her pussy lips, wet, stretched, encompassing his friend's solid penis.

'I can't,' he replied. 'It won't go in, there's no room.'

'Try. I want you both inside me at once. Try.'

Stabbing, stretching, pressing his knob between her glistening folds, he managed to slip the purple head in alongside his companion's hard shaft. Donna gasped, a gasp of pained pleasure as he pressed further on into her tight cavern. 'More!' she breathed, her hands clutching at tufts of grass, her knuckles whitening, her breathing becoming laboured with lust, her eyes wide with pleasure – apprehension. He grimaced, squeezed his eyes shut as he pushed. 'You must do it, push it deeper, fill me!' she begged. Inch by inch his hardness penetrated her hole, stretched the delicate folds of her sex until he was in, deep, fully, to the hilt.

For a while she lay there impaled on the boy, savouring the achievement, the sensations, the thought of two hard penises inside her body, squashed together, throbbing like waiting engines. The two pairs of youthful balls lay against each other – full. 'Now fuck me!' Donna instructed in her euphoria.

Moving his shaft back and forth, the stud on top began his fucking motions, massaging his friend's penis with his, filling Donna's body to capacity as she screamed her delight. As her pelvis bloated, filled to its limits with the rock-hard shafts, she cried out her beautiful words of uninhibited lust. 'Both come inside me together! Fuck me as one!' Quickening his pace, he panted as his coming loomed. Spreadeagled beneath Donna's body, his friend could only enjoy the massaging of another penis, the tightening of a vagina – he was the intruder, his penis a voyeur, spying, watching deep within a woman's cunt as she was taken, brought to orgasm by another penis.

'Both fill me with your sperm!' Grunts came from behind as her sheath billowed with the swelling shafts.

'I'm coming!' the boy beneath gasped, his breathing causing her body to rise and fall with his excitement as he instructed his friend to thrust harder. Pistoning for all he was worth, her young slave on top moaned and grunted and lay across her stomach as his shaft grew and the ballooning head exploded within the quivering wetness of her sheath. Both coming now, they rammed, pumped out their sperm, filling her with their orgasms. Reaching between her splayed lips, Donna massaged her clitoris and cried out with the euphoria of two men coming within her tight fleshy cavern. There were ever new sensations to learn, to delight in.

Their pumping done, their grunting over, her sheath bubbling, she lay still now, the two penises shrinking within her love tube, dying their deaths. Slippery, flaccid, they slipped from her exhausted body, leaving her hole gaping, oozing with the fruits of her slaves. All three lay on the grass, side by side, done, drained, gratified, as the pouring rain cleansed Donna's body, cooled and bathed her inflamed slit, watered her furrow, bringing renewed life as to the flowers.

Reaching out to either side of her, Donna took a penis in each hand. Stiffening again now, they twitched a little in response to her fingers as she ran them round the hard knobs. Which one to suck? Both wet with her come, hard, unblemished in their youth, she eeny-meeny-miny-moed.

Leaning over, she took the chosen one in her mouth, pulling the skin back, drawing the knob deep into the back of her throat where it bulged and quivered. Movements behind her now. Lying on her stomach, sucking hard on the swollen knob, she parted her legs. Fingers fingered between her buttocks, parted them, lifted them to expose the secret hole deep within the dark crease. In her vagina now, massaging, kneading the creamy, velveteen walls. More movements as she continued her sucking to bring the sperm up from the heavy balls in her small hand. She knelt, raised her hips to open her body. Stabbing between her lips, the knob suddenly entered, filled her, pressed fully home against her cervix and lay still, absorbing the warmth, the sensations.

Dreamily, Donna rolled her eyes, moulded her tongue round the quivering hardness ballooning in her mouth, swelling her cheeks. Moving her head up and down the shaft in time with the thrusting in her sheath, she shuddered, moaned and sucked harder, impatient for the sperm to gush. Her young pupils grunted their delight as they felt their climaxes rising, their knobs waiting to explode in their chosen orifice.

In a semi-trance, Donna gave her body totally, in its entirety, to her lovers, allowing them to take her, fill her mouth, her yawning chasm. All three shuddered, let out their cries of gratification as their bodies pumped and drained. Her mouth full of hot nectar, her sheath brimming with come, she rose above her body and up to her heaven where again she was brushed by the wings of the angels of lust. Pumping, ramming on and on, the fledglings used her naked body until they could ram no more and, their balls empty, their shafts flaccid, they fell limp.

Donna rolled over onto the wet grass, sperm dribbling down her chin, over the pink wrinkled lips surrounding the entrance to her full vagina. Every nerve ending tingled with life, every muscle spasmed as she gently fell from the high plateau of orgasm and landed in her senses.

Opening her eyes, she looked up to the trees, green, wavering in the breeze above her, watching. Blue sky broke through the clouds, bringing sunshine to warm her body. A rainbow appeared in the heavens, a rainbow of angels come to bathe her glowing body in light, to shine upon her nakedness.

'That was nice,' Donna breathed as her young men dressed, concealed their spent rods, covered their drained balls.

'We'll do it again,' said one, a tone of pleading in his voice.

'And again and again,' Donna smiled.

'Can I bring a friend?' the other asked. 'Robbie, he . . .'

'No names,' she said. 'No names, no addresses – just sex. Yes, of course you can bring a friend. To prove my existence, is it?'

'Yes. Well, no, not really.'

'He'll have to pleasure me, as you did.'

'Oh, he will – we all will.'

'Tomorrow, then. Bring him tomorrow, here to my little clump of trees by the railway cutting, to my little world, my secret nest of sex.'

The rain stopped and the sun shone hot again as Donna lay naked on the wet grass, watching her young male slaves make their way through the trees. The birds sang, the breeze dropped and the sweet scent of the wood filled her nostrils, her mind. What now? Go home? Had the photographs been taken yet? Was the flat on fire? She was – the fire of lust burned deep within her womb, her swirling womb.

A train slipped through the cutting, bringing Donna

back to the real world. Where was the real world? She hadn't heard the trains. Flying with the angels of lust, she'd heard nothing, perceived nothing of her surroundings – only the quivering, pulsing pleasure running deep within the moist furrow of her cunette, the wet warmth of her sheath, the girlish swell of her clitoris.

Where was she going? Donna wondered. Where were the patches taking her? She'd given up her job, placed a newspaper ad, discovered and enjoyed her body – others' bodies, male and female. But what was it all leading to? Alan had to know about the patches, she decided. It was only fair to tell him. Professor Winmann should have told him – why hadn't he? So many secrets – too many.

Slipping back into her catsuit, Donna pulled her raincoat over her glowing body and walked out into the park – into the real world. She'd need money soon, she was well aware. But to take money for sex? That wouldn't be fair. Besides, hanging around on street corners wasn't her style. She needed something more subtle than blatant prostitution. But what? The money she'd stolen from Lynn Bulmur had been eaten up in the sex shop – money well spent. Her bank account was as good as empty and the mortgage was due. Weren't they always?

The key was still in the lock when Donna returned to her flat. Has he been? she wondered as she crept into her bedroom. Is he still here? The photographs had gone, thank God. Nothing else seemed to be missing, not that there was anything of great value in the flat. Had the walls seen the mysterious intruder? They'd know his identity.

'Money, money,' she whispered as she dialled Steve's number.

'Hello,' Debbie said with sex in her voice. Damn it, why hadn't he answered? Was Debbie wearing a patch? Was she masturbating, fingering herself as she spoke? Suddenly, Donna had an idea.

'If you want the photographs back, it'll cost you,' she said.

'How much?' came the unexpected reply.

'What's it worth?'

Silence. What was she thinking? What the hell would Steve say when he found out?

'A grand.'

'Okay.'

'But you'll have to come here with the photographs. I'm not meeting you anywhere other than on my home ground – I don't trust you.'

'Tomorrow morning, I'll be round at eleven – and I want cash!'

A thousand pounds – not bad. But now Donna had to prepare for an eventful evening. Set up the bondage equipment – but where? The spare room – yes, turn the spare room into a sex parlour, a dungeon of lust where the air would hang heavy with the smell of orgasm. Changing into a T-shirt and a miniskirt, minus knickers and bra, she set to work.

Professor Winmann sat on the edge of Alan's bench and lit his pipe. 'Love, is it?' he asked between puffs.

'Suppose so. But you haven't answered my question. Why have you come back? Surely not to tell me that you think I'm in love with Donna?'

'Partly. But there's something else I think you ought to know. She's been using your patches Alan. She confessed, so to speak. A nice girl, isn't she? You'd make a nice couple.'

'I know about the patches. I realised what she was up to when . . . The first time in the lab when she . . .'

'What do you propose to do?'

'I love her. What can I do?'

'She wants to help inorgasmic women. Why not set up in business with her? The two of you could . . .'

'It's illegal.'

'Is it? Helping women to discover their true sexuality is illegal, is it?'

'True sexuality? I don't know if that's the case. The hormone heightens the libido to an incredible extent. It also destroys the natural heterosexual instinct. Is this bringing out the true sexuality, as you put it? I would say that by destroying the natural chemical inhibitor in the female brain, we are leaving women vulnerable, defenceless.'

'Evolution, Alan. I believe that, over thousands of years, the female brain manufactured the chemical to quell the libido, to curb the population . . .'

'No, no. I'm sure that . . .'

'Adrenalin is a hormone produced when we need to fight or flee. There are many hormones secreted for many reasons and, I would imagine, many that we haven't discovered yet. Perhaps, in the straitlaced prude, the inhibitor is overdoing its job. And in the nymphomaniac, it's not doing its job properly. Balance, Alan. If you work with Donna and produce patches with carefully regulated amounts of hormone, you'll achieve a balance.'

'It's interfering with nature. It's not right to . . .'

'Donna will go ahead with or without you. Elizabeth is using the patches, did you know that?'

'I guessed she was, yes.'

'We are . . . She's coming to live with me, Alan. I'm

older than she is, considerably older. But we've found something together.'

'That was quick!'

'Yes, it seems very quick to those who don't know us. We've worked together for years – your patches have brought out her true feelings, enabled her to open up and tell me how she feels about me.'

'I'll go and see Donna this evening. Better to work with her, as you say. She doesn't know enough to work alone, anyway.'

'Tell her your true feelings.'

'I have, and she doesn't want to know. It's just sex with her now. That's all she wants – sex.'

'Is it? How do you know that? How can you be so sure?'

'I'm not sure about anything any more.'

'Will you jot her address down for me? I want to go and have a word with her, see what I can do to help.'

The spare room was cleared and installed with the equipment. Only a double bed remained, with handcuffs fixed to the four bedposts, ropes and chains in place, ready for the first victim. Wearing her leather catsuit, Donna opened the front door an inch or so and peered at the professor, her eyes wide with surprise.

'Oh, it's you!' she said. 'I'm, er . . .'

'I'd like a chat with you, Donna.'

'Well, I'm busy right now, I . . .'

'It'll only take five minutes. I've come a long way to see you. Surely, you can spare me five minutes?'

Opening the door wider, Donna hesitantly invited him in and awaited his reaction. From her long exposed nipples down to her protruding labia, his eyes devoured the exquisite spectacle. 'Oh, I see,' he murmured as she closed the door. 'I can come back later if . . .'

Like a naughty schoolgirl who'd been caught masturbating by her mother, she hung her head in shame. Send him away? No. Invite him in? What the hell!

'No, no, it's all right. I'm sure you're a man of the world. Besides, you know all about the patches so you'll understand, won't you?'

'Understand, yes, I understand.'

'Come through to the lounge, we'll chat in there.'

What was he thinking? Donna wondered as the professor sat on the sofa. What were his male thoughts? His eyes were locked, transfixed between the softness of her inner thighs. Moving her feet apart she opened her thighs a little more. Now her vaginal lips bulged, her inner folds hung invitingly. What did he think now? More to the point, what did he want?

'Have you seen Alan?' Donna asked, making herself comfortable in her armchair.

'Yes, I went to the lab.'

'Did you tell him about me, about the patches?'

'No,' he lied. 'Look, I know it's none of my business, but he's in love with you, Donna. I've come here to . . . Well, I don't know why I've come, really. I suppose I wondered how you were doing. I hear that you've left the lab.'

'I know he's in love with me, and yes, I have left the lab. I have other interests to pursue.'

'Helping inorgasmic women? Or enjoying your new-found sexual freedom?'

'Both, I suppose.'

Suddenly, Donna found herself wondering about the professor's penis. Was it thick, long? The way his eyes gazed longingly between her thighs, was his penis stiff? He was a normal male, even at his age, with male thoughts swirling, lurking – rising. The girl at his university, had he sucked her elongated clitoris? He'd love to suck hers, she knew. What man wouldn't?

'Oh, I almost forgot,' Winmann said. 'The hormone has another effect. An astonishing effect.'

'What?' Donna asked, wide-eyed.

'Over a period of time, it seems that the brain's ability to secrete the chemical inhibitor is destroyed. In some, it may only take one patch to destroy the inhibitor, in others, several patches over several weeks. In other words, the time will come when there will be no need to use a patch.'

'So I'll be sexually aroused, even without a patch?'

'Yes, your thinking will become permanently like that of the male. The male, as you know, is driven by the sex urge, the libido, and it affects just about everything he thinks, says and does.'

'Men don't think about sex all the time, surely?'

'Most of the time, yes. Sex to the male is, how shall I put it? It's like a hunger, a driving hunger. Orgasm is a necessity for the male – like food. The longer he goes without orgasm, the higher the sexual force rises until it reaches dangerous levels.'

'Dangerous?'

'Well, not in the real sense, but men are driven to masturbation, not because they have dirty thoughts, but because they need the release that orgasm brings.'

'So I have that to look forward to for the rest of my days? Well, it doesn't sound too bad to me. In fact, I quite like the idea.'

'You're a sweet little thing, I wish I were twenty years younger.'

'Why? What would you do if you were?'

'Can't you guess?'

'Yes, I suppose so,' she replied, wondering if it was he who'd made the dirty phone call. 'You haven't been following me, have you?'

'Following you? Good God, no! Why on earth would I do that?'

'You tell me.'

'That's not my style. Anyway, I'm far too old for games. I'll be honest with you. I . . . How shall I put it? Fancy you? Yes, I fancy you. What man wouldn't fancy a young lady dressed as you are?'

Young lady? Young, maybe, but lady? Gazing at the professor, Donna wondered if he masturbated. Poor thing, how he'd love her to take his penis in her mouth and whisk him back to his youthful days – days of sex, of screwing young girls. Did professors screw? In their lecture halls, did they espy the triangular patches of red silk between the thighs of their teenaged students?

Just five minutes of her time would make him a happy man, bring him renewed life. But Donna had to draw the line somewhere, she knew. She couldn't go on and on having her soft sheath filled by one penis, one tongue, after another. But why not? Was not that what it was for? Drinking sperm from the bulging head of a throbbing penis was her idea of heaven. Having her hot tightness filled took her higher and higher to new levels of consciousness – angelic levels. Why not, indeed?

Winmann's eyes glowed expectantly, like a child looking up to his mother, waiting for permission to lick the cake mix from the bowl. How to deny a child? Cruel to be kind? No. The angels had been kind to her – she must be kind to the professor.

Chapter Twelve

A figure crouched in the bushes outside the lounge window. Skulking, spying, peeping, he couldn't be seen from the street. But he could see – Donna kneeling at the professor's feet, the professor pulling his trousers down, his penis, thick, long, half-erect, only inches from the girl's face.

She was strangely aware of a presence as she took the professor's flaccid shaft into her mouth and sucked the soft knob. She knew it wasn't the walls, or Lucifer, or her angels. The same feeling she'd had in the park, the street, her bed, enveloped her – the feeling of being watched, followed. But with only a feeling, some strange intuition, again, she became unsure. Was her mind playing games?

The professor grunted as his penis stiffened and grew to an incredible size in response to the girl's darting tongue. Thrusting his hips forward, he rammed his huge, solid knob deeper into Donna's mouth, dragging her thoughts away from her watcher to the hot flesh ballooning against her tongue.

Gripping the massive shaft in her small hand, she moved the mature dark skin up and down, bringing his stiffness to the full. Gasping, he reached out and took her head in his hands to push further into her mouth. Almost choking, Donna continued her massaging, her sucking, her licking, until the first taste of salty liquid bubbled and ran over her tongue.

She'd decided to pleasure him for one reason – to discover the name of the girl who'd taken the hormone, the girl whose clitoris had grown to an incredible length. But Donna, too, found her pleasure as she pleasured the professor. Young or old, she decided, a wonderfully stiff, throbbing penis brought great satisfaction – especially when spurting its sperm into her mouth, over her tongue, as she drank.

Winmann came quickly, much to her surprise. Grunting, desperately panting for breath as he pumped his sperm into her ravenous mouth, Donna thought he might have a heart attack. Never had she known such huge quantities of sperm to gush from the bulging head of a penis in orgasm. Never had she had her mouth filled with so much nectarous liquid that it overflowed and ran in torrents down her chin. Though she swallowed hard several times, on and on the deluge flowed until she had to withdraw the spurting member, coughing as she brought out the last few dribbles with her hand. He crumpled, clutching his penis as if in pain as he rolled over. His huge balls ballooning between his thighs, his long penis hung limp over his leg, trickling, glistening with milky fluid.

'Did you like that?' Donna asked, wondering if he'd be able to pleasure her clitoris, to extract an orgasm from the now extremely hard and sensitive tip. She had liked it very much.

'God, yes! You certainly know how to please a man! You're far better than Liz . . .'

'Am I? Better than Liz? How do you know that?'

His face reddening, averting his guilty eyes, Winmann hoisted up his trousers and fastened his belt. So, Liz was still enjoying herself, was she? Donna was pleased, pleased that she'd initiated her to the wonders of sex, shown her what her body was for, what beautiful sensations her clitoris could bring. She was happy, too, that the revelation put her in a better position to glean information.

'I . . . Liz and I are living together. We . . . Look, don't say anything about this, will you? I don't think she'd . . .'

'Be too happy to hear that you came in my mouth? Don't worry, it will remain our little secret – but only if you tell me who the girl was that took the hormone at the university. The girl with the long clitoris.'

'She's abroad, I told you.'

'No, no, she's not. You can't fool me. Where is she? I want you to put me in touch with her.'

'I can't do that! For goodness sake, I can't do that!'

'Then I'll give Liz a ring and tell her . . .'

'All right, but you must play this carefully. Meet her somewhere and just get chatting or something. No formal introduction, and whatever you do, don't mention me.'

'Give me her address and I'll not mention you, I promise.'

'Angela Shanks, 21 Brunswick Road, Shelton. And before you ask, yes, she's in the phone book.'

'Thank you. Our little exchange was well worth it, I hope you'll agree?'

'Oh, yes, well worth it. That was wonderful, Donna. Can I see you again? I mean . . .'

'Yes, of course you can. But you'll have to phone me and arrange our little get together first. I don't want you just turning up.'

'All right. I'd better be going, I have a train to catch.

Liz will be wondering where . . . Well, it's been nice, Donna. I can't say how grateful . . .'

'Then don't. Now go, or you'll miss your train and Liz will be one very unhappy lady.'

Donna smiled as she let the professor out. A train to catch? Things happened on trains. Would he enjoy as happy a journey as her college students? Wandering into the lounge, she began to wonder if it had been a good idea to seduce Winmann. He'd be another one who would constantly come back for more, but no matter. She'd got the information she wanted, even though she wasn't too sure why she wanted it. To admire the girl's inch-long clitoris? To suck it into her mouth as she would a miniature penis and bring it to orgasm? A preview, she decided, of the destiny of her own clitoris.

Lifting her skirt, Donna parted her lips and examined her little cumbud. So small, seemingly insignificant – and yet the tiny protrusion was capable of giving such mind-blowing sensations. It had definitely grown, and become far more sensitive to the touch. Perhaps clitorises grew with use, when masturbated several times every day? In her mind, she knew it was the hormone. As she stroked the pulsing tip and pictured the professor's huge penis, the phone rang.

'You like sucking off old men, don't you?' the soft male voice asked as Donna pressed the phone to her ear. 'I've been watching you. You look nice without all that hair covering your pussy. I must get some of that cream that you used on your pussy. You're a little tart, aren't you?'

'And what are you – sick?' she replied coolly.

'I've been watching you, in the park, in your lounge, in your bedroom. I've got enough on you to . . .'

'To what? Look, I can't stand pathetic little perverts like you. Either come round here and prove that you're a man, or sod off!'

'Enjoy your trip to the sex shop, did you? It's a shame that you left your job. But there again, I suppose there's more money to be earned from prostitution than from research work.'

Donna bit her lip. Who the hell was it? He knew everything. How? It had to be someone she knew. Or someone had told him about her. No, no-one knew about the sex shop, and the professor had only just left. How could anyone know what had just happened? Unless it was the professor.

'Look, I'm busy. If you've finished fantasising and wanking, I'll say goodbye and leave you to clean up the mess,' she asserted, banging the phone down. Settling in her armchair, she gazed at the window and suddenly realised that the voyeur must have been there, crouching in the bushes, watching her drinking the professor's sperm as it spurted from his throbbing knob.

Stepping out of the front door, Donna looked at the bushes. There was more than enough room between the foliage and the window to hide, to spy. There were no footprints in the hard, dry earth, but the weeds were flattened. Who? she agonised as she crouched in the hide and looked in through the window. The sofa, and her armchair, were clearly visible through the gap in the net curtains. Moving round the side of the building, she looked through her bedroom window. Again, the bushes afforded good cover for the peeping pervert, and her bed was in full view. She shuddered as she imagined him watching as she lay on her bed, wiping away the depilating cream, stroking her soft, naked lips. The window of the spare room, the sex dungeon, was surrounded by thick, green bushes, providing perfect cover for a man to watch and masturbate. Had he taken photographs? God, not more bloody photographs – was there no privacy for the uninhibited? For private people to do their private things?

Where had he phoned from? Donna's thoughts raced as she closed the front door behind her. The phone box down the road? A mobile phone? It didn't matter. Trap him, set him up and trap him. Shit! Helen and Sophie were coming round. Draw the curtains? No, let him watch the threesome – the fivesome when Charlie arrived with her young boyfriend. Suddenly, the thought of a voyeur added excitement to the imminent orgy.

Sophie arrived at seven – alone.

'Where's Helen?' Donna asked disappointedly.

'Sulked off somewhere.'

'What do you mean? What's happened?'

'We were in the park . . . We argued and she sulked off.'

'Argued about what?'

'She reckons that some man was following us. She's mad, neurotic.'

'Did you see anyone?'

'There was a man, yes. But he wasn't following us.'

'What was he doing, exactly?'

'Does it matter?'

'It might.'

'He was hanging around the trees at the edge of the park.'

'Doing what?'

'Messing around, I don't know. Oh yes, she reckoned that he was trying to climb a tree. I didn't see him, but

what difference does it make whether he climbed a tree
or was bird watching from the bushes?'

'Bird watching?'

'Yes, Helen thought that he was making some sort of
hide, you know, like bird watchers do. He had some
binoculars so he must have been a bird watcher.'

'What sort of birds? That's what worries me.'

'Birds are birds, aren't they?'

'Yes, and pussies are pussies – although they're as
different as chalk and cheese.'

Grabbing her jacket, Donna ordered Sophie to wait
for her while she went in search of Helen. She was sure
the man in the park was her man, her peeping pervert,
and she was determined to discover his identity.

Walking around the edge of the park, Donna wondered if it could be Alan. She hadn't recognised the
voice on the telephone, but that was easy enough to
disguise. Steve, the photographer, sprang to mind. But
he wouldn't bother to play silly games, any more than
Alan. So who the hell was it? Barry had spied from the
bushes on Donna and Sue – perhaps he was the culprit?
But there was no motivation. They already had a good
thing going, so why spoil it?

In the trees, Donna crouched behind a bush and
looked around her. The wood was silent, too silent. No
birds, no breeze, not even a train passing through the
cutting to rouse the still, summery air. But again, she
felt that she wasn't alone. Eyes peering, burning her
with their hidden gaze. A twig cracked, sending an eerie
echo through the trees. Someone was somewhere, lurking in the shadows, under the bushes or high up in the
trees. Remembering Sophie's words, she looked up to
the green canopy high above her. No-one. No bird
watchers.

Suddenly, she caught a faint murmur coming from the fence by the railway cutting. Cautiously creeping on all fours towards the fence she slipped silently through the bushes and peered into the clearing – her clearing.

Sue was lying on her back, her naked body tied over a fallen tree with thick lengths of rope. Between her legs, licking, mouthing, fingering, was Barry – Barry the jogger, Barry the fucker. Two-timing Barry, two-timing Sue. Had he raped her? From Sue's wailed entreaties drifting through the trees, she concluded not. 'Ah, yes, that's nice, Barry! Make me come again, please make me come again!'

No wonder Sue hadn't been round to her flat, Donna thought jealously. With Barry to pleasure her under the trees – Donna's trees – no wonder Sue hadn't needed her between her legs. She'd thought Barry belonged to her. He was her partner in early morning jogging – early morning lusting. Possessions – did anyone possess anyone, anything?

Settling under the cover of the bush, Donna questioned Sue's behaviour. Why was she doing this? With Sue, it would take several patches several weeks to destroy her chemical inhibitor. Without a patch, why was she . . . Unless, she suddenly thought, unless she *did* have a patch on her. Scrutinising Sue's arms, legs, she saw nothing. But focussing on her neck, she could just make out a small plastic disc stuck to her soft skin, releasing its magical hormone, blowing away her inhibitions.

'Where the hell . . .?' Donna thought aloud. Sue must have stolen the patch, there was no other explanation. Or Barry. But he knew nothing about the patches, did he? She glanced around the trees, wondering if the voyeur was lurking, peeping, before remembering

Helen. Where the hell had she sulked off to? Perhaps she was spying on her mother, her mother's naked, tethered body being licked, sucked, fingered, brought to life by Barry?

Donna watched as Sue's body, nearing her orgasm now, shook with pleasure, trembled with the delirium bubbling between her bloated cunt lips as Barry expertly brought her clitoris to fruition. Her own clitoris stirred, tingling between the soft swelling of her smooth nether lips. She'd been wearing her patch for hours, absorbing the hormone since the early morning. Too long, perhaps?

Squatting in the bush, her quim lips parted, bulging, Donna located her bud and massaged its hardness. It seemed bigger now, bigger, harder, more sensitive than ever, and she decided to leave the patch in place, permanently. The hormone would cause her clitoris to grow longer, thicker, and bring her orgasms of unimaginable strength. Two patches, she speculated, would double the effect, force her clitoris to grow twice as fast.

Dragging her milky fluid up her open groove to lubricate her clitoris, Donna watched Sue fly up to her heaven. 'I'm coming! Lick me harder, I'm coming!' Her cries of lust echoed through the wood, reverberated amongst the trees. In the throes of her own orgasmic journey, Donna was jealous. She had been Sue's teacher, teaching her about her body, her clitoris. But now, it seemed, the class was over, Sue had passed her final exam and was out in the world, discovering worldly things.

Gently massaging her clitoris, holding herself on the verge of orgasm, Donna watched as Barry released her pupil and turned her over. Her naked body folded over the fallen tree with her firm buttocks splayed to reveal

Ray Gordon

her thick hanging cunt lips, he re-tied the ropes. Slipping his jeans down to his ankles, he rubbed the swollen butt of his thick penis between her full, creamy lips and eased it into the wet warmth. Gripping her hips, he pushed his shaft deep into her soft tube, filling her gently, opening the centre of her body with his thick hardness until she was completely impaled. Sue moaned her pleasure as he thrust deeper and deeper into her tightening sheath, bringing her clitoris ever nearer to its eruption, her contracting womb to its fruition, until suddenly, Barry withdrew his wet shaft to stab the bulbous head between her open buttocks. 'No, no! No, please don't!' Now cries of fear, the unknown, disturbed the trees as the purple knob trespassed past the tight ring.

Wide-eyed, Donna gazed at the wondrous spectacle as she massaged her aching clitoris ever harder. Barry's shaft slipping deeper into the privacy of Sue's bowels, she again cried out her protests, filling the wood with her screams of pained ecstasy. He drove his solid rod further into her hotness until her buttocks pressed against his body and his balls hung neatly against the swollen lips of her gaping vagina.

Now Barry began his fucking motions, ramming, thrusting his member until he shuddered and his moans of pleasure mingled with Sue's – a sweet musical harmony of debased lust. With each thrust, each gasp, he spurted his sperm deep inside her shuddering body as she cried out in her orgasm. Together, they rocked, writhed, squirmed in their union until he withdrew and collapsed onto the soft grass, leaving her bloated hole dripping with his salty fruits.

Watching in sheer disbelief, Donna cursed Sue, Barry, their debased union of lust. She wanted him

252

inside her small hole, filling, stretching the delicate walls within the dark hotness of her bowels. New experiences, new sensations – she wanted them.

'I didn't want you to do that!' Sue complained.

'But you enjoyed it, didn't you? You liked having your bottom-hole fucked, didn't you?'

'No, yes – I mean . . .'

'Tell me that you loved my cock deep in your bottom!'

'No, I didn't. Well, it was all right, but . . .'

'Tell me that you want it in your bottom again.'

'No, no. I . . . Let me go now, please.'

Picking up a nearby slender branch, Barry began to whip her milky spheres, causing her to yelp. 'Tell me that you want it again!' he gasped. Harder now, he thrashed her tightening buttocks with the leafy branch, reddening her flesh as, at length, she begged for more. 'Tell me!'

'Yes, yes – fuck my bottom again! I like it there, I love you in there, fucking me!'

'Tell me that you want two men inside you!'

'Yes, two men! One in my bottom and . . . Oh, that's good! Do it harder! One man in my bottom and one in my cunt!'

Sue's milk flowed from her spread pussy lips and trickled down her thighs as the beating continued. Donna wanted to drink from her body, push her mouth between the puffy lips and drink. Would Barry drink her come? Would he lap up the creamy liquid coursing down her thighs? Would he press his penis deep into her bowels again? She wanted his hardness in her bowels. Gasping her pleasure as a powerful climax responded to her rude fantasy, she fell noisily into the bushes. Barry halted the thrashing and looked about him. 'Don't stop!' Sue begged, oblivious in her whirlpool of sexual intoxication. 'Do it harder! I'm coming again!'

Donna held her breath as Barry took one last look at the bushes before returning to his victim. Her clitoris demanded more attention, more orgasms, but she knew she'd be caught if she gave in to her uninhibited desires. Creeping away through the undergrowth, she emerged into the park and sighed. Had she wanted to be caught?

Neither Sophie nor Helen were at the flat on her return. Despondency set in. In the cold light of reality, they weren't her slaves, she knew, but free to come and go as they wished, to pleasure each other in the park as it took their fancy. Donna had no say in the matter, but she would severely punish them when the opportunity arose, she promised herself.

Eight o'clock came and went. Where was Charlie? Her beautiful body, her boyfriend, his fresh, young, hard body? Her voyeur wouldn't let her down, Donna thought as she grabbed her silver vibrator and slipped out of her clothes to lie on her bed. Raising her head, she looked between her firm breasts, between her feet at the window. *He* wouldn't let her down, surely?

Aware of eyes spying, gazing, Donna opened her legs as wide as she could and parted her lips with her slender fingers, presenting her wet hole to the hiding eyes. Was there someone there at the window? She couldn't be sure, but she hoped so. Her eyes half closed, she peered through her long eyelashes as she stretched her pinken folds open further and massaged her stiffening clitoris. A shadow in the corner of the window, a shadow lurking. A head, the silhouette of a head – watching, gazing, at her open body. Who?

Pressing the vibrator between her glistening flesh, Donna eased its full length into her hot body and switched it on. It buzzed softly within her quivering sheath and she gasped as she began to thrust it in and out like a huge metal piston within a cylinder – a metal penis within her fleshy tube. Coming nearer to her climax, she raised her knees to her chest, presenting her bloated nether lips to her voyeur as she continued to massage her clitoris and ram her cunt with the huge, buzzing phallus. The powerful vibrations coursed their way deep into her womb as her clitoris engorged with pleasure. The sensations mingled, blended delightfully deep within her pelvis before they imploded, sucking her mind into the depths of her body before exploding, sending her out into the velvety darkness of orgasm. Floating, swirling, flowing in a vibrant world of sexual fulfilment, she passed a new threshold, discovered a new state of consciousness where her orgasm held her, suspended her, in its magical grip.

Floating down to earth as gently as a feather in the breeze, Donna returned to her trembling body and opened her eyes. Had the voyeur seen, watched as her body erupted in the most powerful orgasm she'd ever experienced? Was he watching now as she slipped the metal phallus from her sodden hole and reclined, satisfied as never before?

Slipping from her bedroom, Donna pulled her dressing gown over her shoulders and quietly opened the front door. Creeping round the side of the building she breathed softly, trod carefully, as she approached the bushes. A rustling sound, movements in the bush – a cat? A bird in its nest? Peering through the greenery, she saw the dark hair – a man's head.

As he raised his head to peer through the window, Donna saw who he was. At last, her voyeur, her stalker! Smiling, she quietly returned to the flat and closed the front door. Did he want more, more sex, more female masturbation? What would he enjoy see her doing in the privacy of her room? What could she do to her young body to really excite him – excite him to the point where he'd pull his penis out and spurt his sperm into the bushes?

Grabbing the cucumber from the fridge, Donna returned to the stage. Turning her naked body, she knelt on her bed with her back to the window and leaned forward, her face pressed into the pillow, her buttocks rudely open to the mysterious voyeur. Pressing the cucumber between her sagging inner folds, she pushed it home, filling her pretty cunt to capacity with the cool, hard phallus. He'd like that, she knew. He'd love to see her cunette stretched open by the cucumber – but her bloated pussy encompassing a cucumber wasn't enough. Obsessed, her mind became bent on her debased perversions. What could she do? What disgusting act could she commit for the benefit of her audience? Her mind wandering, she remembered Barry and Sue in the woods.

Grabbing the vibrator, Donna presented the rounded tip to the small hole between her buttocks and began to twist and push. She cried out as the tip slid into the slippery darkness. Further she pushed the metal shaft, deeper and deeper into her abused body until only an inch protruded. What were his thoughts now? The phallic fruit peering out from between her swollen cunt lips, the vibrator protruding from her buttocks, what were his male thoughts? He would be masturbating by now, she was sure as she turned the end of the vibrator to give it life, to transmit life to the very depths of her pelvis. Gyrating her hips, she moved the phalluses so that they frictioned through the thin membrane dividing her stretched holes – her

holes of lust. Was he coming now, spurting his sperm?
She would examine the bush, the ground, later, for
the tell-tale signs of male masturbation.

Rubbing her solid clitoris, she cried out as her
climax ripped through her open body, tore its way
through the depths of her womb and sent her high up
to her heaven. Rolling onto her side, squirming,
panting, she desperately tried to pull the thick pleasure shafts from her body. Bringing her knees up to
her chest, she groped for the end of the vibrator, the
cucumber, but, slippery with her juices, the phalluses
evaded her grip. On and on the sensations welled
from her womb, filled her abdomen, sucked her
clitoris into the dark sea of sex. The angels caressing
every nerve ending in her body, their fingers of love
stroked the inner core of her sex, bringing new life,
new sensations, new meaning to the epicentre
between her twitching legs. Still her fingers slipped
helplessly from the slimy shafts until she could take no
more. Desperate now, deluged in her salt water and
love juice, she rolled over again and like a woman in
childbirth summoned her last energy to bear down on
her cunt and sphincter muscles. Like bullets from a
gun, the giant phalluses were expelled across the
room where they landed on the carpet, used, wet, and
glistening with her come.

Exhausted, she lay still, allowing her body to return
from its incredible trip, her breathing to quieten, her
sheath to shrink, her small, private tube to calm.

The shadow through the window disappeared as she
slipped into her miniskirt and T-shirt. He'd be back, she
knew, to an even more spectacular performance – if
only she could control her slaves. Walking round to the
bushes beneath her bedroom window she examined the

Ray Gordon

dry, flat earth and smiled – globules of mother-of-pearl
splattered around a central pool of sperm. He'd come –
watching her multi-pleasuring herself on her bed, he'd
masturbated and come. Squatting, she circled her finger
in the sticky pool and dragged the liquid across the
earth, making patterns – exquisite patterns of sex. What
a waste, she thought. What a terrible waste.

The time approaching ten, Donna wandered down
the street, her inflamed holes of sex again burning with
desire between her thighs, her womb fluttering delightfully with passion. Intuition, a sixth sense, she didn't
know what, beckoned her to the park, to the trees.
Why? she wondered.

Dusk was falling rapidly, like a blanket to cover the
world – as a goodnight to the good and a welcome to
the wicked. She was wicked, she knew, but she
revelled in it – her wanton wickedness, her new-found
sexuality.

A lone man walking his dog across the park caught
Donna's eye. Where was he going? Most likely not to
take the dog for a walk, as he'd probably told his wife,
but to the pub. Marriages were made of lies – lies made
marriages. She was pleased not to have fallen into the
marriage trap and become a possession. Mrs Alan
Rosenberg – my car, my house, my wife. Not for her or
the women she would enlighten, she thought. For more
than equality even would come power – female power
from between their legs.

Darkness had all but engulfed the wooded area.
Animals lurked, nocturnal animals, for this was their
day, and her night. Donna wanted to be nocturnal – to
sleep all day and venture out at night, seeking out sexual
satisfaction under cover of the swirling darkness. That
would promise new and exciting sensations.

A sound, a rustle. Was someone enjoying new and exciting sensations in the woods? Noises, struggling noises emanating from the blackness. Soft cries echoing as an owl hoots. Young lovers, she decided. Young lovers exploring, touching, feeling, kissing in the dark. Was that why she'd been drawn there? To join in the games of young lovers in the night?

Nearing the railway cutting, the whimpers grew louder, more desperate. And as the moon suddenly peered through a hole in the clouds, Donna saw. Naked, her skin glowing silvery under the moonlight, Sue was tied over the fallen tree. But where was Barry? Donna crouched down, her hands on the cool grass to support her as she looked around, listened above her breathing, her beating heart.

'Sue!' she whispered. 'Are you alone?'

'Who's that? Help me, please help me!'

'What are you doing like this?' Donna asked innocently as she began to untie the ropes. 'Who did this to you?'

'Donna! Thank God it's you! I was terrified!'

'Who did this, Sue?'

'It was . . . It doesn't matter who did it. I've been here for bloody ages!'

'But why? Why tie you up and leave you here?'

'I don't know, do I? He . . . he's obviously got a funny sense of humour.'

'A bloody weird sense of humour if you ask me. Anyway, what do you mean, he? Do I know him?'

'No, no. It's just someone I've been seeing recently. We . . .'

'Were having a bloody good time, by the look of it! Come on, let's get you back to my place and clean you up. Where are your clothes?'

'I don't know, he must have taken them, I suppose.'

'Oh, great! So you've got to walk back completely naked. That'll look good if a police car happens to drive past us.'

'That's a risk we'll have to take. Come on, I'm bloody freezing, and frightened.'

There were no police cars, watchers, followers, as they dashed from shadow to shadow, gateway to gateway, until the safety of Donna's flat. Why was Barry to be Sue's secret? Donna wondered as she rummaged through her wardrobe to find Sue some clothes. He was only a man, a man they'd both enjoyed in the woods. Why the secrecy? And why the enforced bondage? Had he planned to return and take her again – to fill her bottom-hole with his gushing sperm for a second time? Barry was a strange one, an unknown quantity – and as such, a dangerous one.

Donna was thankful to have someone to cuddle up to in her bed that night. She did not tell Sue that she'd seen her with Barry in the woods, that she knew her secret. Instead, warm and naked, they kissed, explored each other's mouths with their tongues, their crevices with their fingers. Had Sue liked her bottom-hole being fucked, as Barry had put it? She wanted to ask her – she wanted a man's throbbing penis buried in her own bottom-hole. Her college students would do it, she decided. Both at once, they would pleasure her holes with their iron rods.

'Have you ever had a man take you from behind?' she asked softly.

'What do you mean?' Sue replied hesitantly.

'Had a man do it to you from behind, you know?'

'No, have you?'

'Yes,' Donna lied as she slipped a finger into Sue's

bottom. 'It was wonderful. You should try it sometime.'

Sue's finger found its way into Donna's tight rear.

'Maybe I will try it – one day, maybe I will.'

And me, Donna thought as she closed her eyes and massaged the sperm within Sue's hot bottom hot – and me.

Chapter Thirteen

The ringing telephone woke Donna at seven the following morning. Sue had gone, flown the love-nest like Elizabeth, leaving only a rumpled pillow as a reminder of a night of fulfilled female desires. Why did her lovers leave her bed before she woke? Were they afraid – somehow fearful of her, what she'd do to them? Surely they couldn't fear mind-blowing orgasms? They must have left because they had their own little lives to lead, their own little worlds to pursue – their thoughts to think. Thoughts of their latent lesbianism manifesting at last, of their sexuality, their powerful orgasms induced by her tongue. Confused thoughts, Donna concluded.

'Is that Donna?' a woman asked as Donna pressed the phone to her ear and yawned.

'Yes, it is.'

'I saw your advert and . . . I'm sorry to have to ring you so early, but it's my husband, you see. He's sleeping at the moment, I don't want him to know that I'm . . . Anyway, can I make an appointment to come and see you?'

Through her sleepy confusion Donna remembered the advert. Why wasn't she ever prepared for anything other than sex? she chastised herself, panicking. 'Certainly, if I can just take your name,' she replied, trying

263

to sound bright and summery.

'Mandy, Mandy Collins. I'm free this afternoon, if you can fit me in, that is.'

'I am rather booked up, Mandy, but let's just have a look in the diary. Ah, you're lucky, I have a cancellation. How does three o'clock suit you?'

'That's fine. May I ask how much you charge?'

You may, but I haven't got a bloody clue, Donna almost said aloud. What's it worth? God, be professional, Ryan! How long will it take? An hour, no, two hours. The phone sucked the words from her mouth before she could think.

'Fifty pounds an hour.'

'Right. I look forward to meeting you, Donna.'

'Er . . . Yes, likewise, Mandy. The first session usually takes a couple of hours so . . .' She wasn't sure why she was trying to out-price herself. Perhaps she wanted the day to herself, to go to the park, to do as she pleased? She half-hoped the woman would say no.

'That's all right. I've plenty of time and I really do need this problem sorting out, believe me.'

'What is your problem, exactly?'

'I'd rather not say over the phone, and besides, I think my husband's awake now. If you'll tell me your address, I'll be there at three.'

Too much sex, Donna thought as she settled on her pillow and brushed her blonde hair from her face. She couldn't rid her mind of sex, her body, her clitoris, sexual thoughts – not that she really wanted to.

A chirping bird dragged her gaze to the window. Was her voyeur there now, in the bushes, crouching, peeping, masturbating? Was he thinking of sex? Where was Alan? Where the hell had everyone got to? She had initiated them all into the delights of sex and they'd got together and deserted her, their mentor – run off with their carnal knowledge.

The sun was hot, burning hot, even through the quilt. Donna kicked it off the bed and spread her legs. Now the sun burned the naked lips nestling neatly between the silky softness of her thighs – warm, moist, girlish lips. To masturbate or not to masturbate? she mused. A quick go with the vibrator before starting the day? It would certainly please anyone who happened to be spying through the window. Why did he want to spy? She wouldn't ask him outright – perhaps drop one or two subtle hints and get him to give her some clues as to why he'd made his dirty phone calls, followed, watched – spied.

Masturbation shouldn't be hurried, Donna thought as she parted her lips and touched the sensitive tip of her clitoris. Her faithful little bud deserved more than a quick go with the vibrator – gentle, unhurried caresses, the slow filling of her sheath with the cucumber, sensations rising from her pelvis, rolling over her body and timelessly crashing through her mind. Masturbation would have to wait, she decided, suddenly remembering Debbie.

The photographs, one thousand pounds – a lot of money to part with in exchange for a few pictures. Why was Debbie so eager to pay out all that money? Who was she afraid of? Photographs of her shapely body, naked, open, her face grimacing in orgasm? Was that something to be ashamed of? Orgasm was natural, healthy. Would Steve be there, waiting to catch Donna when the pay-off was made? Would he tie her down, cane her, punish her? She wanted to be thrashed, to have her buttocks whipped until they burned.

Dressing, she was aware of eyes gazing at her firm, pointed breasts, the smooth plateau of her stomach, her naked cunt lips. The feeling brought Donna exciting sensations – delicious sensations of sexual power, of being in the limelight, beneath the spotlight. Whatever she did now in the privacy of her flat, the openness of the woods, she was aware of constant scrutiny. Whether the prying eyes were always for real or not, she didn't know, but she liked to think that they were there. She wanted the eyes to be there always, watching, sending images of her lewd nakedness to a male brain – impulsed to a stiff penis.

No knickers, no bra. It was a shame most women chose to cover their beauty with clothes, she reflected as she stepped into her miniskirt and pulled it up her slender legs. The male body should be naked, too, the penis free to hang before the eyes of women – hungry women with patches. One day, perhaps. Clothes were inhibiting. What idiot had invented them, anyway? And what fools began wearing them?

Scrambled eggs on toast, fresh orange juice and coffee. With no work to go to, Donna could enjoy her life, enjoy her breakfast without checking the clock every five minutes. Without her inhibitions she had all the time in the world to enjoy her body, her clitoris. She picked and nibbled at her food, thinking, wondering. What would her first appointment be like? Probably an overweight woman with personal hygiene problems – not a fresh young girl desperate to learn of masturbation, of orgasm.

Deciding against an early morning jog through the park, Donna stuffed the photographs of Debbie into her bag and went out to her car. She would drop the pictures round to Debbie and collect the cash after she'd spoken to Alan, she decided. There were things to say, important things that had been left unsaid.

Alan wouldn't be at the lab yet, Donna reflected as she drove to his flat. He'd be surprised to see her – smile, welcome her, invite her in, ask searching questions, talk of love. She'd talk of the truth, the truth about the patches, the hormone, her feelings for him, whatever they were. Strange, mixed emotions – continually changing patterns in the mist of the mind.

'Donna!' Alan exclaimed, opening the door in his dressing gown.

'That's me,' she smiled, tossing her long blonde hair over her shoulder. She was pleased to see him. It gave her a summery feeling.

'You'd better come in, I suppose.'

Suppose? Wasn't he happy to see her? Didn't he want her, her body – her naked, writhing body?

'I'm already late for the lab, what was it you wanted?' he asked nonchalantly as he glanced at his watch.

A good question, Donna thought, considering he'd just shattered her well-rehearsed script, her feelings, with his indifference. I want you, your body, she was about to say, but the look in his eye told her not to. What was that look? What did it mean? Love-hate? Hate-love? Weren't they the same?

'I thought I'd just come and say hello as I was passing,' she lied unconvincingly, the sparkle fading from her eyes.

'Going anywhere nice?'

'Not really. I was . . . Look, Alan, can we talk?'

'We are, aren't we?'

'Come on, you know what I mean.'

'Talk about what?'

'You know about what. You love me, don't you?'

He smiled – at her presumption? He didn't know why he was smiling. He looked at her, into her eyes to discover what lay beneath her surface – the new Donna. But he found nothing there in the misty blue mystery of her eyes. Was there anything to discover?

'I told you of my love for you the other day. I held you, loved you, said that I'd love you forever, remember?' he asked mechanically, as if talking to a child.

'Yes. Yes, I do. And now?'

'I don't know, Donna. So much has happened, so much water under the bridge.'

Bridges crumble.

'What's happened?'

'You tell me. Anything and everything has happened, it seems. You tell me what has happened, Donna.'

Alan knew more than Donna had realised, but how? No, he couldn't know what she'd been up to – or with whom. He kept glancing at his watch, worrying about the time, the lab. She wasn't concerned with the time – nothing seemed to matter anymore. To tell or not to tell? she contemplated. It wasn't the right time to talk of the patches, of love, not early in the morning. But what was time? Was there ever a right time?

'I don't know what you mean,' she replied hesitantly. 'I left the lab, yes, that happened. I've done this and that, made one or two new friends . . .'

'Friends? Is that what they are, Donna, friends?'

'Who?'

'Your new friends, as you call them, is that what they really are to you?'

'Yes, of course, why do you ask? All I said was that I've made one or two new friends, what's the big deal?'

'The big deal, Donna, is that I know everything. And before you open your pretty little mouth – I mean that I know absolutely everything.'

'Good, then that will save me explaining all about Rodrico, won't it?' she bluffed, sure that it would floor him.

Alan moved towards the kitchen, his dressing gown flowing behind him. Filling the kettle, he turned as if about to speak, then turned back again. Donna stood in the doorway, her head to one side, awaiting his answer. Again, he turned to face her, looked her up and down as if trying to decide on a purchase in the supermarket. Male thoughts thinking male things, she mused.

'I know everything about you, Donna. What you've been up to, who with, when and where – I know the lot.'

'So tell me what you know about Rodrico. I met him the other day when I was . . . Well, you tell me, seeing as you know absolutely everything.'

The kitchen was still a mess, she couldn't help but notice. Poor Alan, there he was, fiddling with a coffee jar, trying to think of a way of explaining that he'd never heard of the mysterious Rodrico. There he was, torn by jealousy – love.

'I haven't got all day, Alan. I came here to talk to you and, it seems, you don't want to talk to me. Your conversation so far has consisted of nothing more than telling me that you know everything, yet you seem to know nothing. I asked you if you loved me, can't you even answer a simple question like that?'

'A simple question? You think that love is simple, do you?'

'No, I said that the question is simple.'

'For God's sake, Donna, don't talk to me about love! As . . . as far as you're concerned, love is . . . love is stripping naked and screwing someone, anyone, anywhere, male or female, friends, strangers – anyone who happens to be unfortunate enough to come your way!'

'So do I take it that you don't love me, then?'

'I did. I mean, I do. I love the real you, the old Donna. Not this . . . this . . .'

'This fallen woman, this whore standing before you? You didn't love the old Donna, Alan! The good old, faithful, meek lab assistant who wouldn't say boo to a goose, you didn't love her! The old Donna who tried, God knows I tried, to get you out of the lab, for a drink, for a meal, for anything! You love the old Donna, do you? The one you barely noticed, the one in the white lab coat who jumped at your every word? Get me this, please, Donna! Pass me that, please, Donna! Take this over to cultures, please Donna! Didn't you look beyond the lab coat? *Beneath* the lab coat? Didn't you see the woman – me? Didn't you feel the admiration, the love, yes, the love I had for you? You saw nothing until I seduced you – and then all you saw was a way to pleasure yourself as and when it took your fancy.'

'I . . . Look, Donna . . .'

'No, *you* look! Look at me, a woman, a person, a human being with thoughts, feelings, emotions – and this.'

Pulling her short skirt up and over her hips, Donna exposed her knickerless pussy to his startled eyes. Lifting her T-shirt, she bared her firm, rounded breasts, her beautifully formed, elongated nipples. 'And this, Alan – a body! Yes, a woman's body – tits, pussy and all! I have my wants, my needs, my desires as much as you do – sexual wants, needs, desires. But I have more than you'll ever have. You will never know what it's like to be a woman, or understand women's thoughts, desires, needs. But I have a better understanding of men now, how they think, their sexual thoughts. I'm a woman thinking male thoughts.'

'Listen to me for a moment, please, Donna.'

'No, *you* listen. You make your little patches to help women, to replace their flailing hormones. What you don't realise is that they do far more than that! They . . .'

Breaking off, Donna restored her T-shirt and skirt to their former state. Tears welled as she turned and fled – tears of love lost. Alan called, chased after her as she slammed the front door shut and ran to her car. God, why had she said so much? It was his fault, she told herself as the tyres screeched and she sped down the road. His fault he had an attitude problem. She glanced in the rear view mirror to see him standing in the middle of the road waving her back, his dressing gown flapping open in the breeze like a sail on a lost sailing ship. With Alan at the helm, the crew didn't stand a chance. Pathetic.

She drove – round corners, unknown corners, along unknown roads leading to unknown places. Her stomach churned, tears flowed, mind swimming and then drowning in her tears. Pulling up by a deserted common, she climbed from her car, slammed the door shut and walked. Walked and wandered, aimlessly, without direction, without meaning.

A young couple passed by, hand in hand, laughing, happy. What was happiness – money, orgasm? She didn't know, she supposed she'd never really been happy. Passing by a bench, she stopped, turned and sat down. 'Fucking hell.' The words fell from her lips, slowly, and landed gently on the grass, unheard, unnoticed. 'Fucking hell!' she spat. Louder words, words with meaning, drifting across the common for all to hear. But no-one heard. The angels may have heard – but there were no angels, she decided.

She didn't notice the middle-aged woman moving towards her, moving slowly towards her like a drifting boat towards the shore. The woman sat down, quietly, softly, and gazed out across the common. Donna turned her head and glanced at her. What the hell did she want? A fucking great common like this and she had to sit here! A lone spot on a sandy beach, far removed from the pale faces of the noisy crowd, and someone comes and sits feet away. Why?

'I often come here to think,' the woman said without turning her head. Who was she talking to – herself? Donna let out a rush of breath and raised her eyes to the sky. So bloody what? she thought. 'It helps me to think,' the woman continued. 'Out here, alone with the birds, the grass, the trees, it helps me to think.' Alone – no chance of being alone, not in a world full of people. 'Do you come here often?'

What was it, a chat-up line?

'I've never been here before and I'll never come again,' Donna snarled through gritted teeth. 'I never want to go anywhere, be anywhere again.'

'I felt like that before . . . My husband and I used to come here and talk. We'd talk and laugh for hours, but then he . . .'

'He what?' Donna spat.

'He died. Six months ago, he . . . An accident, it was.'

Donna turned and looked at the woman. Her eyes were red, bloodshot from months of streaming tears. She was attractive, pretty, but looked tired. Tired of life, life alone, Donna surmised. She stood up, looked down to Donna and smiled. 'Whatever your problem is, there's always someone better off than you – and always someone worse off. Remember that.'

Donna watched as the woman walked away, her words of wisdom spoken. Steve had said something similar, she remembered. Smiling, she stood up and breathed in the summery air as she walked back to her car, a spring in her step, new life in her heart. It was meant to be, she knew. Meeting the woman was meant to be.

Pulling out onto a main road, she suddenly realised that she was near to Debbie's house. Glancing at her watch, she grinned. Nine-thirty, plenty of time to see Debbie and then get home for her three o'clock appointment.

There was no car in the drive as Donna pulled up outside the house. Steve must be out, she thought thankfully as she grabbed her bag and climbed out of the car. Would Debbie be in? she wondered, leaning against the car door and pressing it shut. Walking up the drive, she saw the net curtains move aside and Debbie's face smiling at her. Why smile at your blackmailer? A trick? Was Steve hiding, waiting to pounce once she was inside, the door closed and locked? Donna glanced back to her car wondering if she'd ever see it again, if she'd be driving it away, driving home to her flat again.

'Come in,' Debbie invited as she opened the huge oak door, a door that spoke money. Following her into the lounge, Donna looked to the sofa – no ropes, bonds, handcuffs, cane – no Steve, it seemed. 'Drink?' Debbie asked, opening an antique cabinet containing more bottles than the local pub.

'No, I'm driving,' she replied, praying that she would be doing so within ten minutes. 'Here are the photographs.'

'And here's your money,' Debbie replied, holding out an envelope.

Why was she being so nice, so overly nice? What was her game? 'Keep your money,' Donna said. 'None of this had anything to do with you. You were sucked into the mire, so to speak, sucked into the shit.'

'Take the money, Donna. Steve's explained everything to me, and I have you to thank for . . .'

'Thank?'

'Yes, I have you to thank for the patches. Things are so different now. Steve and I are . . .'

'But he said that you were going with anyone and everyone. I don't understand.'

'I did, initially. Mind you, all I did was exactly as he'd been doing for a long time. But yes, I did screw around, as he calls it. I seem to have settled down with him now. I don't want or need anyone else.'

'Oh,' Donna breathed despondently. Gazing at Debbie's short skirt and shapely thighs, she'd half-hoped that she would allow her to open her legs, to kiss the softness between her thighs, to lick and suck her clitoris. Catching her sensual gaze, Debbie smiled.

'I suppose if I were still wearing a patch, I would . . . Well, I would like to . . . Anyway, I'm not.'

'I am,' Donna declared.

'I daren't use the patch again. I promised Steve that now things are all right between us I wouldn't use the patch.'

'Not just the once?' Donna asked dejectedly.

'Look, I like you very much, too much for my own good, I'm afraid. Ring me, we'll arrange something.

Here, take the money. The patches were worth every penny, believe me. And do ring me, I really want to . . . Just ring me – promise?'

'Promise.'

The look in Donna's eye was a look of love – lust. No words passed between them as they walked through the hall to the front door. But their lips kissed, their tongues met, their saliva mingled delightfully. Stomach swirling, breathing deepening, eyes rolling, closing – females exchanging female love.

Driving away from the house, Donna grinned. No more blackmail, no more crap, no more . . . Shit! Lynn Bulmur. Her name loomed from nowhere, a bad penny, a rotten egg, a rotten bitch. Who was her man, her gangster man? More to the point, where was he? Gangstering somewhere, no doubt. Had he prised anything out of Bulmur? Perhaps he'd killed her? That would solve one big problem. Why hadn't he been to her flat demanding patches? Perhaps Bulmur had killed him? Perhaps they'd killed each other in a shoot-out? This isn't the movies, Ryan!

Flopping into her armchair, she tore open the envelope the minute she arrived home. Counting out the crisp twenty-pound notes, she frowned. 'Two hundred and fifty notes?' She counted again, and then again. 'Five thousand pounds? It can't be! Bloody hell! I've got it made!'

Ten o'clock – five hours to go. Prepare, organise, rehearse. Rehearse what? The sex dungeon – apply the patch, talk, drink coffee and then lead her into the dungeon of lust. What was her problem? Perhaps she didn't have a clitoris? Donna found herself thinking. If that was the case, then she'd never be able to come. Vaginal orgasm, or clitoral orgasm? She remembered reading somewhere about the debate, the argument. The G-spot, did she have one? When the woman had gone, she'd experiment. Use the vibrator to locate her G-spot, use it on her nipples and see what happened. She was pleased that she was a woman. Men only had one dangly bit while women had a treasure trove of interesting bits and pieces – all capable of bringing pleasure.

Her thoughts returned to the appointment. What to wear? The leather catsuit? No – she should have asked the woman's age, got some idea of what she was like. Shortish skirt, blouse, and bra – no knickers, of course. If she was anything like Charlie, she'd be happy. Where *was* Charlie?

Her heart leaped as the doorbell rang. 'Shit, she's early!' she breathed. 'Five bloody hours early!' She had no choice – open the door and let her in, or lose her client. Ready or not, she knew she'd have to face her.

'It's me again, Ryan,' Lynn Bulmur spat as Donna opened the door. 'And I've come to sort you out, as I said I would!' Pushing her way into the hall, she slammed the front door, grabbed Donna by the throat and forced her up against the wall. 'You gave him the photographs, you bitch!' she fumed through gritted teeth. 'And now I'm right in the fucking shit!'

Donna struggled to unlock Lynn's hands from her throat. Choking, she kicked out and managed to free herself, but Lynn came at her again, murder in her eyes, evil eating her heart. Quickly jumping to one side, she watched Lynn's fist hit the wall with a loud crack before she doubled up in pain. In a flash, she determined her wounded victim ready for the taking, for her inevitable fate in the sex dungeon. The devil's daughter would be cast into the fire of hell, a sexual hell where multiple orgasms relentlessly tortured.

Dragging her through the hall, Donna grinned wickedly as she realised that, at long last, she had the chance to deal with Lynn Bulmur – once and for all. Her head spun with the fearsome things she was going to do to her prisoner as she marched her into the spare room and threw her across the bed. Lynn put up little in the way of a fight as Donna cuffed her wrists and ankles. More concerned with her aching hand, she either didn't realise what was going on, or didn't care. But her fate was sealed – now Lucifer could only watch.

Suddenly aware of the window, Donna drew the curtains. Her voyeur wasn't going to be given the chance to see Lynn Bulmur chained to the bed, witness her terrible punishment and then blackmail her. Only the walls would see. Only the walls would know.

Donna looked back to her prisoner and smiled. Her hands above her head, her legs spread, Lynn was vulnerable, at last, open to her captor's every whim. No-one must know, Donna knew. No-one must know anything about Lynn Bulmur – her awesome fate. This was to be her terrible secret.

Realising that she couldn't let her prisoner go, Donna began to wonder exactly what it was she was going to do with her. Punish her, yes, but then what? Keep her chained forever? 'I'll get you for this, Ryan!' Lynn spat as she pulled on the handcuffs and struggled to free herself.

'Too late, you're my prisoner, and you'll stay that way until . . . Well, until I've finished with you. You've fucked up a lot of people's lives, my friends' lives, my life, and now you're going to pay for it.'

'When I get out of here, I'll . . .'

'What do you mean, when? What makes you think that you'll ever see the light of day again? You broke into the lab, tricked me and tied me up and had Steve take dirty photographs of me! You stole my money! I've had enough! Set fire to my flat, get your gangster friend to deal with me – threat after threat I've had from you, and it's come to an end! It's finished, Bulmur – *you*'re finished!'

Her hands shaking, her breathing unsteady, she went into the kitchen to compose herself. 'Fuck it!' she cursed under her breath. 'Fuck Lynn bloody Bulmur!' Anger swelled in the pit of her stomach. She should have dealt with her earlier, she knew. But how? There was nothing else she could have done. To tie her up and hold her prisoner was the only way to stop her evil meddling. Fired with hatred now, she grabbed a carving knife from the drawer and returned to the spare room – to the dungeon of sexual torture.

Lynn gazed in disbelief as Donna approached, the blade glistening in the light as she held it in her clenched fist, her knuckles whitened, her face flushed, her eyes afire.

'No, please, no! For Christ's sake, Ryan – no!'

'What's the matter? Don't you want your throat cut? All right, then, how would you like your nipples cut off? Or your clitoris? Yes, that would put an end to your sex life. Imagine it, you're desperate for orgasm and you haven't got a clitoris!'

'You're bloody mad! You've gone crazy! Let me go, I'll never come back, I promise – please!'

Slipping the knife between Lynn's thighs, Donna made a neat cut up the front of her skirt. Peeling the two halves aside, she grinned to see that Lynn wasn't wearing any knickers. Cutting Bulmur's T-shirt, she opened the flimsy material to reveal her firm breasts. The fire in her eyes burning bright now, Donna took a nipple between her finger and thumb and pulled it up, stretching the brown tissue until Lynn cried out for mercy. 'What's the matter now? I'm only going to cut your nipple off,' Donna laughed as she placed the blade against the base of the elongated milk-bud. Possessed by Lucifer? She didn't know, or care. Her only thoughts were revenge for all the bitch had done.

'Please! I'll do anything! Anything!'

'Too late. I'm going to put your nipples and your clitoris in a matchbox so that I can look at them whenever I think of you, whenever I think of all the damage you've done. But not now. I'm busy, so you'll just have to wait until I'm ready – sweat it out.'

Releasing Lynn's nipple, Donna looked at the bag she'd bought from the sex shop. Placing it on the bed, she pulled out the nipple clamps and grinned. 'Do you know what these are?' she asked. Focussing her tearful eyes on the daunting devices, Lynn shook her head. 'They're nipple clamps. They fit over your nipples like this, and you turn this bit, like this, and they get tighter and tighter until . . . I want to prolong your agony for as long as possible, so I'll only tighten them until you squirm a little, until your eyes water and you beg me for mercy.'

As Donna tightened the clamps, Lynn begged her to stop, pleading for mercy. Standing back to admire her work, Donna's mind swirled, wickedness rising to flood her with evil thoughts. Lucifer was there now, coaxing, egging her on, bringing out the animal in her, driving her to torture his daughter. The devil's work was never done.

Observing between Lynn's thighs, Donna smiled.

'I've never really examined anyone's vagina before,' she remarked.

'What do you mean?' Lynn whimpered.

'Well, I've never seen what's at the end of a vagina. I wonder if I can pull your cunt open wide enough for me to see your cervix? I need a tube, a length of pipe to push inside you. Then I can look through it and see what's at the end of your cunt. Good idea, don't you agree? Or I could just cut you open, continue your slit up your stomach and take a proper look. I'll have to think about it.'

Lynn said nothing as Donna left the room to answer the phone. There was nothing she could say. Her pleas had gone unheard, her cries drifted aimlessly with no direction, no-one to hear.

'Donna, it's Alan. Can I come and see you?'

'Oh, Alan. I . . . I don't know. I'm rather busy just now.'

'I know about the patches. I know that you've been using them.' So he did know. But how? Had her voyeur told him? He didn't even know Alan. How the hell could he know?

'What do you mean?' she asked innocently, her stomach churning.

'I mean that I know all about the patches, the effect they have on women – on you. Can I come round and talk to you?'

'About what?'

'The patches, the future – our future. I've left the lab.'

'What!'

'Yes, I've left the lab and I want to work with you on the patches. Since I saw you earlier, I've given it a lot of thought. I want to work *with* you – not against you.'

Donna had no choice. What with Lynn Bulmur chained to the bed, her client coming round, Sue, Helen, Sophie, Barry, Steve, Debbie, the college students . . . She needed Alan. She needed a man. Even with the omnipotent patches bringing her power, she needed the power of a man. Men ruled – sometimes.

'Yes, Alan,' she heard herself agreeing meekly. 'Yes, Alan!'

Chapter Fourteen

'I've discovered an antidote for the hormone,' Alan announced as Donna let him it.

'I don't want an antidote. The patches, the hormone, can bring women power, orgasms – everything. Why take that away?'

'Yes, I know all about the effects. But it's gone too far, Donna. Don't you see what's happening? That Bulmur friend of yours has been distributing patches. Haven't you heard?'

'Heard what?'

'Two women, girls, set up a brothel in a flat in town. When they were arrested and questioned, they told the police about the patches.'

'Who? What girls?'

'Friends of that Lynn Bulmur. And there's more. A girl, I don't know her name, was discovered in the park with three men. She'd paraded herself around the park, naked, in front of everyone, and then taken three young men into the woods and . . .'

'How do you know all this?'

'Jim Slater, a CID friend of mine. He's been to see me in connection with the patches. I dealt with it, thankfully – told him that the idea was ludicrous, and he accepted it. But there's more. The police were called to the college. Apparently, the students have been openly screwing each other. Some of the girls, it seems, have become whores, blatantly stripping off and doing all sorts of things, to each other as well as to the boys.'

'Where did they get the patches from? Lynn only had a few.'

'A man has been selling them. I don't know who he is, or how he got hold of them. Lynn Bulmur must know him and have given him a supply of patches. If we can cut off the supply, I'm sure that things will settle down. The police aren't overly interested now that I've spoken with Jim. They're putting it down to the summer heat, or something equally ridiculous.'

'I've got Bulmur tied up in the spare room,' Donna admitted.

'What? Tied up? But . . .'

'Yes, I had to. Let's question her, find out who this man is.'

Alan gazed in disbelief at Lynn's naked body chained to the bed. Looking at Donna and then back to Lynn he shook his head.

'What the hell do you intend to do with her? I mean, you can't keep her here like this!'

'I don't know. She was causing me too many problems, I don't know.'

Lynn lay wide-eyed, wide-legged on the bed, her swollen cunt lips open, blatantly exposed to Alan, a complete stranger. She turned her head to hide her shame, her embarrassment, but could do nothing to avert his gaze burning the lips between her legs, her exposed pussy lips – her girlishness. 'Let me go and I'll say nothing,' she pleaded without turning her head.

'Who's the man, Bulmur? The man selling the patches, who is he?' Donna asked, her anger rising – her arousal rising.

'There is no man.'

'Don't lie! I'll beat the truth out of you unless you tell me! I bought a nice whip the other day, I'll use it on you unless you tell me!'

'There is no man, I swear. Please, let me go!'

'Where have you been getting the patches from?'

'I haven't. I only had a few, the ones you gave me.'

Suddenly Donna realised who the man was – her voyeur. She smiled at Alan, hurling a salacious grin at Lynn. 'I know who he is,' she said softly, her blue eyes sparkling. 'And I'm going to bring him here and tell him that you told us all about him. He'll be quite upset. In fact, to think that you've told us everything, he'll be more than upset, he'll probably kill you. After he's raped and beaten you, that is.'

Leading Alan out, she closed the door behind them. Taking him into the lounge, she turned to face him. 'I'm going out,' she said. 'I'm going to try to find this man and bring him back here. If my client arrives before I get back, make her coffee and tell her that I've been delayed or something.'

'Client?'

'Yes, a woman with sexual problems. I placed an ad in the paper and . . . Just look after her until I get back, and if she can't wait, take her phone number and tell her that I'll call her.'

Alan wandered into the spare room the minute Donna had closed the front door – a fire of passion in his eyes, a bulge of desire in his trousers. Lucifer was near now, goading him, pushing him to take his daughter's body, to use her for his pleasure. Why not? The walls would contain the debauched secret, the secret of the debauchery. The walls would tell no-one – not even Donna.

'You've a very nice body,' he murmured, stroking Lynn's stomach.

'Get away from me! Don't touch me!'

'It's a shame to let you go to waste. It's not every day that an opportunity like this arises, is it?'

'Keep away from me! Donna will be back soon and . . .'

'Donna won't know anything about it. She won't know that I've amused myself, used you, played with you while she's been out, will she?'

'I'll tell her. I'll . . .'

'No, she won't believe you. You see, she's in love with me. Poor little Donna has fallen in love, she's blinded by love. I love her, yes, but I'm a man – a normal man. And what normal man would turn his back on a fine young woman such as you? You're naked, vulnerable, the sweet little hole between your thighs is mine for the taking. No man could resist such an opportunity.'

Running a finger up her open groove, he smiled as he located her clitoris. Circling the tiny bud, he bent over and kissed her breast, sucked the firm flesh into his mouth until she whimpered. 'Donna thinks that I know nothing of her little escapades,' he whispered, tightening the nipple clamps. 'I've had my fun with her friends. Sophie and Helen, they've been to my flat several times and we've had some fun. Donna thinks that I've been working at the lab, staying at home, being boring. How wrong she is! I've had my spy follow her, tell me everything, her every move. I know all there is to know about the young Donna Ryan! But I haven't had the pleasure of getting to know *you*, the pleasure of using *your* body yet, have I?'

'How can you say that you love her when you send

people to spy on her and you screw her friends? I'll tell her everything about you, what you really are – a bastard!'

'A bastard, maybe. Aren't all men? I'm a normal man, as I said. She won't believe that Alan Rosenberg, her ex-boss, the man who has told her of his great love for her, has used women, girls, for his own sexual pleasure. Never would she believe it of me.'

'She will believe it! Anyway, I don't believe that you've got a so-called spy. It's rubbish!'

'His name's Barry. He'd seen Donna most mornings when he was out jogging and decided that he liked her. He began following her, became obsessed with her, I suppose. Apparently, he'd intended to ask her out but she didn't even return his smile when they passed in the street. That was the old Donna, the Donna without a patch. When they met in the park, he met the new Donna, the uninhibited Donna. He's been keeping me informed of her activities. Funnily enough, we met quite by chance. He came to the lab looking for her after she'd seduced him in the park. We got talking and . . . Well, he's my spy. Will Donna believe that? No, never. I've just given her some cock and bull story about the police – just to worry her. I need her to need me, you see. It's called psychology. Clever, don't you think?'

'I'll tell her everything.'

'As I keep saying, she won't believe a word of it. Anyway, let's get on with it, shall we? There's not much time to enjoy the beauty between your legs.'

Easing three fingers between Lynn's moist, vaginal lips, he pressed them into the wet warmth and massaged the inner flesh of her tightening sheath. 'You like that, don't you?' he asked as he began to caress her clitoris with his free hand.

'No. I mean, yes. Look, let me go and we can . . .'

'Let you go? Why would I want to let you go? You're in the perfect position for what I intend to do to you.'

For what Lucifer intends to do.

Manoeuvring himself between her thighs, Alan noticed Donna's vibrator lying on the floor. 'This looks interesting. Let's try it out, shall we?' he said, his dark eyes mirroring lust.

'Look, just let me go and . . .'

'You'll like this. I'm going to make you come.'

'I don't want to come!'

'Of course you do. All women want to come.'

Placing the cold metal tip between Lynn's pinken lips, Alan looked into her eyes. Fear mingled with desire in the dark pools beneath her long lashes, her tongue licking her lips, dry with heavy breathing, anticipation. Buzzing softly, the vibrations immediately caused her to arch her back and gasp her delight.

'That's nice! God, that's nice! I've never . . . I've never . . .'

'Never used a vibrator?'

'No, never.'

'Then you'll enjoy this.'

The walls closed in like a thick fog to contain the scenario, to hide the debauchery from the prying eyes of the world – a world with no understanding of the base desires locked in the dark, musky dungeon of the female subconscious.

Unaware of the lust engulfing her flat, Donna wandered into the trees thinking of her voyeur. The summer sun was hot in the blue sky. The summer knew nothing of her secrets, nothing of her new life. But the trees knew, she was sure, as she looked up to their protective

canopy and smiled. They'd seen her, naked, writhing in
orgasm as her body was filled with sperm, fresh sperm
from fresh young men. I'll have them again, soon, she
thought as she moved towards the railway cutting, the
deep valley – her valley.

Not expecting her voyeur to be there in the middle of
the morning, Donna decided to leave a note pinned to
the tree – the fallen tree where fallen women gave their
bodies in the name of lust. As she pulled a pen from her
bag and scribbled her phone number on an old envelope, she had the familiar feeling of being watched. Not
by the trees, but by someone lurking, prying.

'Barry!' she called. 'You can come out now, I know
you're there, hiding, watching me, as usual.' Emerging
from the bushes, he smiled. He'd not been jogging, not
in his jeans. He'd been voyeuring, masturbating, more
than likely, thinking of her on her bed bringing her
clitoris to its climax as he spurted his seed over the
ground.

'How did you know I was there?' he asked.

'I've known for ages, Barry. Spying on me, masturbating outside my bedroom window as you watched *me*
masturbate, I've known for a long time.'

He reddened, his mouth falling open.

'Why did you make the dirty phone calls? Did it
give you a kick or something?' Donna asked, to shock
him.

'I didn't make . . . Yes, I suppose it did give me a
kick. I wanted you for myself, you see. I was infatuated,
obsessed with you, before we met. Every morning in the
street. Anyway, my girlfriend finally left me for some
other bloke and . . . Well, now you know. I'm sorry if it
upset you. I didn't mean to . . .'

'Not at all. I found it quite amusing, really. Anyway,

it's not that I want to talk about. You've been selling the patches haven't you?'

'Patches? What do you mean?'

'Come on, Lynn Bulmur told me.'

'I've never met her. I know who she is, but I've never met her.'

Donna frowned. She'd thought she'd known every-thing about Barry, but seemingly not. Looking into his eyes, she saw no lies. Just a man – a man with a good body, a long, thick penis. A man with lust reflected in the dark mirrors of his eyes. A man she wanted, desperately.

Suddenly she remembered Sue, tied naked over the fallen tree with Barry taking her from behind, holding her buttocks apart and thrusting his penis deep into the privacy of her bowels. She wanted him to take her from behind, to take her bottom-hole, to invade the dark privacy there with his hardness and fill her with his cream. Slipping her skirt off Donna smiled at him, a seductive smile – a smile of lust.

'I want you to give me what you gave Sue,' she ordered wickedly, her eyes afire with craving, her vaginal lips bubbling with her milky juices. 'I want you to take me from behind.'

'How do you . . . Were you watching us?'

'I've been watching you watching me. Why did you leave Sue tied to the tree? That was hardly fair, was it?'

'I followed you. I was going to come back. I . . . Well, by the time I did get back, she'd gone. I wasn't going to leave her there all night, if that's what you're thinking.'

'I don't know what to think. Anyway, are you going to give me what you gave her, or not?'

Slipping his jeans down, Barry grinned. His penis was

already hard – long, thick and ready for the secret entrance to Donna's body. He moved towards her, glancing at the fallen tree, giving his silent instruction. Leaning over the tree she spread her legs, exposed her bloated lips gaping invitingly below the tight hole of her young bottom to his hungry eyes. There she waited for her debased pleasure to commence – for her virginal bowels to yield to her desire, to take a penis, to be stretched, used in the name of debauchery.

Pressing his bulging knob between her wet cunt lips, Barry pushed the entire length of his hard shaft deep into her trembling body, lubricating his flesh in her creamy tube in readiness for her smaller entrance. Donna gasped and opened her legs wider as her clitoris stiffened, throbbed delightfully to the gentle caress of its pinken hood slipping back and forth over the sensitive tip. Clinging to the tree trunk, she felt her arousal rising, her nipples stinging, pressing against the rough bark, her womb contracting, her sheath tightening. She wanted to come, to flood his shaft with her juices and come.

Suddenly withdrawing his penis, Barry parted her buttocks and licked her there, wetting the circlet of brown tissue, lubricating the entrance. Standing now, he stabbed his knob at the small, quivering hole, waiting there in the valley between the pale globes climbing up either side of the dark cleft. Her dream dreamed, her time had come, Donna knew. She was about to experience the delight of a man's penis throbbing deep within her bowels, crudely opening and filling her pelvis.

Her muscles yielded a little, allowing the head of his hardness to slip past the defending barrier and bury itself in the hot, velvety darkness. Further he pressed, pulling on her hips, bringing her body ever nearer to his.

Donna wiggled her hips, took half his shaft within her bottom and gasped for more. Further he drove his shaft into the deep warmth until he'd impaled her completely. Her buttocks pressing against him, she gasped, whimpered a little and began to gyrate her hips, revelling in the new and wonderful sensations emanating from her uncharted depths.

Slowly, Barry slid his penis in and out, filling her, emptying her, rudely using her body for his own debased desires. But who was using who? The patches had brought equality, Donna thought fleetingly as her clitoris stiffened even more and cried out for attention. Never before would she have asked a man to take her bottom-hole – never would she have wanted a man driving his penis deep into her bottom-hole. Only the uninhibited know their desires – speak the truth of their desires.

Slipping her hand between her legs, Donna located her yearning spot and began her sensual massage. Barry thrust harder now, desperately taking her bottom-hole, fucking her there with his hardness as she brought her clitoris ever nearer to fruition. Their decadent union brought unknown sensations, locked them in a strangely virginal lust as their naked bodies shuddered under the sensual caress of the Prince of Darkness.

'God, you're beautiful!' Barry gasped, his balls slapping the wet, swelling lips of Donna's cunette, his knob driving deeper into her velveteen hotness. She gasped her gasp of pleasure as she gyrated her hips faster, took the full length of his manhood deep inside hot body and squeezed her muscles around its girth. 'Coming, coming,' he breathed as he groped between her lips and thrust four fingers into the creaminess of her soft tube.

Donna's cries filled the wood, cries of perpetual

orgasm, of a deep lust rising from the depths of her bowels. 'I want two men!' The words bubbled from her lips and drifted through the summery air, up into the green canopy. 'Two men, both fucking me, two holes . . . Fucking my holes!' Her fantasy neared reality as Barry's fingers rammed her sheath and his penis drove deeper into her bottom. 'Two hard . . . Two . . . Ah, yes, yes! I'm coming, coming!'

Her long, low moan of ecstasy reverberated through the trees, swirling, drifting like a leaf on the wind as Donna brought her clitoris to its wondrous climax. Spurting now, the bulging head of Barry's penis swelled and throbbed deep within her pelvis. Pumping, spurting, filling her tightening passage with his sperm, he withdrew his fingers and yanked on her hips. Impaling the open centre of her shuddering body, depriving her of her anal virginity, he took her as she'd never been taken before.

Collapsing over the perspiring skin of Donna's back, Barry rested, swimming in the creamy sensations swirling around his pulsing knob, lost in the twitching of her hot, tight hole. Donna breathed heavily, squeezed the muscles of her bottom, drained the last drop of sperm from his shrinking rod, caressed her clitoris, induced the last flutters of orgasm quivering in her womb.

Slowly withdrawing his penis, Barry moved away and gazed at the creamy liquid oozing between Donna's parted buttocks. Oozing, trickling down between her wet lips, the fruits of orgasm sought their true home, entered her open lovemouth and mingled there with her juices to produce a cocktail of lust.

Lifting her exhausted body from the tree, Donna fell back onto the soft grass and looked up through the green canopy high above her to the blue sky. Smiling a smile of gratitude, she thanked the angels of lust for their precious gift – the gift of her body, her twin entrances of carnality.

Alan wasn't aware that Mandy was ringing the front doorbell as he worked on Lynn's hard clitoris with the vibrator. With Lynn crying out in her orgasm he could hear nothing else, think of nothing else, as he watched her bud swell and visibly throb time and time again in its trembling pleasure. Ignoring her pleas for more, he moved the metal shaft down her open valley and pushed it deep into her soft tube, lubricating the glistening surface with her female milk. The sensations running deep into her womb, Lynn begged Alan not to stop as he slipped the phallus from her burning body and pressed it between her buttocks. The tip rested there for a moment, pressing against the circlet of dark tissue as if waiting for the portal to open – the signal to enter her there.

'No, no! Please, not there!' Lynn cried as Alan pushed and twisted the buzzing shaft, forcing it past her defending muscles. Deeper and deeper into her writhing body the phallus sank, transmitting its wondrous sensual rhythm to the core of her very being. Her vaginal lips bloomed, opened like the petals of a flower to reveal her ripening clitoris within. Her juices flowed as Alan twisted and thrust the cylindrical intruder, opening her tight entrance, stretching the delicate membranes, waking the sleeping nerve endings, bringing life to her body. Like Donna's, Lynn's bottom was full – both stretched and opened in the name of insurmountable lust.

Slipping his trousers down, Alan moved between her thighs and pushed his penis deep into her velveteen sheath. Lynn cried out in her sexual agony but he only pushed his rod further into her consumed body until her abdomen swelled with the hardness within. Alan didn't need to move, to thrust back and forth, to make his fucking motions. Filling her pelvis, her sheath, the vibrations reverberated through her cunt and ran round the end of his penis like a thousand tiny caressing fingers, stiffening him, bringing him near to his climax.

Suddenly, Lynn's cunette tightened, gripping his penis like a velvet vice as she tossed her head from side to side and reached her orgasm. Feeling the stirring of his climax, Alan pressed his knob hard against her cervix, absorbing the tingling vibrations there, sucking the rhythm into his shaft, his balls.

Both locked into the lustful music of the vibrator, they shuddered, grimaced and groaned their pleasure as Alan's penis swelled and filled her with his gushing sperm. Her body contorted, Lynn begged for him to stop, begged for the beautiful torture flowing from the vibrator to leave her. But the sensations ran on and on, tearing her body open, ripping through her mind until she collapsed in an unknown and wondrous sexual haze. At last the devil's daughter was broken – reduced to a quivering heap of flesh.

'You're a bastard!' Lynn gasped as Alan pulled his shaft from her body. 'Using me like that, you're a bastard!'

'You loved every minute of it. Anyway, it's what a whore like you deserves. It's what young tarts like you and Donna are for – for using.'

Uncharacteristic words of a man obsessed, tortured with a debased lust – words of the devil.

'You're a dirty pervert!' Lynn cried, pulling on her bonds. An invitation from a woman tethered.

Ray Gordon

'You think so, do you? In that case, I'd better behave like one.'

Biting the wet lips between Lynn's splayed thighs, Alan slipped the buzzing phallus from her body and waited for his penis to rise and harden again. Licking her clitoris, stretching her soft folds, exposing her intimacy, once more he brought her near to her heaven. His hardness rampant now, he moved between her legs and pressed his penis between her wet lips to lubricate the silky knob. Suddenly he slipped it out and moved down, down below her girlish lips to the dark crease dividing her rounded buttocks.

'No, no!' Lynn pleaded. 'Please don't, not there!' Harder Alan pressed his silky knob against her tight entrance, forcing her open again, breaking past her defences until, suddenly, he slipped deep inside. She groaned, writhed, tossed her head as he took her with a vengeance, thrust his knob deeper and deeper into her bottom-hole leaving her soft sheath void, quivering in its emptiness, yearning to be filled.

'You like it this way, don't you?' Alan gasped as his balls stirred and his sperm began to rise.

'Bastard!' Lynn yelled in her debased ecstasy. 'Pervert!' Her expletives pulling the trigger, the explosion of sperm came, gushing, spurting deep into her bottom-hole, pumping her full of his shuddering orgasm. She wiggled her hips, delighting in the pulsating pleasure deep within her expanding passage, losing herself in the haze of her debased lust. Tight around his shaft, her bottom twitched, gripped like a gloved hand as her clitoris erupted into orgasm. 'Coming!' she gasped. 'My clit, rub my . . . Ah, ah! Rub . . .'

Vibrating his fingers over her hard bud, Alan brought out Lynn's climax as his own gently subsided. Her hot

296

bottom-hole spasmed, gripped, sucked the remnants of his orgasm from his swollen knob before, shuddering her last shudder, she was done. Alan grinned his satisfaction as he released Lynn's body from the pleasure of his rod. At the sound of a key in the door, he quickly pulled his trousers up to cover his guilty secret – his flaccid shaft glistening in its oiliness.

'Sorry I've been so long,' Donna smiled as she breezed into the room. 'I was held up, but I found my man. I was wrong, it seems. He knows nothing about the patches.'

'He fucked me, used me! He's an animal and he's using you, Donna! He lied about the police to worry you! Barry is his spy!' Lynn screamed hysterically from her bed of sex.

Donna looked to Alan, to the innocence in his eyes. 'Really?'

'Yes, he's using you. Barry has been telling him all about . . .'

Alan laughed.

'What an imagination your friend has. I've never heard of a Barry. Good God, whatever will she be telling you next?'

'He fucked my bottom!'

Donna laughed now. Alan wouldn't do that, she knew, not poor innocent Alan. Barry would. 'Don't talk rubbish, Bulmur. I know Alan better than that. He's not a liar, he's a good man. He doesn't know Barry, and neither do you so stop blabbering on.'

'Then how does he know his name? How do I know his name?'

Alan grinned at Lynn and winked, a devilish wink reflecting the devil in his eye. 'Donna mentioned the name when she came in just now,' he said.

'She didn't!'

'I must have done. Alan doesn't know the name, I must have said it. Did my client turn up, Alan?'

'No. No-one's called. Look, I'd better be going. I've one or two things to do so I'll call back later.'

'Yes, we've got a lot to talk about,' Donna smiled. Kissing him, she whispered words of love, sensual words of lust to come.

'I love you, Donna. Don't listen to her rubbish. Just remember that I love you,' he murmured, the normal lies of a normal man.

Turning to leave the room he smiled at Lynn, spitting and cursing him in her anger. Taking his arm, Donna pulled him towards the bed to her prisoner. 'I'll punish you for that, Bulmur, you bitch!' she swore. 'Turn her over for me, Alan. She needs a damn good beating.'

Releasing the cuffs, he turned Lynn's struggling body over and pinned her down. Her legs kicking, her fists lashing out, her naked body fought like that of a woman possessed. With his full weight on her now, Alan held her wrists as Donna chained her. Turning, he gripped her ankles as his accomplice completed her job of bondage and stood back. The walls watched the awesome scenario, the chaining in preparation for the punishment. Naked, Lynn's tight buttocks lay vulnerable, open to Donna's every whim, perfectly positioned to receive the whip – the formidable whip of correction.

Returning to the room after seeing Alan out, Donna took her whip and lightly brushed Lynn's buttocks with the soft leather.

'If you hit me, I'll kill you!' Lynn spat, lifting her face from the pillow.

'Hit? I'm not going to hit you, I'm going to *thrash* you. You've heard of spanking, haven't you? Well, I'm going to spank you with the whip until you come.'

'How will hitting me make me come?'

'You'll see.'

The thin leather met her buttocks with a loud crack. Much to Donna's delight, Lynn's naked body bounced, left the bed in its convulsion. She whimpered and twitched as the whip landed again across the pale spheres. Leaving thin weals across the smooth, unblemished skin, Donna continued the whipping until Lynn cried out for more. 'Harder!' she demanded. 'Much harder!' Grinning now, Donna whipped her for all she was worth, thrashing her burning buttocks until they glowed crimson, the colour of lust, and she cried the warning that her clitoris was coming.

On and on Donna whipped the burning buttocks, bringing them to their strange, quivering fruition. Her arm aching, the whip cracking, Lynn writhing and screaming, her taut flesh on fire, the girls played out their flagellation game until Lynn's clitoris burst once more to pour its sensual pleasure over her shuddering body, her sex juices from her spasming sheath. Gasping, Donna fell onto the bed and collapsed over Lynn's perspiring body. Together they lay there, panting, trembling, burning with lesbian desire.

'You came twice,' Donna breathed. 'Twice.'

'Yes, it was . . . God, I've never experienced anything like it in my life! It was . . . it was absolutely fantastic! Do you want me to do it to you now?'

The thought hardened Donna's clitoris, but Lynn was her prisoner. She daren't let her go, free her to take up her evil meddling again. 'Let me whip you, please,' the tethered girl pleaded. 'I know you'll like it as much as I did.' Temptation circled Donna's mind, swirling, increasingly inviting – irresistible. 'Please,' Lynn begged again, like a child. Never give in to a child.

Releasing the handcuffs, Donna watched as Lynn climbed from the bed, clutching her buttocks, flexing her limbs, grinning with a strange glint in her eye. 'Take your things off and get on the bed, then,' she said, examining the handcuffs. The calling of a powerful orgasm was stronger than the warning bells. Dropping her clothes to the floor, Donna lay face down on the bed and allowed her prisoner to chain her.

'Now,' Lynn said with a daunting growl. 'Now it's my turn, you bitch!' Donna cursed herself, her insatiable clitoris. She should have known better than to trust Lynn Bulmur, listened to the warnings of her inner voice. But, she consoled herself, she'd enjoy the whipping, her orgasms, as they rose from her womb and burst within the hardness of her clitoris. She'd enjoy the debased sex, the perverted use of her young body – the undeniable pleasures of the flesh.

To her surprise, Lynn left the room. Lifting her head to listen to the movements, the sounds, Donna looked to the door. What was she up to? What was the devil's daughter planning? 'Yes, come round now.' Donna caught the mysterious words as they drifted across the room to be captured by the listening walls – absorbed, gone. 'Yes, fifty pounds each, cash. But be quick, I don't want to hang around here for too long.'

Slouched in the doorway, Lynn smirked at her prey. 'I've a little surprise for you,' she said. 'A couple of friends of mine would like to play some naughty games with you – to fuck you.' Donna said nothing. She could only pray that Alan would return to save her from her fate. She thought about the patches – she was still wearing one, but was Lynn? Probably not, she decided. By now she was a natural nymphomaniac. The damn patches – but it was Lynn Bulmur, not them, that had caused so many problems. The daughter of Lucifer.

The ring on the doorbell came all too soon. Donna shuddered as she heard male voices, more than two male voices. How many? Lynn was all shrieks and giggles as she led four young men into the room. 'This is Crude Sounds,' she announced. 'A rock band. And they've come to rock you.'

Donna kept her eyes closed as hands wandered all over her body, seeking out crevices, private entrances no longer private, trespassing, violating. She didn't put up a fight as they released her from the bed and stood her in the middle of the room. Her fate sealed, she accepted it.

They were young, not bad-looking – red-blooded men. They could have been worse, she decided as they continued their fondling. They stripped off quickly, urgent in their desire to take her, to use her, urgent in their rising lust. Donna gazed at the four penises, thick, stiff, red-blooded penises all standing to attention, awaiting the wet warmth of her body.

Two men held Donna's arms as one stood behind her and parted her buttocks, feeling her there, touching her secrecy. The stabbing sensations caused her to wince, but soon her bottom-hole opened to the alien bulbous knob as the hard thickness entered her, filled her. The sheer girth of the penis stretching her, the length violating her, she could do nothing as the stranger pushed his last inch home, pressed his hard body against her buttocks – locked their union. Now another man stood before her and grinned. More stabbing, only this time between her vaginal lips. Another dream was about to come true – she smiled secretly to herself as the penis entered her, filled her body, pressed against the other penis through the thin, dividing membrane. She gasped, her legs weakening as they began their fucking, found their rhythm and sandwiched her trembling body with each pounding thrust.

Losing their rhythm in their frenzy, they rammed Donna in turn as she was thrust first forward and then back like a rag doll, her holes used just as holes. Pummelling her young body, they soon began their gasps of impending orgasm, their grunts of coming, while she, too, panted as she neared the pinnacle of her dream. Suddenly, both men shuddered and gave their final thrusts of lust, almost tearing her in two as they filled her inflamed holes to the brim with their gushing, spurting, sperm. She cried out in her own orgasm as all three shook, rocked and clung to each other in their debased union of the flesh – their abandoned union of corruption.

Before Donna had recovered from her wondrous ordeal, the men had changed places. Now two fresh, hard penises were stabbing between her open legs. Lubricated with sperm, her holes allowed the shafts to slip deep into the warmth of her body, bloating her to capacity. Ramming in synchronisation, far harder than the first two, they lifted her from the floor with every thrust, held her in mid-air, impaled on their hard rods of pleasure.

Grabbing Donna's long blonde hair and yanking her head back, a third man kissed her lips, driving his tongue deep into her mouth as her body rocked, bounced up and down with the pummelling between her legs. Lynn sucked hard on one nipple as the fourth man brought an aching hardness to her other milk-bud. New sensations flooding her young body, every inch of her flesh tingling deliciously, every fibre of her mind wavered in the intoxicating breeze of orgasm.

Grunting now, the men grimaced, their bodies rigid as their bulbous knobs swelled and gushed their orgasms deep into the girl's molten core. Again, Donna's clitoris erupted in sympathy, sending waves of euphoric lust through her mind, electrical charges through every nerve ending in her shuddering flesh. Thrusting until their balls had drained, they filled her with their hot sperm until she brimmed over with the creamy nectar. Pouring from her holes, running down her thighs, the milky liquid splattered on the carpet to collect in a pool of sex between her feet. All done, they collapsed to the floor, a tangle of limbs – shipwrecked, dragged by the tide, left on the sandy shore of a sea of orgasm.

Dragging herself to the bed, Donna was aware of movements, voices in the distant haze of her blurred mind. Kneeling on the floor, her consumed body over the bed, she buried her face in the quilt and breathed in the heady scent of sex. Her beautiful sexual torture was over – almost.

Without warning, she was pulled up by her hair and turned round. Kneeling before a hard penis, she opened her mouth. Slipping the purple head between her generous red lips, it rested against her tongue, awaiting her attention, her sucking, her mouthing. Movements behind her now, someone kneeling between her legs, parting her buttocks, slipping a hardness into her accommodating bowels again.

'Suck it!' The order came from the man towering over her. Donna sucked, ran her tongue round the knob and sensed it swelling. Her bottom-hole filled as its intruder sank deeper and began to massage the warm darkness of her inner flesh. Fingers now, groping, parting her swollen pussy lips, sinking into her wet sheath, searching out her cervix – the entrance to her contracting womb. Now a mouth between her vaginal lips, a tongue licking at her clitoris, stiffening the sore protrusion until she felt it would burst with pleasure. Her body was full, aching, bloated with sex.

Shuddering, Donna choked on the spurting cock filling her mouth as her muscles gripped on the penis plugging her tight bottom-hole, the fingers exploring her used cunt. Swallowing hard, she drank the nectar as it gushed into her hot mouth, as her bowels were filled again with sperm. She shook as her clitoris poured out its orgasm into the mouth engulfing it. She could take no more, she knew. Mouths, tongues, penises, fingers – enough of a good thing. She felt like passing out and leaving her body forever.

Dizzy, her head floating on a sea of sperm, Donna fell to the floor as the penises withdrew from her body and hung limp, drained, satisfied. 'Let's do her again!' The voice floated through the air, bounced off the walls and echoed in the swirling eddies of her mind.

'No more, please!' The words spluttered from her lips, spluttered from the sperm glistening there.

Hauling her body onto the bed, Donna heard the front door close. They'd gone, left her in the wake of their orgasms to rest, calm herself, return to her exhausted body. She oozed, bubbled with bubbling sperm, quivered as her senses slowly returned. Now she wanted more. When men were done, finished, drained, uninhibited women wanted more.

Chapter Fifteen

Donna had slept for hours, dreamed her dreams of lust, wetted the sheets with her juices, with the sperm of strangers. Emerging from the mist of slumber, she opened her eyes and gazed at the walls. Stories were absorbed there, soaked up in the brick, erotic stories of orgasm. She smiled, remembered the hard penises invading her body, violating her hot depths. A rock band, a groupie, a gang bang – another first in the many firsts she was experiencing. Another gift from her angels of lust.

Six o'clock. Time gone, flown, wasted. Stepping into the shower, Donna remembered her client. The first response to the advert, her first real client, and she'd lost her. Would Mandy return? Warm water bathed the stickiness between her thighs, her inflamed vaginal lips. Her clitoris was bigger, definitely bigger, she decided as she pulled back the pinken hood and examined the beauty there. Would her client ring again? Would she allow Donna to examine her clitoris? Arousal came, rising from her womb, swallowing her mind within its warmth.

The phone rang, accompanied by the front doorbell. Her body wet, naked, Donna ran to the door and let Alan in before dashing to the lounge to answer the phone. The client, undeterred, desperate for help, asked if she could come round now. Yes, she could – Donna was more than ready for her, for her body.

'What's that?' she asked, replacing the receiver as Alan lugged a cardboard box into the lounge.

'Equipment,' he replied, gazing at her shapely body as he dumped the box on the floor. 'I thought we'd work together here, in your flat, your spare room.'

'Work?'

'Yes, on the patches, the hormone. I've got all the equipment we need to set up a lab and . . .'

'But the spare room is for . . . Look, there's just no space here, the flat's far too small.'

'No, it's not. One bench, a table in the corner, that's all we need. Your bedroom will do – just one corner in your bedroom.'

It wasn't what Donna had wanted, Alan working from her flat, taking over her plans, invading her privacy – her sex life. She had thought she loved him. Love *was* sharing – but love invaded, intruded. What to do? Tell him about her life, her new life? She decided not. Poor Alan, sensitive, jealous – in love. He thought that he knew everything – the woods, the men, the girls, the wondrous sessions of wanton lust. She daren't risk him discovering everything about her new and abandoned way of life, it was far too precious.

'I can't really have you here every day, Alan. I mean, I just can't live with . . .'

'I'm not asking you to live with me. A table in the corner of your bedroom isn't asking too much, is it? And besides, I thought you wanted us to work together. You need me, don't you?'

'I don't need . . . I do want to work with you, but I can't take this pressure, this intrusion into my life. I've discovered things, discovered myself, my sexuality.'

'You've discovered sex, you mean. Look at you, standing there totally naked. You've discovered what's between your legs.'

'Sex, yes. But more, I've discovered . . . I want to help women. Women shouldn't be second rate, second class, ruled by men.'

'That's the way it is.'

'Yes, and I don't like it. For the first time in my life, I feel free. I thought my life was the lab, that my destiny was to work at the lab, to marry, to have babies, and then go back to the lab. So much has happened to me. Only a short time ago, I would never have believed how much things . . .'

'Would change for the worse?'

'For the better. I've got some money, at last. I've got freedom. I've got my . . .'

'Pussy, yes, I know. I can see it.'

'Look, bring in your equipment and we'll see how it goes for a while. But I do need space, time to be myself. We'll set the times, the hours when you work, when we work here.'

'I know all about . . .'

'What?'

'Nothing, it's all right. I'll bring the things in and get out of your way.'

'You don't know anything, Alan, you couldn't. And you'd never believe me if I told you everything, so just drop this *I know everything* business, will you?'

'All right. It will be nice working together again. I've missed you, Donna. I'll be able to keep my eye on you and . . .'

'I don't want an eye kept on me! Try and understand, please! It's my life, let me live it! Take the gun away from my head and let me live!'

'Sorry. I'll be good, I promise. Friends?'

'Friends? Of course we're bloody friends! Now hurry up and do whatever you want to do, and then go. I've a client coming round soon. I can hardly open the door to her naked, can I?'

'Why not? I thought that was . . .'

'*Don't* think when it comes to my life, Alan. I'll do the thinking, thank you.'

She stood in the hall and frowned as Alan lugged several boxes in from his car and dumped them in her bedroom. She was far from happy, but she had to admit that she *did* need him, his knowledge – his body. He smiled as he left, promising that he'd be back later with a table. Forcing a smile she told him not to hurry back, that she needed a good three hours alone with her client. He raised his eyebrows. Disgust? Jealousy, perhaps? He was a normal man.

Alan had left his boxes in front of her dressing table. Donna kicked them, stubbing her toe and cursing him, cursing herself for agreeing to his idea. Why had he left the lab, a good, secure job? Why keep saying that he knew everything? Perhaps he did know? He couldn't – not her secret secrets.

Donning her short, red skirt and a white blouse, Donna applied her makeup and brushed her long, blonde hair. Colours swirled around her head, around her beauty, as she tossed her head back and thought of sex, her pussy, warm, wet – colours of orgasm, hues of lust. The angels were near.

Standing before the hall mirror, Donna adjusted her hair, scrunched the golden strands, bunched them up and let them fall over her shoulders. Extremely attractive, even though she thought so herself. Rather too much lipstick? She didn't want to overdo it. But why not look glamorous – sexy?

Donna had a sudden change of mind as the front doorbell rang. No makeup would have been better, and a long skirt. The woman would be expecting someone plain, ordinary, someone to listen to her, understand her – not a bimbo.

'Come in, Mandy,' Donna invited with a huge grin that reflected her delight, the instant, quivering arousal between her swelling pussy lips. The young coffee-coloured girl with flowing, jet-black hair and huge dark eyes returned her grin as she stepped inside. She couldn't have a problem, surely? A beautiful model, stunning beyond belief, straight from the cat-walk, with a sexual problem?

Mandy's olive skin shone, glistened. Mediterranean? South American? Wherever she came from, it didn't matter. Nothing mattered, other than the dark delights beneath the girl's short, tight skirt – between her thick, dark nether lips.

A patch in her hand, Donna clasped the girl's arm and pressed it home as she led her into the lounge. 'Sit down, Mandy,' she said hospitably, waving her hand towards the sofa. 'Coffee, tea?'

'No, I'm fine, thanks.'

'So, tell me about yourself, your problem. You're married, aren't you?'

'Yes, three weeks now. We've only just returned from our honeymoon. That's when I discovered that I had a problem.'

'How old are you? Only you look far too young to be married.'

'Just eighteen. Matt and I were at school together. Marriage was a natural progression, I suppose. Our

Ray Gordon

parents expected it, and we wanted it – I think. Things were fine until . . . Well, we'd always enjoyed sex, it was great. But now . . .'

Donna moved to the edge of her armchair in anticipation. But now? But now what? Why had Mandy tailed off? What problem had she discovered on her honeymoon? Donna began to fantasise. How long was Mandy's clitoris? How wet her cunette? How dark and thick the lips surrounding the entrance to her honey-pot? Donna willed the patch to work quickly, to free its hormone and strip Mandy of her inhibitions – so that she could strip her of her clothes.

'But now?' Donna echoed, her stomach fluttering, her wetness trickling between her trembling legs.

'Well, he wanted me to do things, unnatural things.'

'What sort of unnatural things?'

'We've always enjoyed sex . . .'

Yes, *what* unnatural things? Had her young husband wanted to take her little black bottom-hole? Had he asked her if he could press his bulbous knob between her dark, velvety spheres and fill her bowels with his sperm? Donna wanted, desperately needed to know. Finally the truth bubbled from Mandy's luscious red lips.

'. . . but he wanted me to do oral sex.'

Stifling a laugh, Donna covered her mouth with her hand and averted her wide eyes. Soon, Mandy would go home and beg her husband to give her his penis, to push it into her mouth and fill her with his shuddering orgasm. Once the patch had released her, freed her mind, her subconscious desires, she would beg to swallow the sperm as it spurted from his throbbing shaft. But first, Mandy had to taste Donna's female love juice, suck an orgasm from her hard clitoris, understand the

310

sexual delights of the female form before discovering her husband's body.

Mandy uncrossed her slim legs and began to fidget – the tell-tale sign of swelling cunt lips, a stiffening clitoris, a moistening love tube. 'I can understand your apprehension,' Donna said softly. 'The penis can appear as an awesome thing when . . . Did you allow your husband to . . . to give you oral sex?'

'No, certainly not! It's . . . it's wrong, isn't it? I mean, it's just not right to . . .'

'Wrong in whose eyes?'

'Everyone's eyes. Well, all normal, moral, clean-living people, anyway. I mean, it's dirty, vulgar – unwholesome.'

A wonderful word, thought Donna, breathing vulgarity in its own unwholesomeness. How sad the inhibited in their inhibited thoughts! How sad to leave Mandy's generous, pouting lips, her pretty little mouth, virginal, her pink tongue unbathed with sperm! How wasteful to leave her sweet little bottom-hole unattended, unfucked!

Cautiously moving towards her prey, a second patch in her fist, Donna settled at Mandy's feet. Looking up, she smiled. The girl's huge eyes mirrored fear, confusion. She wasn't ready, ripe. The patch had had failed to work its magic. Why?

'What are you doing down there?' she asked, gazing at Donna sitting on the floor by her feet.

'Getting comfortable. I don't like things to be too formal. Just relax and tell me more about your sex life.'

Tell me your innermost thoughts, Donna thought. How you masturbate, what fantasies swim through the caverns of your mind as orgasm rises from the deep to bathe you in lust.

'There's nothing else to tell, really. We both like sex, we both find great satisfaction from sex, but . . .'

'Go on,' Donna said, stroking Mandy's leg.

'What are you doing?'

Donna pressed the second patch to the girl's calf. 'This is all part of the therapy, to relax you, calm you and allow you to open up, tell me your innermost thoughts.'

'Touching my leg like that is . . . is nice, yes. It is relaxing, you're right.'

Moving her hand higher up Mandy's leg, Donna looked into her eyes and smiled as they closed, bringing darkness, warm darkness where thoughts, desires, swirled unhindered by images of the real world. The sexual spell had been cast, the hormone of lust released. Donna's hand wandered now to her inner thigh, explored the smooth, dark skin, the warmth beneath her skirt, and reached its goal – the soft mound of her snug, red panties. Mandy let go, relaxed completely as she slipped into the deepening pool of her arousal. Opening her legs, she allowed her mistress to explore further, to push a finger under her tight panties and feel the moist warmth there – the folds of pinkness between the swellings of darkness.

'I want you to stand up,' Donna ordered softly, desperate in her lust to see the full beauty of Mandy's sable nakedness. Quietly Mandy rose to await the next inevitable instruction of a mistress impassioned. 'Now remove all your clothes!'

Like a leaf blown on Donna's thoughts, following her every whim, Mandy quickly slipped her top and bra off, freeing her firm breasts, her huge, elongated, black nipples. Reaching out to squeeze the round firmness of her breasts, Donna encircled the long, wedge-shaped milk buds. Instinctively she leaned forward and took a nipple into her mouth, running her tongue around the rough tissue as Mandy tugged on her skirt, wrenching it to her ankles where it lay abandoned like a crumpled rag. Now only her panties remained, guarding, concealing her very femininity, the dark secret of her dark, dank sex.

Dropping to her knees, Donna peeled the silky red material from the warm mound and gazed at her treasure. Was Barry, her voyeur, gazing too? Was he masturbating his hard penis, spilling his seed onto the earth as he pried into the secret affairs of two women about to writhe in their secret lust? Perhaps he'd like to join in, to take a young black girl from behind as Donna watched? Or was he in the woods, hiding in his hide, spying on some unsuspecting young couple as they stripped off their clothes, their inhibitions, and made their furtive motions of love?

Tight curls sprouted like patches of black moss from the swell of Mandy's dark, billowing quim lips. She was a rare beauty, a rare catch – a princess of darkness, caught by the angels and delivered to Donna as a sacrifice. Peeling the chocolaty cushions apart, Donna gazed at the moist centre, the pinken, glistening folds of flesh only inches from her mouth, her tongue.

'This is what you've been missing, what you've denied yourself,' she breathed as she poked her tongue out and licked from the bottom to the top of the girl's opening groove. Mandy threw her head back, exhaling her delight as, for the first time, a tongue – a female tongue – gently crossed the tip of her clitoris. Again Donna licked, dragging the oozing warm milk up her valley and over her bud. Now Mandy's fingers joined the excavation, moving either side of her cunt lips to stretch them apart. The pink flesh reddened in her arousal, engorged in her lust, as Donna continued her tormenting licking and mouthing, ripening the crimson flesh, bringing her pert bud ever closer to fruition.

Sensing Mandy's goal in sight, Donna sucked her clitoris into her mouth and ran her tongue round its base. Quivering, throbbing, suddenly it reached its summit, sending electrifying waves of pleasure through Mandy's dusky body, deep into her mind. Trembling, weak, her creamy juices poured, trickled over the wrinkled surface of her inner pussy lips as Donna lapped, savoured and swallowed in lesbian lust until, shuddering, the dark girl pressed her dank centre hard into her face, her accommodating mouth, filling it with her slippery juices.

As Mandy pulled away, her cunt consumed, afire with lust, Donna rose to her feet, her mouth wet with female love juice, her eyes reflecting the burning desire between her legs. Leading her captive into the sex dungeon, she bade her lie on the bed and spread her limbs. Ever willing to please, Mandy spread her nakedness on the bed and awaited her mistress's pleasure.

'You have a beautiful body,' Donna breathed as she ran her fingertips over the deep sheen of Mandy's stomach, over the roundness of her mound, up the dividing groove between the rising hills of flesh. 'A body radiating beauty, sex. A beauty that must never go to waste, a cunette that must never know neglect. I'll teach you, show you how to pleasure yourself, your husband – your friends.'

Pulling Mandy's quim lips open, Donna gazed at the bright pink flesh, accentuated, highlighted by the dark, surrounding skin. Never before had she seen such exquisite folds, such sweet, girlish femininity spread before her.

Pushing three fingers deep into the wetness, Donna felt her own sheath quiver, yearn for her attention, spill sex fluid. But she'd have to wait. It was Mandy who needed her fingers, her tongue, her time, her lesbian skills. Massaging the warm inner flesh, she suddenly remembered the vibrator. What finer way to take her pupil to her heaven, to rouse her latent lesbian instinct, than to vibrate her little clitoris to bursting?

'You're about to come as you've never come before,' Donna whispered. 'You want that, don't you?'

'Yes, very much,' Mandy replied as she made herself comfortable. The buzzing phallus in her hand, Donna pressed the hard tip between the girl's wet pussy lips and grinned. Mandy writhed, arched her back as the new and wondrous sensations filled her cunt, ripped through her pelvis, bathed her mind. Moving the phallus down the yawning fissure, Donna pushed its length deep inside the chasm and pressed it hard against her cervix. Now the girl cried out in her ecstasy, opened her body, her mind, to the sexual power engulfing the beauty between her legs.

Her cream flowing in torrents, pouring down the chromium shaft of the vibrator and down Donna's hand as she pumped the phallus as a fucking penis, Mandy neared her climax. Watching her dark stomach rise and fall with her contracting womb, Donna knew the time had come to focus on the imminent birth of her orgasm.

Slipping the metal shaft from Mandy's sheath, Donna held it against the dusky beauty's ripening clitoris. Pulsing once, it rested. Again it gave a little jerk as Mandy cried out her pleasure until, suddenly, the little bud pumped rhythmically, transmitting its pulses of gratification through the girl's dark body, touching every tingling nerve ending, contracting every muscle. Frenzied, urgent, Mandy grabbed the vibrator to finish the job of masturbation, running the tip round and round, moving the sensations to the right place at the right time, sustaining the flow of sexual euphoria until she fell limp, dropping the magical metal cylinder before rolling up into a ball.

Donna answered the front door to find Sophie and Helen, hand in hand, smiling at her. Three young girls at her disposal, she mused. Three cunettes to play with, to rouse and bring to life – to drink from. Jealousy again, rising from the deep at the sight of their angelic faces, their hands clasped in love.

'Come in,' Donna said, remembering her intention to punish her slaves for not being her slaves. Their smiles broadened as they stepped inside. Would they need the patches? Had they been using patches? She had no idea, but to be safe, she led them into the lounge and sat them on the sofa. 'There's someone I want you to meet,' she said, slipping two patches from her bag. 'But first, I want to hear what you've both been up to, where you've been all this time, especially you, Helen. Now, let me sit between you, and you can tell me all about it.'

'Who are we going to meet?' Sophie asked.

'Someone special,' Donna smiled as she placed her arms behind the girls and pressed the patches onto their necks. 'Someone *very* special.'

'I've been around, here and there, doing this and that,' Helen announced, seemingly uninterested in Donna's 'special' person. 'I've done nothing in particular, really. Haven't seen a great deal of my mum, she's always out. Sophie's been staying with me most nights and . . . Well, that's about it, I suppose.'

Donna wasn't interested. Her thoughts were on her whip, the handcuffs, chains, nipple clamps – Mandy. 'Okay, clothes off,' she ordered, not even sure that the patches had taken effect. As if mesmerised by a hypnotic suggestion, the girls stood up and began to remove their clothes. Donna remained on the sofa, watching, almost with an air of indifference. Blasé? She'd seen it all before and needed more stimulus, more excitement than merely watching her slaves undress, she reflected.

Perhaps Alan moving into the flat wouldn't be such a bad idea? Women together in their sexual enlightenment could share great pleasures – but they also needed men. Perhaps he should move in, permanently. There was no substitute for a penis, a hard, throbbing, sperm-pumping penis, deep within the tightening sheath of a girl's sex. Donna had to admit – she needed Alan.

Leaving the girls undressing, she walked across the room to check the answerphone. The call indicator read sixteen. Raising her eyebrows, she switched it to play and waited.

'Hi, Donna, it's Debbie. Listen, Steve's out this evening so . . . Well, how about coming over for a drink or something? Might see you later, then, bye for now.'

'Hello, Donna. My name's Vicky Woods. I saw your advert and I'd like to make an appointment to see you. Perhaps you'll be good enough to ring me on 636783. Thank you.'

'I wanted to make an appointment to see you. I'll ring back later.'

'Oh, hello. My name's Samantha. I saw your advert. I'll call you back.'

'Er . . . I'll ring back for an appointment.'

She'd heard enough. Switching the machine off, Donna turned to see the girls standing naked, awaiting her instructions. 'What am I doing?' she asked herself aloud. 'I can't cope with all this!' She thought of Mandy lying naked in the sex dungeon – masturbating, probably. Girls everywhere, naked, offering their bodies, their open vaginal lips, open in their arousal, wet in their yearning for orgasm. To add to her problems, the doorbell rang.

'Steve!' she exclaimed. 'What the hell are you doing here?'

'Oh, if you don't want to see me, then . . .'

'No, I mean yes. Come in, I need your help.'

'Heard about Bulmur?' he asked as he followed her into the lounge and stood frozen to the spot, his eyes wide, his mouth open.

'What about her?'

'What the . . . Who are these two lovelies?'

'Never mind them, what about Bulmur?'

'Gone, done a bunk or something.'

'Where?'

'Abroad, done a runner.'

'When? She was only here . . . How do you know, anyway?'

'She called me, got me to drop her off at the airport. She's gone, that's what I came to tell you. Now will you tell me who these beautiful, naked girls are – and what they're doing here?'

Flopping onto the sofa, Donna sighed with relief. Bulmur gone, fled the country. For good? 'Why? Did she say why?'

'Some bloke after her or something,' Steve replied, squeezing the firmness of Sophie's breasts.

'What did she say, exactly?'

'Some bloke from London was after her and . . . She's not coming back, so what the hell? Now, what are these two fine young specimens doing here?'

'Waiting for me. Go and look in the spare room, across the hall on the left, if you really want to see a fine young specimen, as you put it.'

Mandy lay on the bed, her legs outstretched, her fingers between her dark lips massaging her clitoris to another climax. Steve gasped, gazed at the wondrous sight and adjusted the hardness filling his jeans. 'What do you think?' Donna asked, leaning on the door frame with her two slaves in waiting behind her.

'What do I think? I think she's beautiful. Can I . . .'

'Do whatever you want to do to her. She's yours, we're all yours for the taking. Helen, Sophie, remove my clothes, please.'

As Helen unbuttoned Donna's blouse, Sophie tugged on her skirt, pulling it down to her ankles to reveal her knickerless pussy, bulging in its swelling. Donna's breasts free, her nipples grew, hardened, her areolae darkening with arousal. 'Now remove Steve's clothes,' she instructed softly, her eyes catching his.

Grinning, looking down at Sophie kneeling before him, unbuckling his belt with her precise fingers, Steve's mind swirled with male thoughts, thoughts of deeds to come – dirty deeds. Proudly, he watched his penis stand to attention, hard, long, thick in its readiness for lust. 'You may do as you wish with it, Sophie,' Donna conceded as she joined the girl on the floor. 'And you, Helen. Come on, I want to watch, to see what you've both learned.'

Sitting beside Sophie, Helen kissed her lips, pushed her tongue into her mouth, cupped her breasts in her hands. Responding, Sophie walked her fingers up her friend's legs, feeling the warmth between her thighs, touching the oiliness between her swelling cunt lips. 'Is that what you've learned?' Donna asked, anger in her voice. 'A fine penis like this awaiting your attention, and you touch each other?'

Her jealousy was rising, a latent jealousy that had to surface from the deep and show itself – a swirling, engulfing green cloud of jealousy. Grabbing a pair of handcuffs, Donna pulled Sophie's arms behind her back and cuffed her wrists. 'Prefer Helen to Steve, do you?' she asked, pulling the girl to her feet. 'A lovely thick penis like that standing in front of you, and you prefer Helen?' Marching her towards the bed, she told Mandy to move, throwing Sophie across it. 'Steve, there's a length of wood by that bag over there, pass it to me,' she ordered, her eyes glowing, her hands trembling.

Side by side, Mandy and Helen watched as Donna rolled Sophie onto her stomach and tied her feet to each end of the wooden pole. The job done, the girl's buttocks lay open, her puffy quim lips on display nestling below the dark crease, wet and glistening. She wriggled as Donna fixed the leather collar around her neck and connected a chain to the metal hook. 'Walk-ies,' she giggled, pulling on the chain to bring her head up. Mandy climbed onto the bed and sat cross-legged on the pillow, gazing at the wonderful spectacle, fondling between her splayed pussy lips.

Wrapping the chain around the handcuffs, Donna ran it down between the girl's buttocks, rolling her over and pulling it tight. Her head over the side of the bed, her wide eyes staring at the upside-down dressing table, her ankles three feet apart, Sophie begged for her freedom. Donna laughed as she pulled the chain between the swell of her wet cunt lips and up over her stomach.

'What shall I do with this end?' she asked her audience.

'What are you trying to do?' Steve asked.

'Chain her up so that it hurts – punish her, in other words.'

'Then why not fix the chain to the collar? If it's tight enough, it'll hurt her pussy, squash her clit.'

Donna grinned at Steve as she connected the chain to the collar, pulling it tight between Sophie's legs until she yelped. Parting her victim's vaginal lips, she closed the soft pads of flesh over the chain, concealing it neatly. 'And now I'll turn you over again so that I can get to your buttocks,' Donna said, rolling the girl onto her stomach.

Sophie's soft whimpers only heightened the lust filling the room – swirling lust, like a mist engulfing, goading. Helen moved in first, touching, running her fingers up the chain, licking the glistening wetness running down the metal links, nibbling the taut flesh.

Donna looked to Steve and smiled. 'And what are you going to do?' she asked, her eyes darting to Mandy. Returning her knowing smile he laid the girl over the bed next to Sophie. His eyes shone, his penis hardened as he parted her dark buttocks and pressed a finger deep into her bowels. 'You can fuck her there, if you want to,' Donna suggested. He smiled as he relinquished his finger and positioned his ballooning knob between her dark moons. 'Here, let me help you,' Donna offered, taking his penis and pressing it hard against the tightening hole.

Gasping, Mandy thrust her bottom back, offering her virginal hole to the thick invader, desperate to receive her pleasure there. Gripping the hard shaft Donna pushed, twisted, but the girl's muscles wouldn't yield. Moving Steve aside, she licked at the small hole, dribbling her saliva there to lubricate the penetration.

Ray Gordon

Taking his penis she sucked, irrigated the bulbous knob before stabbing again, twisting, pushing the rod hard against the small hole. The muscles suddenly surrendering, allowing the intruder into the creamy warmth, Donna grinned as, again, Mandy gasped, pushing her bottom further up to fill her body with his hardness, to rest her slippery pussy lips against his heavy balls. Donna moved her hand away as the last two inches stretched the tight flesh and disappeared into the darkness. 'Now fill her with sperm,' she ordered, cupping Steve's swinging balls as he moved back and forth.

Helen was happy pleasuring her lesbian lover, easing a finger alongside the chain and into the velveteen heat of her soft tube, bringing hew sensations, wetness there. Steve had pulled Mandy's hips up to meet his pumping penis. On her knees, she rocked to and fro, shuddering with the filling sensations within her tight bottom-hole. All were gasping now, pleasuring each other, finding their heavens – all but Donna.

Pushing Helen aside, she grabbed the whip and brushed Sophie's pale buttocks with the soft leather. 'Now for your punishment!' she hissed. 'Now for the beating of your life!' Sophie wriggled, squirmed as the leather fell across her unblemished skin.

'No, please!' Sophie cried as her buttocks squeezed on the chain deep within her crease. 'I don't want . . . Please don't do it!' Steve gazed in amazement at the thin weals appearing across her twitching flesh as he rammed his penis deeper and deeper into Mandy's bottom-hole. Fired with a new lust, he gasped, shuddered and pressed his penis in to the hilt as his sperm spurted, gushed into the murky depths. Mandy begged for more as he finally came to a halt, his head hanging, his breathing deep, his penis twitching in response to the girl's spasming muscles.

Lost in her lust, Donna continued thrashing Sophie for all she was worth until the girl cried out in her enforced orgasm. 'Stop now!' she begged as the milky fluid oozed from her tight sheath and lubricated the caressing chain. 'I've come, please stop!'

The mistress grinned wickedly as she continued the beating, turning the girl's flesh to a burning crimson – the colour of orgasm. Withdrawing his limp penis, Steve grabbed Donna's arm to halt the torture, but she pulled away to thrash even harder. 'I think that's enough,' he said. 'You're really hurting her.'

'Good, that's the idea!'

Eventually, he pulled her away from Sophie's shuddering body. Taking the whip, he threw it to the floor and kicked it under the bed. 'That's enough of that!' he warned, releasing Sophie's abused body. Looking into his eyes, Donna grinned her wicked grin.

'Get on the bed,' she ordered.

'You get on the bed,' he returned. 'Next to Mandy.'

'No.'

Pulling her towards him, Steve threw Donna onto her stomach. He was about to chain her down when the three girls grabbed him. 'This is Donna's place,' Helen said. 'And we do as she says.' Leaping up, Donna helped to chain Steve over the bed. His penis pointing to the ceiling, his eyes wide with a mixture of arousal and fear, he looked into their eyes – eyes of women uninhibited.

'What shall we do with him?' Donna asked, stroking his penis, stiffening his shaft.

'Let's use him,' Sophie suggested.

'Use him? But I thought that you'd rather have your girlfriend than a man – or has the punishment worked?'

'I . . . I like men, too. But I love Helen.'

Annoyingly, the girl was in love. She'd just have to be whipped again, only the next time there'd be no one there to save her from her fate, Donna decided. She'd be whipped until she fell out of love with Helen – and promised to love Donna.

Returning from her reverie, Donna surveyed her young black pupil. The head of Steve's stiff penis engulfed by her mouth, her voluptuous red lips wrapped around the shaft, she began to suck. Her eyes rolling, her inner desires surfacing, uninhibited, Mandy was delighting in her pleasure. Now her husband would have his way, his normal way as a normal man and they could live happily ever after, Donna reflected.

Sophie moved towards Steve's penis but Donna held her back. 'This is Mandy's treat,' she admonished her. 'Let her discover the delights of a penis throbbing in her mouth, experience the wonders of using her mouth as her cunette.'

The girls watched as Mandy instinctively moved her head up and down, bringing Steve ever nearer to his orgasm, his sperm ever nearer to the inside of her hot mouth. The walls were watching, too, Donna knew. One day they'd tell, tell of their secrets, of the wanton lust that had engulfed the flat, gripped Donna in its arms, never to let go. One day they'd tell of the lewd scenes of lesbianism – tell of normal, uninhibited women.

What would Alan think if he were to see the real Donna? What would he do? she wondered. Join in? Ride the dark girl, take her bottom-hole, fill her dank depths with his sperm? Or would he avert his eyes in disgust? Would he turn and leave, never to see or speak to her again? Why the hell couldn't he use his own flat to work in?

Steve gasped and grunted as his knob ballooned against Mandy's tongue. Returning from her thoughts, Donna watched her pupil with pride as she discovered new sensations, learned of new things. Suddenly, Steve thrust his hips up, pushed the entire length of his shaft deep into the girl's mouth and began his spurting. Choking at first, she soon began to swallow his fruits. Her eyes floating, reflecting her euphoria, she moaned a long, low moan, signalling her satisfaction, the pleasure of her new and wondrous experience.

Milky liquid dribbling down her dark chin, Mandy smiled at her mistress. She was thankful, grateful for the tuition – although it was she who had taught herself. The patches had freed another woman; given the warmth of life where there was cold barrenness, power where there was weakness, sex where there was frigidity. Given Mandy her femininity.

Chapter Sixteen

Donna woke to the birds singing, the sun shining – her naked slaves sleeping by her side. She'd dreamed her dream, a dream where women were free, sexually free, powerfully free. One day.

Her dreamy thoughts recollected the evening's events, and she smiled. Steve had gone home to Debbie, his wife, his new, uninhibited woman. *His* woman? No – *a* woman. He had taken Mandy, Sophie, Helen, and Donna. But he was a normal man, doing normal, manly things – committing normal, manly adultery.

Mandy had returned to her man, *a* man. She had returned a new woman, a woman in control, a powerful woman with a powerful young body – powerful thoughts. Donna had left the patches clinging to her dark skin, secreting the hormone, bathing her mind with the sensual colours of sex. By the time the effect wore off, her transition would be complete and she'd be a free woman. Had she sucked the sperm from her husband's orgasming penis the minute she'd arrived home? Undoubtedly. Had she taken his hardness within her hot bottom-hole? Yes. Why hadn't Alan returned?

Slipping out of bed, Donna stood before the mirror. Her smooth skin was glowing, glowing with sex in the summer sun streaming in through the window. Her curves excited her, her female crevices aroused her. Still wearing her patch, she allowed her fingers to explore between her legs, to feel the oiliness there, the hotness – the sex. She wondered about Alan, Barry, Steve, as she touched her clitoris. She wanted them – all of them.

Eight o'clock. The park would be nice, cool under the trees, naked on the grass. Parks were for female masturbation – early morning girl masturbation. Donna decided to go there, to lie naked under the trees and masturbate. Barry might be there, jogging, spying. She'd give him a treat – a voyeur's delight.

Wandering into her sex dungeon, Donna smiled. Changes. Once romantic novels, now whips and chains. Once the laboratory, now sexy games. Picking up the nipple clamps, she placed them over her milk buds and tightened them. New sensations – pain, sex. Tightening them a little more, she winced, her clitoris stirred. The brown tissue of her niplettes ached, hardened with arousal. Pulling her vaginal lips open, she gazed at her clitoris – it *had* grown, longer, harder. Her mind ached with sex now. Thoughts drifted through her crevices, between her legs. Sex thoughts crept over her body, deep into her wet sheath and found their way to her womb where they roused her innermost femininity. What other delights awaited her young body? What could further heighten her sexual pleasure? A clitoris clamp?

Dressing in her miniskirt and white blouse, Donna smiled at her sleeping slaves. They'd be punished again later, she wasn't sure why. Punished for the sake of punishment, she mused. Whipped for the sake of whipping. Young girls' buttocks were made for whipping, for thrashing.

Pulling Sophie's knee-length leather boots over her legs she gazed in the mirror again at her reflection – girlish. Lifting her skirt, she smiled at her soft quim lips, held slightly open by her inner petals. The soft, red leather boots completed the picture – a picture of girlish sex. She was happy, happy to be a girl.

Lust followed her as she walked down the street. A cloud of lust, swirling through her mind, between her legs like a cool breeze. Her nipples hurt, ached delightfully, brought new pleasures to her breasts as she slipped through the park gates. People were there, unaware that the daughter of Venus was amongst them, wet, aching for sex – orgasm. A man walking arm-in-arm with a woman turned his head. He was unaware that the young blonde was knickerless, that her swollen pussy lips were wet, smooth, without hair. Unaware that her nipples were clamped, stinging, that he could take her young body should he follow her into the trees. The woman yanked on his arm, jealous. Did she masturbate?

The sun was hot, perspiring hot – Donna didn't like it. Beneath the trees it was cooler, sexy cool. She wanted the man, and the woman. Why hadn't they followed her into the trees? She could have taken them both to new, delirious sexual heights. She could have sucked an orgasm from the woman's clitoris as the man filled her bowels with his hot sperm. The woman needed a patch – *all* women needed patches.

Slipping her skirt and blouse off, Donna ran her fingers over her body, her curves, the wetness between her legs. The breeze bathed her, sought the warmth between her thighs and cooled her there. Lying on the soft grass she opened her legs, moved her fingers down to part her cunt lips, to open her body to the trees wavering high above. She liked the trees, rugged, gentle, male trees, sexual in their caressing.

She slept for a while, dreamed her dreams again.

Floating in her dreams she drifted here and there, through pools of orgasm, in and out of sex. She craved orgasm, craved a tongue between the fleshy hills of her female dividing groove. Someone in the bushes, moving, lurking, spying. Her mind returned to the woods. Was it Barry? She hoped so.

Peeling her lips open Donna massaged her clitoris, stiffened the bud, brought it out from its pinken hide. She made her whimperings, her sounds of female masturbation for her voyeur. Was *he* masturbating? A rustling filled the air, a twig broke underfoot, echoed, reverberated through the stillness of the wood.

'You can come out now . . .' She didn't say Barry, she wasn't sure why. A woman's intuition? A woman's sex. Alan emerged from his hide and smiled. 'Why did you follow me?' Donna asked, her fingers still between her lips, inducing a hardness there, sensations.

'I didn't follow you. I was out walking and happened to see you.'

Alan wouldn't follow her. Innocent Alan – lying, cheating, adulterous Alan. Normal Alan. She liked his name, smooth, no rough edges – a man's name.

'Come and join me,' she invited, the sensuality of her slender legs enhanced by the red leather boots.

'Is this your space, your time, your sexuality?' he asked as he sat beside her and gazed at the nipple clamps.

'Yes. This is me, my freedom – my sexuality.'

'Masturbating alone under the trees?'

'My trees.'

'How was your client?'

'She was . . . she was dead – now she has life.'

'A sex life?'

'A sexual life, a free life – unchained, uninhibited.'

'Like you?'

'Like me.'

Leaning forward, Alan kissed Donna's stomach, licked her navel. She breathed in deeply, closed her eyes as he moved down to her mound, a hill rising from the verge of the smooth plateau, sloping down to her symmetrical contours, her moist valley. His tongue sought the valley, tasted the muskiness there – the girlishness. She parted her legs further, opening her groove, her body. He parted her inner petals, sucked on them in turn, pulled them open to reveal the tiny slit within – wet, creamy, glistening pink. Her clitoris protruded, hard, sensitive to his attention, his tongue. She was ripe to come.

Tightening her nipple clamps to heighten the sensations there, Donna licked her lips – dry lips, in need of lubrication. Groping at Alan's belt she released the buckle, tugged the zip down, slipped her fingers into the warmth. His penis throbbed in her hand, hard, solid – sticky. Why?

Pulling Alan nearer, Donna dragged his jeans down and examined his penis, the skin. Soft, hard-soft, whitish, stained, encrusted. Where had it been? Nearer now, she opened her mouth and sucked the purple head into the warmth. Salty, spermy, girlie. Had he penetrated a woman, another woman? Taking the head to the back of her mouth, she ran her tongue round the hard shaft, tasted the starchiness. Juice – female orgasm juice. No, not Alan. Her clitoris swelled and throbbed in response to his darting tongue. This was her life, her new life – her sexuality uninhibited. His penis bulged, filled her tiny mouth with its hardness. She was thirsty for his sperm – impatient.

Working hard on his penis, Donna pictured Helen

and Sophie. Were they awake, licking, mouthing, bringing out their orgasms? She would have them pleasure
her when she got home – then thrash them. Ballooning
with her efforts, Alan's knob twitched and pumped out
its milk. Slurping in her frenzy, Donna swallowed,
mouthed, tongued the slippery cream as it decanted into
her thirsty mouth. As she savoured the bitter-sweet
fruits, her clitoris erupted in orgasm under Alan's
caressing tongue. Now he slurped, too, sucking, nibbling her bud, sustaining her shuddering climax as, on
and on, the shock waves of euphoria rocked her young
body, drained her spasming sheath, shook her very soul.
As she fell limp, the spent penis slipping from her
mouth, Alan moved down her inflamed groove to drink
the nectarous offering from her fountain.

'Lick, inside my cunt!' The words of sex foamed
through the sperm on her lips. 'Push your tongue
inside my cunt and lick me!' Stretching open her
delicate folds, Alan buried his tongue deep within the
creamy hotness and licked there. Her milk flowing in
torrents, Donna's cunt tightened as she approached
her second climax. 'My clitoris now, lick my clitoris
now!' Locating her hard bud, he engulfed it with his
hot mouth and gently sucked her to her climax. 'Ah,
yes, yes!' Moanings of orgasm disturbed the peace of
the wood. 'Coming, com . . . Ah, yes, that's it!' Her
body rigid in the grips of ecstasy, taut in the sensations radiating from her open centre, she breathed her
command. 'God, don't stop! Don't . . .' Floating,
heady, lost now in a haze, her soul gently brushed
against the angels of lust.

Returning to her body, Donna looked at Alan. 'That
was . . . That was wonderful,' she breathed. He smiled
his satisfaction, lips wet with the juice of female orgasm.

'Where to now?' he asked.

'I don't know,' she replied, her mind on the girls and the train rumbling through the cutting – her cutting.

'We have to talk.'

'I must get back,' she said, grabbing her skirt and blouse.

'Why?'

'Because – that's why.' Donna didn't know or care what she meant. This was the pressure, the enchainment, the gun to the head she didn't want.

'Stay a while,' Alan wheedled, a smile curling his lips, a glint in his eye – a glint of sex.

'No, I must go home.'

'Who's there waiting for you?'

'See you some time.'

No possession, no guns. Climbing to her feet she slipped her blouse over her shoulders.

'When's sometime?'

'It's a time sometime in the future.'

Pulling her skirt up over her red leather boots Donna tossed her long blonde hair over her shoulder and smiled a goodbye smile. Alan pulled up his jeans and buckled his belt.

'This is it, isn't it?' he asked, a sadness in his eyes.

'What makes you say that?'

'I'm not sure, Donna. I know . . .'

'Everything, yes, you've told me before.'

'I want to be part of your life.'

'No-one can be a part of someone else's life. A life is a life. Your life, my life, they're different.'

'We can share our lives.'

'We are, aren't we?'

'No, we're sharing our bodies, nothing more.'

'What? You want to share my mind? My psyche?'

'You know what I mean.'

'Yes, I do know. You want to control me, run my life, have a say in what I do or don't do. I'm an individual – a woman.'

All woman – an all-uninhibited woman.

Turning, Donna began to walk away. A heavy cloud hung over her, a cloud heavy with sadness – a longing in her heart, for what, she didn't know. She stopped and turned. Alan was still there, gazing, watching. What were his thoughts? Male thoughts of sex? She moved towards him, slow in her moving, misty in her thinking.

'I know every . . .' he began. 'Sorry, you don't want me to put it that way, do you? Sophie, Helen, Sue, Steve, Barry . . . There's no need to go on, is there?'

'How do you know?'

'Lynn Bulmur, she wasn't lying to you about Barry.'

'You had him spy on me? Follow me?'

'No, no. He was following you anyway. He was obsessed with you, Donna. He probably still is, for all I know.'

'So you do know everything – how interesting.' He didn't know about Rodrico, did he?

'Not quite everything. Steve's wife, for example. I don't know what there is between you and her.'

Debbie wanted her – she wanted Debbie. What was between them? Sex? Love? God, no! Suddenly, she found herself beginning to understand. Love? She was in love with Alan – supposed she always had been.

'I love you, Alan.' Words she hadn't meant to say, had meant to say. 'I love you, Alan.' Repeated words, tumbling from her mouth. Words written on pieces of paper blowing in the wind, catching in the branches of trees, swirling in the eddy currents of life's mysteries. Words of meaning?

Alan looked into Donna's eyes, her misty blue pools. She wanted to hear his thoughts, listen to the clatter of his thoughts as they fell against the memories of years gone by, bounced off experiences. Thinking in his thinking, he smiled. What had he dragged up from the silt lying in the bottom of his mind?

'I was in love once,' he said, his eyes reflecting a pretty girl from the past, the distant past. 'I'm in love now, with you, Donna, but . . .' His mouth froze, his lips hung parted, halted by more memories surfacing. He sighed. 'I don't want . . . I don't want to end up as an OMC.'

'OMC?'

'Old married couple. Contrary to what you may think, what picture you may have built up of me over the years we've worked together, I'm not the slippers-by-the-fireside type. I don't want to be someone's possession.'

The old green-eyed monster – that was her line, not his. He was supposed to fall to his knees, kiss her hand, worship her. What was this, this man? Doctor Alan Rosenberg – not the slippers-by-the-fireside type, not wanting to be someone's possession? Neither did Donna, but she wanted to possess. To her horror, she realised that she wanted to possess him, to own him. She was the contradiction. What's yours is mine, what's mine is mine.

She sat on the grass, her short skirt rising up her thighs as she crossed her legs like a schoolgirl sitting on the floor. He gazed at the nakedness there, the triangular, girlish nakedness. Her groove, still wet with lust, seemed to smile at him, beckoning him. Was this love? he wondered. Love was sex, sex was love.

Donna spoke now. '*I* don't want to be someone's

possession. Anyway, you mentioned Sophie and Helen. They are . . . Well, I call them my slaves, my sex slaves. Do you think someone, a woman who has two female sex slaves, would want a slippers-by-the-fireside type for a . . .'

'Husband?'

Husband and wife – marriage. The all-consuming, devouring, inhibiting, monogamous union. One man, one woman, one penis, one vagina – lies, deceit, adultery. She didn't want that.

'I wasn't going to say *husband*,' Donna said, her eyelids flickering.

'Then what were you going to say?'

'I don't know, partner, I suppose.'

'Is there a difference?'

'Every difference. I can't give up Sophie and Helen, Steve, my clients. I can't give my body to one man and one man only.'

'And I can't give my body to one woman and one woman only.'

She frowned. How had she got Alan so very wrong? He'd taken Elizabeth, yes, but that was different, wasn't it? Suddenly she remembered Bulmur's words – he fucked my bottom. Alan? Had he *really* fucked Lynn Bulmur's bottom?

'Fuck my bottom,' Donna said wickedly.

'What?'

'You heard. That's what you did to Bulmur, isn't it?'

'No, yes. Look, what are we going to do about . . .'

Slipping out of her clothes, she smiled. 'We're going to work together, on the patches, on the clients. Together, we'll make my dream come true.'

'Dream?'

'Equality for women. More than equality – power!'

'But I don't think . . .'

'Good, then don't think. Are you with me, or not?'

Alan slipped his jeans down as she bent over the fallen tree and spread her legs, exposing the tiny hole nestling above her wet, inflamed lips. He moved towards her, his hard penis in his hand. 'I'm not sure that I can do this,' he murmured.

'Why not? You did it to Bulmur.'

'Yes, but I've just taken your sex slaves, as you call them. I popped round to your flat and they answered the door and . . . Well, they were all over me.'

As the head of his penis forced its way past her defeated muscles, Donna gasped, pushed her bottom up, burying her fingernails into the rough bark of the tree trunk. 'You took my girls?' she breathed. 'You shouldn't have . . . Ah, that's nice! You shouldn't have taken my . . . God, that's wonderful!'

'Your girls? You possess them, own them, do you?' Alan grunted, sliding his shaft deeper into her velveteen tube.

No-one possesses anyone, no-one owns anyone – it could work well, Donna thought as Alan pushed his rod fully home and rested his heavy balls against the swell of her pussy lips. If this was the real Alan, things could work out very well indeed. Slowly withdrawing his shaft, he re-entered her bottom hole, filling the dark, hot fleshy cavern, filling her with his stiffness – his malefactor trespassing within the secrets of her body. Rolling her eyes in her euphoria, she wriggled her hips, heightening the sensations deep within her pelvis. This was love, an illicit, wondrous love.

Opening her eyes briefly to gaze at the ground below her head, Donna's stomach leaped. Where she had expected to see decaying leaves were two naked feet.

Looking up, she saw a penis, thick, stiff, inches away from her mouth. Lifting her head, she smiled at Barry. 'Been voyeuring, have you?' she asked sweetly as Alan began to thrust harder.

'You could say that,' he smiled, offering his penis to her mouth.

'You're late,' Alan gasped. 'You nearly missed all the fun.'

'You planned this, bastards! You planned my seduction!'

No-one spoke as Donna took Barry's purple knob in her mouth and rolled her tongue round the silky hardness. It was a good plan, a most welcome seduction. She was happy, happy to be a girl, to have girlish mounds and crevices – happy to give her body to men. Lucifer lurked, grinned as the girl delighted in her double pleasures of the flesh – revelled in taking a man at either end of her used body. Her bottom-hole stretched, her mouth open wide, filled with male pleasure, she was in her heaven. If only Steve were here, she mused as she sucked, aware of the emptiness, the void within her soft, quivering sheath. Another first to be accomplished – three hard penises pumping and filling her trembling body with gushing sperm. Was that what lay over the horizon of her future – three penises?

Their timing perfect, Donna's men grunted together, ballooned within the wetness of her substitute vaginas and spurted. Her head rocking with Barry's thrusting, her pelvis swelling with Alan's ramming, she moaned her satisfaction through her nose as her cunt spasmed and her clitoris erupted between her swollen quim lips. Her lewd ecstasy flowed through her flesh, rippling through the fissures of her mind, reaching out and touching her very soul with sensations of orgasm.

Leaving her mouth full, Barry sat on the grass, his penis glistening under the hot sun with a delicious cocktail of saliva and sperm. Donna didn't swallow, savouring her gift, swilling her mouth until the taste of sex had faded, diluted. Slowly, Alan withdrew his penis from her tingling darkness, allowing the muscles to contract, to close the portal of lust and keep safe the fruits swirling within. Her body limp over the fallen tree, she breathed in the summery air, the odour of sex mingling with the scent of the wood. She was filled with a comforting warming sensation – a sensation of satisfied lust.

Barry had gone by the time Donna pulled her body from the tree to stand on her trembling legs. Gone into the bushes, the undergrowth, she supposed, as voyeurs did. Alan smiled a strange smile, as if unsure of her reaction. She had enjoyed the debased union, he knew, but how would she respond now? Seduced, tricked and seduced by two men, she might well turn against him.

'If ever you plan anything so perverted again, if ever you decide to stick your penis in one end of my body and have a man sneak from the bushes and stick his in the other end – don't tell me about it! That was the most wonderful surprise ever! Thank you.'

Women were unpredictable – always had been, always would be. Alan grinned, happy that Donna was the woman for him, he was the man for her. Their love, their strange, illicit love, had blossomed. She only wished that he'd invited another two men to use her femininity – and a girl. One day, maybe – one day.

'I must get back to my, I mean, *the* girls,' she said, pulling her clothes over her perspiring body. 'They'll be needing me, I hope.

'And what with the amount of clients waiting for me to ring them, it looks as if I'm going to be pretty busy.'

'Want a hand?' Alan asked as he buckled his jeans.

'No, it's all right. You do whatever you have to do to set up the lab and come round later, this afternoon, perhaps.'

Shit! The students would just have to wait.

'This afternoon it is. You look nice like that.'

'Like what?'

'Your nipples, those metal things pressing through your top. It looks as if you have huge nipples.'

Lifting her top, Donna cupped each firm breast in turn and carefully tightened the clamps. The sensations caused her to gasp, to wince, as the clamps squeezed and pinched her brown milk buds. Her aureolae darkening with arousal, her clitoris stirred between her soft, oily pussy lips. She was ready again, ready for sex. Lifting her skirt, she smiled at Alan. 'Kiss me there,' she said, parting her lips to reveal her pinken folds, glistening in the sunlight. Kneeling before her, he licked the length of her slit, cleansing her, taking her milkiness into his mouth, bringing a hardness to her insatiable bud. 'Lick me hard!' Donna instructed as her clitoris began to bloom. 'Lick me like a dog!' The lewd words dribbled from her lips and trickled over Alan, her slave. 'That's it, harder, down a bit! Ah, yes! Nice, nice, that's good! Suck my cunt, my cunt . . .' Throwing her head back, she looked up to the sunlight sparkling like stars through the thousands of tiny holes in the foliage wavering high above. She was coming. Her clitoris was taking her to her heaven again, to her climax – to her angels of lust.

A wind blew, rustling the trees on the far side of the railway cutting, approaching, growing louder, as Donna

The Uninhibited

neared her goal. The branches overhead wavered, closed in to cover the abandoned lust below. The leaves whispered to her, coming, coming, coming. Lucifer moved in the trees as Alan licked, sucked, mouthed the hardness of her spot. 'Coming! I'm coming!' The trees acknowledged her ecstatic screams, waving wildly with new energy as her body shuddered and her juices flowed from her hole. Pulling her wet nether lips open with her slender fingers, she opened her body to Alan, opened her sex to her soul and cried out her wanton lust, filling the woods with her ecstasy.

Trembling, Donna fell to her knees and flopped her head over his shoulder as her climax subsided, leaving her body drained, fulfilled. 'That was nice,' she whispered. 'That was wonderful.' Kissing Alan's mouth, licking her juices from his lips, she took his head in her hands. 'Time for work. We'll do this again. Every day, we'll do this.'

Alan smiled and nodded, happy that he'd brought her happiness, satisfaction.

'Every day,' he replied. 'Every day, I'll make you come. Suck you, lick you and make you come.'

When he'd gone, Donna leaned over the fence and looked down the railway lines. Hard steel, shining in the sunlight, shimmering in the heat, reflecting the summer – hard, solid lengths entering the dark tunnel. She watched a bird settle on the live rail, safe with both feet on the electrified steel. Danger lurked, always lurked, ready to pounce.

Wandering through the trees and out into the park, sperm oozing between her buttocks, cooled by the breeze, cooling her there, Donna contemplated. Clients bringing lesbian sex to her flat, and paying her for it, three men at her beck and call, money – life was

341

wonderful. Would Mandy return with her beautiful, dusky body for more sex, more lesbian orgasms? Probably – undoubtedly.

'Where the hell have you been?' Helen demanded as Donna closed the front door behind her. 'The phone hasn't stopped ringing. We've booked loads of appointments for women who want to come and see you.'

'Appointments? You mean that you've been answering my phone?'

'Yes, we took it in turn to be your secretary. Is that all right?'

'Yes, it's all right. I only wish I'd been here.'

'Where have you been, and why do women keep phoning wanting to see you?'

'It's a long story. What did you say to them, exactly?'

'Just hello, no she's not here, yes I'll make an appointment for you – that sort of thing. It's all written on the pad by the phone.'

'You've both done well, it seems. And I hear that Alan . . .'

'Yes, well . . . He came round and . . .'

'You both had some fun with him, is that right?'

'Sort of.'

'Sort of?'

'He's an attractive man, Donna. I hope you don't mind . . .'

'He doesn't belong to me, or to anyone else, for that matter. Men don't belong to women and women don't belong to men. But you belong to *me*, Helen, and you, Sophie, sitting so quietly over there. Shy, are you? Guilty, perhaps?'

'No, no. I . . .'

'She's been chucked out of home. Her mother didn't

quite understand certain things.'

'What things?'

'Same as my mum, I suppose. When she first found my wet . . . Well, she understands now.'

'Is that why Sophie's been staying with you?'

'Yes. She wants to go home but her mum won't let her. She's one of these Victorian prudes, you see. Just because she doesn't like sex, she thinks that no-one else should enjoy it. My mum was like that, wasn't she? God only knows what changed her.'

'The same thing that's going to change all women, that's what.'

'Do you know, she's just landed herself a top job at that big insurance company by the library – and she can barely type! No shorthand, no office skills, no nothing! She must have something to offer, I suppose – I wish I knew what.'

Donna smiled at her girls. Sophie would soon be back with her mum, once the Victorian prude had lost her inhibitions. And Helen would make a good secretary for the new business venture. Both girls, of course, would remain her sex slaves. And Alan? Helen showed her what he'd done in the bedroom, the mess he'd made, as she put it – a miniature laboratory, set up on a table in the corner of the room.

'You've all been very busy while I've been out. I'm beginning to wonder whether I'm needed here or not. Anyway, Alan will be working in the so-called lab. You, Helen, will be my secretary, taking calls, booking appointments – and you, Sophie, will be forever grateful, forever indebted to me for getting your mum to see things in a different light.'

'That'll be the day!'

'Yes, it will – tomorrow, probably. And by "forever

indebted,'' I mean that you will do exactly as I say, when I say. Do you understand?'

'I'm not . . .'

'Take her to the sex dungeon, Helen, and chain her to the bed!'

'Sex dungeon?'

'The spare room. Chain her to the bed, on her back – naked.'

'I don't want to be chained to the bed!'

'What you want and what you get, Sophie, are two entirely different things – rule number one, remember that. And besides, you know that you enjoy my intimate attention, my tongue between your legs, so don't argue – rule number two.'

'And rule number three?' Helen asked excitedly.

'Rule number three, my dear girl, is that it's your turn next. Now get on with it. Alan will be here soon and he may well be in need of a young girl's body, isn't that right, Sophie?'

'I don't want . . .'

'Rule number one, Sophie. Don't worry, you'll soon learn. Take her away, Helen.'

Donna sat in the armchair, her armchair, and gazed at the rows of romantic novels in the bookcase. The end of an era – eras were ending all the time, and new ones beginning.

A busy life lay ahead, she knew. What with afternoons in the park with her college students, Barry, Debbie – poor Debbie, married to a two-timing bastard like Steve! Shit! The police, the college students, the girls in town who'd opened a brothel. Problems, always problems.

A glint in her eye, a knowing in her heart, she dialled

the police station. 'May I speak to Jim Slater, please?'

'Who?'

'Jim Slater, he's a policeman.'

'Not here he isn't, love, sorry.'

'Are you sure?'

'I've been here for thirty years and there's no-one by that name at this station, believe me.'

'Were two girls arrested recently for running a brothel in town?'

'A brothel? No, sorry. Who is this, anyway? If you're playing . . .'

Gently replacing the receiver, Donna smiled. 'Alan, you naughty thing,' she whispered. 'You naughty, naughty thing.'

Sophie's cries of painful pleasure drifted across the hall and filled the lounge. The walls seemed to return Donna's wicked grin as she lifted her skirt and parted her vaginal lips. Her clitoris was definitely bigger – and in dire need of attention. 'No peace for the wicked,' she breathed as the phone rang and Helen called out that Sophie was ready for her punishment. 'No peace for the uninhibited – thank God!'